Flight
of the
Black Stork

By
Bill Broocke

La Maison Publishing, Inc.
Vero Beach, Florida
www.lamaisonpublishing.com

"...We are reaching out for a new and boundless frontier...of spaceships to the moon...of the ultimate conflict between a united human race and the sinister forces of some other planetary galaxy..."

General of the Army
Douglas MacArthur
Speech to the Corps of Cadets
U.S. Military Academy
West Point, New York 12 May 1962

"Unto thy seed I have given this land..."
Genesis 15:18

"Now go and smite...and utterly destroy all that they have, and spare them not, but slay both man and woman, infant and suckling, ox and sheep, camel and ass."
1 Samuel 15:3

Chapter 1

Fog is one of nature's little reminders that we're not even close to being the hot shits we think we are. It has a way of sucking the life out of machines and can blanket a thousand square miles and humble the mightiest technology into stillness. It cascades through mountains, rolls in from the sea or rises from the earth before dawn, smothering the land until noon when only the sun burns it off.

The visibility plummeted as a tightly wound low pressure over Lake Superior shoved a cold front down toward Washington, uncoiling from its center over Cleveland like a snake about to strike. The prefrontal fog was getting worse. It was three hundred sixty-eight miles from the Trump Tower to the Mall in Washington and Preston McKenna wondered if he was going to beat the weather into town. Interstate 95 had little traffic and as the darkening sky made the night come early, only a few lights appeared in the nearly abandoned homes and businesses along the highway. And while all the exits were open, most of the service plazas were boarded up because interstate traffic was down thirty-five percent. You hardly ever saw carloads of kids piling out of SUVs to get an ice cream with their moms while dad gassed up. In post contact America, people were hunkered down, staying out of sight, like animals quivering in their burrows, waiting for the wolves to move on, or filling the churches, weeping tears in gratitude for their deliverance, however temporary it might be. And even though the defense industry was retooling at warp speed for the next round, the usual salutary effect of billions being poured into the economy didn't happen. That's how bad it was.

Wall Street had cratered with the Dow opening at sixteen hundred when trading finally resumed. Fortunes were destroyed and retirement portfolios wiped out. Even gold was not a safe haven since who could spend the gold if there was nobody left? Banks closed by the hundreds and unlike other war time periods in the nation's history, there was a vacuum of hope. Fear and uncertainly ruled.

The word was sketchy from overseas, but apparently, it was worse. The government was censoring the world news and the BBC World Service was serving up the same sappy crap we were getting. If you watched cable news, the talking heads were full of bravado that bore little resemblance to the facts. The real story was still too much to digest. The RAND studies had been right all along. We had not been ready. People wanted to believe, but fifty years of government duplicity had destroyed too much of its credibility.

Preston McKenna had the 1954 Rolls Silver Wraith slowed to fifty due to the visibility. All he could hear was the sound of the run flat Dunlops lapping the expansion seams in the highway and the soft swoosh of wipers at the end of their arcs, carving the drizzle cleanly from the one inch polycarbonate windshield.

McKenna had been the chauffeur for the Helms family for over twenty years. Mathew Helms got his name out of a New York Times story about the Falklands War. McKenna and another Royal Marine had fired a barrage of Carl Gustav rockets and stopped a battalion sized landing of an Argentine amphibious force. So, the day he mustered out, here came this job offer from the rich American and a green card to boot. Now, what with Mr. and Mrs. Helms having been killed over Lockerbie in the Pan Am 103 bombing, almost all of his driving was for their daughter Leanna, with her robust New York social calendar. *Getting out on the road gives a man time to think,* McKenna mused. The white dashed centerline flitted by like lazy slow moving tracers. McKenna had almost forgotten how well the big limo handled on the highway. It was stable but nimble despite weighing seven thousand pounds plus another thousand pounds of boron carbide ceramic armor in the floors and doors. *Could have used a bit in the roof,* he reminded himself, when a stabbing pain from his bandaged ribs shot up his spine. Mr. Helms had spent eighty thousand dollars supercharging the engine, stiffening the suspension and having the other modifications he wanted in order to make the car a safe transport for his family. *Mr. Helms was a far sighted man,* McKenna thought, *but there was no way he could have guessed we'd be needing the bloody armor in the roof!* Miss Leanna offered to hire another car and driver for the trip to Washington, but Preston would hear none of it. Far too much had happened for him to entrust her safekeeping to somebody he didn't know. *No bloody way that was going to happen!* Somewhere in here, Preston realized that he was all Leanna had in the way of anything resembling family and he started thinking of her more like a willful daughter than an employer. Finally, Leanna had given up after extracting assurances from Preston that he would stop and let her drive if the pain got too bad.

The Americans had saved us again, McKenna slowly nodded his head as the big Rolls ate up the miles. They bloody saved us from the Kaiser, from Hitler and now in this bloody mess. McKenna took off his black livery cap and pushed the remaining strands of his graying hair back off his forehead. He checked his appearance in the visor mirror then flipped it back up. A lot more gray now that was there six months ago, he thought. Then, only out of habit, he checked his side and rear view mirrors. There was no conflicting traffic, no tails and nobody on either side. Then out of the mist, the flash of headlights from opposite direction traffic across the unmowed median, a lonely hello from a fellow traveler. Leanna and her companion stared out opposite windows and had not spoken very much. *Considering where they were going, it was understandable*, Preston thought. Up ahead, he noticed another set of three parallel tire marks on the highway that gradually curved off the shoulder to the right making deep furrows in the earth. He tapped on the division window behind his seat and pointed off to the right. Leanna leaned across her friend to see. It was the charred skeleton of another American fighter jet burned beyond recognition. The American pilots had fought until out of fuel then tried to save their planes by landing them dead stick on the straight sections of the Interstate. Many others after expending their weapons, had died in ramming attacks on the enemy ships.

McKenna could smell the Susquehanna River well before he got there. It was the heavy scent of life caused by the death and birth of a thousand species an hour, in and near the mighty flow of its verdant waters. The glaciers receded, the Bison blackened the prairies and waterfowl had filled the crystal sky. The forests along the river echoed with the glad gabbling of hens on nests

4

and the thin echo of antlers clattering during the rut. The red man came and for thousands of years lived in a quiet partnership with the abundant life that everywhere flourished. Then, along the coastal plains, a thin crust of white arrived. The whites drove inland, mad with greed, their gathering host crushing all resistance. The mighty Susquehanna had seen it all and was unimpressed.

Preston McKenna let all this play through his mind. Now another enemy had to come to grab it all from the victors, the strong taking from the weak…how were they different from any of us? McKenna took a deep breath and messaged his temples with his gloved left hand. *Going to give me-self a bleedin' headache thinking about all this.* He squeezed and released his gloved hands a few times on the huge Bakelite steering wheel. The classic Rolls touring car did not have power steering and needed the large diameter steering wheel for parking.

The ghostly structure of the Susquehanna River Bridge emerged abruptly from the drizzle. The massive steel structure was reassuring somehow and restored a sense of safety and permanence that the recent events had flayed bare the culture like stripped wire. There was no oncoming traffic and none behind. Just over an hour away they'd be picking up the Beltway west. From the bridge to the Beltway was nothing but miles and there was nothing to do but to think; to think about the things that had happened and the things that were surely coming. And like many others who lived in the home of the brave, when the quiet times came, and there was time to think, Preston McKenna was afraid.

* * *

Traffic began to pick up as the black Rolls turned off of the beltway onto Colesville Road and then 16th Street which lead south to the Mall where the Vietnam Memorial was located. Only a handful of oncoming headlights stabbed into the mist like pencil beams of skim milk. A scattered queue of flickering red tail lights could be seen ahead as drivers tapped their brakes joining into the light flow of traffic.

When the Yanks came home from Vietnam it was nothing like when we came home from the Falklands. No bands were playing, no fireboats spraying like when we sailed the fleet up the Thames, McKenna thought. The yanks got pissed on and America was only grateful because it was finally over…but the vets finally got their memorial, McKenna surmised matter of factly. At least they had that. McKenna turned onto Constitution Avenue and lucked out with a parking spot near their destination.

Leanna got out on her side and walked around to the boot to retrieve her companion's wheelchair. McKenna had a strained look on his face as his employer performed what should have been his duties. "You just sit right there and enjoy yourself. Now you can listen to your god awful music," Leanna smiled, still mystified how an Englishman could develop a taste for something so parochial. McKenna shuffled through his CDs, selected one by Confederate Railroad and put on his headset.

The Vietnam Memorial is a holy place for the Vietnam Veterans. Just touching its polished black marble allows its mysterious emancipating energy to flow from the stone through your hand and down into your soul, replenishing some dark and empty place.

There are few dry eyes among those who touch the Wall because it resonates at the secret frequency of the heart. It knows of the wounds and binds them up closing the rings of fire, blood and despair. People leave stuff at the base of the Wall…a canvas jungle boot with a small flag tied in the laces…or a yellowing photo of two guys in flight suits hamming it up in front of a gunship. Somewhere above the photo one of them is on the Wall.

Leanna's slender, powerful body pushed her companion's wheel chair easily down the brick walkway to the place where the monument technicians were working with their etching drills. The man in the chair held an elongated olive drab canvas bag in his lap. The rusty leaves on the walk scattered with gusts from the approaching front and crunched under her steps and the wheels of the chair. The air was rich with the iron smell of coming rain. "This is good," the man in the wheelchair said, and Leanna stopped and sat in the bronze park bench next to her friend's chair facing the Wall. A light drizzle began and beaded up on the black granite of the Wall running down at an angle blown by the wind and tugged by gravity. The droplets changed course zigzagging their way to the base and channeled through the engraved names of 59,163 men and four women who gave full measure in a thankless war. The light was flat and gray menacing rotor clouds raced overhead, their looping tendrils almost touched the ground. It was November 18, 2000 and the Park Service technicians had arrived to carry out a special order of the president. There was no ceremony and only Leanna and her companion were there to commemorate the occasion. The last name that would ever appear on the Vietnam Memorial was being etched.

But he didn't die in Vietnam.

He died in space, in another war.

Chapter 2

Leanna read the message that he had written on the back of a French Aerospace recovery chart for the umpteenth time, her teardrops dripped onto the paper smudging the writing. Rain was often a blessing in disguise for veterans visiting the Wall. Tears go unnoticed with the raindrops that strike your face. The memories flood back of men who were like brothers pitching back dead two feet away hit by enemy fire or were blown out of the sky in big flaming pieces that lit up the night, then a flickering glow in the clouds and a fade to black. Let those who complain about men who can't cry come to the Wall.

A brilliant shaft of lightning branched across the charcoal sky and startled two park police at the far end of the memorial who were collecting up the daily memorabilia left at the Wall. They walked over to where Leanna and her friend were sitting. "Folks, might be a good time to get out of this weather, looks like the bottom is getting ready to fall out," the female officer suggested softly. "We'll be along in a minute, we're almost finished," the man in the wheelchair responded, clearing his throat and wiping his eyes on his sleeves as he kept one hand on the canvas bag in his lap. The Park Police gave ground and left the two people with their thoughts.

Something was learned by another generation in the Vietnam War. We learned that freedom is the natural state of man. And freedom is fragile, like the ice crystals found in the vapor trail of a high flying jet. Change the air temperature just one degree and it vanishes. So, after a hundred centuries of war, the nations of earth in the seasons of time, wrote the lessons of freedom in their blood and for the first time inched toward making war between nations obsolete. But, now, all that had changed.

The soul of a generation is stored in the Vietnam Wall like a massive granite hard drive and to the veterans it represents a nexus in their lives. The Wall became the place where the rape of innocence at last found absolution. The Wall became the alpha and omega, the beginning and the end.

Chapter 3
The Beginning

"About a quarter to nine after Kahr had been speaking for about an hour to some three thousand thirsty burghers, seated at rough hewn tables and quaffing their beer out of stone mugs in the Bavarian fashion, S.A. troops surrounded the Buergerbraukeller and Hitler pushed forward into the hall. While some of his men were mounting a machine gun in the entrance, Hitler jumped up on a table and to attract attention fired a revolver shot to the ceiling."

----The Rise and Fall of the Third Reich
By William L. Shirer

Several interesting things happened on the evening of November 8, 1923. The first one was a phone call received by Matthew Blalock of Marietta, Georgia, amateur astronomer, general science teacher at Marietta High and candidate for induction into the Masonic Lodge.

Matt, his wife Laura and little Matt, lived five miles west of the city square on Powder Springs Road. The Blalock family lived five miles west of town. This meant that the chilly fall sky turned really black when the sun went down and no light pollution from the new Edison Electric street lamps on the square would reach this far. The Autumn night was smoky sweet with the scent of pot bellied stoves. The blazing mills of Birmingham were still in their nascence in 1923 and there was no high altitude haze from their toiling furnaces carried downwind to Atlanta. Later, the mills made so much pollution that the Atlanta sky was a perpetual color of buttermilk with only a little patch of blue directly overhead.

Matthew Blalock, amateur astronomer, had a new telescope that he had ordered from the Edmund Scientific catalog. It was the biggest amateur instrument available at the time and was mounted on a five feet tall wooden tripod with a crank and gear mechanism. It had a small primitive spotting scope mounted on the side of its long tube and compared to something like a Mead ETX150, the purists of today would've dissed Matt's telescope as a piece of Christmas trash. To get a spot with a clear viewing field and stay on the homestead, Blalock had to replant about a dozen of Laura's azaleas and this caused an uproar in the hen house of the WMU at the New Mt. Zion Baptist Church. The church ladies were aghast and told Laura that this was so unfair, and that if Matt really loved her, he'd give up his old telescope. Laura just laughed. She had the novel idea that her man being happy was more important than a bunch of plants.

But back to that phone call. It was not good news. His good friend, Masonic sponsor and probate judge for Cobb County was asked to pass along how the Masonic brothers had voted.

Matthew Blalock had been blackballed.

He shoved back his shock of salt and pepper hair and readjusted the strap on the left side of his denim overalls under his army great coat as he slowly strode back out on the porch, the screen door blam, banged behind him. Laura haltingly followed along after him, still drying the evening's silverware from dinner, but she could not think of a single word of comfort. Matt wasn't showing any emotion, but she knew he was hurting.

The impenetrable, and of course eternal veil of secrecy that surrounded the Mystic Masonic Temple was compromised fifteen minutes later. Maureen Brumby, who was a Bell operator at the central switchboard, called and whispered to Laura that she had overheard the reason for the blackballing. Matt Blalock had been blackballed because he was "too liberal with his ideas about the niggers." When Blalock heard the reason, he started to laugh, but then deep down in his guts he got a warm feeling. It was almost a sense of relief. All he could think to do was take Laura in his arms and hold her. Somewhere in the distance a mockingbird with no calendar and who had not gotten the word it was bedtime was squawking his brains out. Directly overhead, mare's tails raced across the sky like wind blown lace behind a sliver of moon and a star spattered night.

After not very much reflection, Blalock decided that he didn't give a rat's ass about being a Mason if it meant he would have to sacrifice his principles...or have to deal with men of no vision who didn't see the inevitable reckoning of the ledger that was coming.

"Laura," Blalock spoke in a low whisper, "someday the Negroes will have their Moses. And we better just pray to God almighty that he won't be haten' the white man for what we've done.... be hell to pay if they get the wrong one...*hell* to pay!"

She walked part of the way out to the clearing holding hands but as they neared the big refractor she slowly released hers. Matthew Blalock kissed her lightly on the cheek, then returned to his instrument

13

and attempted to find the planet Jupiter once more. Hands in his pockets, he tilted his head back and scanned the inky darkness. *In my father's house there are many mansions*, he thought. *Dear Jesus, what did you really mean when you said that?* The cirrus deck at 37,000 feet had enlarged considerably by this point because now the sky looked like someone splashed milk on the outside of the celestial sphere. Until it blew over, Jupiter was going to be quite a bit less distinct.

He looked up for a moment and thought about his boy, who would be shooting out the front door any minute, after finishing his homework and chores. *The world is going to be a very different place for Matt Junior*, he thought, *different indeed!* Matt junior wanted to be an airmail pilot! Ever since that mail plane had caught fire and crashed down near Macon. The airmail pilot had thrown the mailbags out to save them, then fire balled into the ground like a meteor. "Daddy, why'd the airmail pilot throw the bags out?" Matt Jr. had asked. "Those air mail pilots have a strong sense of duty," Matt answered. This apparently had made quite an impression. Blalock smiled to himself, remembering his harrowing flight from Atlanta's Candler Field over to Spartanburg on Pitcarin Aviation in a Fleetwing. The plane's motor had a stack fire cranking up for the trip home and the airplane had burned up on the ground in minutes. The four passengers had plenty of time to get out of the plane, but it created a powerful opinion in Matt's mind as to the actual status of aeronautics in the real world. *Flying the mail, much less people, in those slow pokin' crates? That's a corker!* Matt stretched, checking the sky for a break in the cirrus as his mind wandered to modern technology. *The Spaniard, Cierva, had a good idea with his autogyro ...could land and takeoff almost straight up...bet the Army could do something with that. But the airplane will never amount to anything unless they get a more powerful motor to make it go faster an get some other kind of fuel that isn't so dangerous...like maybe kerosene.* Matt chuckled to himself at his joke about the kerosene airplane motor as he bent over to adjust the focus on the spotting scope. *Kerosene would never work...unless they could spray it somehow and create a directional explosion...*Matt Blalock's thoughts were interrupted when Jupiter swam slowly into view as he reacquired the planet. *Way too fuzzy with the cloud deck,* he thought...*got to think of a way to keep Matt Jr. out of airplanes.*

Twelve years later, an Englishman named Frank Whittle invented a more powerful airplane motor that ran on kerosene.

He called it the jet engine.

But, by far the most interesting thing that happened on the evening of November 23, 1923 took place during Matthew Blalock's phone call at a point 115.7 million kilometers from the planet Jupiter. It was located on a direct sight line from Earth through the gas giant and out the other side so that the planet was perfectly intervening. If the instruments had existed in 1923, they would have recorded a jaw dropping, meter pegging, off scale gravity wave that rippled the fabric of space. The mythical Jovians, watching from their home planet, would have observed the heavens swim out of focus for an instant, as if a sky sized magnifying glass was momentarily passed from horizon to horizon. The Jovians watching all this would have done the Jovian

15

version of shrugging their shoulders, then went back to doing whatever it is that Jovians do.

The coordinates of this event were not random and anyone analyzing the strategic considerations, would have found that this location was invisible from Earth had people been observing, which they weren't. The event was also shielded from detection by the planet Jupiter from high tech sensors, which of course, had not yet been invented. And if anybody had been counting, he would have discovered a ten thousand metric ton addition to the hundreds of asteroids already in orbit around Jupiter. It had a camouflaged outer hull complete with artificial meteoroid impact marks and the smooth contours imitating those of an ancient space mariner.

Out of the infinite blackness, we had company.

Chapter 4

In other times and places, the towers of Thor on this hazy July afternoon would have been viewed in awe of their magnificence. The boiling cotton balls of cloud bellowed skyward, rolling, changing texture and bubbling in composition and color. The huge afternoon thunderheads were the hue of blush wine as the sun began disappearing over the horizon. The amber sky was caused by light filtered through the atmosphere, stained with dust and smoke and other detritus of civilization. In America's industrial heartland near Detroit and Pittsburgh, the sky looked the same. The sun's rays were colored by the refraction of light through particles spewed out from factories making steel, guns, and other assorted engines of war. But today, the sky was not the colored by factories making things. If air particle samples from the sky were placed under a scanning electron microscope, you would have identified the elements of trinitrotoluene, commonly known as TNT, soot from burning clouds of petroleum at various stages of refinement, vaporized carbon from railway steel, and complex organic molecules from partially incinerated human beings with trace readings of insecticide.

And nothing like thunderclouds in North America, there were no people having picnics lying on blankets gazing skyward at the towers of Thor. Nobody was pointing and laughing imagining the faces of people, dogs, and gorillas. The people on the ground below this particular lightning filled storm were slogging through fields of shell craters, and tangled rubble piles, once the towns and villages of France. They were crawling on their bellies in mud and filth through spider forests of bomb splintered trees, firing and mortaring their way from burning vehicles to hedge rows to bullet riddled stone fences. They fought and suffered and were blown apart by the thousands. But the reaching vineyards of the Rhone Valley were thirsty for the wine of the weeping thundershowers. The heavy rain and occasional hail were welcomed on the ground and gave the opposing legions a momentary respite from the hell and despair.

At 22,000 feet over the fertile pasture lands of Bresse and the rolling Beaujolais wine country with an entirely different perspective, was the crew of 1st Lieutenant Matt Blalock Jr's battle damaged B-24J Liberator of the 487th Bombardment Group.

What the hell are we going to do, Blalock thought to himself as he took an inventory of his woes. *Number one engine was unsuccessfully feathered.* Instead of completely stopping its rotation and turning knife edged into the wind to reduce drag, the three bladed Hamilton Standard prop was windmilling. This caused tremendous drag on that side because the feathering pump had been damaged when the flak burst took out the engine. *Number two engine was running hot because it was at climb power. But if I pull the power back, we sink like a stone. Number three engine was feathered successfully inbound to the target with a shorted out primary, and the number four Pratt & Whitney R1830 supercharged engine was also running hot with the added complication of losing oil.* A rivulet of the black fluid streamed out of the cowl, over the top surface of the wing, then off the trailing edge of the right flap like a skinny, greasy smoke trail. It was just a matter of time before the engine seized from lack of lubrication and welded its pistons to the cylinder walls in an airframe shuddering jolt. The left vertical stabilizer of the B-24's distinctive twin tails was missing two thirds of its control surface and jagged hunks of aluminum whistled in the slipstream. With that much rudder shot off combined with a windmilling prop, heading control was very difficult. *But I have all this under control* Matt thought. Unfortunately there was a far worse problem. There was a scary vibration that intermittently ran through the floorboards of the cockpit and traveled back to the tail gunner's station causing a fluttering low frequency buzz in the yoke. A slow pitching movement of the nose followed the flutter and Blalock correctly diagnosed that something was wrong with the elevator control cables...probably shot through. *Nothing worse than a control problem*, he thought, trying not to show his fear to the rest of the crew. Blalock gently flew the big bomber with the trim wheel and a feather touch not wanting to exert any more pitch control pressure than was absolutely necessary. His guts churned as he nursed the injured warbird along. *I hope to God the rest of the crew can't hear what's going on in my stomach,* he thought. The job was to stay aloft as long as possible, trading a slow loss of altitude for flying speed. Every minute he could pull this off was another two miles closer to home. The idea was to run out of miles to go before running out of feet above the ground. It was a simple but brutal equation. Blalock finally came to the end of his mental inventory. *I'm still alive*, he concluded, *along with everybody else but the new guy.* The new copilot, on his first mission, was lying dead on the catwalk behind the cockpit, pulled out of his seat by the flight engineer. He bled out like a gutted elk and his blood dripped down into the belly compartments, where it partially dried in big sticky pools. He died instantly when shrapnel from the eighty-eight burst blew part of his skull away and flailed his body across the cockpit like a tackling dummy hit by an all-pro. His blood splattered the right side of Blalock's face and all over the inside of the windshield and instrument panel where it congealed then froze. That was an hour ago and they were still flying. *Well, there were some pluses on the inventory ledger*, Blalock thought, as his mind blazed through the short list. *Thank God the Wing Commander had requested the 332nd for their fighter escort.* Blalock looked up through the upward viewing panels in the B-24's Plexiglas windshield and took a deep breath. They were still there…the four red tail angels who had dropped back to cover them. Normally stragglers were left to fend for themselves and the main force fighter escort stayed with the group, the greater good for the many. But the red tailed Mustangs flying escort over Blalock identified them as from the 332nd Fighter Group that always detached fighters from the group to cover the cripples. The big P-51Ds were making wide lazy "S" turns over the wounded Liberator and had even cracked out some flaps in order to fly slow enough to stay with him.

The Mustang flight leader was Captain J.B. McCall, son of a Texas sharecropper who was the son of a slave. A lot of the top brass in the military said the Negroes couldn't fly. Their brains could not handle understanding complex 'chinery it was said. The doubters were gradually muzzled as the kills started coming in. After a few early problems, the 332nd was kicking ass all over Europe and had this freaky record going that they had never lost a bomber to enemy action when they were on bomber escort. Historians will argue that wasn't technically correct, but the 332nd had a damn good record and the bomber crews were plenty glad to see the Red Tails forming up to cover them.

McCall broke radio silence over the strike channel. "How you doin' down there?"

"Not so hot...I think number four is about to run out of oil," Blalock replied.

Blalock's voice was deep and raspy, distorted by the throat mike, designed to allow talking over the radio while wearing an oxygen mask.

"It ain't far to the coast, an we got plenty of gas to stay with you," responded McCall, glancing down at his fuel gages. He then looked over at his wingmen. Number two, Tom "Lucky" Lemuel was slowly shaking his head and Johnny Marks, flying number four, made a corkscrew gesture around his ear with his gloved finger then pointed it at the flight leader. *OK, I get it,* McCall thought. *I'm a liar and a crazy man.* McCall looked back at his own dwindling fuel quantity then down at the lumbering B-24 a thousand feet below them, barely staying airborne. *These guys have enough problems already,* McCall thought. *So what if we lose a little seat cushion up our asses? We can't leave these guys to the wolves.*

"Tail to A/C...bogies at...six o'clock high, no, now six o'clock level...Jesus! Look at em' turn!" Blalock was startled.

"A/C to tail...what the heck are you talking about

Benny? Be specific...how many? Where?" The tail gunner in a B-24 was usually the first to buy it in a tail on attack, since quarter inch Plexiglas isn't much protection against the twenty-millimeter cannon. He was, however, the first to sight incoming fighters. *This is all we need now*, Blalock was angry. *Almost to the channel and jumped by fighters. Shit, almost home!*

Hurtling down from the terminator like three formation flying falling stars the three aircraft made an astounding nearly right angle turn and began bearing down on the Liberator in a sweeping tangential intercept at its six o'clock. The overtake was well over two thousand knots, but nobody thought in speeds that fast back then. In fact, the inbound interceptors had actually halved their speed to position themselves for the attack. Blalock and his crew had seen the jets and the rocket planes, but the brilliant balls of light overhauling the bomber from astern was the most mind boggling thing that any of them had ever seen.

"You red tails see this?" Blalock transmitted, his voice cracking from spasms of fear and dry mouth. "We got em," McCall replied calmly. Could these be the Foo Fighters intel had mentioned in a recent briefing?

"Here they come," McCall said to his flight under his oxygen mask, as he caught a glimpse of the leader in his rear view mirror. "Lets clean up and go," McCall transmitted. The flaps retracted on the four Mustangs and a small cough of blue smoke puffed briefly as each pilot fire walled his Packard-Merlin twelve cylinder engine. Two feet of blue flames poured from exhausts as the flight spread out and accelerated through three hundred knots. The Liberator opened up first, twin fifties from the tail, top turret, bottom, and waist.

"Lead, lead, lead!" Benny yelled over interphone. "They're hauling ass!" Thousands of tracers filled the sky and overheated guns kept firing. Hot, smoking, brass showered onto the floor and became coated with the melted blood from the dead copilot. The deafening defensive firepower of the B-24's guns fully engaged was spectacular as the large orbs of light kept coming.

"Never seen anything that fast," somebody shouted.

"Damn, now they're slowing down," somebody else said.

The four P-51s pulled out ahead of the B-24 and the glowing crescent shaped aircraft passed abeam the stricken bomber on the left blithely sailing through the golden streams of steel. Strangely, the enemy aircraft never fired their weapons, and by the time they went by, their speed was down to less than three hundred knots.

"What are they doing?" Blalock asked over interphone to anybody.

"It's like they're just looking us over," somebody answered.

The three oddly shaped aircraft glided leisurely by the Liberator like old-timer airmail pilots buzzing a nudist colony on a Sunday afternoon. They seemed unfazed as they flew through the Fourth of July fireworks of incendiaries arcing through the sky from the B-24's bristling guns. The four Mustangs shifted into finger four giving the three bandits room to pass on the left. "Let's get 'em," McCall transmitted as he rolled in. His Mustang made a flashing half roll to the left as the sun reflected off its wings. The other three followed McCall and within seconds the three delta shaped craft were raked with a sleet of death from twenty-four machine guns. The sky lit up with tracers as the Mustangs attacked. Packard engines screamed and the staccato muzzle flashes stopped the four bladed props of the P-51s in an eerie disco strobe of fire. Clouds of spent shell casings poured into the sky as the Red Tails swarmed the Foo Fighters like pissed off hornets. Blalock's navigator braced himself in the nose, "Shell casings!" he shouted as the spent brass from the Mustangs clattered into the Liberator.

"Dammit they're getting' away," somebody transmitted.

It was like the German flight leader said, *Time to go.* All at once the three glowing ships leaped forward in a burst of acceleration. Two of the ships went straight ahead in a thirty degree climb then pitched almost to the vertical as if they had ricocheted off a hard surface. The third vehicle began to slow.

"Looks like we winged one of 'em," somebody shouted.

Scales of brilliant blue white arc lit veins suddenly ran over its fuselage, covering it like a cobweb. The ship bulged momentarily like it was inflated suddenly by compressed air, then disappeared in a blinding explosion of intense white energy. Johnny Marks was the closest when the enemy ship blew.

"Johnny, break right, break right...oh shit!" McCall screamed into his throat mike.

Johnny Marks' airplane was engulfed by the explosion and vaporized along with the Foo Fighter in the blast. There were no chutes, no flaming wreckage, no debris. There was nothing left of the two aircraft. McCall and the surviving wingmen made a five G diving turn to the right when the expanding plasma cloud overtook them from the rear. The shock wave hit them with a slam that caused a queer particulate cloud to momentarily form in their cockpits, then dissipate. The shock wave hit so hard it nearly knocked the stick out of their hands.

The bomber crew, witnessing the event from several miles astern, braced as the expanding energy bubble raced directly at them. "Brace for impact," Matt shouted over interphone, "it's some kind of concussion wave!" The bomber lurched violently but the distance had attenuated the blast effect. The control yoke slammed forward then aft in Matt's gloved hands.

Elevator cables, please don't snap, he prayed.

Moments afterwards, the bomber crew and the surviving Red Tails were stunned into silence.

McCall climbed his flight back into position overhead, wagged his wings, and then accelerated away. "The channel's in view...good luck," McCall transmitted to the bomber, much to the relief of his wingmen who were sitting on empty.

Blalock made it across the channel, cleared the Dover cliffs by only five hundred feet and landed the stricken bomber at RAF Strubby, just outside London.

A month later, before his squadron was about to upgrade to the more damage tolerant B-17s, Matt and his crew ferried a war weary B-24 to Soluch Field, Libya on the Mediterranean coast. An unforecast sandstorm obscured the coastline for a hundred miles and a road grader building the new runway, accidentally severed the power cable to the non-directional beacon. Without visual navigation cues from the ground and the radio beacon off the air, Blalock's navigator eventually became unsure of their position. As fuel ran out, they crash-landed in the desert and then attempted to walk out.

In 1965, an oil exploration team found the B-24 in perfectly preserved condition in the zero humidity. It was completely intact and parachutes had been placed on the ground nearby made into the shape of a large arrow pointing in the direction the crew had walked. Matt and his men had hung together until the end and their remains were found within one hundred feet of each other only ten miles from the crash site.

They walked in the wrong direction...not that it would have mattered.

And this is the way it happens sometimes in flying. Seemingly innocuous events compound to overtake the wise and the cautious as easily as the unwitting and unwary.

The exposed part of Blalock's body was a sun bleached skeleton half covered with sand and a few shreds of a wind-ragged flight suit. The oil men found him lying on his side with both arms folded over his chest holding a parched and cracked sun glass case in both hands. Inside the case was a pencil written note and a faded black and white photo of a woman and a baby. The rough tough oil men passed the note to one another without a word after reading it.

There wasn't a dry eye in the house.

Somebody once said that nobody, not even the poets, has ever measured how much love the heart can hold.

After the war, during the intensive interviews of the Strategic Bombing Survey, the Air Force demanded that the Lufwaffe turn over all the technology of their

Foo Fighters.General Herman Kranz, head of Luftwaffe
intelligence responded during the interrogations.

"They weren't ours."

Chapter 5
Leanna

By the age of thirteen Leanna Helms realized that she was quite a bit different from the rest of the girls her age. All of the children she knew and most of the adults more and more each day seemed to be total buffoons. Even when she factored in the probability of her teenage intransigence, there was definitely something wrong with the grownups. Their language, behavior and ability to observe and understand the most elementary of life's events caused her to see the people she knew as total idiots and later almost like insects.

Her intelligence seemed to increase on an exponential basis and her parents, Matthew and Danielle, both brilliant Eastern intellectuals themselves, began worrying about Leanna's development into psychologically healthy channels. One day, Danielle, was discussing her daughter at the bridge club when one of her pals told her about a school in New England that might help. So after checking it out carefully, Matthew and Danielle enrolled Leanna at The Heatherton School for Gifted Children, founded by the late Isaac Heatherton the physicist, in Groton Connecticut. But after the novelty of boarding school wore off, Leanna found the school for the gifted was like running a marathon through wet concrete. Her teachers implored her parents to skip grades and allow her to rise to the level of her considerable ability. Further complicating matters was the fact that she had begun menstruating at eleven and was developing physically into a stone fox looker comparable to her sheer brainpower. More and more concerned about her socialization, Leanna's parents resisted the idea of skipping too many grades.

After becoming sexually active at fifteen the complaints from their daughter seemed to trail off, thus confirming the rightness of their decision. But the complaints weren't trailing off because Leanna was becoming better socialized. Leanna suddenly discovered powerful appetites that dwarfed the simpleminded world of academics. Her high school provided an abundant supply of boys, which she consumed like the Morlock eating the Eloi. The supply was inexhaustible and so was she. She was an equal opportunity Lolita and waded into the boys with a vengeance; hotshot football players, captain of the debate team, rich kids, and off campus she went through several tough guys with tattoos and raked Chevy convertibles and a couple of truly bad ass biker types. She got into their minds like some kind of nympho brain virus and manipulated them with perfect control like sock puppets. She sliced through these guys like a bolo knife through palm hearts and when she got tired of the latest dude, she dropped him so hard that he bounced. You always could spot her most recent ex-boyfriend. He was the one with the zombie purple sacks under his eyes and wandering aimlessly around for a couple of weeks talking in one syllable words. Leanna sucked them dry emotionally and sexually, and the crazy thing was that nobody ever looked at her like an easy punch. Teenage boys can be barbaric, but no sooner had one suitor gone down in flames, another was ready to slam home his bolt, and Leanna was always ready for another shooter.

By eighteen, Leanna was a senior at Georgia Tech sailing through computer engineering and astrophysics barely attending classes. At five feet ten inches, 127 pounds, she had jet black, shoulder length hair and deep violet eyes the color of the sky in Learjet country. She had firm and perfectly proportioned breasts, wore size seven pumps and had tapered powerful legs that went "from the ground clear to heaven," according to the word on the street from the "hads" who were still breathing, and the "wannabe had," who were just panting. She had a great ass, a tiny waist, and her skin, the color of natural cream, was never exposed to the sun unless she was outside actually doing something. Southern women know the stupidity of baking themselves in the solar radiation which makes their pool bunny Yankee bitch counterparts old before their time. Leanna's skin was velvet to the touch and as soft as a deerskin chamois.

When she contracted her stomach muscles, she could make a lightly sculpted six pack, but when she relaxed, it was gone and flat. She worked out every day and did fifty Kegels. She used a tape measure to keep her waist, thighs, hips and calves at the ratios she found in anthropologist Anne Jordan Crane's book. By actual human trials, Crane discovered the ratios that created the most powerful atavistic response in men. And her voice...Robert Tranh, who later became her Project 214 director, used to say that it was soft enough to call wild birds out of trees. Any man she went after was history after two minutes of conversation...before even the first brush of her touch or ignition of her rocket engine sex drive.

Leanna disdained the tawdry bouncing with the

bimbos in exercise classes and enduring the coarse grammar and callused hands of the gauche, muscle-head personal trainers used by other affluent Atlanta women. Instead, she used ballet exercises. She had been taking classes since she was four, and by special permission, generated by a large donation from her mother, Leanna was allowed to train and rehearse with The Atlanta Ballet. Early on, she showed incredible potential and the coaches again wanted her parents to push her into the performing arts. But Leanna torpedoed this idea early in the program. She thought the ballet far too easy and the idea of dancing the same performance over and over was mind numbing.

By the time Leanna was nineteen and commencing her Ph.D., her libido was starting to settle down at last and she now preferred maintaining a stable of five studs, which was continually being selected, used up, and culled. She liked variety, and her studs' ages ran from the mid-twenties to late forties. It was about this time that she figured out there was literally no man she could not have. For example, in 1982, at a faculty Christmas party, accompanied by their wives, two married professors, innocently strayed into her kill zone. One was a dean at the Columbia School of Divinity. It started with the most innocent of conversations, a mild bit of teasing, caused perhaps, by one too many cups of punch. Unfortunately, she became aroused, and before the evening was over, the two profs were ambushed by Leanna in what the uninitiated would have considered a completely random encounter. In a matter of minutes, in an empty bedroom near an upstairs bath of the chancellor's mansion, each man was ruthlessly destroyed in a brain burning spasm of animal ecstasy. Families, reputations, tenure, careers, their whole lives were blown to hell in one wild roll of the bones.

Later on, one of them became obsessed and called her incessantly over the phone for months, in some cases crying, begging to see her again. But upon finally accepting rejection, his mood changed and then he began stalking and making threats. The stalking and threats stopped two weeks later in the garden of her penthouse apartment near the university just off Peachtree and 10th street. It happened late on a Friday night. She was bare-footed, wearing gym shorts and a halter top and had tugged on a pair of black leather driving gloves, holding a roll of quarters wrapped in electrician's tape in her right hand. She waited for him in the swing near the gazebo. The last thing he remembered was turning his head when Leanna whispered his name. She stood up and glided slowly out of the swing and walked softly toward him. She attacked without another word, striking silently like a Cobra out of the darkness. The first blow struck deep into his solar plexus which doubled him over, stunning him with excruciating pain and prevented him from crying out for help or mercy. Then she kicked his legs out from under him in one powerful sweep. His six-two, two hundred and forty pound frame crashed to the wooden deck and she was on top of him instantly, her intense athletic power ramping up as adrenaline exploded her muscular system into overdrive. The bridge of her right foot slashed into his groin with the impact of a soccer kick, her left knee smashed down dislocating his shoulder pinning his right arm to the ground. She then slammed one powerful and carefully aimed blow after another into his face and chest.

An hour later he staggered into the street coughing blood and fell unconscious where the stream of blood was noticed running into a sewer drain by two students who back tracked it to the source. They found his body under a street light on Collier Road and called the paramedics who took him to the ER at Piedmont Hospital, thankfully, only minutes away. His story about being mugged by a big black dude was viewed suspiciously by the police since he still had his wallet. The cops thought it was mighty unlikely that the massive tissue damage, broken ribs and partially punctured lung could have been wrought on a guy his size by just one person. Two years later, plastic surgeons had given him back eighty percent of his looks.

When finished teaching her stalking lover the lesson of his life, Leanna's blood was up and she needed badly to be completed. Handily, one of her current five studs was in the same apartment building, Jerry Baldwin, a twenty-five year old Atlanta Falcon defensive back and runner up for the Heisman Trophy. At six-four and two-thirty, Baldwin was cat quick, could bench press three-twenty, had only five percent body fat, and was hard as a rock. When Baldwin answered his door Leanna was taking deep slow breaths contemplating what she was going to do him.

Baldwin opened the door wearing a USC T-shirt and skivvies. "Leanna, what hell are you doing out this time of …?" He never finished his sentence. "You talk too much," Leanna said huskily, then slapped him across his mouth and melted her body into his, sinking her nails deep into his lats, snaking her hot, velvety tongue halfway down his throat. She used her body as a kind of weapon, driving him backwards, off balance, into his living room. She locked the heel of her left foot into the small of his right knee and applied pressure bending his knee, her firm thighs and groin pressing hard against his. She kept pushing, almost staggering him, until she maneuvered him with a slight pirouette to the left that placed her back to the huge leather sofa in the living room. Baldwin's right hand was holding her strongly at the small of her back and he felt his hand crunching the gold bikini chain around her tiny waist. Leanna brought her right leg slowly up and wrapped it around his left thigh, arched her back to show him the penetration angle she wanted and pulled him roughly down on top of her, dragging her nails slowly across his naked back.

Over the next six hours the newly weds in the adjoining unit had the tables turned and it was they who didn't get a wink of sleep, except for a few intermissions. And if it weren't for the fact that it continued all night, it sounded so violent a couple of times that they almost called the cops.

Baldwin missed practice for the next two weeks with a sprained back.

Leanna bounced out early and went jogging.

The other Christmas party victim, the dean of the divinity school, was only slightly luckier. Divorce papers were served on him six weeks after the party when he couldn't explain the deep red claw marks on the back of his arms delivered by Leanna at the instant she climaxed. His teenage sons were not speaking to him, and as the story began leaking out to the awful places that they go, the worlds in his universe began to spin crazily out of orbit. The mortal sin of suicide began to appear a completely rational solution.

Somebody once said that the obvious trouble with the road less traveled is that it has far too few travelers. In matters of love there is a high road into the light and a low road that disappears into the darkness. Both roads provide the visceral and soul quenching satisfaction all humans need. There comes a time, however, in the lives of men that a choice has to be made, either toward the light or further descent into the night. The light leads toward joy and family and love of the spiritual and profoundly binding kind. The kind that lasts through the mountains and valleys of life and sustains and renews; one that works like a nuclear reactor which makes its own fuel. It is the love that the Apostle spoke of that is patient and kind and never gives up.

The other love leads downward into deviancy and a spiraling dehumanization that thrives on the thrill of doing, having, and taking for its own sake. It takes from others even when it does not need. It takes and takes because it knows it can't be stopped. It is a cyclone narcissistic illusion of love like a sparkling, swirling plasma cloud of pure energy that casts no shadow. People can survive a long time with this illusion, but not forever. When the day finally comes that they see their shadow for that first time, the maniacal, ego driven plasma cloud freezes solid. It goes from ten million rpm to zero in a microsecond. Then it shatters in a blinding explosion, scattering shards of icy glass into a million pieces. From the smoking crater of these ruins, sometimes, a better, stronger person can be constructed, emerging from their empty illusions. But first, there must be the great crash of crystal in the night... to obtain the pieces...to begin the rebuilding.

There was no logical explanation for how Leanna got this way. Perhaps logic itself made her a victim since logic cannot explain good and evil. Without a logical explanation, Leanna would always doubt the reality of anything.

Leanna Helms was happily on the dark road and God was a laughable myth. It was her scientific opinion that all of the so-called higher functions that we call humanity, like love, charity, and kindness, were nothing more than the interaction of neurochemicals in the brain. Outside these intricate molecular chains in the spongy tissue of the cerebellum, love, tenderness, and God Himself ceased to exist. "Once we decode the controlling genes for the neurochemicals, the need for God will be exposed as the hoax it has always been," she once casually observed at a board meeting. Nobody reacted visibly but it was a shuddering experience to several of the new directors.

Matthew and Danielle Helms were killed on Pan Am 103, which fire balled out of the night like a giant meteor over Lockerbie, Scotland in 1988. The terrorist bomb was hidden in a portable radio. The radio was a gift to a young American girl from her summer boyfriend, allegedly one of two Libyan intelligence agents. There was little time for grief and Leanna was thrust into the CEO job of Helms Industries, a high tech international consortium that built everything from laser target illuminators for the Air Force to consumer appliances. She had billions at her disposal and control of a multinational high tech consortium by owning fifty-one percent of the stock. The first order she gave the company president was to mobilize every asset of

Helm's global empire and find out who placed the bomb on the Pan Am jet. Within three months, it was learned from the Mossad, that Syria and Iran had actually been responsible for the bombing. It was in retaliation for the Iran Air A-300 that accidentally had been shot down by the U.S. Navy prior to the Persian Gulf War. The Helms banking contacts in Lucerne quickly confirmed the information when the General Command terrorist organization, part of the Popular Front for the Liberation of Palestine, suddenly logged in an eleven million dollar deposit only two days after the bombing. The trail of the money was incredibly subtle, but the trail was clear to the Swiss bankers. The money irrefutably came from Iran. The State Department could not admit to the American people who was actually responsible, since the resulting uproar would have triggered a demand for retribution, sucking America into a vicious circle of attack and reprisal. This would have undone fifty years of agonizing diplomacy to bring stability and the control of conflict to that tortured part of the world. The Libyan agent story was complete bullshit trumped up by CIA to divert the attention of the public. Two of the terrorists were identified, and Leanna wanted to meet them. The only one that could be located was holed up in Adana, Turkey and the Helms contact in the Mossad went to incredible lengths to prevent Leanna from encountering this extremely dangerous asshole. He finally caved in and she was escorted to a hotel with a hash den in the basement where she pretended to be an American tourist looking for a score. Within an hour she had the guy upstairs in the stale dank room with bad paint and plaster. They were completely naked on the thin and stained shopworn mattress when Leanna pulled the tie that allowed her dark hair to fall down over her face and shoulders. In the barrette, which held her hair, was a three-inch blade similar to a trench knife with three holes for her fingers. The unshaven Syrian was an inch shorter than Leanna with a weak poorly maintained body. He reeked of hashish and body odor as she placed her left arm around his shoulders as if preparing to kiss. His pencil thin right arm was pinned under her left armpit and she clinched her left hand powerfully cupping his left bicep preventing movement of his left arm. He closed his eyes, his thin lips curled back revealing his tobacco-stained teeth as he waited for his kiss. Leanna contracted her body, focusing her strength on immobilizing movement of his torso. "Do you remember Pan Am 103?" she asked softly. Her grip on the Arab was like a warm, flesh-covered vise. His eyes popped open and his shock turned to panic when he realized that the woman physically dominated him and he could not free her grasp. As he started to scream, Leanna silenced him with the three-inch blade buried into his left kidney. The terrorist's eyes bulged, frozen in horror, but Leanna kept eye contact with him and pulled the blade across his abdomen, gutting him like a pig. She stuffed her wadded up panties in his mouth and held him down on the bed with one hand across his mouth until he stopped struggling. She then took a quick shower and within twelve hours was sleeping soundly on a United 777 en route to Chicago out of London.

At age twenty-five, Leanna Helms had become one very dangerous female.

Chapter 6
J. B. McCall

If Leanna was on one end of the spectrum of humanity, J.B. McCall was at the opposite end. After WWII, McCall ended up back in Texas in the oil business. But despite being a decorated fighter pilot and Army Air Force officer, he was also black and they wouldn't serve him a goddamned sandwich at the W.T. Grant's lunch counter in Fort Worth. McCall sent out applications to all the major airlines but was politely turned down. The first job he landed just to keep from using up his savings was as a roustabout on a wildcat well owned by Dooly "Red" Nekkerman. But Red was no redneck. Nekkerman was a straight shooter and McCall figured out that Red was smarter than anybody he was meeting in the business. He decided he was going to learn as much as he could from Red then put a deal together by himself as soon as he found a backer. That, of course, was going to be the big problem what with him being a Negro.

McCall was one of these what you see is what you get type guys. He always kept his head down especially since he was finally getting successful. Then one day, a fat assed, big mouth preacher out of Atlanta that worked for the SCLC, referred to McCall as an Uncle Tom in a newspaper interview. That pissed off McCall, but it made him start thinking. History wasn't finished with McCall just yet and when the sixties arrived, the Civil Rights movement was getting plenty of ink. McCall's fledgling exploration company couldn't withstand any bad publicity with his Texas wildcat buddies much less the seven sisters who ruled the world of the black gold.

At last, the fickle finger of fate, as they say, writ' and moved on, and McCall's life took a sudden change of direction. Over breakfast one morning, his wife, Jessie, handed him a photo she'd cut out of the Fort Worth Star Telegram.

"J.B. did you see this photo? When will the white man ever let up on us?"

McCall took the half-folded front page from his wife's hand and read while he sipped his coffee with his free hand. It was the now famous picture of the police dog going for the throat of the terrified Negro schoolboy during a civil rights demonstration. McCall finished the article and stood up from the table walking to the kitchen window.

McCall took a deep breath and exhaled.

"Baby, I've been sitting this one out too long. I'm going to March with Dr. King. Now don't start worrying…I'll be way back in the pack."

It happened on March 7, 1965. The SCLC was in Selma to promote Negro voter registration. McCall was way back in the column, as promised, when the marchers crossed the Edmund Pettis Bridge over the Alabama River.

Then something happened up at the front. The marchers were stopped by hundreds of State Troopers, many of whom on horseback.

Sheriff Jim Clark raised the megaphone to his mouth, "You have two minutes to turn around and go back to your church." The front ranks of the marchers kneeled and began praying.

Clark raised the megaphone again, "Troopers

Advance."

Then from the same megaphone a more chilling order; "Get those goddamned niggers!" The now U.S. Congressman from Georgia, John Lewis, went down immediately, felled by a police baton. Then, all hell broke loose. Dogs attacked; giant clouds of tear gas wafted through the front ranks, and screams of terror came from those in the front being mowed down by dogs, horses, and police billy clubs.

"What's happening?" some white guy a few paces behind McCall shouted.

McCall ducked when something went whizzing by, barely missing his head. It was a burning tear gas projectile fired by the police that wasn't making tear gas like it was supposed to and instead was on fire. The grenade hit the white man squarely in the solar plexis knocking him to the street. The pain was excruciating, he couldn't breathe and as he rolled his body in agony, he rolled on top of the flaming projectile and burned his left forearm and the back of his left hand. The man screamed in pain as more tear gas rounds rained down on the marchers and people panicked. McCall grabbed the man and dragged him to safety between two cars.

"Don't move, I'll be right back," McCall said just before he ran down the embankment to the river's edge and stripped off his shirt soaking it and his T-shirt with cold river water. He ran back up to the white man and squeezed out the water bathing the burns. McCall ran back and forth for to the river about thirty minutes until the demonstrators had dispersed enough to flag down a passing patrol car.

"What's yo' problem boy?" the police officer said.

"I have an injured white man over here," McCall

41

responded. The cop's attitude seemed to soften, but he didn't get out to check on the man. The cop put the microphone against the tobacco smear on the corner of his lip, "Getta amb-u-lance over here to the Pettis Bridge, we gotta man down."

The white man had second degree burns, was hurting real bad and just about in shock. J.B. stayed with him until the ambulance showed up and loaded him on the stretcher. Just as they shoved him into the back, two pieces of paper fell onto the ground out of the man's shirt pocket. The first piece of paper was the guy's business card. The other was a tattered newspaper article. J.B. put the business card back into the man's pocket. The man took the card back out and rasped..."No, you take it...call me!" The ambulance techs were about to close the big single door on the ambulance when the man called out again,"Don't forget..."

The guy's business card read simply "Helms Industries, Matt Helms, CEO."

The ambulance drove off and McCall remembered the other piece of paper. He picked up the tattered article from the New York Times. It was the same photo of the dog going for the young Negro schoolboy.

Matthew Helms became the first big investor in a McCall drilling deal...and made a twenty-nine percent return on his investment. And so, on a bleary March afternoon in 1965, under a barrage of tear gas, a twenty-year friendship began. The history books later called the day "Bloody Sunday."

Just like everybody else in the oil business McCall fought for his piece of the sky. One observer who wrote a book about big oil said they were like a pack of cats in heat "...you couldn't tell if they were fightn' or fuckin." But there was one thing everybody knew about McCall; a handshake deal with him was as good as a hundred page contract with Arco.

In that first big deal, J.B. and Matt Helms were at the closing table with a shit pot full of lawyers when one young smart ass named Dubois from a from a firm in New Orleans, asked a question.

"Well, Mr. McCall, now that you're a big oil ty-**coon,** where'd you get your first 'sperince with oil?" Matt Helms smiled as he elbowed McCall.

"Yeah, J.B., why don't you tell young Mr. Du-boys down there about your first 'sperince with oil." McCall leaned forward to make eye contact with the young attorney down the long table and started answering matter of factly.

"My first experience with oil was when I smoked my fourth Me-109. Shot him through the oil radiator…was so close it went all over the canopy…couldn't see shit…had to land looking out the side." Dubois' face went blank and there was a sort of embarrassed silence and a couple of coughs. Two of the older men at the table were nodding and smiling as they closed their briefcases.

Two years later McCall's company, TriAmCo Energy, had hit all but two wells it drilled and the money was rolling in. But McCall drove a used Ford pick up, wore a Timex watch and lived in a modest, by Texas millionaire standards, thirty-five hundred square foot home with no pool on only twenty-five acres. It was just a short drive to the new TriAmCo building that was going up outside Plainview, Texas, located northeast of Lubbock, not far from Reese Air Force

Base. And even the twenty some odd acres was basically just for privacy and was pancake flat cotton fields with a couple of rigs pumping around sixty a day. Descended from slaves and sharecroppers, despite riots, social revolution and unlike Dr. King, J.B. McCall had arrived in the promised land, "and by God stayed married to the finest woman in the world for over twenty-five years," he would segue at barely related points in conversations with his staff. McCall's son Duane was at Texas Tech playing football and making good grades and during school breaks ran the real estate department of TriAmCo, such that it was. J.B. McCall had a net worth of over twenty-two million and was the sole shareholder and CEO of TriAmCo Energy, a scrappy independent oil company. TriAmCo had smaller drilling properties in Texas, Saudi, and later Bolivia and Guyana near the place the French later built their spaceport.

McCall was hoeing in tall cotton shore 'nuff.

The Guyana leases gave McCall an in with the French colonial administration and that was what caused Lawrence Feldman of the JPL McCall to later seek out McCall with the incredible results of his twenty-year investigation. Once Feldman had convinced McCall of the truth, he revealed his plans for the mission.

Anyhow, in 1988, McCall made the biggest crapshoot of his career on seven leases down in Bolivia and tripled his net worth.

Only a decade later, who could have guessed that McCall would liquidate most of his vast wealth when he was asked to save the human race?

*   *   *

McCall's mind was wandering again, and as he lost focus on one problem, he turned again to the event that had recently changed his life forever...his wife Jessie...who had died of stomach cancer only ten months before. Forty years with the same woman...it seemed like a huge part of his soul had caved off and gone under like a glacier calving icebergs except his icebergs never bobbed back to the surface. They had met at a bus stop outside Tuskeegee, Alabama in 1941 where he was an Air Corps cadet going through pilot training. One night some German POWs from a nearby camp were being taken into town on a furlough. The Tuskeegee cadets were told that they couldn't ride on the bus with the white German prisoners and would have to wait for the next bus. Inflamed with anger, McCall was about to explode in rage against the Alabama redneck bus driver, when someone out of the group of waiting passengers reached over and clasped his hand holding her finger up to her beautiful mouth with a shush sign. "Don't say anything," she had whispered. She was the most beautiful thing McCall had ever seen. He never let go of that hand. Forty years later she died in his arms.

TriAmCo was a desolate, sad, place for almost a year, the joy was gone from the halls and offices and the sense of doom and gloom only lifted when Duane, his son who was a Navy F-4 carrier pilot, came home from the South China Sea on leave. This pumped up the Old Man and the light would glow dimly for a week or so, but when Duane returned to the ship, J.B. McCall fell right back into the pit.

McCall was at his desk one day, gazing absently out the window. He was surrounded by the one affectation he allowed himself...his fantastically ornate, almost Vatican looking office. His troops referred to it as the Taj McCall. Located at the top of the tallest building in Plainview, Texas. McCall had spent some really big bucks on his office...original Remington sculptures...he owned "The Bronc Rider." He had two original Gauguins from the Tahitian period and a huge Kerman rug. The office had a Nara executive desk, hand carved and assembled in the Philippines. The Mahogany was so hard that it had to be constructed with wooden dowels since nails could not be driven into it. The desk appeared to be long enough to recover jet fighters, according to his son, who was serving aboard the Kitty Hawk. His chair was high backed and made from the modified seat of a Boeing 727 given to him by the president of Continental Airlines. The seat adjusted in seven different axis, but best of all, was its ability to recline for a really good nap...a concept that was vaguely troubling since he flew on the Boeings from time to time when his son had the G-2 while home on leave. But by far the most awe inspiring, mind blowing accessory that was truly Texan in grandeur was the two thousand gallon salt water aquarium sitting behind him on the low boy concrete and steel reinforced credenza. With sponges, weed, lobsters, eels, shrimp and octopus, it had thirty-six varieties of tropical fish and a pair of foot long, baby reef sharks. The tank was maintained by two full time attendants he hired from Marineland who actually dived the tank each week to clean the glass using an electric air compressor connected to a scuba mask and regulator by a long black hose. McCall's justification for the grandiose office was that it reeked power, completely intimidated presidents to Arab princes and was the ultimate intimidator to close business deals.

But since Jessie had died, not much seemed to really matter. McCall knew the Old Testament and thought of the Proverbs. "Place not thy heart into things, for things into nothingness pass." McCall knew the Old Testament prophets, but had never heard of Arlo Guthrie or the newer prophets with their messages on the walls and tenement halls...and predictions that "the times they are a' changin." But a big change was a'fixin to happen to J.B. McCall just the same at 1432 hours on the afternoon of October 17, 1968.

Chapter 7

Reese Air Force Base is padlocked and chained now, a relic of the Vietnam War. Tumbleweeds blow down the narrow streets on the base where once were parked brand new honey gold 1968 Mustangs, Pontiac GTOs and Corvette convertibles that belonged to the second lieutenants of the 501st Pilot Training Wing. Completely surrounded by cotton fields with an occasional oil well in every section or so, the skies north of Lubbock nowadays are quiet. A few buzzards circle silently, the only sound that of cicadas chattering in the blistering summer heat. At night there is only wind and stars and the rumble of distant freight trains on the tracks to the northwest.

The "O" club is blacked out, most of the furniture, oddly enough, still in place and a few of the artifacts are still on the walls of the stag bar. The stuffed Sand Hill Crane with the surprised look on his face is still there over the bar, complete with T-38 pitot boom going up his butt, honoring one of the local threats to aerial navigation. The large twenty pound birds blasting through the thin T-38 Plexiglas windshields at 400 knots, had already killed five pilots by 1968 and four more afterwards until bird proof windscreens were installed. The pool out behind the stag bar, where so many senior officers were unceremoniously thrown fully clothed, is completely empty and the concrete deck is badly cracked in several places. Even though they fought furiously, having the pockets of your flight suit ripped open, then being thrown in the pool by the student pilots, was secretly considered a great honor.

The flight line, where hundreds of jets were parked, is empty. The flight line, taxiways and eight thousand foot runways are nothing more than a white fading desert of concrete with broken yellow lines. The footprints of a cat are still there who bravely marched out onto the wet cement near base ops when it was poured in 1953. Someday, archeologists will look at those footprints and wonder how they got there.

In October of 1968, however, Reese Air Force Base was white hot with activity and the Vietnam War was blazing away night after night on the evening news with its obligatory scenes of bloodied and bandaged GIs being loaded into a Huey. Martin Luther King Jr. and Bobby Kennedy had been assassinated. The Tet offensive made it to the living rooms of America showing North Vietnamese regulars attacking the American embassy in Saigon. The enemy took 145,000 casualties during the Tet Offensive, but the American media chalked it up as a huge victory for the communists. Chicago mayor Richard Daley was calling Senator Abraham Ribicoff a "dirty Jew" on the evening news as his police clashed with demonstrators at the democratic national convention. In December of 1968, Frank Borman, James Lovell, and William Anders made the first manned orbit of the moon. It was the Age of Aquarius, guns and butter, and the flower children were screwing themselves to death, smoking everything in sight...taking the magic carpet ride...and Haight Ashbury St. in San Francisco was the center of the blown universe. There was a lot of shit going on in 1968.

The social revolution which had the country in flames, collapsing the previous order, was accepted in a curious yawning puzzlement and the Reese second lieutenants diverted themselves with frog strangling beer busts and flight suit parties with some of the Texas Tech honeys. The old wooden BOQs were in constant danger of being burned to the ground by rocket battles with fireworks bought from highway stands. Classes which had Norwegian Air Force exchange students were especially lucky. The Norwegian Air Force would ship literally hundreds of cases of Tiengold beer to their guys in the USA.

Never in their wildest dreams or late night debates on the war did any of the Reese lieutenants have the slightest idea that we would pull out of the war five years later, with the job unfinished, abandoning our South Vietnamese allies. They were young Air Force officers in pilot training from good families and believed in their country. In modern history, until the Persian Gulf, they were the last generation to ever do so because of the anger, disgust, cynicism and fear that came much later with Watergate, Ruby Ridge, Waco and the election of the draft dodger Bill Clinton. We didn't get our spirit completely back until September 11, 2001.

One magnificent fall afternoon, 2Lt. Matt Blalock III, was summoned by Major Alcock, the flight commander. "Blalock, I need you to go get point six hours to finish out the solo section of the syllabus," he mumbled between chews on the unlighted cigar that was always stuffed in the corner of his mouth. "Get it today."

It's a great day to go flying, Blalock surmised, noting a crystal blue sky with twenty miles visibility. Of course when you've got a T-38 that will do Mach 1.2 and climb faster than a forty-five caliber bullet, there ain't no such thing as a bad day, he thought, picking up his helmet and gear in the equipment room. The T-38 was a supersonic trainer built by Northrop with a razor edged wing and area rule fuselage and for several years held the world's time to climb record. The "White Rocket" could do 812 mph and was being flown by pilots with only a hundred hours of total flying time. One guy in Blalock's class had his first flight in an airplane when he flew in from Hawaii to start training. The washout rate was usually about forty percent and out of every class of sixty pilots there were at least two guys killed in training. Larry Parsons, Blalock's table mate in the T-37 program had already died in a spin accident.

The pilot class mourned his death, but not for long. Death is a constant companion and many more would take his place before a pilot hung up his goggles. But the task at hand was to get exactly six-tenths of an hour and not more or less. The solution was blindingly obvious to Blalock as he ran down the checklist and cranked the two General Electric J-85 afterburning engines. The plan was an after burner climb to flight level 450 (45,000 ft), fly straight out to the edge of the Alpha High/Low jet training area and do a split "S" and a low altitude penetration return to base for a standard overhead recovery. This was going to be fun.

After lining up into position, Reese tower cleared Blalock for takeoff.

"Beer Can two-three, cleared for burner climb to flight level four-five-zero, cleared for takeoff."

"Cleared to flight level four-five-zero, cleared for take off, Beer Can twenty-three." Blalock read back, huffing a little in anticipation through his mask microphone, with a big shit eating grin on his face under the mask. The Northrop jet surged forward as the brakes were released and the afterburners kicked in and began eating up runway. The concrete flashed by and Blalock rotated the nose ten degrees...then as soon as he noted a climb on the altimeter and vertical speed indicator he retracted the landing gear. The T-38 has such tremendous acceleration that the limiting speed for the gear doors can easily be exceeded just taking off. Asked to describe the acceleration of the T-38, the standard response was, take a hound dog, throw some scalding water on him while simultaneously shoving a bat up his ass and you'll be close.

He held it in a ten degree climb as the airspeed started winding up, two hundred, two-fifty, three hundred, three fifty, now the mach barber pole was alive creeping up to .7 mach, .8 mach., .9 mach. Now the really fun part, Blalock said to himself, as he honked the jet into a thirty-five degree climb. The altimeter was winding up like a stopwatch running amuck. Looking over his shoulder, Reese grew smaller and the sky began getting darker until it was deep purple. Some of his classmates claimed they could see the curvature of the earth at this altitude, but Blalock never saw it. The jet hurtled skyward like a controlled missile.

"Beer Can two-three, Lubbock departure, you're cleared into Alpha Hi/Low squawk twelve hundred and monitor Albuquerque center on 254.5."

"Two-fifty-four point five Beer Can two-three."

Approaching 45,000 feet, Blalock realized he was going to overshoot it badly so he did a half roll to the right, went inverted as he reached an apogee of 51,000 feet and did a slow inverted descent with positive "G" and rolled level again at 45,000 feet. Looking down at his TACAN range indicator he noticed an alarming piece of information. He was now three miles outside the practice area going away from Reese....no time like the present, he thought, was going to do this anyway, and Matt Blalock, second lieutenant United States Air Force was about to meet J.B. McCall and change the course of planetary history.

Going inverted again, Blalock pulled back gently on the stick. The T-38 arced over on its back and headed for the ground. Ohhh man this is greaaat, he was audibly saying to himself under the mask. But before he could enjoy himself another nanosecond, he realized that he had just made a grave error, he hadn't pulled the throttles to idle and had left them at cruise power. Able to climb like a bullet, you can imagine what this jet can do in a dive. Unless he did something fast, he was either going to hit the ground, or go supersonic over the small town that was coming up like lightning over the nose. The "Gs" came on and the "G" suit inflated, doing its job. His abdomen and legs were squeezed by the air bladders in the suit to keep him from blacking out. The altimeter was virtually unreadable it was unwinding so fast...all he could do was to hold on, keep the wings loaded up and into the buffet and hope he had enough room to pull out. Getting behind the airplane...the classic blunder of the new guy in the T-38.

Holy shit, he thought, if that's Plainview on the nose; I've flown twenty miles outside the practice area. Plainview flashed by in a streaky blur of small buildings and toy cars. The altimeter stopped descending and began climbing at somewhere below 3,000 feet. Relief melded into another shock as Blalock as one fuck up led to the next. He looked at his airspeed indicator. It was passing backwards through Mach 1.0!

This meant that Blalock had just committed the most unpardonable sin in the Air Force.

He had gone supersonic, over a populated area at low altitude.

Ohhh shhittttt, now I've done it, he thought.

The all-seeing eye of Albuquerque center would have it all on radar...the time and date and the name of the perp were all on the big reel of magnetic tape.

Beer can two-three's actual altitude over Plainview was just under a thousand feet above ground level, which is the perfect altitude for maximum ground damage from a sonic boom. The ear splitting explosion of the sonic compression wave raked up Prairie Street as Blalock flashed overhead. Shop windows shattered, and almost every rear window in every car parked on the street blew out. The new Piggley Wiggly out on route six was totaled. Every window was blown and it changed instantly from an air-conditioned marvel of modern shopping to a watermelon stand.

TriAmCo Energy was six seconds next only a mile further down the highway.

J.B. McCall was alone with his thoughts gazing at the picture on his desk of his beloved Jessie. The sonic blast wave hit the TriAmCo building like a mining accident. Some of the downstairs windows cracked and the whole building rumbled on its foundations like a mild earthquake. McCall had built the HQ to last and consequently, the special shock resistant tempered glass he had used paid off big time. The huge panoramic controlled polarization windows, which lined one entire wall of the Taj McCall, just flexed mightily bowing in an out a few times until the shock wave passed.

No so lucky, however, was the two thousand gallon salt water aquarium directly behind McCall on the special reinforced concrete credenza. The glass on the aquarium shattered magnificently in a spectacular display and a mini tsunami of perfectly maintained salt water, fish, eels, weed, shrimp and lobsters roared down on J.B. McCall's back. The wall of water knocked him out of his B-727 cockpit chair, body surfed him over the big Nara desk, and carried him around the big sculpture of the Bronc Rider like it was a boulder in a white water river. The foaming torrent tossed McCall over a hundred feet from his desk, all the way out into the reception area. He finally came spinning to a stop in front of the elevators. His secretary was on top of her desk, which had partially washed off to one side. She was kneeling on top like a stranded seaman from a torpedoed liberty ship and was screaming hysterically. Water was four inches deep on the entire top floor and cascaded like a Salmon ladder down the emergency stairwell. McCall, uninjured, slowly came to his feet with seaweed hanging out of one pocket and spitting water out of his mouth, which contained something alive. "Damn, I think that was one of my new Holacanthus Clarionesis," he said as the baby yellow angelfish flopped helplessly on the floor. "....and Anne Louise, for Heaven's sake stop your bawling."

But there was no stopping Ann Louise from bawling...she was pointing at his back. McCall looked around at his backside holding up his right arm..."Oh for crissake," McCall felt a new sensation from somewhere, he was smiling. "Anne Louise, get over here and help me get this shark off my butt."

One of his baby reef sharks bit the first thing that went by and it was the baggy seat of McCall's Bond Street suit.

McCall took a chance on the elevators hoping they

hadn't been shorted out. He hit "lobby" and started to laugh at himself standing there wearing a thousand dollar "diving" suit, spitting fish out of his mouth with a shark chomped down on his coat tail. Jessie would have loved this one. McCall could not stop chuckling as he wiped the tears out of his eyes with salt water soaked sleeves. McCall was still laughing as he waved to Marvin and T.W., the day security guards in the lobby as he headed back to the ranch to change clothes. McCall had no sooner left the lobby when the two security men high fived each other and got on the intercom.

***

The sonic boom was big news in Plainview. But at TriAmCo, the big news that blazed from office to office was that "Old Man" was laughing again.

Blalock called Albuquerque center for clearance back to Reese, he knew he was screwed. "Beer can two-three squawk ident, we've had a radar outage, say your radial and DME from the Reese TACAN."

Let no one kid you on this one...there is a God.

The radar failure at Albuquerque center meant that his major screw up had not been observed on center radar. There was no record on the big reel of tape.

The investigation that followed the flood of complaints from the citizens of Plainview narrowed the field of possibilities down to Blalock, one other T-38 flying solo in the adjoining practice area, and a dual acro mission in another nearby practice area. Tom LaBeau, a classmate, who later became general counsel for Alaska Air Lines was the other solo student pilot. Blalock admitted to Tom that it was he who had done the booming of Plainview but he had to deny it or they'd kick him out of the program. LeBeau agreed. The two guys on the dual mission, of course, were innocent, so of course they would deny everything. LeBeau reasoned that all they had to do was stick to their story and the training command probably wouldn't kick four guys out to get the one offending perpetrator. Blalock told Tom that if they started making noises about eighty-sixing both of them out, that he would fess up at the last minute to keep Tom from getting the boot.

Vietnam was hungry for pilots, and the Air Force being somewhat enlightened for a military service, dropped the investigation with a stern warning to all four officers that if there were any further problems the shit was going to hit the fan. The two completely innocent guys, who were minding their own business on the aerobatic mission, were sorely put with Blalock and LeBeau since they were the only ones who knew for a fact it was one of those two. But now they had the sword hanging over their heads as well for the rest of the program.

Chapter 8
"Oyster"

USS Kitty Hawk
10 November 1968
"Dear Pop:

I got your letter today about the Air Force puke booming the HQ. I posted it in the squadron ready room and everybody that read it laughed their ass off. I'm glad you didn't file a complaint though. That guy was so screwed up by the time he RTBd you couldn't have got a greasy cockroach up his ass with a sledge hammer. Be interesting to find out whatever happened to the dude. You sounded happy in the letter. Since Mom died, frankly, I was starting to get worried what with all the gloom and doom in your letters. Too bad Ann Louise didn't have a Polaroid, that reef shark chowing down on one of your thousand buck suits would have been a hoot.

Everybody here is totally pissed off about the targeting and bomb load selection and frankly, I'll be surprised if this even gets to you. They say nobody is censoring our mail, but who the hell knows what with the way we're fighting this war. The F-4 can carry 8 750lb bombs on a standard mission profile up north. Would you believe they are launching us with 2 (2) TWO! 250lb bombs? Exposing two guys and an expensive airframe to all the fireworks they have around Hanoi to plop a couple of firecrackers in Uncle Ho's lap! It's positively sickening and everybody is furious. One of the rumors floating around is that the whole idea is to keep the sortie rate up so that certain captains can get their tickets punched to make admiral.

The way they're running this war, it makes you wonder if they really want to win it. If they keep this shit up I don't see how we can.

Remember Joe Dickey, my RIO from Fairhope Alabama, I brought home on the last leave? You let us have the G-2 for a week and we had dates in New York, New Orleans and San Francisco? Not to mention giving us the corporate credit card and us staying at the Mark Hopkins and the Ritz Carleton on TriAmCo's tab. Somebody asked this asshole how he enjoyed going home on leave with the only black pilot on the ship. You know what he said? Said he "had never tasted finer watermelon anywhere." The whole briefing room howled. (They knew the true story) I'm telling you Pop, that being the only brother in a sea of whitey is not without its hilarious moments. Uncle Dave was dead wrong about these guys. They don't give a damn what color I am. All these guys care about is can you fly...and to a lesser extent drink...and chase women. Pilots seem to have a lot in common that breaks a lot of the barriers. Nothing like what you guys had to put up with in WWII, of course. You plowed the field for the rest of us. It's up to us to now.

Been working in the maintenance office all day and my two chiefs have everything under control, as always, so I'm going to hit the rack for a few hours. Our quarters on the ship are two levels below the flight deck, and when we're launching and recovering aircraft, which is most of the time, we can hear them hit the deck and the steam cat when it fires. If you can sleep with this stuff going on you can sleep anywhere. When those recruiters came smoking into the parking lot at Tech with their white uniforms and white Chrysler convertible, they didn't tell us about this part.

Bill Broocke

Joe has a bad cold so am flying with a new guy back seater tonight. Have a night mission up north. I'm hoping it will be top cover.

Love, Duane

USS Kitty Hawk
11 November 1968

Dear Mr. McCall:

I'm sorry to have to write you about this, but Duane was injured in a landing accident on the ship last night. The injuries are serious, but not life threatening. The Skipper asked me to write you first since I knew the family. He will be in touch in the next several days when more is known about his exact medical condition. And what they plan to do with him.

I was sacked out when everything happened, but according to paddles (the LSO) this is a fairly accurate account. "Oyster," that's Duane's call sign, got shot off cat number one and fodded both engines. Initially, we all thought that he had ejected, but after several tense minutes we realized that he was still in the aircraft. He somehow managed to level the plane at eighty feet over the relatively rough seas and then was able to milk it up to about 150'. It was 2045 hours and the weather was about a thousand foot broken and really dark. We were going to attempt to recover him at half flaps single engine when he stated that he was only able to maintain level flight in full blower with the gear up. The one engine remaining was having massive compressor stalls that were barking fire out of his tailpipe and were pretty impressive even from six miles. He had already jettisoned his ordinance and dumped fuel down to about two thousand pounds just to stay level.

The next thing we wanted to do was a wave off/approach capability check to see how the aircraft would perform up close to the ship. But, unfortunately he couldn't get enough altitude. We readied the deck and decided to give him a chance at a normal pass. After he lined up, he saw that there was no way he would get down. He went up the starboard side of the ship and once again, everybody thought he was going to eject. The shit coming out of his right engine was unbclievable. Throughout the whole evolution everyone stayed extremely calm and pulled together to make some good decisions. Duane, by now, had burned down to almost nothing on gas and we knew he'd have to get down on the next pass without bolter capability. The decision was made to rig the barricade.

The deck crew rigged the barricade in record time. Nobody had ever seen the men perform so magnificently. We crunched the numbers and he started his final approach.

The approach was high and by the time he hit the glide slope he was way out of parameters and the LSO sent him around. He went by the ship in full burner with the engine making this sickening whine-pop with more shit coming out of his tail pipe like a salvo of flares. He cleared the top of the barricade by only ten feet and nobody could figure out what he was using for fuel since he had to be down to fumes.

His last pass was right out of the book and his stick work was fantastic as he jockeyed the jet right down the slot. The ship was on a recovery heading and couldn't change course with Oyster on final approach. As Duane was about two tenths of a mile from the ramp, we hit a light rain shower. The down draft out of the shower and the normal burble over the fantail was more that he could handle on one engine, however, and he crashed into the maintenance parts storage just below the ramp.

Thank God there was no explosion. The F-4 was demolished and we thought that Duane and his RIO were goners for sure. About five minutes later some guy calls the bridge over the ship's telephone and says that he's Oyster and could somebody come down and pry him out the wreckage. The CAG went ballistic and shouted into the phone that one of our pilots had just been killed and the sick son of a bitch making this call was going to be court martialled. After further conversation, the caller convinced the CAG that it was indeed Duane. There was no light down in that section and the wreckage heap had come to a stop like a giant accordion within arm's reach of a bulkhead where a phone was located. Duane was just sitting there in the dark so he pulled out his flashlight and looked around. He could see the phone right outside the cockpit, so he blew his canopy, reached over and just dialed the bridge.

It appears that his legs were crushed in the crash. They're air evacing him to Clark Field and we should know more within a few days.

Sincerely,
Joe Dickey

12 December 1968
US Air Force Hospital
Clark Air Force Base
Republic of the Philippines

Dear Pop:

I'm OK. Stand down from general quarters! Please ask your buddy Congressman Ben to have his staff stop calling. And NO I don't want you flying out here. They had a small earthquake at Subic Bay and one of the main wings of the base hospital was closed so I got lucky and was sent to the Air Force hospital over here at Clark. It looks like they may be sending me home for some additional surgery in few weeks and we can get caught up then. I get a backrub every night from these Air Force nurses and they're treating me just fine. I'm fairly doped up so I'll write again as soon as I can.

Love,
Duane
PS: It looks like I'll be losing the use of my legs.

And so he did. Duane McCall was confined, although he would object to that term, to a wheelchair for the rest of his life, but it didn't slow him down one damned bit with the ladies, or with his work as the Real Estate Vice President for TriAmCo.

The only brush with disaster that was related to Duane's handicap happened on an Eastern Air Lines B-727. In an emergency evacuation of an aircraft, airline flight attendants are trained to perform a sort of triage as to who gets evacuated. If you are handicapped, they are taught to get all the able bodied people out first and if there is enough time later, to get the handicapped out. The idea is to save as many as you can in the limited time available. It sounds cruel, but it works.

It was in April of 1973, heavy rain showers were sweeping the New York area and the Boeing tri-jet was making the expressway approach to runway 22 at LaGuardia. On short final, it hit a severe windshear. The captain firewalled the throttles and attempted to correct the huge sink rate that had begun, but the airplane kept plummeting for the ground. The 727 barely cleared the dike, and hit so hard that the right landing gear broke off and ruptured a fuel line for the APU. The raw fuel, porting out of the center tank, began spraying around the broken landing gear stump which was rooster tailing a shower of sparks down the runway and ignited a massive wheel well fire. After the aircraft careened off the right side of the runway and smoke started bellowing out from under the wing root, the alert flight attendants immediately began an evacuation and got just about everybody out before the flames consumed the entire fuselage.

Clearing the fuselage, the passengers and crew ran hard as the right side of the jet went up like a huge napalm burst. The second officer, however, looked back and saw the face of a struggling passenger in a first class window. Without thinking, he sprinted back to the airplane, clambered back up the left flap, tumbled through the emergency exit into the flaming fuselage, and dived to the floor to stay under the curtain of fire, smoke, and toxic gas produced from the synthetic, flame resistant seat material. When the Federal Air Regulations were passed requiring "flame resistant" interiors, it was somehow overlooked that in order to accomplish this, the seat covers when actually on fire, produced lethal by products, such as cyanide gas.

The second officer crawled forward to where Duane was struggling to get himself out of his seat when he noticed movement on the floor behind him. He turned and made eye contact with the Eastern pilot.

"You hanging around for the barbecue or would you like to get off?"

"Off!" Duane shouted. The man on the floor reached though a plume of fire curling down from the ceiling and grabbed McCall by the collar of his suit.

Duane saw the man's face wince with pain then felt himself yanked out of his seat onto the floor. McCall worked out regularly with free weights and had good upper body strength.

"You pull, I'll push," the man shouted. Between the two of them they were able to crawl and push their way on the floor to the forward emergency slide. The pilot grabbed McCall by his belt and catapulted him head first down the forward escape slide, like a torpedo, then jumped properly himself, butt first. The flammable honeycomb, aluminum and all the rest of the stuff that burns really good in a modern airliner, finally had their orgasm of fire. The forward exit blew like there were explosive charges in the doorframe.

The fire department was on the scene by then spraying the flames with fire suppressant foam. The paramedics grabbed the Eastern pilot and McCall and put them in separate ambulances. McCall was uninjured except for minor abrasions and some smoke inhalation. The Eastern guy had third degree burns on his left arm and hand and would be permanently scarred. Two fingers of his left hand had melted together and would have to be surgically separated.

Later on, McCall wanted to thank his rescuer for saving his life and even though the airlines are very protective of giving out names of crewmembers, by pulling some strings, Duane got the guy's name. The Eastern guy told the chief pilot that he didn't want to be contacted by anybody and especially anyone wanting to give him a reward. Said he was just doing his job. The Eastern guy was a new hire probationary pilot just out of the Air Force and had only been on the line about four months...some guy the name of Matt Blalock.

Sixteen years later when the great Eastern Air

Lines strike occurred, Blalock went out with the rest of the pilots in a risky and desperate scheme to rid the airline of the corporate vampire Frank Lorenzo. The idea was to join forces with the hated machinists union to force Lorenzo to sell the airline to a legitimate operator who wanted to run the airline successfully instead of bleeding it to death as Lorenzo had planned.

The strike took a deadly personal toll as the bills came due without the high pilot income to pay them. Facing imminent personal bankruptcy, one year into the strike, Blalock got a certified letter one morning from a lawyer in Houston disclosing that he had just inherited two thousand shares of private stock from a Texas oil company and one of his other clients wanted to buy it. The shares, with an estimated value of $ 107.00 each, were in some company he'd never heard of called TriAmCo Energy.

There are some people who say there's no such thing as coincidences. That everything happens for a reason. That there are multiple planes of reality that are continuously intersecting one another in the known universe and that time and space are irrelevant. Some even say that extraterrestrial contact has shaped our history for thousands of years as they intersected human history in the forms of gods, myths, and fables. Matt Blalock, staring down at the letter on a December morning, of course knew nothing of this or would have cared, and of course he couldn't figure out who this distant cousin was and what could have motivated him to bequeath the windfall.

All Blalock knew was that it was a miracle. When his wife Diana did the arithmetic, she hugged his neck and cried. Blalock stroked her shoulder length, honey-colored hair, which had not seen the inside of a beauty parlor in over a year. He held her close. He could feel the beating of her heart and her teardrops dripping on his shoulder.

Chapter 9
Feldman

The family at the adjoining campsite, a mile over, reported to the ranger station the sounds of low flying jets and a strange glow against the low clouds hovering above the towering Sequoias. "Probably sheet lightning," one ranger explained, and this explanation would have been just peachy except for the facts that: One, there's no such thing as sheet lightening. Two, there was no thunder. And three...there was no flash or flicker just a steady glow.

But the King's Canyon park rangers, like park rangers everywhere, take a dim view of anything happening to campers or the critters under their charge, went over and did a ground search of the site and then checked again as the family who had it reserved departed late Sunday afternoon. Maury and Esther Feldman and their boy reported nothing unusual and after a second ground inspection of the surrounding area, the rangers chalked it up.

Maury and Esther, however, over the years that followed, laughingly referred to the holiday as the "lost weekend," since for some reason, over that Memorial Day, two hours had disappeared somewhere. Larry was eight at the time and he didn't remember anything either, but apparently the great outdoors has quite a salutary effect on the lad since when school cranked up the following semester Lawrence Feldman started blowing the doors off the curriculum.

And well he should, since the inferior parietal lobe of his brain was now about fifteen percent wider than normal and the parietal operculum was completely missing. This greatly enhanced his visiospacial cognition and mathematical reasoning. And besides the enlargement of the inferior parietal lobe, the Sylvan fissure had been shrunk. This allowed the brain cells to be packed much more closely together allowing great leaps of creative induction and the ability to cross reference massive amounts of information. Studies made of Einstein's brain in 1996 by a team led by Dr. Sandra Witelson, at McMaster University in Hamilton, Ontario, disclosed a similar arrangement. The restriction placed in the limbic region of Feldman's brain, designed to eliminate his capacity for remorse did not take. And lastly, certain subtle alterations were made in the genes that control the acid tolerance of alveoli in the lungs and the sensitivity to the ultraviolet spectrum in his epithelial cells.

Larry's teachers were surprised and pleased that his previous indolence had suddenly lifted like fog revealing a radiant academic...But Larry was not turning into a nerdy, pocket protector geek. Not just science and math, but he soaked up the great works of literature and poetry and could quote the romantics for hours on end from his photographic memory. At fifteen he was accepted as a freshman at Caltech and made the gymnastics team as a walk-on. His dream was to become an astronaut and when he turned sixteen his parents bought him his dream chariot...a used Chevy pickup...like the one Chuck Yeager drove. He dubbed it Glamorous Glennis II, after the X-1 rocket plane in which Yeager had broken the sound barrier. He practiced his version of what he thought was a sort of Texas drawl so he'd sound like a real test pilot when he talked. He chewed Beeman's gum and completely immersed himself in the evolving technology that was beginning to touch the edge of space. Larry's blessing and curse were his eyes. At six feet even, he had piercing emerald eyes and short and curly oaken brown hair. Despite the age differential problem, the co-eds were goo goo eyed over the guy. That was the blessing part. The curse was his vision. He was a cunt hair short of being legally blind. And even though he had some real Air Force pilot frames for his glasses, when you looked closely, you realized that on a mountain top somewhere, a great astronomical instrument was sitting idle, impotent, because two of its primary lenses had been vandalized for Feldman's specs. This meant he'd never be a test pilot, or an astronaut despite the liberalization of vision requirements.

There was one pivotal event in Larry's formative years: the summer trip to France with his Dad and then on to the Normandy beachhead on the sixth of June. The German coastal guns were all still there, sunk deeply into the mighty bluffs that glowered above the allied forces. In the sand of the rock strewn beaches, was the blood of men who died without a whimper, torn by shells from the towering heights and the rain of fire pouring down without pity. Maury and Larry walked that beach and talked about the men who died, who strove and fell in the deafening din of war in early June of 1944.

"Hitler captured France's munitions industry completely intact and had production running wide open making land mines," Maurey said as they walked down the dark pebble strewn channel beach which was one timed called Omaha.

"What were they going to do with all those mines, Papa?"

"Before the invasion the Nazis had twenty million already planted and the plan was to lay two hundred million mines making the entire coast an impenetrable barrier of death from the waterline up to twenty kilometers inland. The battle that took place here was a vast series of heroic individual actions of individual soldiers against individual enemies. It was total chaos at first that only swam into focus ever so slightly the following day. Larry, one man can make a difference and if you get the right one at the right place in history. It can spell the difference between disaster and a flood tide of victory." Maury Feldman's knowledge of military history bordered on the encyclopedic...and then they went to the cemetery.

Maury had saved this part for last. It was a cool overcast day. There were hundreds of acres of white marble markers in geometric precision extending as far as you could see in every direction...they walked for about an hour, Maury waiting. Larry suddenly stopped...."Papa look how many of the markers are Stars of David."

Of course, being the good Dad that he was, this was the secret agenda behind the whole trip to France in the first place. "You better believe it. A lot of good Jews died for our country. There isn't one Israeli buried in this place." Of course, in fairness, the nation of Israel wasn't around in 1944, but the point wasn't lost on young Lawrence Feldman.

Larry graduated with honors in 1969 with double majors in astrophysics and economics and was at the legal minimum age when he received his ROTC commission in the Air Force. All hell was breaking loose in California in 1969 with anti-war riots and peace demonstrations, and while most of Larry's contemporaries were shouting "baby killers" from the barricades, Feldman raised his right hand, and gave his oath of allegiance to our nation.

The Air Force had been rubbing their hands together waiting for Feldman to graduate because they had literally seen the guy coming and had big plans. After a couple of months of paper shuffling in the Pentagon where they wanted to give him another once over, his initial assignment, finally came through. Feldman was the first second lieutenant ever assigned to the National Reconnaissance Office (NRO).

The next four years were spent on ultra-classified reconnaissance satellite projects. Feldman was the guy who doped out the South African nuclear test on a barge near Edgeman Island in the South Atlantic. Everybody else who looked at the data said it was a "superbolt," an unusually powerful bolt of lightning out of a huge thunderstorm. Feldman said the water was too cold that far south for a big thunderstorm that would produce a superbolt and wrote a computer program to analyze this one particular event. It took him months, but the program worked and filtered out the extraneous bullshit. What he found was the unmistakable EM pulse, an electromagnetic footprint of a five kiloton device. The result of this brilliant stroke of work was the basis for the complete restructuring of U.S. Foreign policy in southern Africa.

The perpetrators of apartheid, desperate and isolated by the world, the perpetrators who controlled the world's primary source of industrial diamonds, chromium, cobalt, and gold, had joined the nuclear club. Overnight, the table stakes went way up in that part of the globe.

The desperate and isolated now had atomic

weapons.

Not a bad piece of work for a twenty-two year old guy.

From that point onward, Feldman's career seemed to be paved with success and all agreed that here was a guy who was really going places, especially now that he was going over to NASA and given a plum assignment in the Apollo Program.

Unfortunately, God sometimes has other plans for us mortals, and the great tests of Job were about to descend. Also unfortunate is that Job ultimately had a better fate than Feldman...an individual soldier...who would pay a price for his victory. A victory which would join those at Concord and Iwo Jima in the history books.

Not all great battles are won by the sword. Some are won with computers, digital imagery analyzers, healthy skepticism, and in the minds of men who don't jump out of their skins when the wind blows a door shut. Feldman never quit and in what anybody else would have called an obsession, he figured out what the aliens were up to. Then, he had a plan. Feldman would make his father proud.

It all started when Apollo 18, 19, and 20 were mysteriously canceled, allegedly for budget constraints. Spending all those years in intelligence made Feldman naturally suspicious of important events explained by barely plausible justifications. The cancellations were surprising by themselves, but combined with the sudden classification of fifty percent of the Apollo photographs of the lunar surface, red flags were flying and alarms were going off in the back of his mind. His civilian coworkers, who didn't have his intelligence training, accepted everything with bovine, civil servant equanimity. Their main interest was how they were going to make the house payment if the program tubed, and how fast they could sell their Sea Ray. The clincher, which greased Feldman's skids out the door at the Cape, was when he discovered that one of the oblique photographic negatives of the moon's south pole was missing and the remainder had been renumbered as if the missing negative had never existed. Nobody but an expert in imagery analysis would have detected it. Within forty-eight hours after bringing this to the program director's attention, Feldman was off the property...but not after a full afternoon with the FBI reviewing the fine print of his security clearance...the part about going to prison.

History recorded that Feldman's relentless search for the missing negative was the triggering event for man's return to the moon...but this time not to take one small step...and this time we would not be coming in peace.

It was right after Feldman's departure from the Cape that the nightmares began. Unsettling dreams, maddeningly incomplete, filled with shadowy threats and fragmented, frightening images that could not be remembered the next morning. There was something back there where nightmares are generated but expertly compressed under layers of what? The dreams were always similar...nebulous, nefarious, ghostly, and perfectly and symmetrically evil. Something really bad had happened, was happening now, or about to happen. The evil was unswerving in purpose, with a sweetly sickening malevolence, totally confident, submerged in its sublime self-awareness of invincibility. It lived in a Biblical scale that dwarfed galactic distances and the cosmic understanding of time and space. A metaphysical war of good and evil was raging in his unconscious and good was being annihilated. A lesser man could not have contained what Feldman was going through. He seized strength from his profound belief that God wouldn't create more than he could handle. He tried to reduce it into an equation he could understand. He was in some kind of battle. He was a soldier. The right soldier in the right place can make the difference between disaster and the flood tide of victory. And he thought of the cool afternoon that summer day in June, walking through the garden with his father...white marble markers in the cemetery at Normandy, the Stars of David among rows of crosses in the green sea of manicured grass. Some nights he woke up crying.

Over a period of five years Feldman consulted myriad experts; psychiatrists, dream specialists, neurologists, Rabbis, a priest, and even an Inuit shaman on the Hudson Bay by short wave. Nobody could unlock the secret of his dreams. The shaman alluded that part of his solution was in the spirit of the Great Aurora...that would be the time when the evil one appeared. "When will the evil one appear?" Feldman shouted into the ham operator's desk mike. "Every eleven years," the old Indian responded.

One positive thing did come of these various consultations, however. He found out that the dreams were originating in the part of the brain that stimulates the higher human functions such as morality, love, self-sacrifice, and philanthropy.

"You mean it's all locked away like in a bank vault?" one of the shrinks had queried.

"Yeah, maybe, but nobody knows the combination," Feldman replied.

"Well, why don't you dream one up?" the shrink

had countered.

The analogy of the bank vault led him to try a totally different approach. He went over to his local bank and asked the branch manager to give him some information on vault combinations. He was then referred to the Ventron Corporation out of Trenton, NJ who stone walled him for three weeks until he was finally able to prove to the president that he was on the level by coughing up all his top secret clearances. All he was able to find out was that all Ventron vaults used a combination of ten two digit numbers from zero one to ninety-nine. This meant that there were literally millions of possible permutations and if there was a combination that would unlock the vault in his dreams, it could take a hundred years of trial and error to find it.

The last shrink he had been talking to received the information with sangfroid aplomb.

"Larry, your mind already knows the combination, all you have to do is permit the creative process to find it for you."

"You mean like a guided missile locking onto a target?"

"You got it. Maxwell Maltz, the late plastic surgeon, discovered this effect in the early sixties, and it's the basis for about ninety percent of the self-help books on the market. Be sure to keep a note pad by your bed."

Two weeks later, for the first time, the images were gone. But he could still hear screaming behind the vault door of his dreams and still no combination materialized.

On his yellow notepad the next morning, he found the message in his own hand.

Find the goddamn negative!

Twenty-five years later, when the dust settled from the national emergency and after the all the other "Feldmans" had been hunted down, that page would be part of a major exhibit at the Air and Space Museum in Washington on the Tau Ceti War.

Feldman's last assignment in NASA was at the JPL in Pasadena, working on Project Clementine, and had anybody in the project known he was clandestinely still looking for the missing Apollo negative, he never would have gotten the job. As it turned out, working on Clementine put him in an information stream that was perfect for snooping around. Clementine was supposed to be a mission to evaluate the mining possibilities of asteroids, hence the name Clementine, daughter of the miner, forty-niner in the folk song. The truth, of course, was a different matter, and Clementine had about as much to do with asteroid mining as it had to do with the Mustang Ranch. Clementine was a joint project of NASA and the newly formed Strategic Defense Organization, set up to take advantage of a loophole in a treaty with the Russians. And here again, none of the young engineers made any global connections with the actual mission of Clementine and anything that happened in the past. This was because while all the history was being made, they were stoned and bombed in various frat houses around the country. Whatever they might have remembered, they saw it on TV.

Clementine was supposed to enter Lunar orbit and do imaging of the polar regions, then fire its rocket motor, swing out of orbit and rendezvous with a mysterious asteroid that had suddenly appeared in a near Earth orbit. Nobody had noticed the asteroid Geographos until it had gotten quite close, which was not unusual, since back then few people were particularly worried about the Apollos, the planet killing asteroids that occasionally crossed Earth's orbit. It's trajectory indicated that it had originated from the vicinity of Jupiter, apparently passing nearby at such extreme speed it readily escaped Jupiter's immense gravity well, then continued its voyage passing near Earth's solar orbit. After intercepting the asteroid, Clementine was supposed to blast it with a powerful laser, the results of which were to be analyzed by ground sensors. Allegedly, the mission was to see exactly what the composition of the object was and how it would react to the most powerful space weapon we had at the time. Feldman was seeing a hell of a lot of pieces coming together on the shocking theory he was formulating about what was actually going on. And then the information got worse. Clementine discovered water on the moon. A lot of it. The data showed that there could be as much as twenty-six billion gallons in the form of slushy permafrost in the polar craters that never saw the light of day. This is because the sun only rises 1.6 degrees above the moon's polar horizons. Calculations showed that in the Aitken Basin, the largest and deepest known impact crater in the solar system, there could be as much 30 square miles of ice. Initially thought as a novel and quite interesting geological discovery, Feldman realized that there were sinister implications if the rest of his research panned out. With this much water on the moon, certain larger barriers to colonization were removed. You could drink the water, use the oxygen out of it for life support and extract the hydrogen for fuel.

Then the fourth ace came out of the deck. When it came time to swing Clementine out of lunar orbit for its asteroid rendezvous, it stopped responding to earth commands. NASA and the JPL made an unconcerned statement that it was decided instead of checking out Geographos, that they would crash Clementine on the moon to do seismic research. They announced that there were some moonquake fault lines in the area that they needed to check out that took precedence over investigating the asteroid.

Jim Clark, one of the analysts, called Feldman over to his desk one day about a week after Clementine augured into the moon.

"Hey Larry take a look at this." Clark was prairie dogging over the top of his cubicle to make sure nobody was coming. "Look at these EM signatures. Ever seen anything like this before?" Feldman examined the graph. Each of the parameters had gone vertically off scale at the end of the tracing...then were flat lined, indicating a sudden stoppage of data flow.

"Where did you get this?"

"Never mind. Do you know what you're looking at?"

"Why, no." Feldman lied.

"It's the last thing we got from Clementine as it went over the lunar south pole."

"Solar flare?" queried Feldman; the goose flesh formed on the back of his neck, he knew damn well what he was looking at.

"Nope, the eleven year Solar Max doesn't hit until late 2000."

"What is this Jim?"

"Clementine, for some unknown reason, experienced a massive off scale pulse of electromagnetic energy at least to the fifth power."

"Very interesting. Refresh me on the Solar Max. That's the every eleven year event right?"

"Sure. Every eleven years sunspot activity skyrockets causing massive Coronal Mass Ejections. Imagine five billion tons of solar matter smashing into the Earth. As you know, we get hit with ejected matter from the sun all the time...that's what causes the Auroras. But the Earth's magnetic field from its molten core catches most of it preventing it from getting through. But what we're talking about is a whole different ball game. It knocks the shit out of communications, fries the circuits in satellites and hell, in 1989 it knocked out fifteen million homes when a CME shorted out the electrical grid of Hydro Quebec, something the engineers said could never happen. And during the Solar Max, we'll be getting six coronal mass ejections per day! At northern latitudes if you're in a plane when one of them hits, it will be the same as getting a hundred chest x-rays. Larry, the solar forecasters are saying that this cycle will be the most powerful solar max we've ever had. We're talking something that could be really be bad. You won't hear much about it on CNN because all it would do is agitate the masses of the great unwashed."

"But you didn't answer my question. What do you make of those charts?"

"Like I said before...interesting."

"Ahh, come on pal...is that your only reaction, a former spook for the NRO? I thought you guys looked at this shit all the time."

Feldman turned to go back to his desk, then stopped and faced Clark, placing his hand on his friend's shoulder...."Yeah Jim, that's my reaction, and it better be yours too."

Feldman sat down at his desk and hit the speed dialer to get his wife. Time was growing short. Did they have until the end of 2000? Feldman asked himself as he drummed the desk with a pencil waiting for his wife to pick up. An eleven year solar cycle was coming, forecast to be the worst in decades, he thought. Communications, Air traffic Control, NORAD, and Space Command will be temporarily blinded during peak activity.

Taken by itself, Feldman knew that the Solar Max would be somewhat problematic, and the various agencies, aware of its repercussions had no doubt already taken precautions. They had already reshuffled the shuttle schedule so they could go up and shove the international space station a little higher so that the solar max wouldn't knock it into the atmosphere. But combined with his suspicions coalescing rapidly into a cogent theory, supported by a growing body of facts, something extremely dangerous was about to happen. Feldman's mind raced. Somebody who could act needed to be contacted. Who could be trusted? The last time he reported something he was gone in two days. If his suspicions turned out to be correct, getting fired would be the least of his problems. But he had a family now and he had to be extremely careful.

Feldman got out from behind his desk and walked over to the window of his office. Traffic was coming and going on the highway and civilians and military personnel were entering and departing the JPL through the main entrance across the courtyard. Nobody had the slightest idea of the shit that was about to come down. Feldman went back to desk and sat down and stared at the phone.

Feldman pulled a small slip of paper out of his wallet and dialed the number that was written on it. The search for the missing Apollo negative was over. He

Bill Broocke

didn't need to see it now. He knew what it must have shown the instant Clark had showed him the EM tracing transmitted from the lost satellite.

Somebody was on the moon and it sure as hell wasn't us.

Clementine had been shot down.

Chapter 10
Yakov

Major Kolya Dimitri Yakov of the 1304th Air Logistical Regiment was sick and tired of riding the train. He was sick of the stench of the leaking toilet and the sweet sickening smell of sweat soaked passengers crammed into the cars on the wood slat benches designed for half the number aboard. And he was especially sick of listening to the young KGB lieutenant in the after part of his car raising hell with an old couple on the way to Kiev whose travel papers had the wrong date stamp.

Lickity clack, lickety clack, crunch, crunch, crunch, lickety clack...the decrepit track system was constantly being repaired, and since no modernization or replacement roadbed had been constructed since the fifties, the train was constantly slowing to a fast walk to get through the many stretches of track too unstable for even the slow speeds of the Ukrainian railroad. That was the bad news. The good news was that he was going home on leave to visit his parents in his hometown of Pripyat, and after passing Slavutich about an hour ahead, it would be only another eighty kilometers.

It was April 25, 1986 and the Pripyat River, for which his hometown was named, was running high, clear and cold. The blooming cottonwoods would be blazing along the riverbanks filling the walking paths with their big white blotchy blossoms. Disheveled, yellow fuzzy ducklings looking more like hairy wind up toys, were being carefully shepherded by their mothers and skittered across the quiet pools of gentle eddy along the river's edge, protected by the huge granite boulders and thick fallen trees.

The rolling fields of the collective farms were green with spring wheat and occasional islands of virgin forest drifted slowly through his vision field. Yakov, at times like these, with not too many nearby, would let his mind drift off into the quiet reverie of treason. He rationalized this as a sort of luxurious mental vacation into sanity, because when he analyzed the Soviet system with his engineer's mind and his poet's heart, the conclusions were inescapable. Deep down in his guts he knew that it was totally, irretrievably, and unquestionably screwed up beyond repair. Unfortunately, despite the inescapable logic, the futility, and the subterranean vein of pure despair that ran deep and long in his soul, Yakov was also a patriot and loved the motherland. Perhaps everything would change under the new man Gorbachev. Perhaps, true communism would finally be implemented by 1990. He laughed, recalling his father's response to that prediction the day they heard it over radio Moscow. "Let's hope they do it to the Georgians first," his father said.

Yakov's father had served on Marshall Zhukov's intelligence staff during the Great Patriotic War and was fluent in German and English. It was his father who had translated and brought to the staff meeting the message from the Americans that they had dropped an atom bomb on Japan. His father remembered that even blooded officers accustomed to the routine death and slaughter of the front were shocked as the description of the attack was revealed. It was generally agreed that the Americans were a truly barbaric race to do something so horrible.

The haranguing KGB lieutenant jolted Yakov back to the present when he finally crossed the line and began shouting at the old couple. Yakov straightened his blouse, put on his hat and walked down the aisle as the car jolted and careened on the ancient steel rails. The KGB officer saw him coming out of the corner of his eye but had no idea what was about to happen.

"Lieutenant may I speak to you a moment?"

The cocky young officer ignored Yakov and continued his diatribe leaning with one arm against the overhead, stopping his lecture to take a long drag from a cigarette he held in the fork of his two fingers the way Europeans do.

Yakov moved over and positioned himself between the geriatric duo and the KGB officer, then stiff armed him backwards into the aisle snatching the cigarette out of his mouth. "You will stand at attention when a superior addresses you," Yakov ordered evenly, attempting to make eye contact with the junior officer. The lieutenant, however was transfixed in confusion as he stared at the four rows of decorations on Yakovs tunic including the Order of Lenin he got in Afghanistan when he rescued a Spitznatz team under heavy fire from Mujadeem. An American Stinger missile had almost shot the tail rotor off. He made a run on crash landing only ten miles away, but it was enough to get everybody out of harms way. The KGB officer finally recovered his wits and was standing at attention at last. "You don't understand, comrade major, these people..."

"These people haven't done shit," Yakov roared. "Furthermore, I want you to take yourself to another compartment and leave these people alone for the remainder of their trip."

"You are interfering with the performance of my....."

"One more fucking word out of your pig face, lieutenant, and I am going to throw you bodily off this train...we'll see if you can perform your God forsaken duties with a mouth full of gravel and a broken neck." The lieutenant grabbed his hat as it fell off his head, his back to the rows of seats, stumbling and back peddling away. The comrade major was completely out of his mind, he thought, and might just do what he was threatening. Maybe it was the post Afghanistan syndrome, he thought.

The old woman, undoubtedly somebody's grandmother, was still shaking, her face soaked with tears as she dried her eyes with her tattered sweater sleeve. Her husband was whispering something to her with his arm around her shoulder, her head on his chest. The old man looked up at Yakov. In his haunting sunken eyes was the collective suffering of generations. "Please accept the apology of the Soviet Air Force for the unpardonable conduct of that officer," Yakov said gently. Yakov straightened his uniform jacket then excused himself back to his section. Before he could leave the old man reached out and clutched Yakov's hand. His hand was rough and his fingernails dirty. There were tears in his eyes as he tried to speak. "Do not worry grandfather," Yakov said softly. The old man's head was nodding in appreciation as Yakov made his way back to his seat. I'll probably hear about that one, he thought, but he'd tangled with KGB pricks before and nothing had ever happened.

While this certainly wasn't one of them, being a Soviet Air Force pilot had its moments of pleasure, even though once back on the ground, the reality of the hopeless state of affairs needed to be placed into perspective with vast quantities of vodka. If it hadn't been for the vodka, he often surmised; the revolution of 1917 would have been followed by another revolution in 1918 throwing out the Bolsheviks. Nobody ever sobered up in the USSR.

The sign read "Slavutich 10 KM." Yakov smiled. The first thing his mother would want to know was did he have a girlfriend and when was he going to get married so that they could have grand children. His standard answer was from an underground book of American jokes one of his squadron mates had lent him. "Mother, I would have no respect for any woman who would marry somebody like me." The thought startled him for a moment and reminded him to recheck the subversive and illegal documents he was carrying. He loved his parents, but knew that they would be in severe emotional distress if they knew what he was reading. So he zipped open his kit bag and made sure his anthology of Robert Frost was secreted within some rolled up skivvies. And God help him, if his father, a public utilities manager and party member for forty years, ever found the other Book.

His father had taught his boy fluent English and German because he thought that someday there would be another war and Kolya spoke a flawless brand of English with a slight British accent. His German was almost as good. He wanted Kolya on a rear echelon staff somewhere deep and safe when the bombs began to fall. His father had also suspected that he had survived the purges of the experienced officers because of his unique multi-lingual capability. The fluency in English, however, had cracked open the door to truth

87

and although Kolya Dimitri Yakov knew he would never betray the homeland, he had finally discovered the reality of the great lie.

Crunch, crunch, lickety crunch, the train slowed to a fast jog as it hit another length of old track. "Pripyat 50 KM" the sign read. Yakov was reviewing his career so far in the Air Force. Was about average as a major, although several of his classmates were already Lt. Colonels. He was a crew commander on the Mi-6 Superlift helicopter and he had hopes of getting transferred to the MiG-17s then maybe later to 23s, although, once in helicopters, many times you became trapped. Not many had escaped to jets after flying rotorwing. As a bachelor, his salary at 400 rubles a month was plenty to have a good life and he was still in damn good shape. Some of the younger women were starting to balk at a guy of thirty-nine, but there were plenty that didn't. Life was good...at least good for the Soviet Union.

"Pripyat 30 KM," Yakov could see his mother in his mind's eye, short and stocky with her faded purple scarf on her head and old pink sweater seeing him off at the station that cold and rainy day twenty years ago, tears streaming down her heavily wrinkled face as he went off to the service. His Father stood ramrod straight trying not to cry...filled with pride...motionless on the platform wearing all his medals...the stoic code of Spartacus embodied. Twenty years, where does the time go, Yakov thought. One day I'm skipping flat river stones across the Pripyat and running barefoot through the heather. The next minute, I'm thirty-nine, losing my hair, still single and not that far from retirement out of the Air Force. What has my life amounted to so far? What happened to becoming a cosmonaut? Being the bottom man in his class in flight school fairly well torpedoed that idea. His academics were stellar, and his flying was good, but the run in with his sadistic instructor had marked him. His instructor had a bad habit of grabbing students' oxygen hoses and yanking them left and right to get their attention for some minor infraction of procedure. One day after the instructor did this to Yakov, he had backhanded the instructor across his visor, shattering the plastic. The sadistic bastard had only said, "take me home, you're busted." The instructor said nothing to the flight commander, but Yakov never made a grade above a "fair" for any of the training after that. This put him at the bottom of the class with only one other person below him.

Let me think of some of the positives, Yakov continued with his life's inventory, as the rickety train approached Pripyat. Well, I've screwed over two hundred women...that's good. I have about 3200 hours of flight time...mostly rotor wing...not all that good. I drink too much...but how much is that? Everybody drinks too much. I'm not in love and nobody is in love with me...that's bad. Seems like the time between girlfriends is increasing as I get older. My parents love me...that's a given, no points. My buddy Yuri loves me like a brother and I him...but aside from that, where are the accomplishments? Where's the meaning in my life? Thirty-nine seems a little early for a mid-life crisis, he concluded.

Yakov watched the golden sun swing down like a pendulum below the horizon. The train was running so late, he would not be able to see the panzer oak just outside the station where he had his first kiss from Valentina Cherevichenko when he was fifteen. The Red Army had made a desperate stand nearby during the

Great Patriotic War, before being routed by Kleist's panzer divisions. Five hundred thousand Soviet troops were later encircled and surrendered.

The eye of history always went into free fall as he got closer to home, flooding his memory with the images and escapades of his youth. The night he and Yuri made the pipe bomb from the contents of a dud artillery shell they had found half buried in the flood plain. Now, that was a close one. The triple cigarette fuse was all that saved them when it went off, rattling windows for two miles in every direction. Their alibis were air tight since they both were with numerous other witnesses who could verify their non-involvement, when the crude Russian tobacco finally burned down to the end reaching the explosive. The waiting was excruciating, but forty-five minutes later; the girls jumped clear out of their skins when that baby finally blew with a thoroughly satisfying FOOF-BOOM! Yakov and Yuri could barely contain their laughter.

Twin vapor trails crossing the terminator at high altitude made two forked tongues of silver and bronze ten miles long. That's where I should be, he thought. The sky was rapidly turning from pink to orange to lavender to indigo. Soon darkness would smother the day and the stars would plunder the night. The pollution free skies of Ukraine allowed almost no dusky interlude and the black void of space, into which he would never fly, soon covered the land in a soft rolling quilt of coal.

Look! A large meteor! Yakov marveled as it arced across the sky heading for Pripyat. No, it was heading a little more northwest. Perhaps his father would see it from his office at the Chernobyl nuclear power plant where he was the plant manger.

In fact, his father, at the moment, was arguing with

two nuclear engineers who wanted to conduct an experiment with the number four reactor during shutdown, which required bypassing four safety systems including the automatic water cooling system and automatic rod inserter. Anatoly Yakov at first refused to grant permission. But, after an hour of withering argumentation and a blitz of engineering techno-babble about how perfectly safe the experiment was, he reluctantly gave his permission.

Lickety clack, lickety clack, Belenko was right and that's a fact, crunch, crunch, crunch, crunch, lickety crunch. Major Kolya Dimitri Yakov smiled again, placing his chin on his folded arms on the rolled down window of his compartment.

"Pripyat 10 KM" read the sign briefly, before it swept into the night.

Crickety rack, Crickety rack, Crickety crunch, crunch, crunch....

It would be good to be home again.

The siege of An Loc wasn't going so hot. Second lieutenant Nughen Tranh was in a left hand orbit at 8,000 feet over the encircled ARVN base just north of Saigon. His guts were so tight, he was starting to cramp from fatigue, and dehydration. The bubble canopy of his propeller driven A-1 Skyraider was like a huge greenhouse with the hot sun of Vietnam baking relentlessly upon him and his flight suit was soaking wet from perspiration. Tranh was angry. The Americans had caused all this. First they came over swearing their undying allegiance to see the war through. "We aren't the French," Westmoreland had assured Big Minh. And we bought it hook line and sinker, Tranh thought in English. Westy's statement was right in one way, however. When the Americans decided they were going to kick some ass, they could do it. The French never heard of the B-52, but plenty of NVA regulars and Viet Cong, now blown to hell had heard the far away whine of jet engines at high altitude, seconds before they were vaporized, along with birds, jungle, monkeys, and all life in a screaming furrow of death that thundered along for miles.

But the will to gut it out had been eroded at home, and the Americans were gone. The ARVN had been crushed by waves of tanks and a relentless assault from the North after the "decent interval" of two years had finally elapsed. Once An Loc was gone, the road was clear all the way to Saigon and it would be all over for little South Vietnam. The NVA now had Russian SA-

6s, a shoulder fired anti-aircraft rocket, and here he was at 8,000 feet trying to stay out of the threat envelope, but not doing anybody any good with his last two 500 pounders. His wingman had already been shot down trying to get in low to support the surrounded base. The war was lost, he thought. Time to go home.

***

Tranh sat at his desk looking an e-mail from Leanna Helms without actually focusing his eyes on the content. He had replayed his last days in Vietnam a thousand times in his mind and still could not think of anything he would have done differently if it had happened over again. More water! Yes, he definitely would have cached more water in the sampan they used for their final escape. Then the Americans again. So easy to hate when they abandoned them, but then the crew on the American destroyer which rescued them after sixteen days on the open sea. Two officers gave up their cabin and he and his family had been fed and nursed back to health with such affection and tenderness by the sailors of the US Navy. They were then taken to Subic Bay and later to Texas where they resettled and Nughen Tranh got a job with an independent oil company near Plainview. Tranh looked at Leanna's e-mail in earnest, leaning forward in his big leather executive chair. It read, "Robert, see me immediately."

How many times had this message flashed across his screen? These particular words usually marked the start of another Helms Industries Special Project. And since Nughen "Bobby" Tranh was the Director of Special Projects, he knew that there was something interesting waiting for him in Leanna's office. Special Projects were handled personally by Leanna, and Tranh was the only person between her and the rest of the company whose gargantuan global assets were available for special projects. The daily operation of the various companies controlled by Helms Industries were controlled by their own CEO and board and reported to Leanna on a monthly basis. This provided her with wide discretion in choosing projects she wished to initiate and the time to see them through. There was just one teensy weensy problem.

Leanna was a sexual predator who went through men in a thoughtless process in which she gave about as much consideration as most women would give to deciding what color lipstick to wear. Rarely was there any objection from her targets, maybe a couple of married ones over the years, but they slowed her down about as much as Belgium slowed down Hitler. She realized after a while that her working on her special projects directly with her male executives was sort of like hiring Count Dracula to run the blood bank. She needed another person, somebody completely unique, to go between her and the drones she needed to carry out the work of the hive. She needed someone who could function flawlessly with her and not be stung to death by the queen bee. Bobby Tranh, came recommended from Uncle J. B. her father's old friend J.B. McCall in Plainview, Texas, and had been with her for a number of years in lower positions, but Leanna gave him a chance and the chance worked. Tranh had enjoyed the confidence of her father, and this went a long way with Leanna. Tranh had an AE Degree from Texas A&M and above all, Tranh loved his wife, and nobody, nobody, would ever put that asunder. And while he glowed like any other normal guy around Leanna with her lethal sexual radiation, she had no interest in him and he gained her confidence. Tranh over the years became the only true friend Leanna ever had and he was the only man she ever talked to about her life. She had a yawning abyss of emptiness she tried to fill with sex, more sex and the exercise of power. "Leanna, you need a boyfriend, a real one," he once blurted out, instantly regretting his words when she looked up. Instantly regretting his words, because he knew that there most likely was no man on the planet who could handle her; and if there was, his presence was a closely guarded secret. Leanna's searing intellect and maddening beauty melted men in her path like a flame throwing tank torching Jap bunkers on Iwo. Nobody could or would, stand up to her and deep down in her soul, whose existence, she of course denied, Leanna Helms was lonely as sin.

Tranh walked into her beautiful office that overlooked New York harbor from the World trade Center where Helms leased three floors of the South Tower. Fourth of July was always breath taking from her office with the parade of tall ships and the fireworks fired from barges near the Lady in the harbor. Leanna's office was minimalist with a smack of Japanese and a little on the dim side, distinctly impressionistic with two original Manets of young girls in ballet classes. Most of the illumination was from the massive floor to ceiling windows that ran along one whole side of the room.

Tranh seated himself in one of the comfortable easy chairs in front of her desk.

"What's up Toots," he queried with a toothy grin and with his slight Vietnamese accent. This was one of the few things that Leanna had ever found even slightly amusing from a man and she looked over at him and smiled.

"Robert," she began, "Have you ever read these two books?" Leanna pushed two books across the table to him. One was leather bound; the other was a paperback. Tranh looked at the two books and became instantly alarmed.

Tranh held up the paperback. "I haven't read this one, and the other one, well, you know I'm a Bhuddist." Leanna reached over and picked the paperback out of his hand. "This one is "Lucifer's Hammer," by Niven and Pournelle. I want you to read it and let me know when you've finished."

"The other Book is a collection of myths, contradictions, and obsolete ideas that comprise the belief system of the largest religion in the world."

"So, Leanna, what did you really think about that book?"

"I read it entirely last week. The last section, which was mainly letters to the early Christian churches put forth a few touchy-feely but mildly interesting ideas which we will discuss at our next meeting in two days. We'll discuss the Hammer book then. Good day Robert."

Leanna's standard dismissal marked the ending of all meetings.

For the first time in his career at Helms, Tranh was very uneasy.

Tranh had noticed a shift in Leanna's special projects over the last several years. At first it was stuff like finding her a one thousand carat opal. That one had him scurrying all over the hot, dusty, Australian out back for months. He found the stone ok, but when it got back to New York, the salutary effect that he expected did not materialize.

Then there was the Trypto Africanus fiasco. And while it was a major failure, it marked the subtle change in direction that Leanna was taking in her special projects. She read an article in National Geographic about the starving children in Somalia. "I can fix this," she announced one day. Leanna directed Steve Webber, the CEO of AgraCam, an agricultural R&D subsidiary of Helms Industries, to develop a corn hybrid that could prosper in desert climates. Webber initially objected, saying that the costs for development and distribution for something like this had been looked into and rejected years before, since anybody who needed the product couldn't afford to pay for it. "That won't be a consideration this time," she told Webber.

"Why's that Leanna?"

"We're not going to sell it, Steve. We're going to give away to the nations that need it, as much as they want."

AgriCam came up with Trypto Africanus, a hybrid corn that thrived on a fraction of the water required by the closest competitor. Trypto Africanus obtained most of its water from the air at night and when fully grown was only about two feet tall. The corn cobs, however, were full sized. Tons of seed corn were given to Somalia and several other countries. The Somali shipment rotted in the Port of Mogadishu and was never distributed. Most of the rest was stolen and resold on the black market as corn for grinding up into meal. At the end of this multi-year effort, the children were still starving in Somalia.

The next project had been the fresh water wells in Central America. Leanna teamed up this time with

Rotary International and by the end of the five year project, two thousand wells were drilled in villages all over Central America. Virtually overnight, dozens of water born diseases disappeared. Teams from the World health Organization went in after the last wells were dug and began monitoring the results. They sent glowing reports to Leanna with photos of children and plenty of stats that showed the irrefutable proof of the good results. The Rotarians made a big deal out of Leanna's contribution, made her an honorary member, and gave her a big tacky plaque at one of their conventions. The change in her overall attitude was a miraculous event that Tranh, frankly, thought would never happen. He just prayed every night that she could keep it up. Leanna put that plaque up in her office, a totally out of place artifact with the million dollar pieces of art already in place. Some vice president of one of the subsidiaries made the comment one day while visiting her office, that the plaque looked a little out of place. He was trying to make an oblique compliment about the quality of the other stuff on the wall, but unfortunately for him, Leanna didn't quite take it that way. The poor son of a bitch didn't even get out of the building with his job. Leanna had security lift his badge in the lobby. For the first time in her life, Leanna Helms was happy.

Tranh, turned the last page of "Lucifer's Hammer" and laid it on his desk. It was a long-assed piece of crap with about a zillion characters and the alien invaders were elephants who had big mud baths on their gigantic ships. They were going to clobber the Earth with a comet. He punched in Leanna on the intercom. "Leanna, I finished the book."

"Come on down, Bobby boy, and let's talk. This

time we're going to do something big." And big it would be, using up the entire special projects budget, and then some for the next six years.

Project 214 was born that April morning in 1987. History has many intersecting seemingly unrelated events and this was one of them. Who could have predicted the immigration of a Jewish patent office clerk to America would result in the atomic bomb? Leanna's Project 214 ended up saving our ass as a species on planet Earth when some interstellar sonofabitches tangled with a feisty backward little planet. After their fifty-year reconnaissance of our planet, the conclusions were obvious. We were primitive, mired in chaos, locked in obsessive self-interest, incapable of united action, utterly savage, and virtually unpredictable.

Our warlike propensities, it was thought, had something to do with the so-called economics of the planet. But they misjudged the hell out of that one or maybe they just didn't give a shit. In fact, we were so savage and unpredictable that we had built two mighty arsenals, either of which, all by itself was capable of removing life from the surface of the planet and rendering it uninhabitable for thousands of years. Each side had its weapons trained on the other, but the aliens' analysis of the silo based missiles revealed that their targeting system could be reprogrammed in minutes to strike anywhere on the planet's surface. Triggering an exchange of theese primitive but gruesome weapons would make the surface unusable and create possible undesirable repercussions in other parts of the solar system. The fifty years of painstaking reconaissance being scrupulously careful not to injure anyone, determined that a method had to be found to disarm one of the two sides, then stand down a significant percentage in the remaining arsenal. These could be easily neutralized when the time came. The plan became slightly complicated when it was further learned that neither of the two major antagonists ever bluffed and on several occasions each was on the brink of commencing hostilities that would have ended their civilizations. All in all however, we were exactly what they were looking for. Our species had DNA pool ripe for conversion. We were exactly at the right stage of development, because had Earth's variouis governments revealed to the general population what was known by the leadership, it would have caused planet wide panic, disrupting every fiber of the social fabric, especially our myriad religions, which already taught intolerance and suspicion. Unification for planet wide resistance was impossible because of the social dynamics. Any revelation of the truth would cause worldwide anarchy and would only advance the alien timetable. In retrospect, assuming the surveyors conducted an after action report, they probably would wish that they had looked a little more into our savage and unpredictable side.

Looking back on the beginning of the Tau Ceti War, there was one school of thought that divine intervention had occurred. This was ok for the preachers, but the hard thinkers just looked back at military history over the centuries and noted that it is composed of myriad seemingly unrelated events that came together at the right or wrong time and spelled out victory or defeat. We had something that they badly needed. They had been searching for five centuries and had investigated then rejected a thousand biped species which exist in proliferation throughout the galaxy.

Our visitors could manipulate the fabric of space and hurtle through electromagnetic waves of time, sleek and wet like dolphins swim the seas. They found us when one of their two million automated exploration ships intercepted a weak amplitude modulated signal and homed on its source. It went into a parking orbit at a nearby planet and waited. When the EM pulse from the first nuclear weapon detonation was detected, the qualification message had been transmitted.

Chapter 12

Yakov stepped down off the almost stopped rail car and looked around. Something was definitely wrong. People were running in different directions like someone had kicked an anthill. Yakov grabbed the arm of one of the station police and asked what was going on. "Something has happened at Chernobyl comrade Major."

Yakov slung his kit bag over his shoulder and headed for his parents` cottage near the outskirts of town. His pace quickend as he got closer to home. A reactor leak? Could it be something that serious? He remembered his father saying over and over how safe the plant was and scoffed at the critique the American team had levelled at the design of the plant built without a containment building. The American designs incorporated a steel and concrete containment shell over the reactor vessel that could contain any runaway reaction and prevent penetration from the outside, even from a Boeing 747 at full throttle. The Americans were always too concerned with the unnecessary and the pretty. Their highly litigious society controlled by the international banks and insurance companies were always wagging the dog. His mother met him at the door with hugs and kisses, but her eyes were red and she was dabbing her face with a handkerchief.

"There's been an accident at the plant, your father just called, thank God he is well. I saw black storks yesterday…just like before the war broke out. This is always a bad omen…."

"Mother, please," Yakov interrupted, taking her

hands gently in his own. "What happened?"

"He could not tell me anything except that it happened yesterday and they are still working on it."

"Yesterday?" Yakov was incredulous. Trains were still arriving and departing. Children were still playing soccer in the schoolyards near the plant. Except for some commotion with the police and a few insiders, nobody was doing anything. Perhaps it wasn't as bad as he thought. If it was a radiation leak, surely they would have evacuated the town by now.

The phone rang. One of the perks of being a nuclear plant manager was that you had your own phone in your home. The Yakovs had one of the only fifty or so telephones in the entire town.

"Kolya, it's me Yuri, how are you doing pal?"

"Just got home. Big commotion at the power plant. Have you heard what's happening?"

"That's why I'm calling. Get your gear together I've already sent a vehicle to pick you up. We're down here at Sarkov Airfield with three crews and three Mi-6s near the big cement plant."

"Yuri, what the hell are you talking about? I'm on leave."

"Nobody's on leave now my old friend. Chernobyl has sprung a leak and we've got to plug her up with cement before the entire Ukraine downwind of the plant is contaminated." Yuri's voice sounded tired and scratchy.

"You mean radioactivity is escaping into the atmosphere?"

"That's right. I've never seen anything like it. It's like a geyser." Yuri coughed twice and then continued. "Last night, the plume of escaping gases was actually glowing …spectacular sight. More when you get here.

Gotta' go now, they have my ship loaded for another run. None of the scientific types from Moscow have arrived yet. We're just flying and dumping concrete until they tell us to stop."

A chill ran down Yakov's spine as he quickly calculated the massive radiation poisoning that was happening every second that Chernobyl spewed into the sky.

Yakov arrived at Sarkov aerodrome at dusk as additional crews were coming in ferrying the big Mi-6 superlift helicopters and bringing in the army of support and cleanup personnel that would eventually swell to over two million civilians and troops. Mi-6s were being loaded with concrete in jury-rigged sling loads and taking off toward the plant just as the slingload cleared the ground, not even wasting the time to climb.

Yakov noticed an ambulance waiting on the parking ramp as one Mi-6 made a bumpy sideways landing, then for some reason didn't throttle back, its rotor blades were flat pitched but still turning at flight speed. Something was wrong. Yakov was the closest pilot to the helicopter and broke into a dead run for the aircraft. He yanked the cockpit door open just as the ambulance pulled up. Slumped over the controls, with vomit running down the front of his flight suit, the pilot's face, even in the dim light of dusk was a bright pink like a bad sunburn. The guy's forehead was resting on his right arm, which was across the top of the instrument panel, like he was just trying to take a nap. His left hand still clasped the throttle handle. Yakov reached in and pulled his hand off the throttle and brought the big helos engines back to idle. A flight engineer clambered up to the cockpit simultaneously and chopped the fuel control levers. His eyes met

Yakov's. "We begged him to stop flying when he first got sick," the flight engineer said. "But he said the other crews weren't here yet and somebody had to do it."

Yakov's eyes went back to the slumped pilot in the darkened cockpit and noticed the partially visible yellow silk scarf around his neck. The scarf was a gift from Yakov.

"Oh God," Yakov gasped, holding his fist to his mouth.

It was Yuri.

He grabbed his best friend, and with the ambulance crew, gently pulled Yuri's body down from his seat and onto a stretcher. The medic with a stethoscope made a preliminary examination then looked up at Yakov, shaking his head.

Yuri was dead. He died in the hover of his final mission. The docs later told Yakov that Yuri had been exposed to over a thousand times the maximum allowable radiation dosage. But, Yuri was only the first.

Quenching the nuclear fires of Chernobyl required hovering directly over the ruptured reactor vessel, remaining stationary directly in the stream of a bellowing geyser of radioactive steam that reached 25,000 feet. Every hour Chernobyl remained uncapped; the equivalent radiation of one Hiroshima sized atomic bomb was released. Tens of thousands downwind eventually died. Hundreds of thousands became sick from radiation related diseases. Fighting this lethal nightmare were one hundred twelve Soviet helicopter pilots who flew and kept flying until the nuclear fires were sated. Millions of people around the globe and especially in Western Europe owe their lives to these men. All the Mi-6s used in the Chernobyl operation have been quarantined, too radioactive to ever fly again.

Within three years, all the pilots except one were dead from radiation exposure.

The Soviet Air Force and civilian pilots used in the capping of the blown reactor building were awarded the Order of the Soviet Union, posthumously in dozens of cases.

The sole surviving helicopter pilot was Kolya Dimitri Yakov. Still not showing symptoms after five years. The Soviet physicians chalked it up to some curious quirk of anatomy and biochemistry. Of course, symptoms could manifest themselves at any time, but by the time he was called to Moscow to meet General Secretary Gorbachev he was still as healthy as an army mule.

Undoubtedly, some kind of reward was in the wind. And if this were the case, Yakov already knew what he wanted. And based on his ongoing hero status, and the major press coverage he'd gotten in the face of the biggest screw up ever made with nuclear power, asking for a slot in the cosmonaut program did not seem like too much to ask. The space shuttle was nearing flight tests and that was what he would ask for. Some American test pilot had referred to their astronauts in the in their conventional spacecraft as "spam in a can." This wouldn't be the case with the space shuttle Buran, "Snow Storm." The Buran could be flown and landed back on earth like an airplane.

Chapter 13

"Play the tape again," Clinton ordered.

The voice was probably mid-western, but had a very slight metallic stiltidness to it that was almost not there. "Undoubtedly, machine generated, but at a high order of fidelity, or maybe a normal human voice made to sound machine-like similar to the recorded messages in the Metro," somebody said from the rear of the room.

"And have we confirmed absolutely that there is something where they say it is?" the President continued. "That is affirmative Mr. President. It is a ten thousand metric ton asteroid exactly where they said it would be and its trajectory shows an origination point in the vicinity of Jupiter. There is no question that it is there." General Troy Hampton, the new chairman of the joint chiefs, rechecked his notes. "It will cross Earth's orbital plane exactly where they said it would and will miss us by approximately half a million miles. That's about double the distance to the moon. We are informed by our people that this is an extremely close encounter, and while it will miss us this time, it may not miss us the next time, whenever that might be."

"Do we have anything that could blast it to pieces when it goes by?" The President queried, looking at General Hampton. "Yes, we do Mr. President, however there are risks. For example, if we do nothing but gather data and then calculate its return date and proximity, it may turn out that this thing won't be a threat for thousands of years. By that time the means will be in place to easily deal with it. On the other hand, if we initiate some highly proactive event, we might find that we not only failed to destroy the object, but by interfering with its natural mechanics we caused it or one of its parts to drill us dead center next time around."

Clinton rotated around in his chair and looked over at the Vice President who had said nothing thus far. Gore looked over at General Hampton, "Is there some middle ground?"

"Yes, sir, there is. We have time to retrofit the Clementine, an already scheduled lunar scientific mission with one of the new lasers. We could hit the asteroid with laser fire and gain a massive amount of information about its properties and weaknesses without significantly disturbing its trajectory. We can analyze the laser hit with satellite and ground based equipment and we would know a hell of a lot more about what or possibly who we are dealing with."

A murmur began in the room and President Clinton held his hand up to bring order. "I don't know about the rest of the people in here, General Hampton, but what I want to know is who sent us this tape and how did they know about the asteroid? I believe the operative word in your last statement was who?" Hampton's head jerked up and made eye contact with the President. "In my opinion, another phase of contact has been commenced and I don't like the look of it. Mr. President, despite what we are hearing from the astronomers, I have a gut feeling that there is at least a small possibility that despite its appearance, this thing is not an asteroid."

Clinton stood signaling the end of the meeting. "Gentlemen, if General Hampton is correct in his suspicions, there will be a quid pro quo from whoever sent that tape. This is only the beginning. I want the FBI to see if they can trace the chain of custody of the package the tape came in, and unless somebody has a better idea, it looks like we're just going to have to wait for their next contact." Nobody had a better idea.

The eight men began filing out of the room and the President sat back down and began to continue his phone call list for the morning. Everyone had left but one. General Hampton sat patiently, waiting. The President looked over and saw him, then slowly replaced the phone on its cradle, thinking to himself that this was not a good omen. Hampton was the first Air Force Chairman of the Joint Chiefs who had come out of Space Command. Hampton was a former astronaut, fighter pilot, scientist and scholar. He was supposed to be the MacArthur of the high frontier and had written volumes on war fighting in space, specifically near Earth space.

"I have a feeling you're not hanging around to talk about the Redskins."

"I'm afraid you're right, Mr. President."

"Go ahead, Troy. What's on your mind?"

"Mr. President, based on several comments you made in the meeting, it appears that you have not been fully briefed on a number of issues."

Clinton punched his intercom button. "Hold all my calls and appointments Linda."

He then folded his hands behind his head and leaned back in his chair...."So, brief me."

"Mr. President, have you ever heard of Area 51?"

"Of course, that's the secret base in Nevada where we fly the Aurora and are working on the X-35, the shuttle replacement right? I signed a national security finding 95-45, to preempt a lawsuit on burning some hazardous materials out there. The place from the movie, Independence Day?"

"Partially correct, Mr. President." Hampton attempted a weak smile at the President's small joke. "But none of the above is the reason we built Area 51," Hampton continued.

"Mr. President, were you ever briefed on Canadian Forces Project Flypaper?"

Clinton shook his head. Hampton kept going, "Project Fly Paper was the Canadian attempt to create a lure base for extraterrestrial contact. We and they were experiencing hundreds of random contacts, but nobody had any idea how to set up an organized meeting so that we could find out why they were here."

"Excuse me, General Hampton, are you telling me that flying saucers are real and come from outer space? I had one of my people looking into this when I first got this job and he couldn't substantiate a single thing…and he had a Top Secret clearance."

Hampton became instantly uncomfortable. An extremely serious breach of protocol had occurred and here he was, first week on the job, sitting in a private conversation with the Commander in Chief, who did not have a clue about the highest state secret of the nation. Unless he was lying…the man was a political genius…but what would be the motivation? This possibility, however, was irrelevant considering the seriousness of the current events. The President had to be told everything…especially now, when a new phase of the game with the extra terrestrial entities may have begun. All the mistakes of the past, the hidden agendas kept from congress and the executive branch…everything had to come out. Hampton shuddered to think how many laws had been broken to keep the secret for fifty years.

"Mr. President, may I suggest that if this meeting is being taped that the recorder be turned off?"

"General, this administration does not engage in such practices," Clinton admonished. He then stepped on the floor button under his desk, which activated the recording system.

Hampton took a deep breath and began. "Mr. President, your man discovered nothing with his top secret clearance because there are twenty-two security classifications above top secret, the highest being Double Gamma. What I am bout to tell you classified above the Double Gamma. It was decided years ago that to place any security classification on the information would subject it to exposure by computer search or the operation of law if a category and location were ever recorded systematically. If only a handful of people knew, there were no traceable files, and if suitable cover stories could be manufactured, it was thought that the secret could be maintained more or less indefinitely. In fact the Air Force ran a program for forty years called Project Blue Book whose sole purpose was to release to the public the fraudulent and easily explainable UFO sightings thus debunking every encounter report including the real ones. In its forty year history, Project Blue Book said they only had ten unexplainable events…and this was out of over 27,000 reports that they processed."

"I always suspected that something like this was going on," Clinton said, as he leaned back in his chair folding his hands behind his head.

"Mr. President, your suspicions were well founded…this gets us back to Project Fly Paper and Area 51. The Canadians set aside as off limits a huge rectangular area around one of their northern military airfields which was not in use. They placed prohibited airspace classifications on all their aeronautical charts and would not allow over flight by commercial air traffic even though it was right on one of the heaviest traveled polar routes. They even leaked to the media that something really hush-hush was going on at the secret base. The base itself had dozens of well camouflaged, high speed cameras and recording equipment manned by researchers and scientists who did not come out of hiding for twelve months.

"Did they get anything?"

"No, Mr. President, nobody showed up, and this is where Area 51 came in. We monitored the Canadians and noticed that their lure base was vacant. Nothing was actually happening that would have interested the aliens. We decided to establish a lure base of our own at a location near Groom Lake, Nevada. We moved some test flying out of Edwards to the new location and set up ruses to hopefully arouse their curiosity. For example, we never put the base on any map. We cut a huge "X" on the ground that was twenty miles long, out of the sagebrush, so that it was distinctly visible from orbit. We set up a network of powerful strobe lights that blanketed the five hundred square mile area of the base. On random nights, we would turn on the strobes for random periods of time. This, by the way, drove the Soviets nuts since they thought we were doing something that violated the ABM treaty. The strobes, which flashed at every frequency of the spectrum from UV to infrared, blinded their reconnaissance birds. The former JCS had to use his personnel friendship with his counterpart on the Russian side to quiet their fears, and in fact, told him what we were doing."

"Un-fucking believable...the goddamn Russians knew more about what was going on than the President of the United States." Clinton punched his intercom once more.

"Linda, cancel my appointments for the rest of the day...looks like General Hampton and I will be a while. So, General, what was the ultimate bottom line on our version of Fly Paper?"

"They took the bait, Mr. President. Big time!"

Clinton leaned back in his chair and exhaled audibly, "Holy shit."

Three hours later the world was a completely different place for the President of the United States. "And, Mr. President, what I have briefed for the last three hours is only the tip of the iceberg. There's a great deal more you need to know, especially the defensive technology we have been able to employ with some success...the EBEs are not invulnerable... for example, we haven't encountered any invincible Star Trek type defense shields around their ships. In fact, we shot down one of them with an old Nike Zeus over in Germany back in 1967. Their spacecraft are built of stuff that we can't duplicate that is extremely tough. The vehicles, however, are very lightweight. We salvaged one off St. Augustine, Florida, that tangled with one of our attack submarines. When we let the water drain out of it and hoisted the wreckage aboard the salvage ship, the report indicated that even though the vehicle was over two hundred feet in diameter, it only weighed about fifteen hundred pounds, not much more than a Cessna 172."

"The son of a bitch was submerged?"

"Yes sir. Their spacecraft are capable of undersea travel as well as space and atmospheric flight. It was inspecting one of our SOSUS stations...they are very interested in the network of SOSUS tracking stations."

"Well, at least the SOSUS net was one of the things I was briefed on. That's the system that can pinpoint the location of enemy submarines in all the oceans right?"

"That is correct, Mr. President...may I make a suggestion, sir?"

"By all means."

"Mr. President, I would like to attach an officer to the White House who is cleared to Double Gamma. His name is Colonel Lowell Bremen and he's currently the Army's deputy chief of intelligence. He knows more about the extraterrestrials and all we are doing to stop them, than anyone we have. He was in New Mexico, when we salvaged the first one of their ships in 1947 and served with distinction since World War Two. He's only six months from retirement, but would be the ideal resource to begin getting you completely up to speed."

"You mean the story about Roswell and the crashed flying saucer is true?"

"Yes, Mr. President, it is all true except that it wasn't a saucer...it was a crescent- shaped craft with small aerodynamic surfaces on it...capable of space flight, but we think it was designed as a scout or reconnaissance vehicle."

Hampton made several mental notes to himself as his driver drove him back to the Pentagon...President thinks the X-35 is a shuttle replacement...still thinks all the secret flying is at Groom Lake...thinks the G-1 engine is still experimental. It's going to take Bremen days to get it all laid out to the man.

Colonel Bremen got his orders by fax the next day in his office at the Pentagon. "Report to White House

Chief of Staff, Mr. Harold Dempsey, immediately. Verbal instructions will be issued by the Office of the President on your specific duties." Signed, Troy L. Hampton, Major General, Chairman, Joint Chiefs.

Bremen looked out across the rolling lawn of the Pentagon to the golden oaks and

amber maples on fire with the flaming colors of fall. It was autumn in Washington and the autumn of his last year in the service of our country...the twilight of his long career culminating as Deputy Chief of Army Intelligence. The secrets he had so carefully guarded for almost fifty years were struggling to be free. As the Cold War began to thaw, Bremen finally met his Russian counterpart at a reception at the Russian Embassy. Both were fluent in each other's language, but he had laughed when he looked over at the interpreter to get a translation of something the Russian had said to another officer standing in the group. The interpreter looked at the Russian intelligence chief who gave him a nod. The Russian interpreter translated. "Colonel General Fourman said to Major Alexanderov that you are the dirtiest playing bastard and trickiest son of a bitch he's ever come up against." Bremen and the three Russians then laughed hard and long. General Fourman looked around the room for a moment then leaned over to Bremen with his hand up next to his mouth..."Of course that doesn't include the eight piles of bear shit I have to put up with in the Politburo." The comment resulted in another long laugh by the four officers and a call for more Vodka. Bremen recalled one of the teachings of the Dalai Lama. "Always live a noble life, so that when you are old you can enjoy it once again in your memories." Fourman's remark was logged in there right along with his Legion of Merit and his two dozen other decorations. What could be more noble than bamboozling the arch enemy of your nation and preserving the hope of freedom for an entire world? Yet, having served in three wars, his greatest battle with the mightiest, most amoral, and evil foe was yet to come. Every trick he'd ever learned in forty years of intelligence warfare would be needed.

Chapter 14

In 1991, Eastern Air Lines died the death of a thousand cuts. The hated machinists union and their decades of guerilla war against the company had finally been victorious. The day that the airline closed, the machinists staged a victory celebration at the airport with a huge banner that gloated "We lasted one day longer." The pilots of the other carriers turned their backs, just as Diane had predicted. Matt Blalock heard, "I told you so," a dozen times a day until the day of the big announcement. Diane had applied, and been accepted at the Emory Law School.

Diane, being in school, caused a physical separation of the combatants that actually started working for them. Things settled down to a steady grind until the second semester of her first year. Two of her professors were rather strident feminists, and in the course of the remainder of the year aroused some interest in Diane to learn a little more about what they were talking about.

The series of seminars opened Diane's eyes to an entire universe of experience that had been happening all around her and she had been too naïve to even know what was going on. How could she have been so stupid? And Matt, oh God, Matt! How could she have been so blind? Under her clarified and defogged vision, her husband was, without doubt, the most oppressive, dominating, chauvinistic, and emotionally abusive man she could have ever picked. What in the world had she been thinking? Insisting she stay home with the children and be a housefrau until they were eight…unbelievable…how much time had she lost? All her friends were moving forward, getting their MBAs, starting businesses, and becoming successful and financially secure in real careers. She had spent eight grueling years baking brownies and being the family chauffeur to Cub Scouts. Matt's argument that him being out on trips two weeks per month made her being home essential, was pure bullshit. All her friends had used day care, and the children had turned out fine…well except for Eileen and Ted's boy, but that was the exception.

Over time, as the workshops gradually opened her eyes, Diane began to realize that the institution of marriage itself was actually a type of slave owning system invented by men, and its roots went back thousands of years. The Bible had been written by men and they were not going to let anything get in it that would challenge their power and control that had been literally been inspired by God Himself…another male! Diane began to see the irrefutable proof that for thousands of years men had brutalized, raped, bullied, and controlled their women, using them nothing more as baby making machines and servants to assure their lives of ease would continue without too much discomfort. In the past, she used to have sex with Matt, even during the times she really wasn't in the mood. Diane began to understand that this was actually a type of rape…raped by her own husband! The implications of her increased understanding were staggering.

While Diane was finding the new meaning in her life, and coming to grips with all the underlying issues which had made her so unhappy for so long, Matt had finally started hitting a few long balls in real estate. He was now making more money than he had ever made in his life as an airline pilot. The long green was finally coming in again, but Diane was still drifting away. He sensed something was dreadfully wrong between the two of them but was angrily rebuffed every time he tried to talk to her about it. She would shake her head and angrily assert, "You just don't get it do you?" Diane finally agreed to go to counseling only if she could chose the counselor. After months of joint sessions, the woman therapist asked Matt to come in alone.

The shrink's names was Arlene Galt, Ph.D. and while she herself was a divorcee twice by the time she was forty, seemed to have a special connection with Diane that Matt thought would be good. At least Diane would talk to somebody, and maybe the somebody could then pass along to him what he had to do to save his marriage. It was a Wednesday afternoon in July of 1995. Atlanta was hot as hell with the heat index hitting over a hundred for the last week. He and Diane had been in joint counseling for about four months and Diane had already had several individual sessions with Dr. Galt. Matt was enthusiastic about his individual session because this would be an indication that a potential breakthrough was on the horizon. He was already sawing off his twelve-hour days at the office and had been coming home to help with the housework by three o'clock, even though his new income permitted a housekeeper that came four times a week. There really wasn't that much to do anymore. The thought is what counts, was his rationale, and by this point in the matter, he was getting scared to death that he was losing Diane…a woman he would literally die for if he had to.

Dr. Galt got up from behind her desk and came

around to the other rocking chair and sat down next to Matt. "Matt, I want to tell you how pleased I am with how you're coming along...I've dealt with you airline pilots before and frankly, I wasn't too sanguine about being able to do anything with you, the road ahead is going to be rocky," and then she smiled. Blalock was fantastically relieved. It looked like he had turned the corner at last. Dr. Galt reached over and touched his hand.

"Matt, you've lost Diane."

Chapter 15

Major Kolya Dimitri Yakov followed the development of the Soviet shuttle with intense interest as he completed the basic comosnat courses. Gorbachev passed the word that he wanted Yakov to go to the head of the line for assignments and so he was selected to fly as second in command on the Buran's maiden flight. This really pissed off the rest of the cosmonauts who'd been waiting for years to fly. One day at an astrophysics lecture, one of them verbally confronted him with the question how somebody so inexperienced was getting to fly the first launch of a new spacecraft. The room became quiet and after a pause, the instructor walked in about then and bent over the mike at the lectern. "I can answer that for you," he said. "It was easy comrade colonel," the instructor looked to his left off the platform at Yakov's interrogator. "All you have to do is hover an Mi-6 seventy-nine times in a boiling cloud of radiation, then watch all your friends die of cancer." A hush fell across the room. The phrase, deafening silence, was invented for this occasion. Several minutes elapsed and no one spoke. Then the inquisitor, a Lt. Colonel who Yakov had only seen a couple of times, gathered himself slowly to his feet on the other side of the auditorium. "Major Yakov, I would like to apologize to you for my comments and to your comrades who died for the motherland." He then came to attention, slowly saluted and held it. One by one, the rest of the cosmonauts came to their feet facing Yakov, each bringing his hand up with a salute…the sound of heels clicking together echoed in the half full room.

Yakov's face flushed but he quickly gained his feet and returned everyone's salute. Yakov turned to face the Colonel across the room, "Forget it comrade colonel, it will be an honor to fly with you."

And that was the last time anybody bitched about Yakov's lack of experience.

After dozens of designs were evaluated, the team at the Tupelov design bureau suggested that to save time and costs, that they just copy the American shuttle. The Americans had studied forty-seven different configurations and had settled upon the winged aircraft design. And while the debate was furious, cooler heads prevailed and it was decided that it would be ridiculous to go with an inferior design because it was original. Besides, copying western technology was a time honored tradition in the Soviet Union and they had usually come out well. There was the one major disaster with the SST, but that was only because of British treachery. Soviet agents had been able to steal copies of the complete plans for the Concord and it had been considered a major intelligence coup at the time. The gloating ended seven years later, unfortunately, when after hundreds of millions of rubles had been spent building the supersonic plane; the aircraft had a pesky habit of crashing. After it was permanently grounded, a team from Mikoyan discovered subtle flaws in the plans intentionally placed by British intelligence.

Nobody thought they'd have this problem with the Americans. Besides, they were already flying prototypes of the design being copied. The key to the shuttle was reusable components. This would allow resupply of the Mir station, restocking ozone in the atmosphere, dozens of scientific projects, and of course the military imperative of denying the use of near orbit to the Americans. There was widespread belief that the American shuttle was actually a space bomber that could swoop down from orbit lobbing nuclear bombs with impunity. The Americans, to quiet these fears later suspended shuttle flights from Vandenberg AFB, which flew the shuttle by polar orbit over the most sensitive areas of the Soviet Union. Just in case, however, work immediately began on another smaller shuttle-type vehicle called the Uragan. This spacecraft was a space fighter designed to shoot down the American shuttle with an on board recoilless gun. The change in shuttle launch sites to Florida became permanent and the Vandenberg launch site was dismantled. This took the wind out of Uragan development and the prototype was never completed.

Yakov began his intensive training into the Buran's systems. The mass of the complete system which included the Energia booster and the various modules of the orbiter, was at first staggering. The mated Energia-Buran spacecraft was incredibly complex with its millions of moving parts, the smallest of which could turn the towering structure of titanium, ceramic tile, and electronics into the worlds biggest napalm cloud. It was made all the more complex because there was insufficient experience in solid propellants, outside a few submarine launched ICBMs and surface to air missiles, to build the kind of solid rocket boosters used on the American shuttle. The decision was made to go with liquid fuel engines for the system and the RD-170 was born, the largest liquid fuel rocket engine in the world. The Energia boosters with the RD-170 engines later became a source of excellent cash flow when NPO Energia, the builder, began selling the boosters to the European Space Agency and most notably the French, who used them extensively from their spaceport at Kourou, French Guyana. The French spaceport, on the equator, could take advantage of the earth's higher rotational speed, which enhanced the Energia's already huge payload capability. It became the work horse of launch vehicles, and the shuttle attach system was on all of them since changing the design would have cost more than leaving the brackets in place. The booster was also easy to handle since the only tricky part of the propellant system was the liquid oxygen. The fuel used was Syntin, little more than a synthetic type of kerosene, cheap, safe, and easy to handle. Yakov developed an affection for the big Energia, much like any pilot develops with the aircraft he is flying. Soviet engineers had been working with and refining liquid fuel rocket propulsion for decades, and had achieved a quite high level of safety and reliability. And depending on the payload you wanted to carry, up to five stages could be added on top of the Energia. This made the payload bay for almost any conceivable mission cube out before it grossed out. The Soviet tradition of the big boosters was alive and well in the Energia, called by the cosmonauts as "Big Ed." The use of an American nickname in what was supposed to be the competitive response to the great capitalist enemy of the communist state, ruffled a few feathers, but Russian pilots, like their American enemies, had an irreverent streak nourished by their untouchable hero status in the hierarchy.

The first space plane arrived shortly thereafter in pieces. Assembly crews from MiG arrived in the hundreds and within ninety days, the Buran was ready. Yakov began to submerge himself into the nuts and bolts of the spaceplane systems. The construction schematics were the first documents he studied. A spacecraft is far more complex than an aircraft. It was explained that if something goes wrong with an airplane, you can usually land in fairly short order and get it fixed. A spacecraft, however, might not be able to land due to landing point weather or perhaps the malfunction would affect the reentry. Consequently, there were hundreds of emergency procedures to solve malfunctions of the labyrinthine plumbing, and electrical systems.

Of course the cockpit was of particular interest, and like the rest of the ship, it was crammed with equipment. Yakov stopped by the MiG contractor office one day with two questions. One of the MiG engineers that he had become friendly with was working in the shop that day so Yakov cornered the guy. "Mikhail, in the cockpit here there is a console titled Console Twelve, but there appears to be no electronic plumbing going to and from it."

"You are looking at plans that include the number three shuttle," he said. "The one you're going to fly won't have Console Twelve. So don't worry about it."

"Oh, I see. So what does it do?"

"You don't need to know that. It's classified."

"Ahh, come on, don't leave me in the dark here. We're on the same side you know."

Yakov, fumbled around inside his jacket. "Before you tell me, Mikhail, I'll even turn off the tape recorder…there it's off."

"Very fucking funny Dimitri." Yakov was laughing.

"You said you had two questions?"

"Yeah, here in the payload bay there are ten locking devices entitled magazine locks…that's not where we store the old issues of Izvestia is it?"

"Dimitri, you are single, a cosmonaut and are untouchable. I have a wife, a kid, and could disappear tomorrow if I pissed off the wrong people."

Yakov knew that what his friend was saying was true. The old days were not entirely gone. "Can you tell me anything?" Mikhail looked out the office door and both ways down the hall and came back into the room. "My friend, all I can tell you is that the when the magazine locks are engaged, Console Twelve will be active and that's it. Don't ask me anything else."

Out of concern for his friend, Yakov didn't press any further. I'll just keep my ears open, he thought, maybe somebody will slip.

One by one, Yakov and his classmates went through the systems of the sophisticated spacecraft. The flight guidance system was where the big let down happened.

The Buran was going to be flown out of a place designated IVPP that was a first class airfield with a huge runway that was 4500 m by 84 m and could accommodate aircraft of up to 650 tonnes in gross takeoff weight. The really bad news for the cosmonauts was the revelation of the automatic landing systems. It was all fully automated and no cosmonaut would even touch the controls, unless there was an emergency where the automatic systems failed. There was no option to using the automatic systems and no exceptions to the rule.

The Buran used five different automatic landing systems that handed the ship off by computer control one to the next until touch down. After the hypersonic turns were executed by the onboard computer and the orbiter got within 400 km of IVPP, the ship automatically selected the Volkhov-P radio landing system. At 300 km the Volkhov-P, disengaged only after Ilmen airfield locator was locked on. The Ilmen stayed engaged to just inside 200 km where the Skala-MK took over to within 50 miles of touch down. From that point the Svecha-3M guided the ship to within 10 km where the Vympel took over sort of like an approach coupler on a modern airliner, and guided the Buran all the way to touchdown. The system sounds unduly complicated, but on the first flight, it landed the Buran in a thirty-four knot crosswind within five feet of the centerline.

It was later released that the first flight would be unmanned. Chief Cosmonaut Volkov and every other guy in the program sent a signed letter to the central committee's Directorate of Space Science demanding that the first flight be manned, just like the Americans' first flight. The letter was completely ignored and the program plowed ahead with four planned unmanned missions. Nobody was going to ride until mission five. Everyone was by now getting concerned because of budgetary constraints and the weakening economy. In 1993, nobody was very surprised when they announced that the program had been cancelled.

Volkov tried to cheer up the twelve cosmonauts who were in training to fly the shuttle. "Don't worry comrades, they'll find a place in space for us...they have too much invested." But Yakov and the rest were beyond cheering. They knew that the cancellation of the program was only the beginning of big, bad things to come. The motherland and everything that was familiar and good would soon vanish. Bad had long ago turned into worse, and the fall of the Soviet Empire began.

Shuttle number one, Buran, which completed one

Bill Broocke

two orbit mission was dismantled and shipped to Gorky Park just outside Moscow where it sits today as a space theme restaurant. Several members of the original Tupelov design team are now tour guides at the restaurant making ten times more money in wages and tips than they ever made as aerospace engineers. Shuttle number two, the "Pticha" (Little Bird) and number three, with its mysterious Console Twelve, were completed but then covered with tarps and placed in storage at their production site. The plant then retooled and went into production making buses, syringes, and airliner interiors for Aeroflot.

Volkov went into space again and spent six months at the Mir Station. The rest were given as good assignments as could be found. Yakov was promoted to Lt. Colonel and given command of a MiG-25 Regiment, and besides Volkov, would be the only one in his cosmonaut class to ever fly in space again.

***

The 777th Interceptor Regiment, based outside the town of Scapino on the Kamchatka peninsula, was the pivot point of the entire Soviet southern air defense. And while the planners felt that an American bomber attack would likely come over the pole, the Americans had the ability to come through the door anywhere they pleased. The 777th's job was to block the back door and to reinforce the Northern or Eastern sectors if directed. The 777th, as well as the other units, did not suffer from parts shortages or any of the other myriad hardware needed to run a MiG-25. They didn't have anything else, but fuel, spares, and personnel were in abundance. The triple seven was a historic unit that

128

traced its lineage all the way back to the Great Patriotic War in which the triple seven was flying L2 Sturmoviks, a tank busting low-level nightmare for German armor. The unit had an unusually low loss rate and gained the reputation of the lucky triple seven. When Yakov arrived as the new commander, the luck had long since run out for the triple seven and the unit was in horrendous condition in every department except hardware.

"Why was there was no sentry at the gate?" Yakov inquired politely of the outgoing regiment commander. "I don't know, comrade colonel. If you'd like I'll look into it before I leave."

"Never mind. So, I understand you've had a lot of problems with morale here. Is that correct?"

"It's the worst I've ever seen, Colonel Yakov. The insubordination has become so bad that I had a corporal shot about two months ago. I had to set an example for the rest that we would not be pushed any further. It helped for a short time. You may have to shoot another one to keep their attention."

Oh God! Yakov thought to himself.

"And we've had desertions as well. Five in the last month."

"Where the hell would they go?" Yakov demanded incredulously. "It's nothing but wilderness out there…"

"We think they're living in the forest," the outgoing commander explained.

"What else?" Yakov asked.

"You might as well know it all. There also have been two suicides since we shot down the Korean airliner."

"This was the unit that did that?" Yakov could not believe that he had not been informed of this. "Yes, comrade colonel. It happened before I took command, but the pilot and the ground intercept officer killed themselves within a week of each other. The morale went to the bottom of the well after that and we've never recovered."

Yakov leaned back in his chair in front of the colonel's desk and exhaled a long breath. "Is there anything else?"

"I'm afraid so."

"Well, let's have it."

"Our KGB political officer is the most dangerous one I've ever had and he is the nephew of somebody on the Central Committee. He was the one behind the execution of corporal Tysbin. I had to authorize it or he would have had me relieved, or worse. Everyone from private to major cringes when they see him coming. He reported me every time I tried to do anything to improve this mess around here…and to mix shit with the piss, this bastard has a hard on for pilots."

"And why's that?"

"Well, when this guy was a lieutenant, he had some kind of run in with a pilot on a train to Pripyat one night. He said the guy was some kind psycho Afghanistan veteran who threatened to break his neck and throw him bodily of the train. He's hated our guts ever since."

Yakov leaned back again in his chair with his hands folded behind his head and looked at the ceiling. What was the line in Casablanca, the American movie with Bogart? "Of all the gin joints in the world…" Or something like that.

Yakov said nothing for several minutes.

"Is there something wrong, comrade Yakov?"

Yakov rocked forward on all four legs of the chair

and put his elbows on the commander's desk.

"Yes, there is a problem, and it's going to be the first one I am going to solve around here."

For the first week, Yakov and his operations officer conducted a detailed inspection of the base. It had a hundred and four officers and twelve hundred forty enlisted troops, mostly technical, and a few security police. The Regiment had fifty MiG-25s and a hundred spare engines in crates, the tank farm was brimming with fuel and alcohol, and the maintenance warehouse had plenty of parts. There were two hundred twenty-two air to air missiles, AA-6s and AA-8s, some of which were getting a little old. The food in the officer's mess was barely edible. They had a bowl of wheat porridge with one egg for breakfast …every day the same thing. And the second meal was a weak broth-like soup with one albino looking sausage in the bottom. There was rarely any variation and there were only two meals a day. The enlisted mess consisted of some kind of porridge looking watery gruel for breakfast and some kind of soup for lunch with a piece of meat in the bottom of the bowl if they were lucky. On several occasions, the men had rioted in the mess hall, when the meat going in the soup turned out to be rotten. The enlisted barracks had bunks stacked together so tight it resembled something in a submarine. The latrines were woefully inadequate and the stench from the pits permeated the entire enlisted barracks when the wind was out of the northwest.

The base had zero recreation facilities, not even a soccer ball. Going into town on the weekends was no good because the town people hated the military. This was because when the base was built, it required a lot of power for its defense radar and aerodrome facilities.

The base builders didn't include its own power plant but instead used power from a hydroelectric grid that came off a small dam on the Kamchatka River. The hydroelectric plant barely had the capacity to provide electricity for the meager consumers on the four surrounding towns and the larger town of Kamchatka. When the base opened, it caused brown outs and random blackouts in all the towns on the grid. The small clinic in Kamchatka became a terrifying place if you happened to be hooked up to a life support device that used electrical power. The two surgeons refused to work at night.

Yakov made a list of the staggering problems. He used the blank back side of an area navigation chart and tacked it up on his office wall. On one side he listed the problems and drew a line down the middle of the chart. On the other side he listed solutions…so far it was blank

On Monday of his second week in command of the 777th, Yakov asked his chief administrative NCO to type up a set of orders requiring the political officer to report to the commander at 0700 the following morning. Normally a phone call was all you'd need in case like this, but Yakov wanted the effect. It was time to take care of problem number one.

KGB Captain Vadim P. Lukashevich sauntered into the commander's outer office at 0735 and sat down putting his boots up on the sergeant's desk.

"You can tell him I'm here," he said, lighting a cigarette and taking a long drag, then blowing the smoke in the direction of the sergeant.

"Go tell Yakov I'm here." he repeated when the sergeant didn't get up quite fast enough to suit him.

Sergeant Chernyshov nervously opened the

commander's office door.

"Uhh, Colonel Yakov, Capt. Lukashevich will see you now."

"Will he now? Well aren't I lucky." Then Yakov shouted, "Tell that pig-faced son of a bitch to report to me in front of this desk immediately!"

Lukashevich, was startled at first, but then regained his composure, slowly got up out of his chair and took his time walking across the foyer to the commander's office. He helped himself to a chair in front of Yakov and took another long drag from his cigarette..."Welcome to the shithole of Air Defense Command....and I don't appreciate that tone of....."

Yakov drilled the KGB officer with eye contact. "Nobody told you to sit down Vadim Petros Lukashevich...you will stand at attention when a superior addresses you...."

"I am the political officer of this base and you have no right to....."

"I told you to shut your pig face six years ago, I see you haven't learned your lesson...get rid of that cigarette. You will not smoke in my presence from now on." The political officer started to slouch after he threw the cigarette onto the wooded floor and crushed it with his boot. That voice, it was familiar.

Oh shit it was him! The psycho Afghanistan veteran on the train.

"Stand at attention when a superior addresses you!" Yakov roared. Lukashevich was now at rigid attention heels together, toes apart and eyes straight ahead. Yakov came out from around his desk and looked into the side of the KGB captain's face, his nose about six inches from the KGB man's ear and continued bellowing. "And don't you ever speak to my administrative sergeant, or to any of my enlisted personnel in that manner…but you're right about one thing…this is a shit hole…a shit hole you helped to dig, you worthless bear turd."

Yakov made a complete circle and was seated again behind his desk.

Sergeant Chernyshov had already been on the phone to several other of the senior NCOs. Now there were four of them in the reception area, listening at the closed door of the commander's office to the KGB guy getting his ass kicked.

"Capt. Lukashevich," Yakov lowered his voice to an angry and sinister growl. "I have ordered you here this morning to inform you that you are in grave danger at this base, grave danger. Do you know why?"

"No comrade Colonel, I do not know why." Lukashevich could feel his right hand starting to tremble.

"You are in mortal peril Captain because your new superior is a desperate man, Desperate! Do you know why I am a desperate man Capt. Lukashevich?"

"No comrade colonel I do not know why you are desperate."

"I am desperate captain, because have nothing to lose. I have been radiation poisoned and I could die in two weeks if a cancer developed. I fought a thankless war in Afghanistan and was spit on when I came home. I was selected for cosmonaut training and then the program cancelled after I had trained intensely for two years. My father was killed at Chernobyl and my mother died of broken heart. I have no wife and few relatives…and what is my great reward from the motherland? This godforsaken base in the middle of nowhere. And you know what else? I have an American ally who is eager to help me deal with you…his name is Samuel Colt." The political officer's brow crinkled in confusion. He had never heard of Samuel Colt, but if it had to do with the Americans, it could not be good. Yakov slowly half opened his top desk drawer to reveal the only thing of value his father had left him…a vintage 1944 U.S. Army Colt .45 automatic, given him as a gift from an American officer after the war. Lukashevich let his eyes drop to the desk drawer. When he saw the pistol, his eyes widened about twenty percent and noticeable color drained from his face.

"And when I get ready to blow your fucking brains out, comrade captain," Yakov kept talking, "I have plenty of ammunition for this pistol. But it's getting a little old, so just to be sure it will be good when I need it, I'm going to test fire it every Monday at noon. When you hear a pistol shot, comrade shit for brains, remember what I'm going to do if I get one squeak out of Moscow because of a report from you. Now get out of here!"

The KGB man perfectly executed an about face and marched for the office door. There was mad clomping of boots outside the commander's door as the four NCOs scrambled to different chairs in the reception grabbing old magazines to look nonchalant. But Lukashevich never noticed; all he wanted was to get the hell out of the commander's office before anything happened.

The following Monday, Yakov made good on his promise and fired the American pistol through his opened office window into some empty vodka bottles sitting on cartons placed on the ground. Clear across the base, the KGB officer jumped six inches off his chair. At the enlisted mess, however, a loud cheer went up, and for the first time since anybody could remember, there were smiles.

Yakov slid Mr. Colt back into his drawer and locked it. He then walked across his office to the wall where he had the area chart tacked up and made a notation. "Problem number one---solved for now." But he knew that Lukashevich would just bide his time until he could screw him in some way.

The two lieutenants waited nervously in the outer office after being summoned to see the commander. "Sergeant Chernyshov, what does Colonel Yakov want with us?"

"I could not say for sure, lieutenant. All I know is that he has been in black mood ever since he arrived...you must have done something really bad...you know he almost shot Capt. Lukashevich last week."

Yakov came out of his office about that time with some signed requisitions and plopped them on the sergeant's desk, who looked up with a startled half grin.

"That's quite enough sergeant...don't be messing with the minds of my pilots," Yakov said. Yakov took both lieutenants by the arm and walked them out onto the gravel roadway that connected all the buildings. After getting out of earshot from his office, Yakov turned to the two men.

"OK, are you guys up for some skullduggery in the interest of morale?"

"Yes sir," they both responded in unison. Yakov peeled off a hundred rubles and handed it to one of them. "I want you two to take the two-seater and go find some soccer balls. I don't care if you have to fly all the way to Moscow...don't come back until you've bought or stolen as many as you can find."

Five days later, the MiG 25PU came swooping in on the long runway with Lt. Grosovich in the back seat almost invisible, completely submerged in deflated soccer balls, eighteen baseball gloves, ten softballs, five bats, and two American type soccer balls that were pointed on each end ...all donated by the United States counsel general in Kiev... where the two pilots had hustled two local honeys in a bar that turned out to be secretaries that worked for the Americans.

"It was a very successful mission," Grosovich saluted Yakov who was waiting on the parking apron when the two-seater roll to a halt and whined into silence as the engines were shut down. Yakov looked at the booty, and in obviously mock anger looked over at Grosovich climbing down the cockpit ladder. "So lieutenant, what would have happened if you had to eject with all that stuff in the cockpit."

Grosovich looked over at his coconspirator who was just taking off his helmet standing next to him, and said, "We talked about that Colonel Yakov. The soccer balls would have been no problem, but we were al little concerned about where those bats would go."

Yakov made the two lieutenants the intramural sports officers and began setting up soccer teams. He simultaneously had the base engineering office mark off part of the drill field into two soccer fields and build goals out of the wooden crates and nets that came with the spare engines.

Next, he had the administration office divide the number of enlisted personnel up into a hundred and four groups and assigned an officer to each one. Yakov made that officer responsible for the well being of his group and the focal point for any personal or professional problems.

The rest of the problems were too complex for just one man so Yakov had an officer's call in the officers' mess. Yakov brought along his aeronautical chart with problem number one and its resolution covered over with tape. Yakov went right down the list.

"What about the food? Don't expect any help from upstairs…"

A section leader stood up and said, "Colonel Yakov there is plenty of food in the forests…there is boundless supplies of elk, deer, and moose in this area, not to mention the streams, which are brimming with trout, grayling and salmon. Why don't we go bag some? It will also give our boys some recreation in the field and get them off the base."

Yakov looked over at the operations officer. "Get that man's name and put him in charge of the hunting parties."

Another officer stood. "Colonel Yakov, I have a degree in agriculture from Moscow University. This base has an area of almost a hundred square kilometers and the soil is a rich loam that is a meter in depth. We can grow our own vegetables. We're sitting here at fifty-five degrees north and have a super long summer just like the Susitna Valley in Alaska. The Americans grow cabbages there that are two meters in diameter…and our soil is better! What we don't eat right away we can wrap in plastic and store in the arctic research hangar." The adjutant recorded the man's name and suggestion.

"Ok men, put your thinking caps on now. Is there anything we can do about those brown outs the base is causing on the hydro grid?" A hand went up slowly in the back.

"Yes, in the back, go ahead."

One of the newly assigned pilots slowly stood up. "Colonel Yakov, I have an idea, but it is probably against regulations."

"I'm starting to like it already," Yakov said, to a round of laughter from the officers.

"Colonel Yakov, may I speak to you in private tomorrow?"

The KGB officer looked around, wrote the man's name down along with Yakov's statement. The window of opportunity had finally opened.

The next morning, second lieutenant I. G. Chugunova, a graduate electrical engineer from the University of St. Petersburg, who had asked for the private meeting with Yakov, laid out his idea. The guy was also assigned to the assistant director of maintenance for the unit. The young lieutenant walked over to Yakov's desk and unrolled a large diagram hand drawn by pencil. "Colonel Yakov, we have the necessary resources at our disposal to not only to relieve the kilovolt shortfall on Kamchatka's hydro grid, but to create surplus power that we may be able to sell back to the peninsula co-op, maybe even trade for something we need."

"By all means man, keep talking," Yakov was enthralled. The lieutenant traced his conclusions by pointing to the subsystems and components on his hand drawn plan.

"Colonel Yakov, the power requirements for just one MiG-25, to operate the entire ship's electrical systems is enough to supply the power for the whole town of Scapino. Two Tumanski engines at 42% thrust, just above idle, running two paralleled generators with constant speed drives, would supply one hundred percent of the electrical demand for Scapino and the town of Mil Kovo."

"But what about the hundred hour time between overhaul limitation on the engines? Wouldn't we have to replace the engines every hundred hours like we do in the airplane?"

"Actually, no, comrade colonel. The hundred hour TBO requirement assumes operation at flight and afterburner EGTs and eighty-seven to one hundred twenty percent N2. And, it assumes that one of our valuable Soviet pilots has his butt strapped in as well. The hundred hour TBO figure is a very conservative manufacturing specification and has no application to an unstressed non afterburning engine running at just above idle and not mounted in an airplane."

"So how long could we run the engines, Chugunova?"

"Six months easy," the young officer replied, grinning from ear to ear, "And we've got plenty of engines, more fuel than we could burn in five years…and more of both on the way."

Forty-five days later, in contradiction of at least twenty Soviet Air Force regulations, Yakov's team of maintenance experts and three guys from NPO Hydro-Kamchatka adapted the two systems together with an ingenious technology. Lt. Chugunova's system used two RB30 engines running paralleled generators and a third shut down engine as a standby. It wasn't pretty to look at, like a lot of Russian engineering, but it worked. Hitler had learned that lesson the hard way. Up and down the peninsula at the five towns being served by the hydro-grid, the new power and the elimination of the brownouts and blackouts turned the guys at the base from electricity stealing villains to folk heroes overnight. Two months after coming on line,

Chugunova, and a five junior officer team met with Yakov with the final touch on the system. After an intensive engineering study, they found that by coordinating with Hydro-Kamchatka, and actuating only twenty seven switches at the hydro plant, the base could run the standby engine using its own generator as an emergency backup to the hospital when a series of operations were scheduled. The use of military resources in this manner without prior approval was an egregious offense. It was just a matter of time.

The KGB was conspicuously absent off base when the telex came in from KGB headquarters in Moscow. Colonel Yakov was to report immediately to Colonel General V. N. Kobelyev to present explanations for crimes against the state. Yakov read the message as his administrative sergeant looked on with worry. Yakov could feel his stomach churning as he read the message. The word spread quickly around the base and Yakov was to fly to Moscow the next morning to present his explanations. A small committee of junior officers was waiting for him on the flight line; Lt. Grosovich was one of them and was suited up in flying gear. "With the greatest respect, Colonel Yakov, what do you think you're doing?" one of the pilots asked. Yakov was in no mood for any lip and said, "I'm flying to Moscow for a date with a woman with big tits." Yakov kept walking toward his aircraft, filled with despair as he strode across the pavement.

The group of young officers fell into line behind Yakov. "We regret to inform you Colonel Yakov that ship number two thirty-four is grounded for maintenance."

"What?" he said, stopping in his tracks. "Why was I not informed of this...find me another aircraft

141

immediately."

"Colonel Yakov," another lieutenant piped up, "All the single seaters are down for maintenance."

"That's impossible," Yakov argued.

"Sir, the PU is the only aircraft that is available."

"Well then, get me the two-seater…I don't know what you people are up to, but when I get back…."

The words when I get back, had a chilling hollowness to them. The young officers dreaded the idea that Yakov would not be returning…a not uncommon event.

Another lieutenant Yakov did not recognize had the nerve to interrupt him. "Colonel Yakov, there is another problem. Bat Man's…errr… I mean Lt. Grosovich will lose his landing currency if he does not get two landings today. The training cycle will have to be reset. It will cause a great deal of paperwork, and Air Defense Command would have to be notified with an explanation. Sir, I'm afraid the only solution is for you to have Grosovich fly you to Moscow."

It began to dawn on Yakov what was going on. The young officers were concerned that he was unsafe to fly himself in his agitated frame of mind and when he got to Moscow he would be alone against the KGB.

"Look, gentlemen, I appreciate what you are trying to do, but I can handle these KGB bastards….so don't worry…I can fly myself just…."

And that was the last thing Yakov got out of his mouth. The lieutenants' gang tackled him, grabbing him like a log and began carrying him down the flight line where the ground crew and Grosovich already had the MiG-25PU two-seater preflighted with one engine already started. Yakov struggled…"There's no point in resisting Comrade Colonel," somebody said, "we are desperate, desperate men with nothing to lose." They all laughed hard at the secret slogan that spread like wildfire around the base after Yakov had busted the political officer's balls. They stuffed him into the back seat and handed up his helmet to the crew chief. After Grosovich got the taxi clearance and pushed up the power to get the big jet rolling, Yakov pushed the canopy lever forward bringing down the plastic bubble for the rear seat pilot then looked over at the mutineers. They were standing at attention, saluting. Yakov's eyes started burning...Oh no, not that again. He returned their salute. Why do my eyes always start burning at times like this?

He keyed the interphone switch on the rear throttle quadrant. "Grosovich, let's go to Moscow." The MiG's two 25,450 pound thrust engines roared as Grosovich shoved both throttles into afterburner. The sleek, steel, forty ton jet thundered into the morning sky. Grosovich pulled it out of burner quickly for the long enroute climb to 15,000 meters.

Minutes later, the green mountains of the Kamchatka dropped away into the gray foreboding sea. The sky turned darker, from a crystal powdery blue, and softly slid to a deeper blue and then to indigo, the deadly hunting ground of the MiG-25 Foxbat.

Yakov leaned his head back against the headrest, put his visor up, and looked up at the sky. Yakov let his arms rest on the canopy rails. This is the last time I'll ever fly the Foxbat, he thought. He thought of his friend Yuri, and his mother crying at the train station. He saw the blood-streaked young faces of the Spitsnatz commandos that he rescued in Afghanistan. He remembered the staccato thuds of Taliban weapons fire raking his helicopter and the loud whump of the Stinger missile that blew off part of his tail rotor. It'll be a hell of a note to get it from state after going through all this shit, he thought. If this is it, he concluded, I've had a damn good run.

Yakov closed his eyes and lowered the tinted visor of his helmet. He dreamed of black storks flying low over the clear cold waters of the Pripyat River.

Chapter 16

"Somebody turn the machine off."

The president was the only one who seemed to have any presence of mind. The cabinet sat in stunned silence, trying to wrap their minds around the incredible message they just heard. No event in history could ever approximate the one they were experiencing. About four minutes went by and no one said a word.

"Mr. President, why don't we play the message again? I think some of us, at least us thick-headed military types anyway, would like to hear it a second time." Colonel Lowell Bremen was at the very end of the table, according to protocol. Being a Rhodes Scholar with a doctorate in history would hardly make Bremen thickheaded, but the trick worked. It unfroze the group and started the neurons firing again. The second playing did not improve the message, but some of the fear seemed to have bled off, at least to the point that the cabinet could begin to speak.

"Does anybody here see any options to their demands? I need your best thoughts. Speak your mind without hesitation." A long silence started anew while everyone began to consider the demands.

"Does anyone here question their credibility?"

The Secretary of Defense was the first to speak. "Mr. President, their fore knowledge of the arrival of the Geographos asteroid, and exact prediction of its trajectory, would make one believe that their credibility is beyond reproach."

There were several heads nodding in agreement.

The president looked at the Secretary of Defense.

"Lamar, can we defeat their technology?"

"No, Mr. President we cannot. Analysis of all available information concludes that they have an unknown source of power that can be used for propulsion and most likely weaponry. There are scant reports of overt action on their parts aside from some sort of heat ray they used in Brazil at an Army fort near Brasilia and one other instance in the Florida Everglades. Undoubtedly, they are not revealing their actual capability, a prudent tactical and strategic procedure that we use ourselves."

Clinton had a follow-up question. "But what about the high powered laser weapons we're working on at Los Alamos?"

"Mr. President the EBEs presented themselves only twice, so far, on a reconnaisance of Los Alamos. We fired the Pace Lantern on both occasions with sustained, full power, multiple bursts at each of the two ships. Every time we fired at one, the other spacecraft would emit a massive EM pulse that bent the laser beam causing it to miss. Even in the multiple target mode which can attack up to ten targets with only microseconds between bursts, the EBEs stayed right with us like they were somehow synchronized, each ship shielding the other one with an EM pulse."

The president continued. "What about their motives? Are they up to no good, or are they just here to study us and move on as they say? Have they killed any humans?"

Again silence. There was not one single record of a human being killed except for several airborne incidents in which our interceptors had been destroyed in flight along with the pilots. There was absolutely zero data which supported an aggressive overtly intentional act on the part of the EBEs. The Aerospace Defense Command pilots were known for their aggressiveness, and it was quite possible that they got too close and flew into the wake of the alien ships or some other proximity effect which was unintentional on the part of the EBEs.

The president continued his line of reasoning. "So what would be the downside of complying with their orders?"

"We'd lose a year of research at our weapons labs, there would be more abductions, and we'd have to explain a few more flying saucer reports," said the Secretary of State.

"They might recognize that we are not as savage as they probably think we are, since we are willing to give peace a chance and let them go on their way...it takes two for a fight." Secretary of Transportation Alice Hayes-Udall was well known for her stance for gun control, repeal of the second amendment, more power to the police, women's rights, and more women in combat roles in the military. She had a running feud with the Commandant of the Marine Corps who refused to allow women in front line combat duty, and refused to allow women to train with the men.

Maureen Harrison-DuPont, the Secretary of the Treasury nodded her head in agreement and then added, "Mr. President, the way of peace is always the hardest. The way of conciliation is always unpopular. The way of cooperation so often seems impossible. I say we have very little to lose by conceding, and if they are right about 2022, as they were about Geographos, we will have saved a billion lives."

The consensus was building for accepting their demands.

The aliens stated that they were almost finished with their peaceful survey of our system but were afraid that our weapons technology was advancing to a point that it was becoming a threat to the completion of their project. In return for our suspending all defensive action and military research for one year, they would agree to deflect a large asteroid that would be hitting us in the year 2022. If we did not comply, the EBEs bluntly stated that no such deflection would be made and we'd be on our own.

Lowell Bremen looked at his watch. Where the hell was the Chief of Staff? He thought of General Marshall out riding with strict orders to not be disturbed on December 6th 1941, when the Japanese attack message on Pearl Harbor had been decoded.

"May I assume we are in agreement on the course of action then?" The president looked down each side of the table. Colonel Lowell Bremen slowly rose to his feet. "Mr. President I have a comment before we finish."

"By all means Colonel Bremen, give us the benefit of your political acumen," cracked Alice Hayes-Udall, referring to Bremen's zero political experience.

"Colonel Bremen, please continue," said the Vice President.

Bremen began. "Mr. President, John Stuart Mill once said that the work of the world is also accomplished with scissors as well as the sword. Mr. Mill, however, did not say that the sword would never be necessary. What has been suggested here in nothing but complete capitulation and appeasement. If there is one lesson that history has taught us in the twentieth century, it is that appeasement never leads to peace…only an interval before the conflagration.

Secretary Hayes-Udall and others here think that this is a political matter, a political event, some kind of negotiated settlement of equals. It is not. For the last fifty years they have been conducting a planet wide reconnaissance of our military, repeat military defensive capability."

Bremen looked at Hayes-Udall for his last sentence, then returned his gaze to each face in the room one by one.

"We and the Soviets responded to this surveillance by building the mightiest arsenals of destruction ever compiled on our planet. Sure, our two systems were in competition, but the most superficial examination would reveal the truth. One squadron of twentyB-52s could lay waste to the entire Soviet Union. We had a hundred three squadrons. One ballistic submarine, with its MIRV warheads could do the same, yet we kept twenty-seven missile submarines on continuous patrol. One Minuteman ICBM squadron out in Montana, with eight missiles and sixty-four MIRVs could make the Soviet empire a pool of molten glass, yet we had a hundred and twenty-two missile squadrons... And the Russians had the equivalent number of bombers, missile submarines, and ICBMs that we did. For fifty years, the EBEs did nothing but fly around and look us over. And how did we win the Cold War? By our superior technology. And how did we make these massive leaps of technology? We harvested it from three of their ships, which conveniently crashed and fell into our hands. Microcircuits, lasers, fiber optics, Kevlar, all reverse engineered from the alien technology. The first one crashed in New Mexico, right next to our best weapons laboratories. Isn't it odd that no alien ships ever crashed behind the Iron Curtain?

149

The Soviets shared with us that they had fired thousands of missiles and hotly pursued the alien ships every time they appeared. Now, the Russian arsenal has been virtually dismantled, and we have cut our own by fifty percent. My forty years of military intelligence has taught me that when it comes to the important matters, there's no such thing as a coincidence. They then fly what they claim is an asteroid by us, and then demand that we stand down for twelve more months so that *they can finish their peaceful survey and be on their way.* If their goals are peaceful, why have they systematically analyzed every defensive system that we own? Why are they threatening to permit this asteroid to hit us in 2022?"

Hayes-Udall butted in and answered his question. "Colonel Bremen perhaps they observed the rabid barbarity of our citizens who hunt and kill innocent animals in the forest...or our sending two million soldiers to commit genocide against an innocent population in Southeast Asia. They became afraid of us, and wanted to protect themselves."

Everyone's eyes were now switched to Bremen, like a tennis match.

Bremen levelled his gaze at Alice Hayes-Udall. "Madam Secretary, for fifty years, when they were afraid of us, with all our bad old Bambi killing things that go boom-boom, how many ultimatums like this did they send us?"

President Clinton raised his hand to stop the exchange. "Colonel Bremen, Alice, please...Colonel Bremen, I think we get your point. It might be best if you waited in the reception until the cabinet meeting has finished."

"Yes sir, Mr. President." Bremen picked up his hat

off the empty chair where Hampton should have been and went out the door. Major General Troy Hampton would not make the next cabinet meeting either. This was because General Troy Hampton, astronaut, scientist, soldier and patriot, husband and father of twin baby girls....was dead, by his own hand. They found his body the next morning in a small roadside park near Arlington, about half a mile from where they found Vince Foster.

Air Force CID did an intensive investigation, and while there was no note, which they said ninety percent of the time was present in suicides, foul play was ruled out.

Hampton came up with a system to defend our cities from alien attack. He called the system the Triple Threat. The system consisted of an outer defense with remotely piloted

Mach ten space fighters that patrolled out to five hundred miles, a middle altitude defense using kill vehicles known as the SDI, and an inner ring of ten advanced Pave Lantern lasers paired with Pave Pebble particle beam projectors and a high and low altitude missile compliment. The inner ring low altitude system for city defense was code named the Bear Trap. The mated systems could be placed around a city or region we wanted to defend. The ring was large, almost a hundred miles in diameter. At four locations inside the ring were hypersonic rocket batteries which protected from 100,000 to 400,000 ft. code named Night Rider, and twelve low altitude missile batteries, code named Flechette which covered from 10,000 feet to 100,000 feet. The Night Rider was a big missile that accelerated to 12,000 miles per hour in less than 6000 feet of altitude. The highest speed ever recorded by the alien scout ships, so called "Sport Model," was 7,000 knots. Each warhead of the big rocket had a cluster munition of twenty, advanced neutron warheads about the size of a cantaloupe. Each of the individual warheads was a one kiloton weapon. With the advanced neutron warhead, you get a traditional nuclear blast but with enhanced neutron emissions that will kill any living thing and devastate electronic circuitry. The other benefit of the advanced neutron warheads was that they created zero fallout to endanger people on the ground. The weapon would not arm below 10,000 feet and if it missed, each individual warhead would disarm itself and glide back to the nearest Bear Trap battery, using a microwave homer and parafoil which unfolded out of the shell casing. When an enemy spacecraft flew into the effective envelope of the Bear Trap ring, all the lasers and particle beam projectors would lock onto the target and open up simultaneously, catching the target in a fantastic cross fire of concentrated of energy. If the alien ship was at or above 10,000 feet, he also gets a nuclear tipped missile up his ass at 12,000 knots complete with special surprise neutron suppository. If the enemy spacecraft was below 10,000 down to 1,000 ft above ground level a Flechette engagement would happen with similar shotgun type warheads that instead used T-5, a chemical explosive with approximately fifty times the explosive force of a similar weight of TNT. One second before arrival of either missile, all the beam weapons would cease fire to avoid prematurely detonating the warheads. Two seconds after warhead detonation, all ten sites would switch to the multiple target engagement mode and vaporize whatever pieces were left as they fluttered to earth. If any of the pieces exhibited controlled flight characteristics as they passed

10,000 feet, the process began all over again with a Flechette engagement. This thing was nasty, and based on the tests that they made on the structures of the captured ships at Wright Patt, it was believed that the Bear Trap would be extremely effective. A Bear Trap system with only the low altitude sector active was finally approved for testing near Groom Lake, Nevada. But, for the obvious reasons, it was never tried out against the aliens. Hampton said that if they became hostile, then, and only then, should we show them our stuff.

Hampton's theory centered on the fact that they were a long way from home. We're fighting on our home turf with tight lines of internal communication and logistics. We would not have to defeat their technology, just by superior numbers of weapons, demonstrate that attacking us would be a price they would not be willing to pay. This was the theory behind the arms race. If the EBEs were able to render inoperative ours, or the Soviet arsenal, the other side could still fire everything they had. This would make the earth's surface unusable for whatever nefarious purpose they had in mind. As dangerous as it was, it had kept them at bay for fifty years.

After hearing the bad news, Bremen immediately went to the acting Chairman and suggested the Hampton's personal files on war fighting in space be preserved and protected with the maximum security possible. The acting chairman told Bremen that this was the first thing he ordered when he got the news himself. Unfortunately, General Hampton had just received a brand new system for his office the day before and had not yet transferred all his files.

"And his old computer...back up tapes?" Bremen

asked.

The new Chairman's forehead crinkled with worry.

"Everything is missing."

Bremen put his retirement papers in the same day that the president and his cabinet approved acceding to the aliens' demands. There was nothing he could do. Going to congress would have eventually leaked to the public creating a panic. Two different studies, the latest by the Rand Corporation, had demonstrated with high confidence that massive disruption of society would occur if all that was known about the EBEs were made public. This was what had kept the government silent for five decades despite overwhelming evidence that the EBEs were here.

Bremen was cleaning out his office when the phone rang.

"Colonel Bremen."

"Colonel Bremen, my name is John Good, and I work for a well known company in the Washington area." Bremen knew by Good's accent on the word company, exactly which company it was. It was the Central Intelligence Agency.

"I'm familiar with your company. Speak your piece, I'm as short as they get." Bremen was curt with the guy because it was well known that CIA had been penetrated by the KGB. The standing joke in Army Intelligence was that the fastest way to communicate with the Kremlin was not the White House hot line. It was a fax to the CIA stamped Top Secret.

"Colonel Bremen, I realize that this may be a bad time, but we hear that you're a save the world kind of guy…"

Chapter 17

Robert Tranh poured over the latest discovery data from project Skyguard. The day in 1989 when Leanna announced that "this time we're going to do something big," seemed like five minutes ago. Here it was 1997 and the program was successful beyond anyone's most optimistic projections. Leanna had been continuously evolving into a higher form of life. The Leanna of today would not even be recognized by anyone who knew her before I they had not witnessed the transformation themselves. For example, take the guy she fired after he made a crack about her Rotary plaque. Even though he eventually found a job and then retired in another company, the guy's age precluded him from ever hitting the big salary numbers he was making for the Helms subsidiary. The guy had four kids in college. Leanna restored his full retirement package. But then, she wouldn't take any of his calls, which was more like the old Leanna. "I haven't got time for that loser," she said. Few solutions are perfectly symmetrical, Tranh thought. The few male subordinates she had personal contact with were floored when about a year ago, the steely eyed killer had said thank you to one of them. Tranh had no idea what was happening, he just hoped to God that it would continue.

The day eight years ago, when Leanna made her proclamation, was the day that Skyguard began. After an exhaustive research effort that Leanna herself conducted only aided from time to time with outside consultants, Leanna had determined that the planet Earth needed an asteroid detection system that would give advance warning of huge asteroid or comet collisions. She was heavily influenced by the research of NASA space engineer John S. Lewis. Lewis had published a highly important book entitled "Rain of Iron and Ice." The book was a publishing flop and wound up on the bargain book counter at Barnes & Noble. The book contained, however, some of the most important research ever compiled on the threat of an Earth asteroid collision. Lewis maintained that bombardment theory probably was more important in changing the evolutionary history of life on Earth than anything Darwin could have imagined. Tranh recalled making the comment to Leanna that he thought that the money envisioned could be far better used for more concrete humanitarian uses since the earth doesn't get hit by an asteroid but once in billions of years. Leanna quoted heavily from Lewis book on the first meeting. Workers on the Trans-Siberian railway in 1908 witnessed a brilliant fireball that disappeared over the northern horizon. The massive explosion made a nuclear mushroom cloud, which spread dust that lit up the skies of Europe for weeks. Even the primitive seismographs of that period registered the explosion all over the world. It wasn't until 1927 that the Russians got up there with an expedition. They found no crater, but 2000 square kilometers of coniferous forest had been devastated by an airburst of an asteroid.

"Robert, imagine the death toll if the Tungaska asteroid had exploded over Los Angeles."

"But surely there's some kind of effort already underway to find these things if they're so dangerous."

"There is," she responded. "An astronomer named Tom Gehels at the University of Arizona has come up with a brilliant plan he calls Spacewatch...but it is woefully under funded and it will take them fifty to one hundred years to find every near Earth asteroid that might hit us. Lewis says in his book that conventional photographic methods of finding NEAs can't identify any that are less than 250-300 meters in diameter....using current technology, these sized asteroids could go undetected forever."

"And the problem is what?" Tranh knew Leanna wasn't through talking.

"The problem, my dear Bob, is that the Tungaska asteroid and many, many others that have hit us in recorded history were approximately 250 meters in diameter."

"Uh oh, I wasn't aware of that." Tranh felt his throat constrict slightly.

"Virtually nobody is, outside of the scientific community," Leanna continued. "And now the interesting part. Bob, did you ever wonder what happened to the dinosaurs?"

"They got whacked by an asteroid?"

"Precisely. It was only in 1981 when a team from Berkeley headed up by Lewis Alvarez discovered a one millimeter thick layer of iridium, are rare metal found mostly in asteroids, covering the entire Earth. It was ten feet thick near Haiti and included micrometeorite and soot. The iridium came from a one kilometer in diameter asteroid that hit off the Yucatan peninsula creating a two hundred kilometer wide crater. The hit of that rock marked the end of the dinosaur's Cretaceous period and the beginning of the Tertiary...the rise of mammals...us. Lewis' research suggests that impacts of one kilometer sized asteroids is very rare...but it only takes one...and Robert, as we speak, nobody is looking. Nobody! With the federal budget under intense scrutiny, spending hundreds of millions to look for asteroids when children in Mississippi don't have access to Head Start because of funding...it becomes almost politically impossible."

"So what are we going to do?" Tranh had asked. Leanna then pulled out the completed proposal she had labored over for months. Leanna's plan, after her independent verification, followed NASA engineer Lewis's plan from his book.

Leanna set aside $300 million for the installation of 150 state of the art 72 inch telescopes all over the world. Tranh delegated the site selection to a Helms subsidiary that had built a worldwide satellite tracking system for the Air Force. The interesting twist was that Leanna allowed the host nations to use the observatories for any research they wanted except at those times of the night when conditions existed for asteroid tracking. At those times, the telescopes had to be devoted to 100% asteroid hunting. Within weeks after the last site was completed, the NEA hunters were finding 950 per month and well over 12,000 per year, almost exactly according to Lewis's forecasts. The tracks of the Apollos, the name for the Earth threatening asteroids, were sent to a Helms Industries central computer base that began to analyze the orbital characteristics to estimate the threat level of each Apollo.

Eight years, Tranh thought to himself. Time flies when you're having fun. Eight years and we've got 99% of the Apollos identified and analyzed. The only one we think will hit us is a 200 meter nickel iron that won't be here for over a thousand years...and we'll sure have something by then to zap the son of a bitch before it causes any problems...and our data is at the

.999999 confidence level....ahhh, now I'll be able to finally get a good night's sleep, Tranh chuckled to himself.

Chapter 18

The year 1997 was also a good year for two guys named Bob. Bob Gomez was somewhere within the confines of the United States with a Ford Econovan and an Airstream trailer having a blast with his wife. Last seen, Gomez and Linda were on a barge with over 150 Airstream trailers heading down the Mississippi from St. Louis heading down to the Big Easy for Mardi Gras. The license plate on the front bumper of his truck more or less summed up his current attitude after twenty-five years in the Navy, the last twenty in the SEALs. The license plate read, "No Phone, No address, No Bills, No Shit!" The bumper sticker on the back of his Airstream further clarified his various political and social sensitivities. He saw it in a T-shirt shop in Kalispell, Montana. It read, "Nuke the Gay Unborn Whales."

The barge pulled up for lunch one afternoon in Oceola, Arkansas, where the tow boat crew had some family, and the captain had a girlfriend. So, it worked out peachy for everybody. The Airstream Travel Club got to walk around a quaint little fly over American town, the crew got to spend a few hours with their families, and the captain got laid. After they pulled out of Oceola and been underway for about fifteen minutes, the word reached Gomez that way in the back of the barge, a pack of bonafide Hells Angels from the Oakland headquarters club had decided they were going to hitch a ride. There were five of them on the way to a convention in New Orleans and to check on a couple of their distributors there who were skimming some of the dope money. The average age of the Airstream tour group was about seventy, the bikers were in their thirties and forties. There five of these shit birds, tough looking, tattoo covered hombres with two sissies along for poke bait...to keep everyone's morale up on the long lonesome highway. They didn't waste any time showing their ass and getting mean with some of the older folks at the back of the barge, who were already giving them beer and food. Lenny Purcell, the Airstream tour coordinator had a worried look on his face when he finally made it through the tightly crammed trailers up to the front where Bob and Linda were playing gin rummy.

"Uh Bob, we got a problem in the back," Lenny began.

"Gin!" Linda pronounced, smiling, putting her hand face up on the card table, which folded out of the side of their polished aluminum Airstream trailer. "You owe me another two hundred forty-three thousand bucks!"

"Jesus," muttered Bob Gomez, tossing his cards into the center of the table in mock disgust. "What's the problem Lenny?" Lenny laid out the problem. Gomez got up from the folding table, stretched and yawned. "Be back in a minute honey," and then put his arm over Purcell's shoulder. "Actually, I have some experience dealing with undesirable characters," Gomez laughed.

Purcell seemed relieved and the two of them began winding their way back through the densely packed trucks, SUVs and assorted other vehicles hooked up to their Airstream trailers which had been backed in. The five bikers and their bitches were parked in the left rear corner of the barge and had already confiscated a card table and chairs from somebody. They were crapped out with their feet up, slugging down Bud, throwing the cans overboard and playing grab ass with their babes. Bob stopped Lenny about three car lengths from the commotion to recce the situation. Right in front of the bikers there was a big old Chevy Suburban pointed aft still hooked up to its Airstream. Gomez crept forward, looked in the cab, Oh yeah! He thought. The keys were in the ignition. Lenny Purcell was an old geezer who had served in the 4th Armored Division in Europe and had flown Piper Cub spotter planes. A German tank shot his tail off, but since it was shooting armor piercing rounds, it didn't explode and just made a big mess and he crashed the Cub and got away….

"Yo Lenny," Gomez whispered. "Can you unhook this trailer for me on this Suburban?"

"Can do," Lenny whispered back.

Purcell pulled the safety latch pin on the trailer hook unscrewed the connector and gently lifted the tow bar clear. He then tapped the back of the truck twice.

Bob Gomez eased into the cab of the Suburban, started the engine, gunned it a couple of times, and slammed the transmission into low gear. The bikers looked up when he gunned the engine and started to rise from the table.

"What the fuck you doin' old man," the leader of the group shouted, as his pals all started to put their feet down and get up from the folding chairs.

The biker assholes weren't quite fast enough, as Gomez floored the accelerator. The big SUV burned rubber for about twenty feet and plowed into the table, bikers, sissies, and the five beautiful 30,000 dollar chopped Harleys, like it was pushing a bale of balloons. The five motorcycles, five bad asses, and two screaming sissies were literally catapulted off the deck. Last seen, the seven hitchhikers were swimming for shore trying to hurtle invective and keep from drowning at the same time.

"That fat un' really got a mouth on em' don't he?" a little gray-hair said.

"Yeah, fuck the pricks, somebody quick, throw em' an anchor!" cackled a purple-hair standing next to her, in a high whiney voice. The whole thing took about four minutes.

Gomez shifted the Suburban into reverse and backed it precisely to its former position. There was only one fairly decent ding in the bumper and hardly any other damage. The Suburban's owner came over and profusely shook Bob and Lenny's hand, looking over at the dented bumper he pronounced loud enough for everybody to hear, "I ain't never gonna take that dent out."

Bob and Linda had reservations at the St. Charles guesthouse just for a change of scenery when they got to New Orleans. Linda plugged in the laptop into the room's terminal. "Bobby," she called to Gomez who was in the bathroom luxuriating in a long Hollywood shower.

"What honey?"

"Bobby, you've got an e-mail from Mike."

"No shit, open it. What's that son of a bitch up to? He got out of the SEALS six months before me and Palmer and disappeared for God's sake."

"Oh, I don't like this at all," Linda called back over the roaring shower.

"Just read it honey, you've known the guy as long as I have."

"OK. It says, The gunfighter rides again, wire PaladinCorp@aol.com."

Gomez abruptly shut off the shower and wrapped a

towel around him and came into the bedroom dripping with water. "Honey, how about going out and getting me a six pack will ya? I need to make a phone call."

"Please Bobby, don't agree to do anything without discussing it with me ok?"

"Don't worry honey…Mike's just probably setting up a reunion or something."

"Yeah, so why are you sending me out while you talk to him?" Linda's voice was tinged with fear.

Bob Gomez went over to the door and hugged her, then put his hand under her chin and pulled it up gently…then he kissed her lightly. "Baby, there is nothing on this planet that can keep me from spending the rest of my days with you...no matter what Mike Mancusso wants…now scoot." Gomez laughed and half heartedly popped her with the wet towel as she went out the door.

Linda half smiled, wanting to believe him with all her heart.

The door shut and Gomez picked up the phone…Nothing on this earth, he repeated to himself. That's the fucking least I owe that good woman…and started dialing. Now, Captain Mike Mancusso, just what the hell are you up to?

* * *

Bob Palmer's dive shop was doing great. Not only was the dive business good, but as an agent for Mel Fisher, the famous salvage diver who found millions in gold on the Maria De Atocha, Palmer was selling salvage permits to scour the Spanish wrecks right off the beach near Vero Beach, Florida. Fisher, of course, had suctioned up everything on the site that was valuable, but there were always a few suckers who thought that they could get out there and find something that Fisher had missed. The permit business was good. Palmer had his own personal Navy SEAL museum in the shop which made it a must see for divers in the area who at the same time, filled their tanks, rented equipment and bought the expensive doodads that they sell in dive shops. A nice easy life...until the call from Mike Mancuso.

Chapter 19

The year 1997 was hell on earth for Matt Blalock. For the first few months after his divorce from Diane he lived in a quixotic state of denial when he was asleep. At night he was able to escape the gut wrenching pain and self-recrimination that inhabited every corner of his waking day. His real estate business was suffering, and if it weren't for two of his top producers not defecting to ReMax, he would have already gone down at the bow with the band playing on the poopdeck. One of them had actually starting managing the office while Matt came rolling in at two PM, made a couple of phone calls, then left by four without speaking to anyone. Blalock hardly seemed to notice when checks made out to the phone company, the multi-list providers, and the other vendors appeared on his desk for signing. He just signed them and left. Oblivion would have been a good word to describe the guy.

Diane had her law degree and when it came down to the nut cutting in the divorce, she realized that to assure a really fair settlement, she had to go after Matt with a sublime impersonal vengeance designed to shock him into complicity by the shear ferocity of the attack. She and her attorney waded into him like a giant circle saw in an Alabama lumber mill. Blalock's attorney, a guy named John Peck, a former Eastern pilot who had a law practice was a former Air Commando. He saw what was happening and tried to rally Blalock into battle. It was a fruitless effort for Peck since his client was an emotional rubble pile at the bottom of a smoking crater that was once his life. All Blalock seemed capable of saying in their conferences was, "Give her what she wants John, I don't think I can last much longer."

Blalock was living with a divorced buddy down off Collier Road in downtown Atlanta. He had his expenses down to about seven-fifty a month including his half of the rent. Fortunately, his Lex 400 was paid for, so that the ends were meeting just fine…at least that was good. The days were endless hours of pain, confusion, and anger. One night over at Houck's, one of his hangouts, he noticed the surface of his mug of beer shimmy a little. Oh Christ, he thought, this has got to be some kind of landmark event. Teardrops were running down his face and into his draft. Literally, crying in his beer. For God's sake, he said to himself, grabbing a couple of napkins. This has got to be the rock bottom that they talk about, he concluded, wiping his face with the napkins.

Here's where all those people who don't believe in coincidences will all jump up out of their chairs and yell, "See, we told you so!" Shit, who knows, but it sure as hell happened. Not more than five minutes after Blalock had used those napkins, a big black Lincoln limo pulled up in front of Houck's. The driver piled out, ran back to the trunk, and began assembling a motorized wheelchair, then rolled it around the left side of the limo for the passenger to climb into. The lean muscular black guy in the chair looked around to the driver and called out, "Tex, don't forget my elephant gun."

"Got it right here Duane," Tex yelled back pulling the elongated green canvas bag out of the trunk and handing it to Duane McCall.

"Tex, you want to come in for a cold one?"

"No thanks, you go have your reunion with your

167

buddy...but you could have somebody send me a burger with some fries and a Coke."

"It's a done deal," Duane answered.

Now, let's see if this guy remembers me, he thought, plugging the speed controller of his chair into the position marked "AB" for afterburner. Duane motored up the handicapped access ramp through the double doors and stopped in front of the hostess station.

"I'm looking for Matt Blalock an ex-Eastern pilot that hangs out in here, you know the dude?"

The two angelic teenage hostesses were sitting on the bench next to the reception stand rolling up silverware into cloth napkins. "That's Matt right there," one pointed. "He's the only one with the long sleeved shirt."

McCall buzzed up the ramp and into the darkened bar and rolled up to an empty spot next to Blalock. He hit the spring loaded elevation switch on his custom chair, which was professionally placarded "Ejection Seat." The seat slowly moved up to the height of a barstool, and Duane motioned for the bartender. Blalock was still staring down into his beer mug. McCall nudged him with his elbow a little harder than what would be considered polite. Blalock looked over without saying anything, then back into his mug.

McCall nudged him once more. "Excuse me pard, I think I'm lost."

Blalock looked over, this time with mild irritation.

"Yeah, I think I'm lost," Duane continued with total indifference.

"Getting lost sounds like something you should do," Blalock quipped, taking a deep chug without even looking up.

"No seriously," McCall continued. "I think I made

a wrong turn someplace. Now I'm gonna' be late for my Klan meetin.'"

Blalock slowly turned his head to his right to get a better look at his new bar buddy. "From the look of you, I'd say your sheet needs a bleach job."

"You don't know who I am, do you?" McCall was smiling.

"Don't know, don't give a shit," Blalock took another long slug.

"We met at LaGuardia Airport on May 5th 1974. It was raining...you were so handsome in your uniform...I was on fire."

Blalock's head jerked to his right; then he embarrassed himself.

"Nice trick, they teach you that in the Air force...the spitting of beer out your nose I mean?"

Blalock wiped himself off with another handful of napkins. "I didn't recognize you," was all Blalock could think to say, still coughing a little, his voice high pitched...the beer went down the wrong hole.

"I'm not surprised. It was a, shall we say, 'fleeing' encounter?"

"Fleeing wasn't half of it." Blalock was beginning to lighten up.

"When I got up there and saw that you were...uhhh..."

"Mobility challenged?" McCall helped him out, chuckling.

"Yeah, mobility challenged, I thought we were gonna' be the salt and pepper on a cooked goose."

"Why don't we get a table?" Duane suggested.

"Sure, why not."

Duane engaged the elevation down switch on his chair then hand peddled himself over to a table in the corner. Blalock pulled up a chair.

Two and a half hours later, they were both completely shit faced. You find out a lot about a man when he's drunk. The underlying true personality surfaces. If a man is filled with hate, it comes bubbling out with aggression and meanness. If he's basically an amiable sort, he laughs a lot. He's a happy drunk. If he's basically melancholy, booze tunes him quiet and reflective. And when a man is fighting for his life, after losing something that he loves, and his life is in ruins, you got a guy like Blalock. Momentarily lucid and seemingly in control, but the next minute in the bottomless well of despair and beyond rescue. Being with Blalock in this condition, felt to McCall at the end of the evening, like he had been beaten half to death with rubber hoses then run over by a truck. McCall found out what the man had been going through alright. Hell on earth didn't even come close. Blalock was an emotional train wreck and unless he came out of it, Duane knew that the group would never accept him as the replacement.

"Look, Matt, lets link up tomorrow and have another talk. There's something going down that you might be interested in. Something really important…history book stuff."

"What is it?" Blalock suddenly seemed a lot more sober.

"I can't talk about it here. I'd like to fly you out to my Dad's company headquarters in Texas and let you hear it from the horse's mouth."

"When?"

"How about tomorrow? I mean how can you turn down an all expenses paid trip by private jet to Plainview, Texas? Ever been there?"

"Flew over it once," Blalock was instantly suspicious and began wondering...nahh it's been too long...it couldn't be that.

McCall remembered his package, and thought to himself, Captain Matt Blalock, it's time for some play therapy. "Matt, gimme some popcorn willya?"

Blalock got up from the table, stumbled across the room to the popcorn machine, filled up a big basket and stumbled back to the table.

"That's so disgusting," commented one of the four perfectly coifed Dunwoody queens at the next table. "Probably beats his wife," another one said.

McCall took out the elephant gun. "Oh shit, I ain't seen one dem sumbitches since Cam Ranh Bay."

"Gimme some nabkins," McCall slurred.

The elephant gun was ten steel beer cans with both ends cut out taped together with duct tape so that it made a long tube. The last beer can only had one end missing with the end remaining with two triangular holes punched by a church key. McCall reached down in his bag and produced a travel-sized can of Right Guard.

"You aim, I'll fire," Duane said. Matt stuffed a big paper napkin into the muzzle, then shoveled the whole basket of popcorn in, followed by another napkin.

Blalock had the elephant gun on his shoulder like a bazooka. McCall sprayed Right Guard into one of the two church key holes and stuck a lighter up to the hole. 'Fire in the hole" he yelled. The elephant gun made a huge *"KA FOOM!"* A short blue flame poofed out the muzzle as the elephant gun blasted popcorn to every corner of the large steakhouse. The Dunwoody society matrons at the next table shrieked, two of them wet their pants and one went running off to the ladies room.

"I believe that one did a number two," Duane observed expertly.

"Number two? Yes, yes, I think you've got something there," Matt answered scientifically. The fun didn't last long.

"Show some respect, I'm handicapped," McCall shouted as four bouncers gave him and Blalock the muy rapido eighty-six out the front door. Waiting with open arms, Tex grabbed both of the drunk pilots and stuffed them in the back of the limo, apologizing profusely to the bouncers as he folded up Duane's wheely and shoved it in the trunk.

"Thas was brillian-puurrfect timing Tex," Duane said. "Yougottharight," Blalock agreed. Tex put his shoulder harness on and cranked the big Lincoln.

Not that brilliant, Tex was thinking, as he checked his side mirrors and pulled out of the tree-lined lot. Duane ain't never stayed in a club more'n five minutes before they throw'd his ass out once't he fired the dang elephant gun. Oh, now ain't this cute, Tex Lambert looked in his rear view mirror. McCall and Blalock had passed out in the back seat and were propped up against each other in the middle like an "A" frame.

Chapter 20

Leonard Peerless Trask was by far the most colorful of the drab geniuses who had head up the 38,000 employee National Security Agency. The NSA, also known as Crypto City covers a hundred acres of countryside and is protected by earthen berms, anti-truck barriers, remote censors, a thousand miles of razor wire, and black clad commandos with automatic weapons. Crypto City has computers that can perform one septillion operations per second. (1,000,000,000,000,000,000,000,000) Serious people work here. Some found Peerless Trask a little disturbing. Trask had a sign on his office door that read "Land Office," in an old timey western movie font that would have been used with the word "Saloon." Underneath it was one of these hokey plastic signs that sticks on with suction cups you get at Office Depot that slid back and forth that said open or closed. Leonard P. Trask was a old west aficionado of the early genre that starred Tom Mix, Johnny Mack Brown, and Bob Steele. Many of those early formula westerns always had a new school marm who was rescued from a runaway stage coach by the hero, and a really bad ass machiavellian black hat named Trask, who ran the land office. Trask was always trying to cheat the honest ranchers out of their water rights and steal their homesteads for ten cents on the dollar. Leonard Trask had come to the attention of the president when he blew the whistle on Operation Northwoods; the most corrupt plan ever cooked up by the United States military. Outraged over President Kennedy's loss of nerve at the

Bay of Pigs, the joint chiefs cooked up a plan to mobilize public opinion in the nation to support a war they had in mind against Cuba. The plan included the random shooting of American civilians and framing alleged Cuban agents. The plan's piece de resistance was to blow up John Glenn on his historic mission and blame it on Cuba. Trask later discovered that Kennedy had "sort of suggested" that he wanted an excuse to invade Cuba and perhaps we "could consider manufacturing something that was generally acceptable." That Trask would report immediately what he knew, considering the lethal ramifications of disclosure, impressed the young president who marked him for advancement.

To get into the "Land Office" when it was "open," you had to have a special code on your National Security Agency badge, which went though an optical badge reader and unlocked the door. Once you were through that door, you were in the reception of the NSA Director Trask's twenty office suite on the top floor of the NSA building located just off the Baltimore-Washington Parkway near the small town of Annapolis Junction, Maryland. The receptionist and his two associates were armed Marines with no sense of humor whatsoever. To get in to see Trask, you had to be on a list stored in the computer and pass a photo examination by the Marines using a picture on file, which you had to update every six months. Once past the Marines, you had access to all the facilities in the Land Office and there was no more Mickey Mouse you had to put up with. Carson Francis Benchly, Yale 81, thought to himself, yet with all these precautions, the KGB had penetrated us twice over the last twenty-five years. But, he knew Trask needed to see some interesting satellite imagery that had just come up from the NRO and he had long since outgrown his irritation for the intense security required in the building.

"Leonard, take a look at these…This is the Tupelov factory outside St. Petersburg yesterday just after high noon." Trask put the photos under his desk magnifier. "Great flick, Gary Cooper, Grace Kelly…Do not forsake me oh ma'darlin'" he hummed.

Uh Oh…what's this?"

"They've taken one of their space shuttles out of storage. It's been pulled out on the ramp for about twenty-four hours based on the CIA's ground asset."

Benchly leaned over Trask's shoulder pointing with his retracted Mount Blanc ballpoint. "Notice the smaller payload bay doors right behind the crew cabin."

"Yes, what about them?"

"The small set of payload doors were only built on the number three and last model of their shuttle fleet. They can open these doors without opening the entire cargo bay…possibly for EVA, although they seem a little large for just that alone according to our people."

Trask turned off the light on his desk magnifier and looked up at his deputy director. "Do they still have the capability to launch one of these? Didn't they sell off all the hardware for this system when they started commercial production of those big boosters?"

"You're ninety-nine percent correct. They have been supplying Energia boosters to the French since they cancelled their shuttle program in ninety-three. And the French purchased the second and only other erector they had that could handle the Energia."

"Carson, you think the Russians are getting back into the shuttle business? Maybe they just pulled it out to put down linoleum."

Benchly smiled…"Leonard, hows about I mosey on down to the Long Branch and get Miss Kitty to retask one of the K12s for multiple passes for the next week or so."

Miss Kitty was Katherine Foxe, a forty-five year old, Vasser Phi Beta Kappa, who ran the satellite reconnaissance liaison office…Trask and Benchly's inside joke tagged her office the Long Branch. This was because Katherine ruled with an iron fist in the recon office and knew instantly if even single paperclip was removed.

"Carson, by all means mosey. Get Miss Kitty to get some more pics, and just for grins, why don't we send this photo over to CIA and see if their Remote Technical Viewers get anything….although, as you well know, I don't put much stock in that stuff."

"Me neither Leonard, but you remember they found Colonel Tate, the kidnapped guy in Lebanon?"

"They sure did," Trask responded. "How the hell did they do that?"

Chapter 21

"Yep, boys, I'm taking off in a whole new business direction and I need some top hands to negotiate a deal for me down in South America." Mike Mancusso and the two Bobs looked at each other sitting at the small conference table in J.B McCall's ornate office at his Plainview, Texas HQ. "Did you read the employment agreement gentlemen? Was the compensation satisfactory?" There was no problem with that, McCall had doubled their Navy retirement and thrown in profit sharing and a medical and insurance package that was something you'd hear about in Fortune Magazine for some hot shot CEO. At the end of the contract, all three guys had an option to continue working at the same salary but as employees, starting a new international security division at TriAmCo with Mike Mancusso as director. The new assignment was supposed to only take about ninety days and McCall had thrown in an all expense paid thirty-day vacation for the three wives to Tahiti. The only stipulation being that all three went together. That cinched the deal on the three home fronts and everything was copescetic all the way up to the present meeting.

"Well, if everything is acceptable to you fellows, I'll brief Mike on the details and you'll be on your way tomorrow morning out of Dallas for Bogota." J.B. rose from his chair and the meeting was over.

The two Bobs filed out, Mancusso remaining behind. Mancusso leveled a hard look at McCall. "J.B., if I was the Oscar committee I'd put you in for best actor...now maybe you'd better tell me just what the hell is actually going on."

McCall, smiled, and sat back in his custom Boeing cockpit chair.

"Mike, I want you to go down to Bogota and buy me a good lot to build a restaurant on a main drag...good visibility...plenty of parking...be sure it's easy to make left turns into the location. I'll give you a real estate guy down there you can work with and a power of attorney...it will all be in a package I'm going to give you to study. No kidding, we're going to call it La Estrella Fugaz, The Fallen Star...French cuisine. We're going to make a pile of dough on this deal. These Colombians can be tough, that's why I need you."

Mancusso just sat quietly never breaking eye contact with McCall.

McCall started squirming in his seat almost imperceptibly.

"OK Mike, I'm going to level with you. This is going to be a one of a kind restaurant in South America. Myself and another investor, the daughter of an old friend, have purchased a non-flyable Russian space shuttle and we're going to make a restaurant out of it just like one they have in Moscow...the damn thing makes a bundle. Here take a look at this." McCall shoved a photo of the Buran Restaurant in Gorky Park across the huge mahogany desk to Mancusso.

Mancusso gave the photo a nanosecond's worth of glance then returned making eye contact with McCall. Mancusso was now smiling, his hands together with his chin resting on his thumbs. McCall let several minutes go by and the two of them just sat there. Mancusso hadn't said a word yet, just smiled.

Then McCall said "Ahh shit," and punched his interphone button. "Anne Louise, ask Colonel Bremen and Mr. Good to come down to my office if they're not busy."

"Sure thing J.B.," Ann Louise answered. "I told you he wouldn't go for it."

"Thank you Anne Louise," McCall answered, with a touch of irritation. If Bremen and Good knew he had asked his trusted secretary of twenty-five years with a high school diploma and who was a charismatic Pentecostal her whole life, for advice on this project, they would have gone ballistic. But, after twenty-five years, Anne Louise had proved her instincts about deals had a lethal accuracy, regardless of how complex it was.

McCall laid out the entire plan to her one night. Anne Louise started shaking but then closed her eyes and prayed for ten minutes. J.B. just sat quietly waiting. Then she rendered her opinion. She squinted her eyes and lowered her voice. It was a different Anne Louise than he'd ever seen before. It was the first time he'd ever heard a profane word come out of her mouth...somebody once said that inside every woman there's an evil twin sister you never want to meet. "J.B.," she hissed, "It ain't our time yet. We ought to get up there and kick the dogshit out of em' or die 'tryin."

She then had started crying and said she'd wish he'd never told her. The world was now a totally different place for Anne Louise...more fragile...more vulnerable...many certainties evaporated...and now a deep abiding fear for the souls of a whole world, where it never existed before. That was the confirmation McCall needed for the massive investment he was about to make with Leanna Helms, the daughter of his old friend killed on Pan Am 103.

Bremen and Good arrived about then and looked Mancusso over.

Good spoke first. "Mr. McCall are you sure you want to tell him? By informing Captain Mancusso we further increase our potential of exposure before we are ready to act. In addition, we increase the danger to his life and possible prosecution after the operation."

"Tell him," J.B. answered.

"Yeah, tell me," chimed in Mancusso. "This is starting to sound fun."

Colonel Bremen began the briefing. "Captain Mancusso, we are going into competition with NASA and the United States Government and will be breaking at least two dozen federal statutes. Are you familiar with geophysical orbital surveying?"

"Looking for oil with satellites right?"

"Exactly," Bremen continued not missing a beat. "We have arranged to lease a package of just declassified equipment that can be used in space to search for oil. There is only one such package in existence and it might be that declassifying this technology might have been a clerical mistake."

Bremen shot a knowing and conspiratorial look at Mr. Good who just nodded.

"We intend to take advantage of this clerical mistake and use this sensor package by flying it into space before the mistake is discovered and it becomes reclassified and unavailable. The, shall we say, sensitivity of the equipment we plan to use, makes using a commercial booster from any nation, and obviously our own, impossible."

Mancusso was running with the bait like a Marlin with a Wahoo in his mouth. "So how are we going to get the son of a bitch into space?" The reel was screaming as the line paid out.

"This is the most dangerous part of this briefing Capt. Mancusso, the part you have no need to know," Bremen intoned with total credibility. "Do you still want me to continue?"

Mancusso started tapping his foot, this was about as hyper as Mancusso ever got.

"You're killing me, man...what the hell are we going to do?" Mancusso's voice was as high as McCall had ever heard it even during the Bolivia operation.

"What we're going to do Capt. Mancusso is fly our own ship into orbit that we have preloaded with our exploration gear. We're going to use a Russian space shuttle we have purchased and launch it from the French base in Guyana where Mr. McCall is well connected with several of his oil interests. The imagery we expect to obtain during a three day mission will keep exploration companies busy for ten years, after they have paid TriAmCo handsomely for the data, of course. I believe your compensation agreement includes profit sharing does it not?"

Bremen paused at this point to let Mancusso digest the information. Several minutes went by. You could almost hear the slot machine in Mancusso's brain hit the giant jackpot, pouring out a deafening waterfall of money.

"That is a fan-fucking-tastic idea," Mancusso was now leaping into the air behind the Bremen's cruiser.

"Your job, Capt. Mancusso is to create a highly believable ruse to explain to the curious what we are doing in South America with a Russian space ship."

"When do we saddle up and get this show on the road?" Mancusso said as he got to his feet, realizing the briefing was over, his voice back to normal. Mancusso was now gaffed and pulled over the transom by Colonel Lowell Bremen, Director of Army Intelligence, (Ret.) a forty-year master harpooner.

"Of course, you understand that Gomez and Palmer are not to know what we have told you in this briefing."

"Of course," Mancusso had regained his composure by this point.

Going down to the lobby on the elevator, Mancusso was figuring…those other oil companies are going to pay millions for this data…and the three of them with profit sharing…how good could it get?

J.B. McCall sat back in his chair, marveling at the performance he had just witnessed. Bringing in Good, who then recruited Bremen, had to be one of his greatest strokes of brilliance. In the cutthroat world of Arabs and international oil, McCall had seen some devious genius bastards in his almost fifty years in the business. Compared to the Good/Bremen team, however, the worst bastards he'd ever dealt with were like a plate of oysters taking on the Packers.

Anne Louise interrupted his train of thought. "J.B., Sir Edmund is on the line from Cambridge fer' Lowell, he says the translations are finished." Lowell Bremen came closer to McCall's desk so that the speakerphone would have better reception.

"Anne Louise, could you please have Sir Edmund fax the data to me on the encrypted line and could you please tell him thanks so much and that I will get back to him before his first class tomorrow."

"Will do Lowell, I'll put a team on it," and she clicked off.

There was a new player that McCall hadn't heard of. "Colonel Bremen, may I ask who Sir Edmund is?"

"Of course, J.B. Sir Edmund Massey, teaches at

Cambridge twice a week...he's the last living scholar who reads and writes Indo-Croatian."

McCall waited for more. More was not forthcoming. All he could think to say was, "Oh, I see...just curious."

Chapter 22

Yakov bounded up the long flight of steps to the old KGB headquarters two at a time. His blood was up. There's only one way to deal with these pricks, he thought. Admit nothing and attack. Lieutenant Grosovich was bounding right after him disobeying another direct order to wait at base operations for his call. He was supposed to wait in the flight planning office until he got a phone call. If Yakov hadn't called him by 1700, he was supposed to refuel the two-seater and fly back to Scapino before anyone could come out and arrest him as well. But, here he was instead, traipsing along behind Yakov right into the lion's den. The Lubayanka was conveniently adjacent to SVP head quarters and it was perfectly possible that both of them would go in the front door of the building and never be heard from again.

A uniformed official with no rank insignia sat at an old desk flanked by two guards with AK47s at the separate stairwells. He sat out in the open in the expansive marble floored lobby. Peeling murals of the great worker's struggle covered a massive plaster wall directly behind him. Heroic Soviet workers driving steel for railroads, heroic Soviet workers pouring steel from huge ladles, heroic Soviet workers working steel in huge skyscrapers. There was a lot of steel in the mural.

"Colonel Yakov, you are on General Kobelyev's calendar and can go right up, it's the stairwell to the right. You," the uniformed bureaucrat pointed at Grosovich with his pencil without looking up, "will have to wait outside with the taxi drivers and other nuisances." Grosovich leaned over and put both hands on the reception table and got his face down about six inches from the nose of the SVP guy. Before Yakov could stop him, Grosovitch cut loose. "Listen very carefully to me you pig-faced son of a bitch. I am Colonel Yakov's adjutant and I go where he goes, if I want any shit out of you, I'll kick it out of you."

Yakov just shook his head, Oh Christ! What have I created, he thought. We'll be lucky if we get out of here with only a tenner. A tenner was ten years in a labor camp, the standard sentence for political crimes not deemed serious enough for the wall.

The SVP guy reeled backwards in his chair and for a moment was speechless. Grosovich was still leaning on the desk just getting warmed up. The rankless security officer then shouted through Grosovich's withering verbal barrage. "Go, go, go with your colonel…just get out of my sight!" Pounding up the long stairs Grosovich had some more to say.

"You're right about these bastards, the way to deal with them is to…."

"Shut up, you idiot." Yakov stopped on the stars and turned to his lieutenant. He was furious. "From here on, I'll do the talking. You stupid fool, you don't know these people. These people are killers. Have you forgotten what they did in Western Command?" That was a chilling and sobering reminder. Grosovich's big mouth closed with a slam. In 1967 another Korean Airliner got "lost" in Western Command's defensive sector and it took three hours to intercept him. Pilots were drunk and others supposedly on alert duty could not be found. The KGB arrived the next day and put two regiment commanders and the wing commander up against the wall and shot them.

Colonel General V.N. Kobelyev's office was a grand reminder of the decadence of the Czars, complete with polished black maple furniture, magnificent, well-preserved tapestries, and a warm blazing coal fire in the fireplace. Large original oil paintings of military campaigns unknown to Yakov hung above the mantel and all over his office. It stank of the Romanoffs. How many people had entered here and never seen the light of day again, Yakov wondered. Grosovich waited calmly in the reception, thankfully, General Kobelyev had a female secretary, a pretty one, that would not, God forbid, be confrontational with Grosovich.

Yakov saluted the seated Kobelyev, who delayed momentarily, signing something, before standing and extending his hand to Yakov.

"Colonel Yakov, thank you for coming and thank you for your service to the motherland at Chernobyl. Please accept my condolences for your many fallen comrades."

Yakov took the general's hand. His grip was firm, his hand warm and soft, definitely a paper pusher. Yakov experienced a conscious and invisible sigh of relief; perhaps he would avoid the wall after all.

"Yakov, let me apologize for that message that we sent concerning certain severe irregularities that needed explaining. That's not why you're here."

"You mean that the reports that Lukashevich sent were..."

General Kobelyev held his hand up, with a half smirk on his face. "Oh, we received his reports alright...firing your American pistol out the window of your office every Monday at noon was truly terrifying to comrade Lukashevich. It was pure genius on your part. Colonel Yakov, members of my staff who read the reports from Scapino were quite amused and always looked forward to what you were going to do next." The general then allowed himself a two chuckle laugh and then became serious again.

"In the old days, Colonel Yakov, you would have made an excellent KGB officer…but it is now 1997 and the old days are gone. Did you notice anything different about the facade of the building?"

"No sir, I was thinking about this meeting."

"I imagine you were…Iron Mike is gone…and so are many of the old attitudes…it appears that for seventy years we lived with a delusion, possibly a nightmare. The massive criminal record of its depravity is housed within these walls; the horrific chronicle of death, torture, misery and despair that we perpetrated on our citizens is here in this building, a monument to everything that was evil about the old system. We murdered millions…we starved millions to death…on two occasions we very nearly started a nuclear holocaust that would have annihilated western civilization. Colonel Yakov, this building represents the worst that has ever occurred in the long bloody history of the motherland. But we have begun anew…turned a new leaf if you will. The economy is a disaster, but the struggle for freedom, that's right Yakov, freedom, has been won. I've only had this job for a year…but I can tell you that the path we are on is the correct one." The general stopped speaking and rotated his chair around ninety degrees to contemplate some weighty matter while staring into the blazing fireplace beside his desk. After a minute, he turned back to Yakov.

"Unfortunately, Yakov, another threat to the motherland has arrived. The portents of the new threat pales into insignificance anything that has happened in the past."

"Not the Americans again!" Yakov blurted incredulously.

"It's not the Americans, Yakov. I now must ask you if you are willing to make another grave sacrifice for our country. You have already sacrificed too much for one man. Unfortunately, you are the only man we have who has the specific skills for the dangerous job ahead. If you say no, I have instructions to order you to accept this assignment. But I will ask first."

Yakov gave the matter a moment's consideration. What were the options? There weren't any. He was screwed. "General Kobelyev, it would be my honor to be of service again to the motherland."

"Excellent, Colonel Yakov…Now, do you still want to fly the space shuttle?"

I have truly stepped in shit and come out smelling like a rose, Yakov thought to himself.

"Unfortunately, Colonel Yakov, it will be necessary to preserve the cover story that we used to get you here. Your lieutenant coming with you will prove useful. You must tell him that while you have not been arrested, you have been relieved of your command. He can return home with the story and we'll have a replacement out there as soon as possible."

"General Kobelyev, could I have a say in selecting my replacement? My junior officers have been allowed to use a great deal of initiative and while extremely dedicated, they are, shall we say impulsive? I am concerned that a heavy hand will dampen the morale. I would also like to have Political Officer Lukasevich transferred to another unit or perhaps duty here in Moscow where he can't do any more damage."

"It is done," the general said, making several notes in his daily planner.

Grosovich was devastated. "How can they do this to you, Colonel Yakov?"

"Do not concern yourself Alexi, I will be fine." Yakov put his hand on the young officer's shoulder. It was the first time Grosovich had ever heard a senior officer use his first name. "Look, you must now do your duty and report back. The Deputy Regiment Commander will keep all the great programs you guys came up with in place as long as possible. Take care of our enlisted troops and guard the Eastern sector with vigilance...you helped me restore the honor to the 777th, now concentrate all your thoughts on your duty to the motherland...God bless you, son."

Yakov put his arm around his shoulder and walked him to the down staircase. Grosovitch was startled by Yakov's last statement. He looked back one more time at his commander, grabbed his cap off the receptionist's desk, and made for the long winding staircase and started down. The sound of his boot steps echoed on the marble as he left the building.

Chapter 23

Blalock finally came to after his long nap on the oh so smooth flight on the TriAmCo G-IV. Cruising above ninety-nine percent of the weather at 41,000, the big twinjet Gulfstream was the epitome of executive aircraft. With only eight seats, in a cabin that could comfortably take twice that number, TriAmCo had spent almost as much on the interior as it spent for the aircraft all by itself. The captain began gently pulling the power back. Blalock knew that they were thirty-five minutes from the ramp from the moment the power was reduced. It always seemed to work out that way.

Blalock rubbed his eyes and looked out the window, the three parallel runways of Reese were sliding under the right wing…man, does that bring back memories, he thought. He felt a tap on his shoulder.

"Captain Blalock are you thirsty?" It was the TriAmCo knockout gorgeous black girl who was the executive flight attendant.

My God, this girl is telepathic, he thought. "You don't by any wild stretch of the imagination have any Gatorade do you?"

"Yes we do, Captain Blalock. Do you want lemon lime, strawberry kiwi, or orange?"

For the first time he noticed Duane sitting across the aisle…

"Yes mam', that sounds great, how about a lemon lime?"

She scampered back to the galley. Blalock noticed she was wearing khaki tennis shorts expensive running shoes and a royal blue polo shirt with the TriAmCo logo across the front accentuating her beautiful and unsupported breasts. He looked across the aisle again and made eye contact with the smiling Duane McCall. "I see you hire the flight attendants on this airline."

"You bet your ass I do…her name is Sheila and we have two more just like her…one of them is her twin sister."

The Gatorade arrived in a large crystal ice tea glass and Matt gulped it down. Sheila refilled his glass two more times. The ice in the glass was funny…very clear…and didn't seem to melt. "Duane what's with the ice?"

"You're very observant…it's glacial …we buy it from a guy up in Alaska."

Sheila was back with a damp, scented linen towel and Blalock wiped his face with it. Seconds later Sheila magically reappeared with a pair of bamboo tongs and placed the used towel into an ivory inlaid walnut box and was gone. Blalock twisted his head in a circle. "Man, I can't believe I got so plowed last night…my back hurts like hell and my head feels like there is a troll inside trying to get out with a rivet gun."

After loading up, they hit the Burger King for some real murican' food…an imminently practical suggestion by Tex Lambert, since both hung over pilots slept right through the Duck L'Orange that had been catered for the flight. An hour later, the black Lincoln limo pulled up to the security gate of the sprawling campus of TriAmCo Energy. There was another manned security desk in the lobby. Then in order to access the main security Duane used a special card slide and punch code that was being changed every three days. Once on the elevator, they had a palm reader right out of James Bond. Duane put his hand on it, it pinged twice, a green light came on, and Duane punched in the floor. The elevator then began its quick ascent to the twenty-fifth floor and the Taj McCall.

Blalock leaned over to Duane as the elevator took off. "When does the bomb sniffing dog check my crotch."

"In your case we'll skip that," Duane said in total dead pan. "Bomb dogs are expensive…hate to lose one just 'cause he got grossed out."

This was a good sign, McCall was thinking. Blalock was going to have to get a grip if he was ever to be of any use. And since two military test pilots and two former astronauts had turned down the job, time was running out for a replacement. They could not just keep interviewing applicants and laying out the plan, then relying upon a confidentiality agreement on a piece of paper to keep something of this magnitude secret. Mr. Good and Colonel Bremen had been very specific about that. The second astronaut was a guy named Duke Demming, a cocky hot shot shuttle pilot who quit the space program after one flight to take a job with United. Demming had come close to a mental breakdown when he was briefed on the mission. Mr. Good said that if Demming became a problem, that it would be taken care of. John Good was a shadow of a man with no personality. His presence had an aura to it like some kind of futuristic and deadly holograph. Touch the hem of his robe and you would die. Members of the Group were deferential to Good and it was a prevalent opinion that his real name was cloistered in a secret file in a nuclear bomb shelter deep inside a mountain…there was a darkness about Good…a lethal essence refined from years of the dagger. Lawrence Feldman at the last Group meeting had also voiced the concern that the number of people who had been compromised was unknown and possibly large. There was no known way to detect who they were. If the plan was accidentally revealed to a compromised person in the recruitment process, it would be lethal for everyone and their families. Time was also running out. It might have to be Blalock or no mission.

The tricked out G-IV, the fabulous Sheila, glacial ice for drinks, and three flavors of Gatorade might give one a hint of the opulence to come, but Matt Blalock joined the ranks of the mind blown when Anne Louise ushered him and Duane into the Taj McCall, to meet the big man himself, J.B. McCall.

J.B. circumnavigated his huge Nara mahogany desk and warmly shook Blalock's hand. "I always wanted to thank you personally for saving my son's life...but the airline said you did not want to be contacted. Sit down, sit down please. Can I offer you something to drink?"

"Thanks so much, Mr. McCall, could I have some coffee with a package of the blue stuff?"

Anne Louise heard the order. "One black with a package of the blue stuff...I'll put a team on it." Duane rolled over to a cabinet and opened a built in refrigerator and popped a can of diet Coke.

Blalock kept talking..."You sent me the TriAmCo stock Mr. McCall?"

"It was Duane's idea actually...said you boys at Eastern were fightn' a skunk...couple of bucks always comes in handy in a skunk fight don't it?"

"Couple of bucks? Mr. McCall, it was over two hundred thousand dollars...you saved me from bankruptcy and it almost saved my marriage."

"Well, I'm sorry you didn't save your marriage...I

was married to the greatest woman in the world for over twenty-five years. She's gone now...I was a mess around here, I'll tell you. Wasn't I Duane?"

"I heard that, Pop...everybody was worried."

"You got that right J.B.," chimed in Anne Louise putting Blalock's coffee down on a porcelain coaster. "J.B. you gonna tell em' about that there sonic boom what busted out yer fish tank and sent you 'sailin?" Anne Louise now had up a head of steam and looked at Blalock. "That was the day he finally come out of his gloom & doom...it was God sent, that boy in his little white jet." Anne Louise padded out of the Taj and closed the door behind her.

"Please forgive my secretary Captain Blalock, she's been with me for a long time. I'm not going to bore you with the fish tank story...we're here on another matter of grave importance to our nation and to our world. I think you may be able to help us..."

Blalock noticed the beautiful P-51D Mustang model on McCall's desk. It was a Red Tailed Mustang of the 332nd Fighter Group...the Tuskeegee Airmen. My God, Blalock thought, Mr. McCall flew with the red tailed angels!

"But before I go any further...may I call you Matt?" J.B. asked.

"Of course Mr. McCall...Matt is fine."

"Great, Matt. Now before we get into this I would like you to take a look at a secrecy agreement. If you don't think you can sign it and comply with it in a clear conscience, please tell us now. The matter we are about to discuss will be the most fantastic and important event in your life and the life of every person on this planet...Duane pull up a copy of the agreement would you?" Duane went over to a terminal in the corner of the office and went to the document library.

Blalock scanned the Taj and the many magnificent examples of sculpture and art and then noticed a larger rectangular section of oak paneling between the rows of bookshelves on one wall of the office. There were five yellowing black and white photos beautifully framed in non-glare glass. One of the photos caught his attention. Blalock walked across the room. It was a crash-landed B-24 Liberator with bent back props, oil all over the cowling of the number four engine, and its left vertical stabilizer almost completely shot away. A youthful J.B. McCall was standing there with his elbow leaning on a white pilot who was doing the devil's horns with his fingers behind McCall's head...presumably the B-24 aircraft commander. They were both giving the thumbs up to the camera, with the rest of the bomber crew and two other black pilots kneeling in the foreground. Blalock stared hard at the photo. The white pilot looked very familiar.

Duane rolled over to where Matt had been sitting in the big brown and black cowhide chair. "Matt, here's that agreement."

Blalock turned to walk back to his seat...then stopped. He went back to the B-24 photo and stared again. He then very slowly turned and walked slowly back to his chair.

"Mr. McCall do you know the name of the B-24 driver you were posing with in that photo?"

"No Matt, I don't. We escorted that guy all the way home and damn near ran out of fuel ourselves. But that wasn't half of what happened that day. If you decide to join us, I'll tell you the rest of the story, as Paul Harvey might say. The B-24 group commander was on us as soon as we showed up at the base...told us to take our pictures and get the hell out of there...he didn't like Negroes associating with the white pilots. The B-24 crew got really pissed off at the guy and started to really get on his case...I intervened and said we'd be leaving right away...things were a lot different back then...in the old days."

"And may they never come again," Matt answered. "Where's that agreement? I think we have some business to take care of."

***

As Matt signed off on the confidentiality agreement in Plainview, Texas, at the same time, on the other side of the world, Colonel General Kobelyev had just finished a two hour discourse. He reached into his pocket and produced a pair of keys and went to a safe in the floor under his desk. He inserted the keys, dialed the combination, pulled out a file and handed it to Yakov. Within seconds of pulling out the folder, a deafening roar of a low flying jet at near sonic speed boomed and echoed through the miles of corridors at the old KGB building. Rusting cell doors sprung open in the Lubayanka, pictures of Gorbachev went crooked on walls in a hundred offices, and what little glass there was in the building shattered into splinters. The pain in the ass in the downstairs lobby jumped off his chair and shit in his pants. General Kobelyev leaped to his feet. "What the hell was that?"

Yakov said nothing and rested his forehead in the palm of one hand slowly shaking his head, then uttered a slightly too audible sigh. General Kobelyev looked down at Yakov with a puzzled look, then started a deep, barrelchested laugh.

"Comrade Yakov, I believe someone just sent you a vote of solidarity."

"Soccer Ball four-two, Moscow departure, we're still not getting your squawk." The air traffic controllers at Turalin Air Force Base were having trouble finding Grosovich's MiG-25PU on their scopes because the gadget in the airplane that enhances the radar return, called a transponder, was in the O-F-F position. "Reset transponder, squawk Alpha, Tango, Zulu."

Grosovich reached over and turned his transponder to the O-N position.

"Okay, we got you now Soccer Ball four-two, confirm altitude passing flight level seven thousand meters?"

"Soccer Ball four-two affirmative, now out of eight thousand."

Grosovich pushed the throttles smoothly forward and the twin Tumansky R31s answered instantly with fifty thousand pounds of thrust. The steel rocket accelerated effortlessly through the Mach without a ripple. Pancake layers of altostratus flashed by the cockpit at a forty-five degree angle as the Foxbat vaulted for the top of the sky. The sun was gone and the stars were like diamonds adrift in the black ocean of space. Designed to hunt and kill the American B-70 and the SR-71, the razor winged interceptor climbed at 25,000 feet per minute. Grosovich glanced down at the Mach meter easing through one point two. Climb you stripe-assed ape, he said to himself under his mask. Well, Grosovich, he thought, enjoy it while you can. You really fucked up this time... Yep, you'll be hearing about this one.

Chapter 24

The number three shuttle had been towed over to the paint shop, disappearedfor three days, then reappeared back on the ramp with something painted on the side of the fuselage. Carson Benchly had the new photos and took them down to Director Trask's office, although this time it seemed a little less important…always good to wrap things up in a nice package, he thought.

Leonard Trask looked through his desk magnifier at the already magnified oblique photographs. "Interesting, so somebody is going to make a restaurant out of it? Their first shuttle, Buran, is a restaurant in Gorky Park you know. Food tastes like shit…little tubes of space borsht."

"So it would appear, Leonard…and by the way, if your Spanish is a little rusty,

La Estrella Fugaz means the fallen star. Restaurante Francese is obviously self explanatory.

"Fallen Star, hmmm does that make a little too much sense?" Trask looked more closely at the photos. "What's this in the finer print under the name."

"I believe, Leonard, that that is the address they're going to put it."

"So where is Avenida 15 de Octobre?"

"There are two of them, Leonard. One is in Bogota, the other is in Ayacucho, Peru."

"Well, I think we can scratch Ayacucho…nobody down there has two pesos to rub

together, much less take a senorita out for a French dinner. Have somebody on the ground in Bogota see if they know anything about this."

"I gather you're concerned about something you're not sharing with me?"

"Carson, my old sidekick, I guess I am. I'd have been a lot happier if the Colombians had bought the Ptchika, the number two shuttle, instead of the number three."

"The rumors?"

"That's right," Trask looked back at the photos. "Why would the Colombians want to buy a space ship we think the Russians built to be an attack bomber...one that can be refueled in orbit? I think we oughta' round up a posse, and check up on this a smidgen' more."

Chapter 25

Yakov read General Kobelyev's file while sitting in front of his desk. It outlined the entire history and inventory of death still possessed by the Russian Federation in its many underground arsenals. He had no idea of the numbers and types of weapons that were available.

"And we had about thirty percent more before we signed Start II with the Americans," Kobelyev added after Yakov handed him back the folder. "The first part of your mission, Yakov, is to become expert in the tactical deployment of each of our primary chemical, biological, and nuclear weapons."

"But, General Kobelyev, you said this would not involve the Americans."

"This is still correct."

"Then who will we be using the weapons against and what does this have to do with my flying the shuttle?"

"All that in good time, Yakov, first, here are your orders."

Yakov's orders were to report to Dr. Yevgeny Lukin, a pipe smoking amiable scientist in his early sixties who wore the same old brown tweed jacket every day under his white lab coat. Dr. Lukin was the Director of Biopreparat's research and weapons production laboratories at Omutninsk, deep in the forests near the city of Kirov. Omutninsk was built near two other primary weapons facilities which assembled nuclear and chemical warheads into the various delivery vehicles, then shipped them out to ordinance depots to attach the rocket or artillery casings which would actually be used on the battlefield or attached to missiles and aircraft. The first thirty days were spent with the chemical and nuclear weapons engineers and was basically just a quick refresher course on weapons Yakov had already studied before reporting to the 777th.

The bio-weapons were another matter. Omutninsk was Russia's last remaining bacteriological weapons test and production facility and was completely in violation the Biological Warfare Convention of 1972 signed by The Soviet Union, The United States, and a hundred forty other nations. The factory was expansive, covering five hundred acres with its central feature being building 107, which had multiple buildings within buildings like a matryoshka doll. Inside the doll is another identical but smaller doll. Zone One, the outer building was all administrative, and people working in Zone One had no idea what was being perpetrated deep in the interior of the rest of the building. The deeper you went into the building the more arcane things became until you arrived at Zone Five, the manufacturing core in which hydrogen peroxide was constantly being sprayed into the closed circuit air conditioning system to kill stray airborne bacteria. The interior zones contained the hot laboratories and giant twenty ton fermenters for producing the lethal soup which was freeze dried into powder for the delivery mechanism of the bio weapons. Personnel wore self-contained space suits, thick rubber boots and gloves to work in the hot areas within Zone Two.

Yakov was later shocked to learn that viral agents were employed in the Russian weapons like Marburg,

Machupo, Glanders, and VEE…agents for which there was no known cure or vaccine. And as incredibly gruesome as these four were, another weapon was almost ready for testing that was genetically engineered. The new weapon was called R-T-E, a diabolical combination of Rift Fever, Tularemia, and Ebola, which was projected to be the most toxic biological agent ever conceived. By recombinant genetic engineering they had created a doomsday bug which contained the worst features of the three most virulent diseases known on the planet. Developing a vaccine or cure was estimated to be well beyond the capabilities of modern medicine in the United States or Russia. Section "K" was the large complex of laboratories set aside for its manufacture and was off limits to Yakov. Even the experienced technicians were rotated out of section "K" at twice the normal rate. As they learned more and more about the properties of RTE they got spooked and became accident-prone. At least this was Dr. Lukin's opinion. Section "K" had an unusual network of pneumatic plumbing that was similar to a test chamber Yakov had observed at the Cosmodrome at Baikonar. Lukin let drop a casual statement one afternoon, that one liter of RTE, could in theory, kill every human on Earth. After observing the look on Yakov's face, Lukin hastily added, "Of course that is only theoretical." Yakov had learned at Lukin's knee, that just three aerosol particles of the Marburg, all by itself, was enough to begin an epidemic that would only be limited by the size of the population that was targeted and how fast the enemy figured out what had hit them. The weaponeers at Biopreparat estimated a fatality rate, just for Marburg, of ten thousand for each person initially affected, and Marburg was a first generation bio-weapon. RTE was fifteenth generation and genetically altered and Lukin's theoretical number of everybody on the planet seemed perfectly plausible. Yakov later learned from one of the chemical engineers that four hundred liters of RTE had already been manufactured and production was being suspended when they hit fifteen hundred liters.

The six month school at Omutninsk was the most intensely nerve racking experience in his military career. How the weaponeers, scientists, and technicians worked around the dangerous substances day in day out completely baffled him.

***

"Dr. Lukin, why are we still making these toxins? Who is the enemy we could use them on?"

"Well, it's not the Americans, I can tell you that." Lukin tapped his pipe upside down on the corner of his desk so the ashes would fall into the wastebasket.

"Why do you rule out the Americans? Aren't they dedicated to our destruction just like always?"

Dr. Lukin Laughed. "Hardly, Yakov. I was on a team last year to check on their compliance with the 1972 Convention…What a joke. We're over here making this shit as fast as we can and I am sent to America to assure that they are not doing exactly what we are doing. They gave us a jet and let us go anywhere we wanted…we even changed the destination several times in mid-flight so they would not have time to hide what they were doing…we looked in any building…any facility…nothing was off limits…anywhere in the entire country. The GRU gave us a list of places to search generated by our best intelligence, and we found nothing. The Americans kept the treaty to the letter as best as we could determine."

***

The last day at Omutninsk, Dr. Lukin asked Yakov to his office for a cup of tea. Dr. Lukin closed the door and seated himself behind his dilapidated desk piled high with papers, old scientific journals and several crusty and well incinerated ashtrays. "You asked me the first week you were here who the enemy might be for our bio-weapons...do you recall?"

"Of course, Dr. Lukin."

"Based on what you have learned here, what is the major drawback to the effective use of bio-weapons?"

"The weather, Dr. Lukin. Unpredictable winds and precipitation can cause the agents to lose potency or blow back upon our own forces as the Germans learned in World War I when they attempted to use Glanders against Romanian cavalry."

"Precisely, Colonel Yakov. Now, are you aware of what the Americans found inside a camera case on the moon left over from a previous Apollo mission?"

Yakov shook his head.

"I thought not. What they found were found live streptococcus bacteria which had survived without nourishment, water or sunlight for two years, under continuous bombardment by cosmic and other solar radiation at temperatures of −150 degrees Celsius."

Yakov was beginning to get that 'oh shit here it comes' feeling down in his gut.

"Yakov, I still can't answer your question with certainty. But I can tell you this. Section "K" where we are testing RTE, has a space simulation chamber. The specifications for the weapon require that it retain ninety-eight percent of its potency in a vacuum under an extreme range of temperatures. I do not know the reason behind this specification, but perhaps combined with the classified information that you have, you can make some sense out of it. This, of course, is highly confidential, but I thought I'd share what I knew. I hope it helps."

Yakov just sat and digested the information. No combination or permutation of his experiences could make any connection among the disparate pieces of information that he had. One thing was for sure, however. Whatever they were going to do with the shuttle, they weren't launching a cell phone satellite.

This deal was definitely not any getting better.

Chapter 26

Carlton Benchly, Yale 81, slid the ten 8X10 high density glossies into a manila envelope and headed down the hall to the Land Office. His daughter had her first piano recital at three that afternoon and it being Friday, it would be good to beat the traffic and the rest of the thundering herd scramming out of the NSA complex for the weekend. The mystery of the Russian shuttle was finally solved and he knew Trask would gladly let him bail out early. Trask pulled the photos out of the envelope and started going through them. "Check this one Leonard." It was a ground level shot by the US Military attaché in Bogota."

"Translate that for me Okay?"

Carleton began the translation of the big sign on a recently cleared lot on Avenida Bolivar, one of the main streets in the affluent suburbs of Bogota. "Coming Soon! The Fallen Star French Restaurant. Opening January 2000."

"So what happened to the original location on Avenida 15 de Octobre?"

"You got me boss, maybe there's better parking on this one. But no doubt about it, this is where they're going to put it." Trask mumbled something and started shuffling through the rest of the photos.

"Who are these guys?"

"This one is Raul DeSavedra a well-known local commercial real estate broker," Benchly moved his Mont Blanc from figure to figure.

"This one is Felix DeLopez, a Puerto Rican, one of the restaurant investors. This one is an American name of Terrence Neidlman from New York, the second investor. And the last guy, on the end, is a Canadian named Rupert Ward...he's the deep pockets according to our information."

"Oh fuck," Trask grabbed his desk magnifier and yanked it over to magnify the photo. He studied it for about thirty seconds and pushed the big lens out of the way and shoved his chair back from his desk and stood up. He then sat back down again and looked at the photo once more with the magnifier.

Carleton Benchly had never seen the chief act with such a lack of deportment. "Leonard what's wrong."

"Deep pockets my ass, that's Mike Mancusso. Now, what the hell is that cowboy doin' down on the south forty?"

"And Mancusso is whom?"

"Benchly, old side kick, Mike Mancusso is one of the toughest and smartest sumbitches ever put into the field by an intelligence organization...any organization. I worked with this guy at the company. He was TDY from SEAL team five out of Norfolk....lemme see...yep, he must be retired by now."

"Maybe he's consulting with the restaurant guys...perhaps it's a security issue of some kind."

Trask laughed out loud. "Shit, Benchly, what the hell did they teach you at Yale? See this guy DeLopez? I never met the guy, but I'd bet the ranch that this is Master Chief Bob Gomez. Mancusso never went on an op without him and another guy named Palmer. Shit, I lay odds your New York Jew boy is probably Palmer! What we got here Benchly, is the spook equivalent of the Cisco Kid, Roy Rogers, and Rooster Cogburn himself! But, there is some good news in your pictures here Benchly...know what it is?"

"Hmmm, quimo sabe...me thinkem` all good guys?"

"Tonto, I don't know how the Cavalry licked you bastards, because you are exactly right, and I take back all those mean things I ever said about Yale. But, now we have a real mystery on our hands, and prudence would dictate what, old side kick?"

"We need to find out just what the hell they're really doing down there. Chief, can I get on this thing first thing Monday?"

"No problemo Benchly, enjoy that recital. But, I'll tell you something, if the guy in the picture happened to be one of a couple of other banditos I know...you'd be burning the week end oil."

Chapter 27

"That's all I can tell you at this point Matt, what do you say? Are you in?" J.B. McCall steepled his big hands under his chin and just waited. It was time to close the deal. The first one who speaks loses. Blalock had retreated into a kind of denial about what he had just heard. He sat back in the big leather brown and black cowhide easy chair and let out a huge breath of air. The two thousand gallon salt water aquarium dwarfed the six-one McCall in his fancy seat from the Boeing jet.

I wonder what McCall would say if I at this point confessed to being the one who boomed him back in sixty-seven, Blalock wondered. The money, these guys bailed him out when he was desperate, McCall Sr., WWII vet and Jesus, a Tuskeegee airman, millionaire many times over, Duane, the crash at LaGuardia, is my score even with these people? I think my score is even with the McCall's, Blalock concluded.

"Mr. McCall, with the greatest respect, I'm going to have to say no. As much as I'd like to get into space, I don't think my six months in NASA hardly qualifies me to command your oil exploration mission. You know they busted me out as an attitude case? And Frankly, I'm at a loss why you can't find somebody more qualified...what about the Russians...surely they have some guys who were in training to fly the thing, get one of them."

"We have one of them now Matt, but we want an American to command the mission because it's OUR money. We're buying the ship, the booster, and paying the French to put it up for us. We're talking close to a hundred million here, and I need somebody I know and trust to take care of my investment…not some Boris I ain't never even heard of. If what happens is what we hope will happen, your compensation package will run into seven figures."

"Duane, what were you talking about when you said this was history book stuff?"

Matt looked over to his right as Duane came motoring over to rejoin the conversation.

"It will solve the energy crisis Matt. The government has been holding out on us. We have a window of opportunity to use a piece of equipment that will find the fields that they have known about for decades but won't share the information because the big oil companies want to keep prices up. The glut we expect to produce will cut oil prices in half and the smaller companies, whose cost of doing business is a fraction of the big guys, will make a killing. Matt, we'll make the history books by eliminating the energy crisis and wiping out our dependence on the Arabs for oil."

Duane looked at his Dad who was nodding in his mind about the killing part. Yep, there's sure going to be some killing going on alright. McCall's conscience was knotted up like a rubber band on a model plane. Good and Bremen ought to be doing this, not me. They're the one's who have spent a lifetime lying so that the symmetrical logic of the end justifying the means always makes its neat little circle. Man, I'm not cut out for this stuff, he thought, maintaining his poker face. There was entirely too much shit coming together. Maybe this was too much for the small group of warriors he had assembled…maybe it was a one way suicide mission as Bremen had postulated. What if the Kremlin was using him to harm his own country in some way? But what were the options? What were the odds that Feldman, Good, Bremen, General Hampton, and the four Russian scientists were all wrong and our own government was right? What if the aliens' intentions really were benign? Just peaceful explorers who came our way and then departed. What message would they take with them about who we are? How much corroboration do you need to start a nuclear war with beings from another star?

Blalock stood and approached McCall's carrier sized desk. McCall stood up and walked way around to shake Matt's hand. "I'm sorry Mr. McCall. I don't think I could help you right now, my head's just not on straight enough to jump into something as important as solving the world energy crisis."

McCall's decades of salesmanship locked on like radar to two statements by Blalock...he had said "not right now," and "I don't think...because my head's not straight enough..."

Blalock's hard no had softened to a possible maybe.

"Matt will you do an old fighter pilot a favor?"

"Sure Mr. McCall, name it."

"Matt, will you think about it for two weeks before you give me a final answer?"

"Yeah, Matt, think about it, that's all we ask," Duane chimed in. "Besides I've got some stuff to do in Atlanta for the next two weeks, we can stay in touch, maybe hoist a few horns."

"Yeah, sure, why not...two weeks I'll give you my final answer."

"Well, that's what happened, I'm sure you were listening in." McCall explained to Ann Louise what had happened in the failed recruiting interview with

Blalock. Anne Louise made a completely phony surprised look on her face. "J.B. I am shocked, shocked, that you would think I'd do such a thing."

"I want this guy Anne Louise…he's as straight as a die, but his mind is messed up over his divorce. Duane says he's up and down like a yo-yo…when he's up, he's really, really, up…when he's down, he's burning wreckage on the end of a runway…what do I do?"

"I liked him too J.B. I ain't never heard NOBODY in your office ceptn' Duane, say yes mam' and no mam' to me. But that ain't all that important. What I want to know is this…has this guy got the gray stuff between his ears and the guts to git this job done when it comes time fer the nut cuttin'?"

McCall flipped open his file on Blalock and started reading to Ann-Louise. "The guy has an AE degree from Florida State, did some production test flying for Lockheed. Flew over a hundred sorties into Khe Sanh when it was under attack over in Vietnam. Was turned down by NASA as psychologically unfit. Has about 15,000 hours of flying time and was a pilot for Eastern for 17 years…flew captain the last five of those."

"This guy ain't exactly no Buzz Aldrin is he?" Anne Louise said.

"No, Anne Louise, Blalock don't sound much like an astronaut does he?"

"But you know J.B., there's something steady about this guy…I trust him…I think he's lucky…If you're askin' me, I say hire em' if he'll take the job…but don't wait too long to tell him the truth."

"Anne Louise, OK, lets assume for a minute that we talk him into this insane operation…how do we get his head together with this divorce mess?"

Anne Louise pondered the question. "How long's it

been since they split the sheets?"

"A year since everything was finalized," J.B said.

"Well, Mr. J.B. McCall, savior of the world, you have come to the right place for that problem...I have the solution that will fix his wagon perfect."

"What are we going to do?

"Where do you get that we stuff, Paleface?"

McCall heard himself belly laughing for the first time since his first meeting with Lawrence Feldman. "Ok, you handle it...but if you don't mind...if you're going to spend any of my money...keep me in the loop OK?"

"Ain't gonna spend a nickel of your billions J.B...but say, you mind if I make a long distance call?"

Chapter 28

Robert Tranh was pouring over some late arriving data from the Skyguard Project. He was getting behind in organizing the voluminous pile to be presented to the team that Leanna had selected. The Team was supposed to suggest profitable means to turn over the networks of observatories for private use when they weren't in the search mode. The team had eight preeminent people from various disciplines. International law, diplomacy, scientists, philosophers, a former United States Vice President who was the chairman, of course, and a Presbyterian minister.

A call came in on the main switchboard for Tranh, which was unusual, since everyone that did business with the Helms Corporation at his level had his personal phone number and called him direct. Tranh kept his two secretaries busy doing actual work and in fact given them quite a bit of authority to solve problems they felt comfortable and competent to solve. His instructions had always been to take the bull by the horns and inform him later of what was done. He said that in some cases we may have to do an instant replay or go over the game films, but he would never criticize them for taking the initiative if that resulted later in a mistake.

"Bobby Tranh is this you? Mr. high and mighty making six figures project director for Helms Group?"

"Anne Louise?"

"Yes, this is Anne Louise...I wanna speak with the Bobby Tranh who worked for J.B. McCall as a roustabout then went off to be a college boy at night. I wanna talk to the Bobby Tranh who used to steal ALL my spearmint candy when he was up brown nosin' his boss."

"Anne Louise, I can't believe it's you. How the hell are you?"

For the next hour, Bob and Anne Louise got all caught up...

"Now Bobby, I had an ulterior motive for calling you besides wanting to fuss at you for not staying in touch any bettern' a Christmas card. Has Leanna got a boyfriend yet?"

"You're kidding, right?"

"No Bobby, I'm not kidding. Is she still a total pain in the ass?"

"I'd say total would be a little strong." Tranh looked around to make sure Leanna wasn't creeping up on him with a memo or something. "I'd say 99% would be more like it."

"Sounds like she's had an epiphany iffn' it's anything less than a hunnert' percent."

"Actually, there have been some startling changes."

"Hmmm that's good Bobby. OK, are you up on the err...'foreman' problem we're having with well number...uhh..214?" Project 214 was the code name for the joint purchase and flight of the Russian space shuttle between Helms Industries and TriAmCo Energy. Tranh became gravely serious as he was only recently brought into the inner circle on Project 214, the matter that TriAmCo and Helms were financing...the totally illegal use of classified military technology for oil exploration with a Russian launch vehicle. It would have been far better, he thought, if he had been able to maintain some plausible deniability. These kinds of things are always come out and it was the underlings that ended up in prison.

"Yes, I understand we are having difficulty in hiring a qualified site manager."

"Well, I think we've found one, but his head is all messed up over a woman...went through a divorce over a year ago...still all tore up. When a boy loses a puppy, the best thing you can do is git em another one."

"Anne Louise, I hope you're not going where I think you're going."

"Well, I guess I am, Bobby. This guy I'm talkin' about is a straight one and he won't be takin' any crap off of anybody...even you-know-who. This might be our golden opportunity to fix everything at once...you know that blobal solution you big shots are always talking about."

"Anne Louise, this guy will be worse off after meeting you-know-who like every dude she's ever met....and by the way it's global solution."

"Well, he ain't in no shape now...what do we have to lose? Whatever...listen to me Bobby, this is your sixty-seven year old grandmother talking, I'm the expert on women here, certainly not you...now here's what I want you to do..."

Chapter 29

This was undoubtedly the high point in Jim Charlesworth's career and that of the twenty-three other engineers and technicians at Harley Davidson's factory in York, PA. The representative from Mt. Marilyn Mining was coming to take delivery of their two, two man lunar surface explorers. Harley Davidson had turned out the vehicles according to the rigid specs set forth by the customer in only fourteen months. They looked like a fifty percent oversized four wheeled ATV and were constructed of titanium honeycomb and graphite. Powered by a powerful set of dual lithium ion batteries, they could travel at speeds easily to sixty miles per hour over level terrain and were stable going downhill at a hundred and twenty. This was accomplished using an extremely responsive inertia dampening shock absorber filled with xenon gas and a special highly sensitive spring ordered from Rolex. The rest of the suspension was from a modified 1974 Harley Baja 100, a competition dirt bike. The engineers joke was that an exploration vehicle that was supposed to go sixty miles an hour must mean that the miners knew where the gold was already…it was an engineer's joke and consequently few others found it very funny.

When the contract first came in, the customer made a one million dollar down payment to finance the research and development and of course to bring on the staff for the time period involved. At first, nobody believed that there was any place on the moon named Mt. Marilyn. Looking it up, however, disclosed that the mountain was real and was named after Marilyn Lovell, the wife of James Lovell, one of the astronauts on Apollo 8.

The Harley Davidson LEX Lunar Explorer was supposed to be used as a promotional tool to raise venture capital for a mining expedition that would begin the first baby steps of commercialization of the moon to bring back certain rare metals discovered in abundance by the astronauts. NASA later admitted classifying a number of Apollo photos in order to "protect future mineral rights and claims by the United States." It was rumored that the lunar South Pole was especially rich in rare metals since all photographs of this region had been classified Double Gamma.

The Harley LEX was beautiful to behold. Painted in metallic cherry with ornate flames curling up and around the center pedestal, it had flat silver coated graphite fenders to protect the astronaut-miners from flying dust. It had small pick up truck bed with the specialized attach points for carrying the yet undisclosed pieces of mining equipment. All the controls were on the hand grips per the customer specs. No footwork would be required and the dual side-by-side saddles had a special folding back for extra stability over rough terrain.

But by far the most interesting technical feature to the Harley Davidson LEX was the Parasol Orbit Engine. The LEX could actually be launched from lunar orbit and make a soft landing with astronauts aboard and ready to rock hunt when they hit the surface. The parasol engine looked something like a beach umbrella on a long pole with the umbrella being only a foot in diameter. The long pole was attached to a roll bar looking apparatus that ran fore and aft. As the LEX went through the automatic de-orbit sequence, the parasol engine rotated from the aft trailing position as a retro rocket to directly overhead as it became a landing thruster, lowering the LEX like a parasol-looking parachute like in an old Mickey Mouse cartoon. The Parasol engine had twenty-six small nozzles spaced completely around the axis of the common combustion chamber. The exhaust was aimed at fifty-two degrees to the thrust axis so the astronauts would not be scorched. The system was possible due to the relatively slow lunar orbital velocity of only three thousand miles per hour, an orbit altitude of only seventy miles and the advance of computer microprocessors since the sixties to figure all this stuff out. The parasol engine and fuel tank was a single unit that was disconnected once on the surface and the LEX was just driven off and away you went. When it was time to go home, you just drive back into the Parasol chassis, tighten up four big locking wing nuts and raise the Parasol tower to the Takeoff/Land position. You then waited for the launch sequence from the ship in orbit. Everything was completely automatic from that point on.

Charlesworth and his team were especially intrigued when they were asked that the LEX be built as a completely operational system including drop and launch tests using the parasol engine. And that they did. It was somewhat of a new problem for Harley Davidson, building a classified product, but they pulled it off since no foreign agents had any interest in the Harley Davidson plant in York, PA.

It was a closed, very private ceremony when the president of Mt. Marilyn Mining, Harold Jacobson, arrived with the chartered Southern Air L-100 to pick up the two LEXs, carefully packed in a huge wooden box laughingly stenciled "Farm Machinery." Southern

Air had transported "Farm Machinery" all over the world and nobody ever asked questions. President Jacobson and the senior management of Harley smoked Cuban cigars and drank five bottles of Dom. The distinguished looking, snow on the dome, president of Mt. Marilyn Mining then had a few puzzling short remarks.

"The use of these vehicles which you have built for us in the traditions of your great company will have repercussions far beyond the specifications which we gave you. Some day soon, I pray that you will be able to realize the great service you have rendered to our nation. God Bless you all." At that point President Jacobson, also known as Colonel Lowell Breman U.S. Army, (ret), waved to the group, walked up the ramp of the L-100, and left.

One of the LEX team leaders nudged Charlesworth in the ribs. "Hey Jim, what'd Jacobson say when you showed him the rumble switch?"

Charlesworth's face flushed. His buddy noticed. "Jim what's wrong?"

"Oh shit! I forgot to tell him."

Chapter 30

A. G. (Chewbacca) Watson was a great guy, as long as you didn't have to fly with him that is. But the problem took care of itself automatically when he hit age sixty. The Federal Air Regulations kicked in and one day he was a seasoned and wise United Air Lines Boeing 777 veteran captain, and the next day by way of the operation of flipping the page over on a calendar, he was instantly too old and unfit. It was so unfair. But, like many retired airline pilots, Chewbacca Watson was in good health, had about two mil in his retirement account, an abundance of piss and vinegar, and was stamped with the standard airline pilot weird sense of humor. Flying with A.G. was tough, because it required that you never look at him in the cockpit. He chewed tobacco and spit into a rubber stopped coke bottle he carried in his flight kit. It was absolutely disgusting and while all the flight attendants and pilots loved A.G. Watson for a layover, flying with the guy made you want to hurl. But, that problem was over. After retirement, A.G. bought himself a vintage North American AT-6 and flew all over the west with his four buddies who also had T-6s. He kept it at Stead Field the old Air Force Base outside Reno where they hold the National Air Races. Stead was the hangout of a group of guys who were the aviation world's version of the Flat Earth Society and the Aryan Nation all rolled into one. Now these guys weren't Nazis, because on the relative political spectrum, compared to these guys' multitude of opinions, Hitler was a pussy. These guys were just, shall we say, frequently wrong, but never in doubt? Maybe "objectivity" challenged?

So, it was one afternoon in the Fall of 1997, when A.G. Watson noticed something very interesting on Cirrus, his internet flight planning and weather program. So he called up one of his other retired buddies with the T-6 group.

"Zarkoff, are you up yet?"

"Chewy, it's two o'clock in the frigging afternoon."

"Yeah, I know, but I know you old farts need to get your beauty rest."

"Hey, I'm only six months older'n you…say, you're unusually full of shit today …maybe we ought to double your Geritol dosage."

"Very funny. I like Geritol, especially with gin...Say, guess what the winds are at 8,000 over Reno today?"

"Seventy-five knots out of the west?"

"Nope, eighty."

"Oh really?"

"Yeah, really." They then both laughed a phony conspiratorial and sinister kind of laugh.

"Zarkoff, do you think it might be too soon? It has been over a year right?"

"More than a year…it's time. Let's do it. I'll hit the Bat Signal and see if I can organize the Interplanetary Space Patrol and drinking society."

A.G. Watson and his four wingmen in their vintage T-6s were about to present to the citizens of Reno and towns all over Nevada another visitation from the "Giant Alien Spaceship." They would form up their T-6s in a huge "V" formation at night, then switch on each of their powerful airplane landing lights. From the ground, it looked like a huge delta winged craft was flying by at fantastic speed at a very high altitude. They could then switch off their landing lights simultaneously, since they were in radio communication with each other. This sudden extinguishing of the landing lights created an illusion that the "Giant Alien Spaceship" had zoomed away at "fantastic speed…beyond anything known by Earth science. " WE ARE NOT ALONE" screamed the headlines of the Reno Gazette, after the last visit of the "Giant Alien Spaceship." The beauty of the 80 knot winds out of the west was that for the first time, they could all slow down to 80 knots in their T-6s, heading into the wind, but this time, they could make the Giant Alien Spaceship appear to hover right over downtown Reno. They had been waiting for these ideal conditions for two years.

"They'll have a helluva time explaining this one," Chewbacca chortled.

A.G. was holding in a left turn over Stead at fifty-five hundred feet as his buddies started arriving and joining up in formation. They kept their planes dispersed at several nearby airports so that it would be difficult to tell when all five guys were getting together. It was getting dark, so they kept the formation really loose. There's nothing like a mid-air collision with a friend to louse up a great night of spoofing the natives.

Unfortunately, for Watson and his pals, this night was going to be quite a bit more than they bargained for.

Chapter 31

The Helms Corp Falcon III squeaked to a landing at Atlanta's Peachtree Dekalb airport, the executive field in the heart of Atlanta's expensive northern suburbs.

"Robert, this is the most preposterous thing Uncle J.B. has ever asked me to do. I do not fly to other cities to interview potential employees who have already turned down a job offer…it's asinine." Robert Tranh was extremely uncomfortable with the secret plan cooked up by Anne Louise with Mr. McCall's blessing. Tranh had always shot extremely straight with Leanna and that was the bedrock foundation of her high degree of trust she had in his judgement. If Leanna ever found out the truth, there was no telling what might happen. He had long since ceased to be astounded at her capabilities in the ruthless department.

"Given the time frame and the fact that the other four candidates turned down the job, I suspect Mr. McCall was motivated at least partially by the dwindling options," Tranh offered feebly.

"If it was anybody but Uncle JB, well, I think I've made my point. What is the itinerary?"

"I thought we'd keep it informal, Leanna, and just meet the guy for dinner over on the north side at one of his hangouts. Blalock and Duane are going over about five for happy hour, and I thought we'd meet them about seven for dinner. Keep it short, you get to look the guy over…err I mean evaluate him for this assignment if Duane and his father can persuade him to take it. I have his file right here…college transcripts, military records, his short tenure at NASA, and some stuff we dug up on him from his days at Eastern and the aftermath including the lowdown on his divorce."

Leanna took the file from Tranh and began reading as the jet taxied to a stop in front of the Epps Air Service executive terminal. She was still reading when the limo picked them up for transport to the Buckhead Ritz Carleton. "What's the attire for this place we're going Robert?"

"It's casual."

"How casual?"

"Like jeans and a blouse casual."

"Oh God, Robert, don't tell me there's a pinball machine and a pool table in this place."

"No Leanna, it's a steakhouse with a big deck on the back, live band...oldie goldies...you'll like it."

"Yes, I'm sure I will. Lets just get this over as soon as possible...I have the reception at the French Consul tomorrow afternoon...where they do not play oldie goldies on the big deck. The more I think about this entire trip the more disgusted I get."

Well, she's got that right, Tranh thought to himself. In New York, Tranh's office was, thankfully, two floors below Leanna's and he didn't have to put up with her on a continuous basis. Going on business trips was terrifically stressful because of her constant complaining and demanding everything from everyone. Nothing was ever accomplished for her fast enough, conscientious enough, detailed enough, blah, blah, blah. Being around Leanna on a trip was like being back in the Skyraider running low on fuel but not being able to disengage from the mission to go get some. His stomach was knotted up within a few hours of listening to her continuous bullshit. And the trip home was undoubtedly going to be more of the same.

They changed clothes at the Ritz and met back downstairs about six-thirty where the limo picked them up for the drive over to Houck's Steakhouse & Saloon overlooking the Chattahootchee River. Leanna wore a pair of black raw silk slacks and flats. The top was also silk, but a pearly shimmering cream unbuttoned down the front by two buttons. The blouse was tied just above the navel revealing about four inches of Leanna's waspish waist. She wore one of her small pearl necklaces and simple pearl earrings…and like always, she wore no bra. Her perfectly proportioned breasts were beautifully sculpted under the custom tailored top. There was a scent of Obsession, her favorite perfume. Named just for her, Tranh had always suspected after observing her in action with the defenseless opposite gender.

Blalock, you poor bastard, Tranh thought, welcome to hell on wheels. When you regain consciousness after the blast hits you, you'll know you've been chainsawed by one of the best. Shit, this isn't going to work. I can't believe I went along with this.

Leanna handed the folder back to Tranh in the limo as the drove the tree lined avenues of North Atlanta. The afternoon sun filtered through the forested suburbs, occasional shafts of light hitting the car like a laser beam as it moved from shadow to light.

"Is this the best we could do?"

"Leanna, he was our fifth choice and we were running out of time."

"Did you see the NASA psychiatrist's comments about his inability ability to deal with authority?"

"Which part?"

Leanna opened the folder and pointed to the transcript of the interview.

Dr. Ilene Greenbaum: "Captain Blalock, your Meyers Briggs Personality Inventory discloses a poor relational index with authority and a very low score on your ability to follow proscribed directives. Would you say that this is a correct assessment?"

Capt. Blalock: "Well gosh, Miz Greenbaum, you might just have something there. Whenever I buy a new mattress, the first thing I do is tear off the tag and mail it to the Department of Commerce with a signed confession daring them to come shoot it out with me."

"Robert, not only is this idiot anti-authority, but he is fantastically immature."

"Leanna, I'm certain you are absolutely right about Captain Blalock, but pilots say things like that sometimes…it's a put on."

"Frankly, Robert, I see nothing in this file that impresses me and I can't understand how he even was contacted in the first place."

"Well, there's a good question we can ask him isn't it?"

Friday afternoon happy hour at Houck's was cooking as the limo pulled up to the front door. The parking lot was packed, and you could hear the Banks & Shane band halfway down the street. "Oh, they're playing so loudly," Leanna complained. "How will we ever have a conversation?"

"Oh gee, I just don't know what we're going to do," Tranh said sarcastically, slipping a little. Leanna darted one of her fixed bayonet looks at him. Just get me through the night, Tranh prayed.

They made their way into the crowded bar, passed the old timey fully operational jukebox that played real 45 RPM records, passed the popcorn machine, and looked for Duane in his wheelchair. Houck's was murmuring with the inane drivel of bar speak and the smell of cigarette smoke and steaks on the grill filled the room.

"It's soo smoky in here," Leanna whined.

"Let's go look on the deck," Tranh suggested. "There they are," Tranh pointed. "Ahh, good, the band is playing inside, at least we'll be able to hear ourselves think."

As Tranh and Leanna approached the table, Duane McCall was pulling a long cylindrical object out of an olive drab zipper bag under the table.

The deck was densely packed with standing patrons trying to get to the bar, and Tranh found that they were being wedged along by the crowd as they made for the table.

"Hand me the elephant gun trusty gun bearer," Blalock intoned with one finger held up in the air for emphasis.

"The zipper is stuck on the bag…hold your horses," replied Duane struggling to get the long tube out of the canvas bag. By this point, Leanna and Tranh had been pushed almost right up next to the Blalock and McCall's table. "I haven't got all day Oyster, the elephants are escaping," Blalock announced looking down at the struggling Duane trying to get the zipper unstuck.

"Why don't you go screw one of the elephants and have your people contact my people," Duane retorted.

Blalock looked over at the bar then back at Duane still unable to get the elephant gun out of the bag. "This elephant hunting is thirsty work. I'm going to get us a couple of beers." Blalock stood at the table and turned to make his way through the throng and bumped immediately head on into Leanna. "Ooops! Pardon me," he said. Then said to Leanna loud enough for Duane to hear, "Isn't this a fine thank you? We let out Mandela and now all the gun bearers are acting like they got a union."

Duane said, "You're gonna need more melanin to negotiate my contract...and make it a Foster's this time...try to get one below room temperature this time for chrissake."

Blalock squeezed by Leanna, but before completely by, he leaned over and whispered in her ear, "Don't go away baby, I've got to go get my son some refreshments. Yes, yes, I know he's a black, depraved alcoholic...but I'm more liberal than you might think...it's the white man's burden you know." Blalock then ankled off to the bar. Leanna stood there with her mouth open, completely speechless for one of the few times in her life.

Duane heard the whole thing and was laughing. The humor was completely lost on Leanna, however. She looked down at Duane who had by now extracted the elephant gun and had craftily hid it under the table for use later.

"Duane, was that Captain Blalock?"

"Sit down Leanna, take a load off. Yo, Bobby how you doin' man?"

"Yo, Duane, long time no see."

Leanna was furious. "Duane, you asked me to come down here for this? This is our mission commander? This total fool?"

"Leanna, come on, lets give the guy a fair hearing...hell, you're already here...Jesus, girl, lighten up for once will ya?"

Blalock returned with the beers and couldn't believe his luck. Duane had somehow lassoed the babe and her pal and they were seated at the table. No way that could be a duo…a short chink and a tall round eye? What the hell, here goes nothing, he said to himself. The chair next to Leanna was open and Matt pulled it back and sat down. Leanna looked over to see who it was. Blalock said, "Hi, my name's Matt. Has anyone ever told you that you look a helluva lot like somebody that I wish I knew?"

Duane jumped in right then to prevent Blalock from completing the self-destruct sequence. "Matt, er Matt, I'd like you to meet Leanna Helms. She's an old family friend and also the other investor in the venture. This is Bobby Tranh one of her directors."

"Pleasure to meet you sir," Blalock said coming to his feet. Tranh rose, reached across the table, and shook hands. Matt then extended his hand to Leanna who with obvious disdain barely extended hers. Blalock clasped it gently and softly pulled the back of her hand to his lips. But instead of kissing her hand he kissed the back of his own.

"It is a great honor for you to meet me," he announced. "So what brings you kids to Atlanta?" Blalock continued, as if Miss Manners had been totally sated.

"I was just asking myself that same question," Leanna shot back, snatching her hand out of Blalock's who hadn't quite got around to releasing it. "Look, I think we're all wasting our time here," Leanna continued. "Mr. Blalock, I have a considerable investment in this enterprise with Mr. J.B. McCall, who seems to have a completely misplaced opinion of your capabilities. Frankly, based on what I have seen so far, I am underwhelmed. Mr. Blalock, I wouldn't let you take my trash out, much less command a mission of this importance. I flew down here from New York this morning at the request of Duane's father to interview you for this assignment…and as for you Duane, maybe you could tell me what you see in this bozo."

Far from getting mad, Matt Blalock found the blunt, tough guy in silk tremendously amusing and sat there smiling throughout her entire diatribe.

Duane, on the other hand was getting steamed. "Well, Leanna, I'll answer your question." Duane reached over and grabbed hold of the cuff of Matt's long sleeve shirt and snatched back the sleeve of his left arm. Blalock's forearm starting at the wrist was hideously scarred from the burns sustained in the 727 crash…alternating patches of white and normal skin void of hair…the follicles long ago burned below the roots. Leanna stared at Blalock's arm, her mouth partially open. "Leanna, he got that pulling my ass out of the burning wreckage of a jet."

Blalock started, "Hey, what the hell," pulling his sleeve back down and buttoning the cuff. Leanna was completely caught off guard. She had a momentary memory flash and remembered her father shaving one morning and she remembered the grotesque burns on his left arm from the tear gas projectile. She forever remembered his explanation. "That's when Daddy met uncle J.B., honey. He took care of me until the ambulance came." Burned into her six-year-old mind, her father's explanation forged a massive debt of gratitude to her uncle J.B.

"This man saved my ass once, and crawled half way down a burning fuselage to get to me…that's what I see in this bozo."

Leanna heard the story years before but nobody had told her that Blalock was the guy. There ensued at that point a somewhat long silence; the term pregnant pause was invented for these situations. Leanna said nothing but looked up into Matt Blalock's eyes for several seconds...there was something familiar about this man... But she caught herself quickly and started anew with Duane. "This changes nothing in my view. I was not informed that Captain Blalock was the individual who rescued you."

"Well that's a relief," Matt butted in. "Heck, I thought you were going to apologize there for a second. That would have been such a shame...I mean you've been a one hundred percent perfectly unmitigated bitch the entire thirty minutes you've been here. What a shame it would have been to ruin your record. Look, Duane and I are going to have a few more beers then have dinner. You and Mr. Tranh are welcome to join us, but you're going to have to conduct yourself as a lady, in a civilized manner, for the rest of the evening. Now, if you can't reach real deep and pull that out, perhaps you better just scoot your magnificent butt right back to New York and whoever it is up there who has to put up with you."

Leanna was shocked. Tranh was in ecstasy...how long had he waited for some guy to tell her like it is. Duane was eating the whole show up, but realized that now the mission was dead and they would be in serious difficulty. With no commander, the mission was facing certain cancellation and the awful consequences that would follow.

Leanna never registered a further reaction, she just looked over at Tranh and said, "Robert, we're leaving." And they left.

The flight back to New York was a living hell for Robert Tranh. A Skyraider on fire and out of fuel would have been preferable. "Robert, did you hear what he called me? An unmitigated bitch! He called me a bitch to my face. He said I would have to reach deep to be a lady! I've never met a man like this. I hate him! I despise the bastard. Did you hear the first thing that came out of his mouth? He called me baby! Baby! I had no idea that the male gender contained men like this. He makes me nauseated just thinking of his name." And so it went for the longest hour and forty-five minutes that Tranh had ever spent in an airplane.

The next day Tranh reported in to Anne Louise and J.B. who was on the speakerphone. He reported the encounter in vivid blow-by-blow detail about how the big plan had collapsed in minutes with Leanna leaving before dinner after being called a bitch...the flight back...and all the next morning proclaiming her hatred for the man named Blalock. "So what do we do now," Tranh wanted to know. "Is there anybody else we can get?"

Anne Louise was the first to speak. "Somebody else? Are you nuts? The plan is working."

J.B. chimed in incredulously. "Ahh come on, Anne Louise, you've got to be kidding. How can you say that? We're dead."

"I agree with Mr. McCall." Tranh added.

"That's because both you guys are men and don't know beans about women. Give it a few more days Bobby. Let me know what she says next about our boy."

Two days letter, Tranh got an instant message from Leanna. "Robert, see me immediately."

Tranh popped into Leanna's office about fifteen minutes later. "So, what's up Toots?" Leanna smiled weakly from behind her neatly organized desk. Were her eyes red? Could she have been crying? The thought appeared, but vanished immediately based on what Tranh knew about her. That would have been another first.

"Robert, I need you to be really honest with me about something."

"Sure Leanna, you know I always shoot straight with you."

"I know, Bobby." There was a softer tone to Leanna's voice...she was also calling him Bobby...that was new.

"I have to ask you a serious question."

"Sure, Leanna, what is it?"

"Bobby, do you think I'm an unmitigated bitch?"

Chapter 32

The cabinet meetings had been getting more and more depressing as the clock counted down to the end of the EBEs' peaceful survey of the planet. Acting Joint Chief, Major General Collier McVey continued reading the latest intelligence. "Twelve ships in lunar synchronous orbit over the Shard, twelve more over the Tower and surface movement in crater Langrenus. Amateur astronomers are bombarding NASA with reports of "Y" shaped formations of moving shadows on the near side. "We now estimate that there are two hundred fifty three alien ships of four types parked in Lunar orbit and two thousand plus elsewhere in the solar system." Fear hung in the room like a pervasive cloud permeating every square inch. Members of the cabinet were afraid. The president and vice president were afraid. General McVey was afraid.

Secretary of Transportation Alice Hayes-Udall and Secretary of the Treasury Maureen Harrison-DuPont, however, were not afraid. Hayes-Udall listened placidly as McVey continued with his latest threat analysis. Glancing down at her arm, she brushed her forearm lightly with her opposite hand. The epithelial cells of her body had long ago been genetically altered to withstand the lethal cosmic rain that was coming. She looked across the table in the situation room at Harrison-DuPont. DuPont responded with a thin smile…sisters, she thought. In a few short months, we will be the only ones in this room left alive.

"And we have received no new tapes, is that correct?"

"That is correct, Mr. President," McVey responded.

"Has Colonel Bremen turned up yet?"

"No, Mr. President, Colonel Bremen seems to have disappeared."

"Kinda' wish he was here now."

Me too, thought Hayes-Udall. We should have done him at the same time we did Hampton.

"So what can we do if they become hostile?" queried the vice president. "What about the stuff that General Hampton was doing?"

General McVey seemed a little uneasy. "Mr. Vice President we do have two defensive systems which we think would be effective. One is the Bear Trap. The other is the X-35."

"Can we commence a crash program and get them ready in time?"

McVey knew where this was headed. "Mr. President, may I speak freely?"

"Of course, General, speak your mind."

"Mr. President, the Bear Trap could be deployed around our major cities if we had the manufacturing base to do it. Unfortunately, when NAFTA was signed, too much of our technology and heavy manufacturing went off shore. The Bear Trap, for instance, requires two large shockproof flat plate liquid crystal displays in the command center to be used by the battery commander and weapons coordinators. Argon Electronics was the only U.S. based manufacturer of this component before NAFTA. Argon closed its doors a year ago. Now, the only people who make what we need are the Japanese and the Koreans. The Korean plant is under heavy siege right now by a labor strike. The Japanese have informed us that before they could commence production of this weapon component, the Diet would have to approve since it might be unconstitutional. And even if rush approval could be obtained, the Japanese could not make the number needed fast enough. The X-35 space fighter is the other system. This was a pet project of General Hampton. While touted as a test platform for the larger X-34, so called space shuttle replacement, the X-35 is actually a geospace fighter designed to control the near Earth space out to five hundred miles. It uses a Pratt & Whitney G1A Gravity Drive once in space and the Raytheon M8 ASAT Laser slash particle beam as its primary weapon. The ships can be flown by onboard crews, but in actual combat, the twenty "G" maneuvers and Mach 8 speeds needed to dogfight the EBEs, requires an earth based duplicator/simulator whose control inputs would be duplicated in space by the X-35. Building the duplicators and training the crews would take at least twenty-four months."

Heads shook around the room and pencils tapped on the conference table nervously.

McVey plowed on. "Hampton had the plans drawn up in eight different languages of the nations that could produce the X-35. The idea was to build thousands of ships and saturate near Earth space with remotely piloted weapons platforms. Again, with NAFTA, the US aerospace industry scaled back domestic operations and subbed out a great deal of the construction of commercial airliners and military hardware to foreign companies. America just doesn't make things like it used to."

"OK, I think I've got the picture, General. So what can we do NOW?" The president was growing slightly impatient.

McVey put down his folder and gazed evenly at the head of the table. "Mr. President, we have enough hardware to build one complete Bear Trap system. I suggest that we place it around NORAD at Cheyenne Mountain and move the government to that location. I further suggest that we immediately take all our ICBMs off stand down and begin spinning up all missiles until we can get to at least DEFCON 2. They were very interested in standing down ours and the Soviets' arsenals, I suggest that we get as much stuff up and ready as we can. The Russians are already at Defense Condition 3."

Hayes-Udall broke in at this point. "General McVey, have the EBEs actually done anything? I mean all we have is some images of a few ships in orbit around the moon. Haven't we known about their Lunar base for some time? Couldn't all the so-called activity, be nothing more than a resupply mission? Or perhaps they're here to remove all their equipment from the moon for transportation home?"

There was a general relaxation at the table with Hayes-Udall's different slant on events. Harrison-DuPont caught her cue. "Any of those explanations certainly makes more sense than an imminent attack from outer space. Frankly, with due respect to General McVey, I think we're all teetering on a little paranoia perhaps tinged with hysteria. Why don't we all take a deep breathe and come up with some better explanations on what is going on." Harrison-DuPont then poured herself a glass of water, took a sip, and finished her comment. "You know, the military always takes the darkest interpretation of events…always looking for the next enemy we're going to have to fight…and I realize that this is what we pay them for...but for the life of me, I think we're really overreacting here."

Everyone's eyes turned to McVey.

McVey was still standing. He walked over to the holoprojector and switched it off. The wall sized sat photos of the orbiting ships went dark on the huge screens of the situation room. The lights in the room slowly came up to full strength.

"Ladies and gentleman, if there ever was a time for overreaction, this is it. Unfortunately, there is little we can do at this late date. The situation is further complicated by a forecast for year 2000 of the most disruptive solar max ever recorded. Seven to nine coronal mass ejections are expected daily, any of which can completely blind our satellite missile detection systems. We believe that the sudden arrival of all these ships coinciding with the Solar Max is not a random event. The decision to stand down our R & D and defenses, made earlier this year based on the promise of good will from the EBEs, may be our epitaph. I have made my recommendations and have nothing to add. Are there any further questions?"

Chapter 33

The five plane formation in the shape of the giant "V" stood motionless in the sky over Reno. The five T-6s had their landing lights and the red passing lights illuminated as they slowed down into the strong eighty-knot westerly winds. Their navigation lights and rotating beacons were turned off to make the Giant Alien Spaceship as realistic as possible. People on the ground were pouring into the streets around the residential areas of town. Throttled back, and at eighty-five hundred feet no engine sound could reach the ground. "Chewbacca" Watson, "Zarkov" and the others were chattering back and forth over 123.45 MHz.

"Let's see em' explain that one," somebody laughed.

"Gentlemen, we have plenty of fuel. What say we give the good citizens of Las Vegas a chance to see the Giant Alien Spaceship?" Everybody thought that was a good idea and Watson then lead his merry squadron of hoaxers down the airway from Reno to Vegas.

About half way, Pete, "Commando," Cody piped up over the radio, "What's all that over to our left...down on the ground? It looks like a million fireflies."

"Isn't the Groom Lake facility over there somewhere?" Zarkov queried.

"The truth is down there," somebody else said.

"Hey Chewy, what radial we supposed to be on out of Vegas?" somebody else asked.

Watson looked down at his horizontal situation indicator. Holy shit I'm full scale to the left, he thought.

Fucking eighty-knot wind had blown them right smack over the western part of Area 51, the most secret and sensitive prohibited area in the country.

"OK troops lets tighten up this formation, we're making a big turn to the right."

* * *

"Are those individual targets or a single target?"

"The computer will tell us in a second," the Bear Trap battery commander Colonel Bill Richardson responded, his eyes searching the large Tactical Situation Display's hundreds of symbols.

"The drones are fifteen minutes early, is that normal?" Battery second in command Lieutenant Larry Dawson wanted an answer. Standing behind the row of seated weapons controllers, he sloughed his senior NCO on the shoulder. "Sergeant Mestres, get hold of range control and see what the deal is on the drones."

"Started calling the minute we picked them up, Lieutenant...the line is busy."

Colonel Bill Richardson had his eyes glued to the large flat plate displays that projected the tactical situation. His young first lieutenant deputy battery commander had a habit of asking annoying questions, but Richardson was not old school and always listened and evaluated what he was getting from his people.

"Why don't I go outside and use the Mark One Eyeball?" Dawson pressed.

"Good idea, Larry, go take a look," Richardson clenched and unclenched his fists as acquisition data raced down the Track Mode window on the right side of the TSD. The computer seemed to be having trouble identifying the target. The Bear Trap test battery was installed in eleven large air conditioned trailers and was not deep underground like the operational squadrons would be. The beam weapon sites were semi-hardened around the command center at twelve locations radiating out from the middle where the tracking and command trailers were parked.

Larry Dawson threw open the back the door of the command trailer and looked around in the cool desert night. There in the sky, directly overhead, almost stationary was the huge "V" shaped craft, its leading edges clearly defined by alternating white and red points of light. "Son of a bitch, he's right on top of us," he shouted.

Richardson bolted out the door and was immediately next to Dawson leaning on the rail of the observation platform. Dawson pointed up at the alien ship. Richardson took one look and his brain switched to the combat mode as the orders came out of his mouth. "Lieutenant, get back inside. The bastards are trying to pulse us…can't let them get away with any intel on the Bear Trap."

Richardson calmly picked up the PA. "Everybody inside that can get there or take cover in place. Field monitors start your cameras, don protective goggles, and prepare for enemy engagement. We're firing the battery in thirty seconds!" The attack computer picked a hell of a time to malfunction because it suddenly showed five independent slow moving targets instead of the single alien ship. Just to be on the safe side, Richardson armed the Bear Trap with the red guarded commander's arming switch and rotated the adjacent selector to "automatic engagement." This theoretically would optimize the beam weapons' deployment and the computer ran the engagement.

"Chewbacca" Watson was the only one who saw anything. For a nanosecond, his eyes registered a bright flare of red from immediately below. But before his brain could send a response to his body, faster than the firing of synapse, the hypersonic Fletchettes had scattered a hundred high explosive projectiles into the center of the T-6 formation. Direct hits and proximity bursts blew all five aircraft out of the sky in an explosion that lit up the mountains miles away. An instant later, the two hundred megajoule lasers and particle beams blazed through the falling wreckage, vaporizing every object they hit in a lightning storm of blinding ionization. The deafening Jurassic roar of the beam weapons ceased as the fleeting cloud of T-6s parts fluttered through seven thousand feet above ground level. The identifiable pieces of the five aircraft would only half fill two fifty-five gallon drums.

Richardson's heart pounded as he typed an entry in the test log. "Successful Bear Trap engagement at 2243 hrs, 29 November 1999. " V" type alien ship completely destroyed. Computer malfunction prior to engagement. Used automatic engagement position for Pave Lantern. Attack computer self selected the multiple target mode after direct hit by Fletchette. MJ12-SVS-XP notified per AFM 201-202." He then printed a hard copy for his boss and made a hand written postscript. "I guess this proves the bastards aren't invincible."

The people of Reno and Las Vegas wouldn't be seeing the Giant Alien Spaceship again. In eight seconds, A.G. "Chewbacca" Watson, "Zarkov," and the rest, in a withering stream of hyper excited atoms, had returned to dust from which they came.

Chapter 34

For only the fourth time in his career with the NSA, Carson Benchly was getting a queasy feeling in his stomach as he reviewed the data he was about to take to his boss down at the Land Office. Director Trask's instincts were dead on about the so-called new restaurant owners in Bogota. The three guys were definitely Mancusso and his two pals. But the grand opening billboards were all over town; radio spots were appearing during morning and afternoon drive. Plumbing, electrical, and gas lines were going in and a giant concrete and steel reinforced pedestal was being built. Apparently, they were going to mount the shuttle like a jet in front of an Air Force base, like a big model plane, and not use the landing gear. The local promoters said that being on the low hill, the added elevation of the pedestal would give diners a dramatic view of the city lights. TV Bogota even had a special one night about the fantastic new restaurant concept. The former Chief of Staff of the South Vietnamese Air Force owned a big liquor store in Los Angeles. Was it really all that hard to see how these guys had teamed up, pooled their resources and gone for the gold? Given how much ass these three had kicked in the drug wars, it was easy to see why they might have wanted to use false identifications. But, unfortunately, that didn't explain the other matters.

"Leonard, this just might be one of those deals that looks spooky but when you rub long enough it turns out to be legit. Look at all this site preparation they're doing." Benchly was leaning on his chief's desk looking over his right shoulder as Trask shuffled slowly through the documents.

"Stranger things have been true," Trask mused. "What about their company? How'd that check out?"

"Problem on that one, boss. They have Fallen Star Restaurant Corp. on their passports. It's a Delaware company whose head offices are a post box in Wilmington. And to make things more confusing, there is a string of other companies listed as investors, directors, stock holders and the like and they all check out to be post office boxes all over the country. The only investor that could be verified was a small independent oil company in Plainview, Texas. I talked to the CEO, personally, and the entire story checked out."

"This is getting curiouser and curiouser," Trask began. "Benchly, I think it's time we had someone look up Mancusso and have a little talk with him to see what's what."

"I'll put in a request at CIA and get right on it," Benchly said, making a notation in his daytimer.

Trask pushed himself back from his desk, and began fumbling around in his desk until he found his cigars. He tossed one to Benchly and then used his cigar cutter until his cheroot was perfect for enjoyment. Trask lit up, sucked a long drag, and let it out filling the room with the pungent smell of a fine El Presidente. "Benchly, old steed, forget the company. I want you to go down there and check this out yourself."

Chapter 35

Date: 4-16-99
From: Lhelms@helmscorp.com
To: ATLpaladin@Sonic.net
Subject: Misunderstanding

Dear Captain Blalock:
After discussing the matter with my director of special projects, it appears that we may have had an unfortunate misunderstanding at our meeting in Atlanta last month. If any intemperate impressions were made, I would hope that should we choose to go forward in the subject enterprise that this would not interfere with our ability to work together.
Sincerely yours,
Leanna Helms, CEO
Helms Industries

***

Date: 4-20-99
From: ATLpaladin@sonic.net
To: Lhelms@helmscorp.com
Subject: Work for you? You're kidding, right?

Dear Miz Helms:
Imagine my surprise getting this e-mail from you. Intemperate...indeed you were. But before I respond any further, let me just say that were we the last man and woman on earth surviving in the jungle, I wouldn't swing ten feet on my vine to hand you a banana.

Unless, of course, an actual and sincere apology was forthcoming…something, no doubt you have never had to do. It might do you good to try one sometime. Do it in a mirror first…you know, practice moving your lips. Undoubtedly, there is a vast universe of people out there to whom you owe an apology. I doubt that there are enough years left in your life to get around to everyone, but before I even fire another neuron with your name on it, I'll be needing one from you.

I guess it's just a guy thing…go figure.

MB

***

Date: 4-24-99
From: Lhelms@helmscorp.com
To: ATLpaladin@sonic.net
Subject: Your last message

Dear Capt. Blalock:
I believe my last message to you, in fact, was an apology.

Leanna Helms

***

Date: 4-27-99
From: ATLpaladin@sonic.net
To: Lhelms@helmcorp.com
Subject: Your last message:

Your last message, in fact, was complete bull (bleep)!

Blalock

Bill Broocke

***

Date: 4-28-99
From: Lhelms@helmscorp.com
To: ATLpaladin@sonic.net
Subject: Your last message

Mr. Blalock:
Your arrogance is only exceeded by your ignorance on how to treat a woman. You have received all the apology you are going to get.
Leanna Helms

***

Date: 4-30-99
From: ATLpaladin@sonic.net
To: Lhelms@helmcorp.com
Subject: Your last message:

I gather from your last that by some tortured convolution of logic that you consider yourself a real woman. Medically, I'd say you have something there, but as far as the rest of the definition of a woman…you know the kind nurturing feminine stuff, you're going to need a frontal lobotomy then a consciousness replacement transferred by mind meld from a Vulcan. I wish I knew who to send you to. Tsk, tsk, it makes me sad to see such a huge pain in the ass trapped in that beautiful body. Somewhere way back when, baby, you took the low road. When you're ready to change lanes give me a shout.
Blalock

***

Date: 4-30-99
From: Lhelms@helmscorp.com
To: ATLpaladin@sonic.net
Subject: Your last message

Blalock:
You are the most incredibly difficult and stubborn man that I have ever met and your last e-mail really hurt me. I don't know if it was because nobody has ever spoken to me in that manner or perhaps you made me see some things that I have never seen or at least admitted to myself. When Duane pulled your shirtsleeve up at the restaurant, I thought of my father, he was burned on his left arm as well. I loved my father very much, but when he died in the Pan Am bombing, I knew that I'd have a lot of responsibility. I have always steeled myself against emotions that I knew would get in the way of what I wanted...and I always get what I want.
Leanna

***

Date: 5-3-99
From: ATLpaladin@sonic.net
To: Lhelms@helmcorp.com
Subject: The beginning of a journey?

Leanna:
As somebody said, journey of a thousand miles begins with one step. Off in the distance, when the wind is just right, I thought I heard violins...was there was

something else you wanted to add to your last note?Matt

***

Date: 5-5-99
From: Lhelms@helmscorp.com
To: ATLpaladin@sonic.net
Subject: Addendum to my last

Dear Matt:
You never quit do you? Ok, yes, let me add this to my last note. Please accept my sincerest apology for my incredibly boorish and thoughtless behavior at Houck's. I earnestly hope that even if we do not work together on this venture that we can at least become friends. Your rescue of Duane was an act of tremendous courage that I respect greatly. If you are ever in New York, I hope you will let me know. I'll take you out on the town and we'll "hit the ville," I believe is what you and Duane call it.
With kindest regards...
Leanna

***

Date: 5-7-99
From: ATLpaladin@sonic.net
To: Lhelms@helmcorp.com
Subject: I can't believe it

Dear Leanna:
Well, I must tell you that you are a woman of many surprises. Of course, I accept your apology, but you

know, the fact that you have the guts to take the dishing out I gave you and come back like this…it makes me think I was a little too harsh in the first place. One of my great handicaps, or so I tell people, is that I know too much about women. Partly, I say this to get a rise out of women. But, partly? Mostly? It's true. But, I'll tell you girl; you surprised the hell out of me! I called Duane this morning and told him I was reconsidering the job.

Matt

***

Date: 5-10-99
From: Lhelms@helmscorp.com
To: ATLpaladin@sonic.net
Subject: Your last message

Dear Matt:

Am on my way home from Bermuda where we had our annual bored' meeting, and I just checked my mail. I am so thrilled to hear that you are reconsidering the job offer although the mission seems a little different to me now. What would you say to this? Why don't you come up to New York for the weekend? Since you so astutely pointed out my deficiencies, don't you owe me a chance to practice my persuasive powers on you? In view of the many areas in which I need to improve upon, I think that a weekend in New York is the least you could do to help me start my way on a new path. (place laugh track here).

Name the date and I'll send a jet to pick you up.
Leanna

Blalock narrated the month long e-mail correspondence to Duane over the phone. As Duane listened to the unfolding events, his respect for his father's secretary was reaching hitherto unknown heights. Compared to these devious women, we're like lambs being lead to the slaughter, he thought. There was an animation and clarity in Blalock's voice that was not there a month ago. There was a kick ass purpose in the guy that reinforced Duane's decision to recruit him. And check this, Blalock wanted to know everything Duane knew about Leanna. Unfortunately, little of it was good and McCall pleaded ignorance to just about every question. The next question in Duane's mind was when would Matt be briefed on the actual mission should he accept the job? Mr. Good and Colonel Bremen did not think that the revelation of the actual mission would be a problem.

"Consider what we're trying to do," Bremen began.

"Doolittle's raiders didn't know the actual mission when they volunteered, and they went ahead to a man. We don't expect great results, just a pause to reflect on the part of our adversary, a disruption that will buy us time...time to build the X-35s and put Bear Traps around our cities. It will buy us time to prepare the people, and time to kill the bacteria that has slowly infected the highest levels of our government. Our enemy is a long way from home...we're going to make him homesick. Blalock will see the wisdom of this after we have laid out the facts. The logic of our plan is irrefutable. I expect no resistance from Captain Blalock."

"Yes, resistance is futile," smiled Mr. Good. "I am not concerned."

Duane started to smile.

"You see, we know where his children are." Good said.

Chapter 36

Las Tres Gringos was bustling as Carson Benchly scanned the people coming and going on a Friday afternoon at the popular Bogota watering hole. At one time Las Tres Gringos was owned by three Americans, but they had been kidnapped and shot years before. The bar had been a favorite target for various guerilla organizations and political factions for twenty years and had the singular distinction of the being the most blown up building in the world, second only to the Hotel Metropol in Belfast. Since then, it began a succession of local owners, the last being connected to Carlos Lehder. After that, a veil of protection had descended and Las Tres Gringos was now the safest place in town.

Mancusso walked in between two flowery shirted touristas with San Juan Samsonites (plastic shopping bags) crammed with stuff. Benchly waved and Mancusso headed for his table. The two tough looking touristas were bellying up to the bar, but undetected by Benchly, were watching events closely in the huge bar mirrors and listening to their Walkman radios.

Benchly stood up as Mancusso approached and extended his hand. Mancusso's firm grip and buoyant personality were relaxing to Benchly, who with virtually no experience in the field was handling this one personally…as it were. They ordered a couple of Aguilas, the local beer, and after a very short series of pleasantries came to the point.

"Mr. Murdock, I believe we have a mutual friend."

"Oh really, who?"

"Leonard Trask."

Mancusso's demeanor changed. "So, how's tricks at the Land Office? Still trying to steal the grazing rights from the peaceful ranchers?"

"Mr. Murdock, Leonard asked me to come down here and find out what you are doing. Based on your superlative record of service, I thought I'd dispense with the usual horse manure and just ask you."

"A wise choice of action," Murdock said. "No doubt you're wondering about the Stork."

"Ahh yes, the number three Russian shuttle, they named it?"

"Correct, the Russians named it the Stork, and we're in the process of removing the guts out of it for a restaurant, I'm sure you know all the details."

"And that's it?"

"Yep, that's it. We have two big backers, one out of New York, and another one in Texas that are fronting the money."

"Can you give their names?" Benchly pulled out his black Mont Blanc ballpoint and pocket calendar.

Mancusso's brow furrowed, "I'll have to get back to you on that, I'm not at liberty to disclose that information on my own. The politics are brutal down here, if the backers were exposed; the grease we'd have to ante up to get all our permits would triple. In fact we've gone to some lengths with dummy corporations and the like to disguise the identity of these people."

"Sounds logical," Benchly nodded.

"Is there anything else you'd like to tell me that I can pass along so as smooth down everybody's feathers? Leonard has this vision of a space bomber in the hands of Colombian drug lords raining death from above."

"Yeah, there is," Mancusso continued. "We looked

255

at all the numbers, and it is forty percent cheaper to fly the shuttle over here on the An-225 carrier aircraft. We won't have to dismantle and crate the ship at then put it back together when we get it here. It's going to save us a pile of dough. The only runway that can handle the weight of the shuttle and the carrier aircraft is over at Aghanna, the French spaceport in Ghana. From there we'll transport it by flatbed trailer to the location on Avenida Bolivar. Tell Trask that you'll also start noticing a few Tupelov technicians on the ground to help with the final preparations to mount the stork on the concrete model stand."

This is easy, Benchly was thinking, of course these men were not enemies of the United States and were being fully cooperative. But field work, how tough could it be?

Murdock/Mancusso opened his briefcase and pulled out a parchment menu with astronomical symbols on the cover and a photo the Russian shuttle heroically poised for flight on its concrete stand.

"If we're through with the bullshit, Benchly, take a look at this menu. You seem like a French restaurant kinda' guy. Gimme your opinion on this OK?"

"Well, I, as a matter of fact I am something of a gastronome and do know something about this." He was trying not to sound pretentious. Benchly placed his notebook in his attaché case and closed it, then picked up the menu and perused it in detail. "These prices seem awfully high...."

After Benchly had departed with all his notes, the two touristas came over from the bar and sat down at Mancusso's table. "Did you get it all?" Mancusso queried.

"Loud and clear," Bob Palmer responded, Gomez

nodding in agreement.

"So, what do you think?" Mancusso whispered.

Gomez leaned over the table and after clearing the area said, "I think it's time you told us what the fuck is going on."

Trask read Benchly's report with Benchly sitting in rapt attention in one of the chairs next to his boss's desk. "Send all this over to the company with my recommendation to closely monitor Mancusso and his team of restaurateurs until the day the thing opens for business. This deal smells to high heaven and I'm not going to believe this bullshit cover story until the first steaming Duck Motard comes quacking out of the kitchen."

Chapter 37

"Bobby, if you have a minute. Could you please stop by my office."

Tranh read Leanna's message on his monitor and recalled that it was sometime before she met Blalock that a whole different not near as polite animal lived in the tower office of the Helms Corp. CEO. It was a kinder gentler Leanna Helms that was the buzz of the building. The various executives that had to meet personally with Leanna had reported back that Leanna's long lost identical twin, the missionary, had seized control of the company and that the real Leanna Helms was wearing an iron mask somewhere in a French dungeon.

Tranh popped into Leanna's office about fifteen minutes later with his customary toothy, "What's up, Toots?"

"Bobby, come look at this." Leanna was pointing at something outside her window.

Tranh went over to see what it was. She was pointing to a large bird's nest couched in one of the modern ornamental facades adjoining but just below her expansive picture window.

"There's some kind hawk using this nest," she said. The one in there now is the female. The male has been out hunting. He's been back several times since I began observing this morning."

"They're peregrine falcons, Leanna, one of the former endangered species. Now they have been downgraded to threatened only. The populations are taking hold all over the country. You can tell the peregrine by the stripe that comes off the head and their white throats. Supposedly they are the fastest birds alive and reach speeds of two hundred seventy miles an hour. The use of the pesticide DDT almost wiped them out…had something to do with the shells of their eggs…weakening them I believe. " Everybody in the building knew about the birds taking up residence and the Audubon Society had handed out flyers in the lobby on a couple of mornings. They later put up a display in the coffee shop.

Leanna was too busy with matters of importance. They'd been there for two seasons already and Leanna had never noticed. "How wonderful! What else do you know about these birds?"

"They keep the same mate for life and copulate in flight. The male covers the female with his wings and they plummet thousands of feet…"

"Now that's exciting…maybe I'll try it sometime." Leanna looked over at Tranh whose face was a noticeable red hue. "Did I embarrass you," she asked.

"No, not at all." Tranh was asking himself why he had mentioned that last part. He tried to change the subject. "Leanna was there something else you wanted to discuss besides the falcons?"

"Actually, yes," she said. "I wanted to share some recent developments with you of a positive nature."

"Such as?"

"Such as, guess who has a date with whom next Saturday night?"

Tranh feigned surprise since he'd been talking to Duane McCall all week, who in turn was talking to Blalock on a daily basis.

"Don King?"

"No."

259

"You bailed out Michael Milken?"

"Stop it."

"OK, I got it." Tranh was on a roll. "OJ?"

"Come on Bobby, you're not trying."

"Tony Robbins?"

"Oh God! Not that idiot. You keep this up and I'm going to get sick," she laughed.

Tranh caressed his chin and with his most inscrutable Asian concentration looking up at the ceiling. "Hmmmm, it's coming to me now…yes, I think I'm getting it…got it. Nahhhh couldn't be. It'd never be THAT guy."

"Which guy?" Leanna played along.

"Couldn't be," Tranh said. "It wouldn't be the bozo in Atlanta, the guy you said you hated, would it?"

Leanna laughed again. Tranh had heard more laughter out of his boss in the preceding fifteen minutes that he had heard in…come to think of it he could not ever remember Leanna laughing. There had always been a profound sadness about her that sublimed her power and purpose that caused fear and loathing from everyone who knew her. Leanna had a soft beautiful laugh not too loud and it reminded him of the tinkling of a Tiffany chandelier when somebody left the French doors open on a balcony.

"That is correct, Robert." She was still smiling. She lowered her head and looked up at Tranh with her flowing dark hair silhouetting her angelic face. The dark blue of her eyes looked straight through him.

"And I'm planning an evening he won't soon forget."

Being the only passenger on the Falcon, Blalock spent most of the trip on the jumpseat bullshitting with the Helms Corp. crew, two of over a hundred pilots and a fleet of sixteen jets that chauffeured the Helms executives and the subsidiary companies' VIPs all over the world.

Approach control vectored the Falcon onto a right base entry and handed them off to tower at the outer marker. Off to the north the twin towers of the World Trade Center were visible and the concrete canyons of Manhattan. Spring had sprung and the countryside was alive with the emerald of new life. People think that agriculture is something that happens in Kansas, but Blalock always marveled that right here near Teterboro, New Jersey, a helicopter hop from the power center of the universe, just a few miles outside the downwind, the furrowed patterns of farmers' fields dominated the gently rolling land. Blalock buckled his seat belt and put his head to the window. Damn, I miss this, he thought. He felt an odd sensation in his chest. He put his hand over his heart. Was it pounding a little more than it should? He was thinking of the steel princess.

The limo driver shut the door on the classic 1954 Silver Phantom and walked back to his driver's station. The passenger door thumped closed with safe like precision. Calley and his copilot were still waving as they drove off.

"Let's stop at the closest VFW so I can get a drink will ya? Need to get my nerve up…big speech at the Garden…Shriners convention tonight."

The driver glanced in his rear view mirror at his passenger then back at the road. Then with a thick cockney accent chuckled, "Haw! Bloody good one, Cap'n Blalock, sir. But Ms. Helms is already warned us 'bout your keen sense of humor."

And so Mathew Blalock motored into Manhattan on a magnificent spring afternoon. You don't drive anywhere in a Rolls, you motor. "What's your name, driver?"

"Preston, Capn' Blalock."

"Preston, is this a Rolls or a Bentley?"

"It's a Silver Phantom, sir, a Rolls Royce most assuredly."

"Preston do you know the difference between a Bentley and a typical female flight attendant?"

"No sir, don't believe I do."

"The difference is that not everybody's been in a Bentley."

"Oh, haw, haw…another good one, Cap'n Blalock."

They drove on into town with Blalock giving a running commentary on how Guiliani was going to clean up New York once and for all, the Mets, the Jets, and a number of other subjects. The sound of the tires lapping against the pavement is all you could hear as they purred across the George Washington Bridge. Not much shipping traffic in the harbor, Matt thought, but the stevedores had brought it all on themselves. They got their twenty-five dollars an hour for unloading ships, but just as their union president had promised, there were no more ships. Just about everything on the East Coast now went through Savannah, Norfolk, and Jacksonville.

Preston wasn't paying much attention to what Matt was saying and the only non-professional thought that was going through his mind was that maybe, just maybe, this chap might be up to the job of taming the wild heart of Leanna Helms. Yes, Preston old lad, he thought to himself, tonight is going to be a most interesting evening.

Chapter 38

Mr. Good, Col. Bremen, Duane and JB McCall were having the weekly staff meeting two days early due to the new intelligence funneled to the working group that Good and Bremen had assembled for the project. Bremen started reading his notes. "According to General McVey, after the last cabinet meeting he was invited back to speak privately with the president and vice president. According to McVey, they are becoming suspicious of the continued objections by two members of the cabinet on even the most elementary precautions against hostile intent by the EBEs. Mr. Feldman, according to his sources, says that the number of facilitators could be as high as seven percent of the U.S. population and it is perfectly possible that they have reached into the cabinet and beyond. That's the bad news. The good news is that we have recently learned that the facilitators can be identified using ultra violet light. Their skin glows slightly, for reasons only suspect to us at this time. We told McVey to expose the cabinet to ultra violet radiation and see if anybody glows in the dark." Bremen paused to notice half smiles on two faces. Levity was gradually giving way to grim realization of the stakes and risks in the mission.

McCall sr. was experiencing a dawning understanding that once the Stork was launched, he might never see his son again.

"It might be possible, according to McVey, in the situation room, which has ultraviolet capability. More later on that. McVey also reports that the president is siphoning off seventy-five percent of the black budget to commence building X-35s and is distributing the plans to specified aerospace manufacturers in two other countries."

"Is it possible we won't have to fly the Stork, Colonel Bremen?"

Bremen closed his folder in front of him and looked at McCall. "Unfortunately, no, Mr. McCall. We've rechecked our data and everything we've got is pointing toward an attack during the peak of the solar max between March and May of 2000. We'll be getting blasted with at least six coronal mass ejections per day. NORAD and Space Command will be blinded as each CME washes through our satellite warning systems. Each one of the CMEs contains five billion tons of solar matter crashing into the atmosphere, and Mr. McCall, this is only a year from now. We feel that there's no way we can build enough X-35s and train the crews to mount a credible defense. Our only hope is that the Stork mission will buy us the time we need."

McCall exhaled a big breath of air and folded his hands in front of him on the conference table.

Mr. Good pulled out his notes and put on his reading glasses. "Thank you Lowell. Now, here are the latest data concerning hardware and launch preparations. The Group's representative in French intelligence has assured us that the arrival of the Tupelov technicians in Ghana has been carefully prepared by the four facility contacts. And the launch preparation and actual mission departure should be underway well before detection of our actual intentions will result in a diplomatic shut down of our effort. Next item, payload. Colonel Bremen?"

Bremen opened another one of his folders that was marked with a red diagonal slash on its cover and started reading. "The Russian have reported that the weapons magazine has been preloaded, sealed, and installed in the ship. Console twelve and all weapons delivery systems have been checked out and are mission ready. And here's a wrinkle." Bremen looked over his half glasses making eye contact with the others at the table. "We have continuously over estimated the Russian threat for decades, mainly to keep defense spending up, but we had a genuine surprise last week. The Russians began discussing the Stork's defensive systems with our group at Tupelov."

"Defensive systems? I didn't think the Russians had any defensive systems on their shuttles. Defense from what?" Duane asked.

Colonel Bremen looked across the table at Duane. "That's was our impression until last week. It appears that the Stork is equipped with a Nudelmann recoilless gun with a sixty round magazine. Very ingenious, very crude, very Russian. Also it is extremely lethal out to two thousand yards. Its main limitation being the sighting system. After two thousand yards, the circular error probability increases significantly, due to the requirement to aim the entire spacecraft like a jet fighter using an internal cannon. Tupelov says they took it off the Uragan, a space interceptor they were working on to shoot down our own shuttles. As to the second part of your question, Mr. McCall, one only has to remember the Soviet mindset. They have fiercely defended their borders and truck no interference from anyone, be they the Wehrmacht or people from another world. Our Russian sources inform us that they have fired literally thousands of surface to air weapons at trespassing alien spacecraft and have hotly pursued them with fighters at every opportunity. Oddly, they had no success shooting any of them down, and never obtained samples of ETE technology with which to make the breakthroughs that we were able to achieve. As you know, the microcircuit, lasers, fiber optics, and Kevlar are but a few of the examples of their technology we have been able to exploit. And, I would add that for some reason, the EBEs only seem to crash or get themselves shot down on our turf. This little fact has been somewhat troubling to some of us in the intelligence community. In my opinion, they wanted us to win the Cold War and let us get our hands on their technology. But getting back to your original question, the Soviets had many encounters with ETE ships in their space program, and the recoilless gun was the logical extension of their philosophy to resist interference wherever it was encountered."

"It sounds like natives with spears going up against a modern army. What chance would we really have?" J.B. McCall asked.

Colonel Bremen picked up the ball. "That question, of course, cuts to the core issue of the entire mission. Members of the Group who have extensive knowledge of the EBEs strongly believe that they have never encountered anyone like us. The EBEs believe that our race's principle occupation is violence, warfare, and the destruction of the environment. We are an unpredictable and savage species, and that unpredictability, gentlemen, is our ace in the hole. The natives have won before, Mr. McCall, as Ketchner learned at Isandlwana and Custer at the Little Big Horn."

John Good's cold emotionless gaze levelled at Duane. "What is the crew status?"

Duane's arms were folded over his chest as he

spoke, unsuccessfully trying to hide his dislike for Good. "Mathew Blalock, our last choice, has agreed to command the mission, although he has not yet been briefed on the actual target and still thinks it's an oil hunting expedition. Colonel Kolya Dimitri Yakov will be the pilot and second in command…who also hasn't been briefed yet. Yakov trained on the original Russian shuttle program and will be the training officer for me, Blalock, and another Russian mission specialist. We'll be bringing Blalock and the Russians here to the GIIQ for the two day mission briefing as soon as we can get Russians' orders cut."

"What about the psychological status of Commander Blalock?" Good inquired. Not that it mattered. Good had already determined that Blalock would be going regardless and had made some rather unpleasant arrangements should they become necessary. The trouble with amateurs, he surmised, looking down the table at the McCalls, was that they were universally embued with a touchy feely sentimental view of the world. When it became time to cut the balls off your opposition, they would always come up short. Bremen understood, but the McCalls? Time would tell on what he might have to do.

Duane answered Good's question. "As far as Commander Blalock's mental status is concerned, as we speak, he's getting his shit together."

"Thank you for that colorful description," Good replied in his routine cold-blooded, sarcastic monotone. "See that he is ready when the time comes. If there is no further business, this meeting is adjourned." Good stood up, closed his briefcase, and departed the conference room with no further comment. The McCalls and Bremen were left at the table.

"What a fucking asshole," Duane said.

Bremen exhaled and raised his eyebrows, then looked over his shoulder to be sure Good was gone. "Do you remember your E.J. King, Mr. McCall?"

"Ah yes, of course," J.B. McCall nodded. Bremen half smiled, gathered his notes and followed Good down the hall.

Alone with his Dad in the conference room, Duane asked, "What the hell was he talking about?"

J.B. steepled his big hands leaned back in his chair and looked at his son. "After the attack on December 7th, the Pacific fleet was smoldering at the bottom of Pearl Harbor. Our technology was ten years behind the Japs, and the Army was training in Louisiana with wooden rifles. They brought an ass kicking admiral out of retirement named E. J. King and made him Chief of Naval Operations. King said, "When they get in trouble, they send for the son's of bitches.""

Chapter 39

About eleven in the morning on the Friday before Matt Blalock was supposed to arrive in the Big Apple, Bobby Tranh got an e-mail from Leanna. "Bobby, come look at something." Going in to see Leanna these days was turning into almost a pleasure since the bozo in Atlanta had told her where to shove it. Nothing lasts forever, especially men, with Leanna Helms, Tranh thought. But what the hey, enjoy it as long as it lasts. Tranh bounded into Leanna's office with his usual "What's up, Toots?"

"I'll tell you what's up Bobby. How about a five thousand dollar Badgley Mischka from Bergdorf's?" The dress was in a clear plastic bag hanging from the engraved cedar coat rack she had moved out of the corner to over in front of the massive picture window.

When Leanna held it up to the light, Tranh's mouth gaped. You could almost see through the black silken diaphanous material. Almost backless with thin criss crossing spaghetti straps holding up the not too plunging neckline, Tranh had to ask. "Leanna, you can almost see through it. What are you going to wear underneath?"

"Why, nothing, of course." She smiled. "You think he'll like it?"

Tranh's heart leaped into his throat again. "Yes," he coughed.

Leanna spent Saturday morning at Frederick Fekkai having her hair and nails done. In the adjoining salons were Ivana Trump and several other powerful New York women that she knew as nodding acquaintances. Leanna had years before rejected the snobbery and idle waste of New York society though it was generally agreed that she would have been the toast of the town had she wanted to play the game. She only did the embassy and international scene to show the flag for the far-flung Helms empire.

Matt should be checking into the Four Seasons about now, she thought, and indeed he was. Preston at the moment was handing Matt the handwritten note from Leanna with the evening's festivities laid out like a military operation.

"I'll be driving you and Ms. Leanna tonight Cap'n Blalock. I'll pick you up at six-thirty. 'Ere's me cell phone number…just ring me up if you need anything."

"Preston, I thought everybody took cabs in NuevoYork."

"When you hit a couple of bloody billion, you don't take cabs no more."

"Yeah right. I see your point."

7:00 PM   Meet me for cocktails at the Boathouse in Central Park. 9:00   PM   Dinner at Daniel. 11:00 PM   Dancing at the Rainbow Room until? Nightcap at Sartino's

Blalock looked over the itinerary. Man, I'm glad she's buying on this one. The Boathouse was a fabulous restaurant with full jazz quartet on the lake in Central Park. The outdoor tables faced south down the park with a view that would knock your socks off. A bottle of beer in this place was eight-fifty. No way two people could get out of there for less than two bucks. And Daniel? Jesus, this was the hottest restaurant on the East Coast, and dinner for two in this joint could hit five hundred bucks in a New York minute. Blalock had never been to the Rainbow Room, on top of the

Rockefeller Center and reputed to have a terrific view of Manhattan, or Sartino's, but knew they were fan-fucking-tastic places to go or Leanna would have had nothing to do with them. "City girls with independent means...we rode in limousines..." he hummed to himself. Yep, Franky boy, you Mafioso puke, you had it right...1999 was going to be a very good year. Things had finally turned the corner. "Nothing but blue sky smiling at me..." he mused to himself as he crapped out on the king sized bed, his hands folded behind his head. Now, for a little practice nap prior to the festivities. His buddies back in Atlanta were never going to believe the story when he got home.

Preston dropped Matt off at the Boathouse at six forty-five. Preston yanked the door open and Matt stepped out. "Cap'n Blalock, I've got a news flash for you," he whispered. Preston held his hand up to his mouth even though there wasn't anybody within fifty feet.

"The staff say that she is really looking forward to seeing you tonight."

"I feel the same way." This seemed to please the chauffeur and Preston jumped back in the big Rolls, thumped the safe like door closed, and motored silently over to the taxi and limo stand.

The Boathouse was alive with the happy murmuring of the trendy and rich. There were guys in there that paid more for their shoes than Blalock paid for his whole wardrobe. The jazz quartet was just about right, not too loud but loud enough to be enjoyed. They were playing "Take Five," by Pete Desmond. There were about forty white linen covered tables, most clustered within twenty feet of the water's edge. Leanna made the reservation in Matt's name and the maitre d' ushered him quickly to a table overlooking the lake with a down park view. Matt took a chair to one side so that he could watch for Leanna and also enjoy the scenery. He ordered a Tanqueray and tonic and leaned back. Decks of tangerine-colored altostratus drifted behind the man-made mountains of steel and glass that surrounded Central Park. Soon the tangerine would melt into magenta and then a deep purple as the sun finished his work for the day. Somewhere up there the stars were waiting. The stars…yes, he was finally going to get a really good look from a ship on orbit. How good can something get? The family at the next table was dressed for church even down to the toy blazers and ties on the small boys who were happily tittering with one another about their Pokemon collection. A little heartbreaker of about five with a white taffeta dress and a red ribbon in her hair was throwing big gobs of French bread into the lake where the huge, well fed, mossy-backed turtles paddled slowly from one snack to the next. Blalock was wearing his charcoal brown goatskin Air Force flight jacket over a navy cashmere turtleneck and dark gray flannel slacks. His recently shined cordovan Rockports were no match for the Church, saddle-black lace ups the guy at the next table was wearing. Man, there were some people in this town who had some dough. The table by the entrance was getting a little rowdy. Some Wall Street guys were celebrating their stock picking genius in the greatest bull market in history. Masters of the universe…better watch those off ramps in the Bronx, Blalock thought.

The fourth serving of oysters on the half shell was being carried out to their table when a sort of hush fell over the big family right behind Blalock. There were three couples plus all their kids, but the adults were all looking toward the vine covered restaurant entrance. Blalock followed their line of vision until he zeroed in on the object of their interest. It was probably well that at that moment he had not been hooked up to the EKG, since any competent cardiologist would have diagnosed a heart attack and raced him to the nearest hospital.

It was Leanna. The almost transparent black evening gown lightly outlined her body. She radiated feline erotic energy that took your breath away. Her eyes were so violet that you could tell their color from a hundred feet off. She looked briefly around the patio until she noticed Matt waving. The guy with the five hundred dollar shoes at the next table tilted his chair back whispered behind his wife's back,"Hey man, you're one lucky dude."

Leanna smiled and started toward their table, Blalock couldn't believe the feminine grace and carriage of this woman. Obviously, she had studied the ballet at some point. She seemed to levitate as she walked and she seemed to have an inspiring calm intent and magnificent efficiency that wasted no motion. Leanna was about abeam the big table, which contained the masters of the universe when her left heel came down on an inverted spoon dropped just as she passed by one of the stock brokers. There was no way she could have seen it in time. Her ankle collapsed to the left and the two-inch spike broke off simultaneously. Leanna fell to the concrete and slate-tiled deck and struck her head on the edge of the marble table at which the brokers were seated. The marble table catapulted up on the far end sending two full orders of oysters into the air, which then arced over and fell onto Leanna's chest and chestnut curls. The rest of the food on the table, some shrimp, and cocktail sauce got in on the act by sliding down and splattering onto the lower part of her dress and legs. It was something right out of a Three Stooges episode.

There was a momentary urge to burst out laughing, but this vaporized in a microsecond when Blalock noticed that Leanna did not move after the fall. Matt bolted from his seat like a hurdler and was at her side in seconds. One of the Wall Street guys was saying, "Grab her, somebody call a cab...we gotta get her to the hospital." The other two masters started to reach for her.

"Leave her alone," Blalock ordered.

"Yeah, but we gotta get her…"

"Touch her and I'll kill you," Blalock shouted. One idiot attempted to push Blalock aside and reached for Leanna's arm. Blalock caught him with an upper cut to the jaw, and the guy folded up like a crash test dummy. The other two guys backed slowly away as Blalock checked Leanna's pulse and respiration then jumped into one of the chairs and shouted, "Is there a doctor in the house?" Three men and a woman were throwing down their napkins and making their way through the tables within ten seconds. The old stories about the New Yorkers standing by while little old ladies were being mugged are now nothing more than urban legends. Maybe true at one time, but nowadays, New Yorkers rally like cavalry to people in trouble. So much for the bullshit stereotypes. The four people got to Matt and wanted to know what happened. He told them. She fell, hit her head on the marble table edge and now she's breathing with a strong pulse, but not moving.

The four doctors kneeled over Leanna and the fifteen-second conversation went something like this:

First guy says, "I'm Dr. Healy, cardiologist."

Second guy says, "Dr. Goldstein, internal medicine."

The woman says: "I'm Dr. Sullivan Mt. Sinai ER."

First guy says, "Excellent. Dr. Sullivan you're in charge."

Sullivan says, "I'll take care of her, you people check the guy."

Blalock stepped out of the way and got Preston on the cell phone. "Preston, standby. Leanna has had an accident."

Dr. Sullivan made a cursory examination and determined that heart and respiration were normal, pupils normal. "Any known medical conditions?" Dr. Sullivan looked up at Blalock. Matt pushed the cell phone into her hand, "Talk to this guy; he's known her for years." Dr. Sullivan ascertained from Preston that Leanna was about as perfect a physical specimen as there was in her gender, with no known defects or medical history.

Up close at the curb only half a block away, red and blue strobes were blazing away but the sirens were winding down as the paramedics jogged toward the restaurant with their equipment and a stretcher.

Dr. Sullivan said, "I'll ride to the hospital with her."

"I'm going with you." Matt piled into the back of the ambulance and the EMTs slammed the doors.

Dr. Sullivan rechecked Leanna's pulse as the EMTs made their examination and began calling ahead the vitals to the ER physician. She then looked over at Blalock's drawn and worried face. "It's well that you didn't move her...if there's a problem with her neck, she could have been paralyzed for life."

"Yes, I know," Blalock said.

One of the EMTs held Matt's right hand for a second. "Better let me wrap those cuts on your knuckles," he said.

"Here let me do that," Dr. Sullivan interrupted. The EMT handed her the scissors and the bandages. Sullivan wrapped Matt's hand gently then held it. "I think she'll be just fine."

Blalock noticed his eyes suddenly begin to burn...then start getting a little watery. "Darned New York smog…always makes my eyes water."

Dr. Sullivan smiled, "Yes, it's amazing how that happens, isn't it?"

The ER doc wanted Leanna admitted for the night for observation and maybe some tests. "We'll need authorization for some of these tests. Are you her husband?"

"No," Blalock said.

"Well, then how about her parents?"

"Both dead."

"Next of kin? Who do we notify in case of emergency?"

By this point Blalock was dialing his cell phone. "Preston, get your ass over to Mt. Sinai if you aren't here already."

"I'm five minutes out," Preston responded instantly.

"Good, who's Leanna's next of kin?"

"Capn' Blalock, as far as I know she don't ave' any."

"No brothers, sisters, aunts, uncles? How about cousins?"

"None. She's the end of the line of the Helms clan. Mr. Tranh is probably the closest thing she got to kin."

"Get Tranh on the phone and tell him what's

happened. Tell him to call me at 678-727-7272." Blalock folded up his phone and stuffed it back into his jacket.

The ER doc was still standing there with his clipboard. "So what's the verdict?"

"Doctor uhhhh," Blalock looked down at his nametag then made a missile lock eye contact with the physician. "Dr. Zimmer, I am authorizing you to perform any procedures or tests which in your professional opinion need to be accomplished."

"All-Right!" Zimmer said, with obvious approval, handing him the clipboard pointing where to sign. "Leave us a contact number and we'll give you a call when she regains consciousness."

"I'm not leaving," Matt said. Dr. Zimmer looked down at the clipboard. "Mr. Blalock, the waiting room isn't very comfortable here. Why don't you go home and get some rest, we'll call you, don't worry."

"I won't be in the waiting room…bring me an air mattress, I'm staying with her."

Zimmer coughed. "Mr. Blalock, we don't have any air mattresses….we're not really supposed to allow…"

"Don't argue with me doctor. She has no family. I'm staying."

The look in the man's face had a cold chisel brittleness to it that convinced Dr. Zimmer that the discussion was over. "Well, you're going to have to sleep on the floor," Zimmer said weakly.

The sun creeped up over the horizon and tendril shafts of light, amber at first, then turning the white of morning began filling every space of Leanna's room. There was the sound of crispy fresh sheets rustling with the creak of a mattress spring. Blalock was curled up on the linoleum under the window with his flight jacket rolled up under his head for a pillow. The sound of the rustling cotton sheets brought him out of his half sleep like a bomb blast. Leanna was stirring.

Standing beside her bed, he searched furiously for the nurse call. "May I help you?" came the metallic voice out of the speaker by the bed.

"Nurse, get the doc, she's coming around."

"We're on our way."

Leanna stretched and yawned as if coming out of an ordinary night's sleep. Matt sat on the side of the bed looking into her face, stroking her hair when she opened her eyes. Their eyes met and she slowly raised herself up in the bed and gently placed her arms around Blalock's neck pressing her cheek to his. "I fell down," she whimpered like a child.

"That's right baby, you fell and bumped your head, but now you're just fine," he whispered tenderly as he continued stroking her hair.

"What happened?" Her voice was so soft he could barely understand her.

"You were mugged by two dozen pissed off oysters...meanest bastards I ever saw."

She tried a weak little laugh, but then touched her forehead. "Ohh, I have a headache," she whispered.

Dr. Zimmer, needing a shave and now at the end of his twelve-hour shift in the ER, came rolling in with the duty nurse. "I see why you wanted to stay, Mr. Blalock. Looks like a love story to me...well, let's have a look at the pretty lady. Mr. Blalock will you *now* go to the waiting room...looks like she'll be checking out shortly."

"I'll be right out here baby, if you need me," Matt said haltingly, pointing in the general direction of the door.

Leanna had sustained the mildest of concussions and was going to have zero repercussions from the event except for a temporary little bump on her head. And even then it was unnoticeable unless you touched it through her thick dark hair.

Tranh and Preston were waiting in the lobby when Leanna was rolled out in her wheelchair. Blalock noticed the shock on Tranh's face.

"Don't sweat it, this is standard procedure for some damn reason."

Tranh noticeably relaxed. "Leanna, you need me for anything?" He asked.

"No, Bobby you were so kind to come down here on a Sunday morning. Go home."

"Will do, Toots, looks like you're in good hands." Tranh shook hands with Blalock and Preston then jogged out into the street to catch a cab.

The big Rolls whispered out of the hospital driveway onto the quiet streets of a New York Sunday morning. Matt tapped on the glass then rolled down the chauffeur partition window so he didn't have to use the absurd telephone the Rolls had for communicating with the "help."

"Trump Tower, Preston."

"And lets go home through the park," Leanna added.

"That'll be an extra ten quid," Preston replied dryly, glancing in the mirror. Preston couldn't believe what just came out of his mouth...Bloody hell, that was something Capn' Blalock would have said.

Leanna looked at Matt and started laughing silently, holding her hand up covering her mouth. Leanna leaned forward in her seat and hit the down switch on the chauffeur partition window, rolling it all the way down leaving it there. Then in mock anger and with a perfect cockney imitation she said, "Ten quid! That's bleedin' highway robbery! I'll pay you a fiver and not a penny more!" Blalock had his arms folded, laughing to himself. Leanna leaned back and took Matt's arm snuggling up next to him. He looked over and they made eye contact, then matter of factly she whispered still in perfect cockney, "Cheeky bugger...you ear' that? Ee' tried to rob us!"

The big Rolls motored through the park as the sun began his daily grind through the sky. Life renewing radiation was pouring down bringing energy to all the living things on earth...all the plants and trees and all God's critters big and small.

The solar max was beginning its eleven-year cycle and as long as the master species on the planet stayed on the ground they would be alright. As long as the numerous precautions that were in place did what they were supposed to do every thing would be just peachy. But unfortunately, someone had another agenda that would glide in behind the coronal mass ejections. It would attack silently like the wings of an owl and would destroy the planetary ozone layer in seconds allowing an unfiltered bombardment of lethal ultraviolet radiation to kill the master species and his women and children, his sheep and oxen, and all that breathed in his land. Their god said it would be so.

Leanna and Matt rode in silence for the next few minutes until Leanna broke the silence. She turned to Matt and said quietly, "The nurse said you slept in my room all night."

"Actually, well, uhhh...the Four Seasons is such a dump...you didn't really expect me to go back there when I had a perfectly good floor to sleep on did you?"

"Uh Huh. The nurse also said you stayed because you didn't want me to be alone."

"Oh Jesus," Blalock muttered.

"She also said that you punched somebody in the nose at the Boathouse who tried to move me which might have paralyzed me for life."

Blalock let out a big breath of air and looked out the side window, "Ya know, sometimes nurses talk too damn much...know what mean?"

Leanna wore Matt's flight jacket. She hugged the well-worn leather to her body and put her nose to the collar. She inhaled deeply the man scent of the jacket. She smelled his body oils and a musky compound of perspiration, turbine oil and jet fuel. She felt an arousing sensation of invincibility and a wonderfully warm feeling of safety.

She tugged on Matt's arm then kissed him on the cheek. "Yes, my hero, I believe I'm beginning to know exactly what you mean," she smiled.

The bells of St. Patrick's were ringing faintly in the distance as a cool breeze wafted through the rolled down windows of the big Rolls. God was in his house and Matt and Leanna motored on toward the Trump Tower. Neither gave a wit about God on that Sunday morning in the spring of 1999. But in twelve short months a lot of people who hadn't prayed in decades would be on their hands and knees praying for all the help the Big Man would cough up, along with a good many others who knew what was happening.

Of course, this time, God was not on our side, or so we were told.

Capt. Bob Calley and First Officer Lenny Santo had the Falcon all vacuumed, Plexiglas polished and waiting when Preston pulled up on the departure ramp at the Million Air terminal. Most of the jets based at Teterboro were all coming home to roost on a Sunday evening, but with any luck, Bob and Lenny would be home by ten PM. Preston grabbed Blalock's one overnight bag and took it over the base of the air stair of the jet where Lenny Santo picked it up and put it in the cabin. Matt turned to Preston, "Well, until the next routine, uneventful night in New York." They shook hands warmly.

"I'm bloody well glad you was around last night."

"Hey, no big deal."

"Oh, almost forgot," Preston reached inside the breast pocket of his black uniform

and produced a small wax-sealed envelope with a twenty-four carat gold engraved return address. "Ms. Helms asked me to give this to you." Blalock stuck it in the side pocket of his flight jacket. "I'll read it later," he said.

Blalock didn't sit on the jumpseat on the way home. He was tired and stiff from the night on the hospital floor and leaned his passenger seat as far back as it would go and tried to sleep. He awoke when Calley pulled the throttles back to begin the descent. Matt could see Rome, Georgia below with Lake Lanier up ahead, named after the poet and Confederate soldier. The Falcon began a long throttles idle descent into Peachtree Dekalb airport and Matt pulled out Leanna's envelope and broke the wax seal. He wouldn't have a chance to see her again until after the training in Russia. The scent of Obsession began to lightly permeate the cabin as Matt unfolded the heavy parchment bond and began reading.

Chapter 40

Yakov was staying with relatives in Pripyat when his orders arrived by courier. He was being temporarily assigned to the Gagarin Cosmonaut Training Center near Moscow. There, he would be working with two rich American playboy types who had bought the cosmonaut course. Cash-strapped Russia was selling everything it had. From flights to edge of space in a MiG-25 at eighty-five hundred dollars US for a forty-five minute hop, to astronaut training sold to piecemeal to western high rollers. A zero G flight on the TU-144 was forty-five hundred American dollars. Centrifuge training was twenty-five hundred. The basic cosmonaut course including orbital mechanics, astrophysics, and space physiology was eighty-five thousand US and included room and board. They had taken a one-year program and crammed it into ninety days, which of course was no problem, since the graduates would never be tested, let alone fly in space and need an actual command of the knowledge. Yakov would be training his own crew for the shuttle mission and it was to appear that the Americans were just two more rich capitalist customers. After the Gagarin Center, Yakov and the two Americans were going to the Tupelov factory for another condensed course on shuttle systems. No shuttle simulator had ever been built for crew training, but he figured that the higher ups had that under control and that was a problem that would be tackled when the time came. After systems school at Tupelov, he and the two Americans were going to America to a classified location for the actual mission briefing. General Kobelyev authorized Yakov one junior officer as an aid for the American phase of the mission or for the entire operation if it was deemed necessary. Kobelyev wrote on the bottom of the document in long hand. "Suggest Grosovitch. There's a colonel in Air Traffic Command who's going to kick his ass if I ever get around to processing the arrest order."

Yakov called General Kobelyev by phone thanking him for looking out for Grosovitch and asking that he be assigned to Yakov immediately and indefinitely. Kobelyev suggested that Grosovitch's military specialization ID code be changed from 0008 (interceptor pilot) to 1677, (special agent for state security), then be placed on classified mission status. This would make him not only immune from prosecution, but also virtually impossible to locate. Yakov further requested that Grosovitch be trained as a back up mission specialist since he was going to be there anyway. Everything was approved and the Americans were going to be arriving by United Air Lines in Moscow in four days where Yakov was to meet their flight and go through all the motions of treating them like any of the other students in the commercial side of the training center.

Working with the fucking Americans, he thought. Bad enough that the old Soviet Union was being raped little by little as the imperialists got their tentacles into our oil, lumber, and mining. But, I have to work with these assholes as well. Rethinking the matter, however, Yakov remembered that what the hell, there had been no options, either volunteer or be ordered was the deal from Kobelyev. God, I hated the old system, he thought, but I never figured it would come down to this.

The Gagarin Center limo pulled up in front of the exit doors from immigration at the Moscow International Airport. The enlisted driver popped out and ran around to open the door for Yakov and Grosovich. It was a cool morning and the smell of jet exhaust could be smelled when the wind was right. Yakov turned to Grosovich and poked him in the chest with his finger. "Now, listen Grosovitch, we're going to be working with these Americans for many months to come, so I don't want you shooting your mouth off like you did at KGB headquarters. I don't like these bastards any more than you do, but it is in everyone's interests to establish an excellent professional working relationship. No doubt these men are highly trained astronaut-scientists who will be all business from the beginning. Don't forget that the western technology is what in the end finally defeated us...and you can bet that the Americans will be sending the high priests of their technology for this mission. We will be working with the elite of the American rocket engineers and test pilots."

"I'll do my duty, Colonel Yakov," Grosovitch replied without a great deal of enthusiasm.

"See that you do. These are serious men and we are embarked upon a serious mission. The motherland demands our best effort...are we clear on this?"

"Yes sir, crystal clear."

Even in late spring, Moscow had chilly blasts of wind roaring relentlessly into town from the northwest. The big swinging doors from the immigration building swung open and a steady stream of mightily relieved passengers began pouring out after the harrowing experience of Russian customs and immigration. Grosovitch held up a small neatly printed sign as the people swelled out of the building into awaiting busses and taxis. A tall slender guy wearing Ray-Bans, a leather flight jacket, and faded blue jeans walked up lugging a bulging, banged up A-3 bag, and announced, "I'm Blalock."

"Welcome to Russia, Commander Blalock. I am Lieutenant Alexander Anatoly Grosovitch and this is Colonel Kolya Dimitri Yakov."

Yakov clicked his heels, made a slight bow and extended his hand.

Blalock shook firmly. "Glad to meet you gents. It looks like I'm finally getting some respect, and it's about damn time I might add."

"What did he mean by that?" Grosovitch shot to Yakov in Russian.

"I have no idea…perhaps paranoia left over from the Cold War."

"Duane should be out any minute…yeah here he comes."

Duane rolled up with his short sleeve Jimmy Buffet yellow flowered party shirt unbuttoned down the front and flapping in the breeze with only a white T-shirt underneath. He was wearing his black Outer Rim hiking shorts and of course his signature red-rubber flip flops. He had his carry on satchel on his lap, and when he rolled to a stop at the long, slinky limo there was a look of total shock on the two Russians' faces. Yakov and Grosovitch were speechless.

Blalock leaned down, "Oh, Duane, I don't think you are exactly what they expected."

"Let the games begin," Duane whispered out of the side of his mouth.

A porter brought out the rest of the baggage about then and Blalock broke the silence. "Comrades Yakov and Grosovitch may I present comrade mission specialist Duane McCall."

"You may address me as planetary agent Klaatu," Duane replied in total deadpan.

"My God he's CIA," Grosovitch sputtered, still in Russian.

"This is worse than I thought," said Yakov. "I will contact General Kobelyev when we reach the center and inform him of the American duplicity. He will give us instructions on what to do. The Americans are obviously attempting to create an international incident by sabotaging this mission. Just shake hands, get into the car and let's go."

The two Russians walked over to the front of the limo and let themselves into the front seat as the driver assisted Duane into the rear with Matt.

"My, my, what do you supposed they're talking about, Mathew," Duane said quietly.

"Perhaps something about regretting the day they were born?" Matt said.

"Ah yes, at least that, I would surmise."

"And look at the hour. Why we have the rest of the day to become better acquainted with our hosts…"

"And a fun-filled day it will be," Duane finished Matt's sentence.

The limo driver collapsed Duane's chair and stuffed it in the trunk with the rest of the luggage. Yakov looked at his watch and started improvising. "We're not due at the center until fifteen hundred and I see that your itinerary provides for a brief tour of the city…I suppose, however, that after such a long trip you are ready to get some well deserved…"

"Au contraire," Blalock held one finger in the air for emphasis. Special planetary agent Klaatu and I would love to see a few of the sights."

"How far is Lenin's tomb?" Agent Klaatu asked.

"It's only about thirty minutes from here. Would you like to see it?"

"Not actually, but I would like to piss on it."

Another flurry of Russian. "Colonel Yakov, why don't you let me punch this asshole in the mouth now and save us from having to do it later."

"What was that Lt. Grosovitch?" Blalock queried.

Yakov forced a smile, "What the lieutenant said was that on a nice day like this there would be long lines waiting to view comrade Lenin and that it would be inconvenient. Perhaps another day."

"Yes, another day when I'll shove you and your fucking wheel chair down the three hundred flights of stairs at the tomb so we could see how fast it would go."

Blalock looked over to Yakov for another translation. "My aide was merely expressing his interest in seeing that agent Klaatu would be suitably entertained at our next earliest opportunity."

The afternoon wore on. Damn, these guys were tough nuts to crack, Duane was thinking. We're dishing out the shit by the bucket and they're being nice as can be. "How about Red Square, Colonel Yakov? I've always wanted to visit Red Square...the northwest corner to be exact."

"That should be no problem Commander Blalock...it is right on our way to the center."

The big Zlin limo zoomed into the traffic rectangle that surrounded Red Square. The plaza was massive, several miles square easily. The four men got out of the limo, the driver helping Duane get his wheels together. They walked briskly for about fifteen minutes and

Yakov held his hand up for the group to stop. He checked the sun, looked at a couple of buildings and pronounced that they had arrived at the northwest corner of Red Square. "Here we are," he announced. "What is the significance of this location? The view of the Kremlin, I see, is excellent from here. Did you wish to take photos?"

"No, comrade, I just wanted to stand on one of our aiming points."

Grosovitch was approaching the breaking point. "Is he referring to bombing the motherland? Is this pig-faced son of a bitch talking about where…?"

Yakov began to slowly chuckle to himself, then became mock serious. "Gentlemen, excuse me while I speak to my aide in Russian."

"Grosovitch, the Americans are putting us on."

"What?"

"Yes, they've been putting us on all afternoon."

"You mean they're joking?"

"Yes, and the joke has been on us."

"Shit, these pricks have had us going for hours."

"Yes, I'm afraid so."

Yakov looked at his watch and pronounced that it was time to head for the center to begin the in-processing. "Oh, by the way, I need to check your passports to fill out some of my paperwork." Matt and Duane pulled out their passports and handed them to Yakov. Yakov leafed through the passports then stopped suddenly, a scowl crawling across his face. He picked up the cell phone in the limo and made a phone call. General Kobelyev answered. There was a brief exchange, Kobelyev agreed to Yakov's proposal, laughed a couple of times and put his phone down. Yakov turned toward his two passengers and serious as cancer said, "Comrades, your papers are not in order. I'm sure there has only been a clerical mistake, but unfortunately they wish to question you at the Ministry of State Security, I believe you know it by the old name…the KGB."

Cold chills blazed up and down the spines of Blalock and McCall. "What! That's impossible! We're on official business! Everything was cleared by your embassy in Washington…you have no right…"

The black Zlin pulled up in front of KGB headquarters and four armed escorts came pounding down the steps toward the car. The police were helping Duane and Blalock out of the car when one of the guards asked Yakov, "What are we supposed to do with these clowns, Colonel?"

"Put them in the most rat-infested cell you can find then bring them back out to the curb at 0300 and we'll have the limo waiting. Be sure you fire your Kalashnikov a few times during the night to let them know we haven't turned into a bunch of pussies."

One security officer slung his automatic rifle over his right shoulder. "Don't worry, Colonel. Before I was conscripted, I was a drama student at the Moscow School of the Arts. We will be sure your friends have an unforgettable evening in the Lubayanka."

Duane turned to Yakov. "What'd those guys say?" his tone revealing the significantly more contrite planetary agent Klaatu.

"They wanted to know if either of you has ever had an allergic reaction to sodium pentathol."

Blalock and McCall's sphincter slammed shut with a clang. You couldn't have got a greasy cockroach up there with a sledge hammer.

"For God sakes man, we haven't done anything! I

thought you guys didn't do this stuff anymore!" said Blalock, his voice about two octaves higher.

"Old habits die hard," Yakov said sympathetically.

"Yeah, tell him we're both allergic as hell to the stuff," Duane was thinking fast.

The guards grabbed the two Americans by the elbows and started them up the steps. "Better not tell them that unless it's true," Yakov called out. "They still use el telephono."

Blalock and McCall disappeared into the massive tomb of the former KGB headquarters with visions of hand-cranked electric generators and alligator clips attached to their nipples.

As the limo pulled away, Yakov, Grosovitch and the driver were laughing their asses off. Yakov at this point had achieved beatific status in the eyes of his aide and the enlisted driver. Yakov looked over at his admiring proteges. "It doesn't pay to tangle with desperate men with nothing to lose, eh Tovarish?"

The following morning, Blalock and McCall had somehow dragged themselves to the scheduled 0830 breakfast at the Gagarin Center even though they had been up all night listening to the gunfire of firing squads in the courtyard and some poor bastard being tortured somewhere off in the darkness. Both pilots were whipped, needed a shave, but were wearing the sky-blue Russian flight suits that had been laid out for them when they finally got to the center at 0500.

Duane stirred his coffee slowly, having trouble keeping his head up. "The next time I make the suggestion that we fuck with the Russians, just bitch slap me ok?" he said.

"I don't think you have to worry about me making that suggestion," Blalock slurred, the jet lag and lack of sleep finally catching up.

Duane looked up when he noticed the double doors of the cafeteria swing open. "Oh shit, here they come. You do the talking *commander*."

"Great, thanks." Blalock tore a small square of his white paper napkin and folded it into a small flag and attached it to the top of his stirring spoon.

Fresh and cheery, Yakov and Grosovitch changed course to their table when they spotted the two Americans. "Good morning comrades, did you sleep well?"

Matt came to his feet with a tired smile and extended his hand. "Call me Matt, OK? You too, Grosovitch." There was a new round of hand shaking, quite a bit less stiff than the day before.

Duane looked up. "It's just Duane. Skip the Klaatu."

"Sit down guys, lets have something to eat," Matt suggested.

"Excellent idea, all this pissing on Lenin and phony firing squads all night long really builds an appetite doesn't it?" Mused Yakov airily.

McCall shot a look at Blalock. Blalock shot a look at Yakov. Nobody said anything for a couple of minutes. Yakov sipped his coffee in complete nonchalance. He then reached across and took Matt's spoon with the little white flag.

"Does this mean we are declaring a truce or are you surrendering?"

Matt chuckled. "Let's just say that for the moment, we're even."

Yakov took a long look into Blalock's face. Matt met his gaze evenly.

These guys aren't all that bad, Yakov thought.

Chapter 41

Carson Benchly, Yale man, Father, and Leonard Trask's hand picked successor was beginning to doubt his own initial opinions about the Estrella Fugaz Restaurant. Benchly had a bit higher opinion of the nontraditional sources of intelligence, even though most of the time it was very difficult to figure out what they were saying. On several occasions the Remote Technical Viewing teams had been very specific and, for example, had located the Army colonel kidnapped in Beirut. In too many other cases, they could only provide sketchy information about the target that was shadowy and impossible to interpret in enough specificity to be of any use. Trask had requested again and again to find something hard that could be verified with other sources, but the RTV teams kept coming up with teaser information. A case in point was when Benchly tasked the trained paranormals in the RTV department to target the Colombian restaurant gig with the Russian shuttle. The twelve, seven person teams were alarmingly similar in their assessments, especially since they were physically separated in their shielded building. They kept getting Lunar-Apollo mission and nuclear Armageddon scenarios. Neither of which could possibly have anything to do with the Russian ship being converted into a gourmet French restaurant. Now, to make matters even fuzzier, they were getting impressions about something to do with crop circles, the most widely exposed hoax in modern times. The two British farmers had confessed that they had started it all, and in fact went out and made some more circles right under the noses of the BBC news reporters they asked to come out and catch them. The nut cases went wild over the crop circles. One theory advanced was that aliens from outer space were writing complex messages explaining how to build an advanced machine with an unknown purpose. Another theory was that the crop circles were energy field patterns caused by a flying saucer landing. One expert claimed that the grain beaten down in the crop circles had been genetically altered. The crop circles were incredibly elaborate and were being found in Europe, Australia, Canada, Argentina, Russia, the Ukraine and other parts of the world.

And then the so-called simple/bisector crop circles began to appear.

The simple crop circle looked like a big circle cut in a wheat field with a straight line bisecting its center oriented north south. The simple circles were being mentioned by the RTV teams in connection with the Russian shuttle assignment, although nobody in the teams could focus on a meaning. It was just more nebulous information that didn't seem to fit anything. Benchly sent the info on the simple circles over to Central Intelligence to see if they could come up with anything concrete.

Ten days later he got a call from Mike Aberdeen, his contact with the agency. "Carlton, better come over to see what we've got on your request."

"What do you have Mike?"

"No telephone on this one OK?"

So Benchly hopped in his old Taurus and headed over to Langley. An hour and half later, after the usual screening to get in the building, Benchly padded into Aberdeen's office.

"Must be good to put me through this."

"Good, might be a stretch."

"What do you have?"

"Carleton, birds won't fly over your bisector circles."

"Really?"

"All your circles are exactly the same diameter and this north south bisector line through the middle of the circle is oriented to *exactly* true north. And I mean exactly to the tolerances of our equipment to measure. We're talking hundredths of a degree. How would hoaxers do that? The CIA man started pointing all over his wall map with a laser pointer on his key chain. Further, every one of the bisector circles from down here near Sydney, to northern England, to Toronto, to Omaha, one hundred eighty-six to be exact, are all exactly oriented to grid north. Every damned one of them."

"It gets more interesting. Carleton do you fly? Private pilot stuff?"

"No, sure don't."

"OK, let me explain this in simple terms. Back in the eighties, the airspace all over the USA was reclassified into either A, B, C, D, E, or G. Class A was from 18,000 feet up to 60,000 feet. Class B was from the ground up to 10,000 feet. I don't want to bore you with the details, but all the airspace except G is under some kind of surveillance by Air Traffic Control and its big radars. Class G is *uncontrolled* airspace where the radar would not reach, either too far out in the boonies, or no air routes or airports nearby. In other words, G airspace is the chink in our armor of coverage. And there's lots of G airspace all over the country, more out west than in the northeast, but there's little patches of it everywhere, where for some odd reason the radar can't see or doesn't need to. Guess what Benchly, old pal? Every one of your simple bisector circles is on the ground under a parcel of class G airspace. Other countries have similar uncontrolled airspace and the trend on the circle locations is consistent everywhere in the world."

"Oh shit," was all Benchly could say.

"Don't say oh shit just yet," Aberdeen went on. "Your simple bisectors are also located at the closest point of a straight line connecting the class G airspace above the crop circle to the metropolitan center of the one hundred eighty-six largest cities on the planet. The two exceptions are where the city is on a coast line or located at these three spots." Aberdeen squeezed something on his key chain and a red dot began jiggling on the enormous wall map in the room. Know where this spot is old chap?" The red dot was jigging around a small town in western Colorado smack in the heart of the Rockies.

Benchly swallowed hard. "It's Cheyenne Mountain, the headquarters of NORAD and Space Command."

"And here?" The dot swept across the map and stopped near an obscure rail junction near the town of Kuransk in the Ural Mountains.

"That's the Russian NORAD."

"Well, done, my friend. Go to the head of the class. You know all the answers. Unfortunately, what we lack are the questions. And just for the record, finding the meaning of your bisector circles has been made a top company project."

"Carleton, hoaxers didn't make these."

A sense of visceral alarm began down in

Benchley's guts. He was glad he had skipped lunch. Being scared shitless can sometimes make you want to puke. Benchly gathered his wits after a moment. "Wait a minute, what about the third point? You said there were three exceptions."

Aberdeen punched his key ring laser pointer again and the dot swept to upstate New York. "This is the town of Hudson, and right next to it is the town of Iron Mountain. Ring any bells?"

Benchly removed his steel rimmed glasses and rubbed his eyes. "I give up. So what's at Hudson, New York?"

Aberdeen put his pointer back in his pocket and went over to his desk, sitting down on the front of it dangling his legs off the front. He put both hands in his pockets and shrugged. "You got me by the balls."

Meanwhile, back at the Land Office, there were a few more interesting developments. The NSA/FBI coordinating committee had received some curious information that was being passed around to see if anyone could make anything out of it.

The NSA in its mandate to maintain the security of the United States has some capabilities of which the public is not aware. For example they can simultaneously monitor every active telephone conversation in the entire country. Same goes for the internet. In order for an Internet Service Provider to be licensed, they have to agree to provide a back door to the NSA to monitor all communications. Same same for bank transactions, credit card use, pay roll transactions, and seventy other activities. "Sixty Minutes" made a hullabaloo about this guy Zimmerman's commercial encryption programs and how terrorists and drug cartels were using them to defeat eavesdropping. The truth is

297

that the NSA super computers slashed through these programs in seconds and read the encrypted messages as fast as they could be transmitted. NSA analysts used four super computers operated in series to run another program called the HSDI or The High Speed Data Integrator. (four trillion operations per second) The insider name was the "Slot Machine." They called it the Slot Machine because in a way it worked a little like the old one armed bandits. But instead of having only three windows which paid a jackpot if you lined up three cherries, the HSDI had 350 "windows" which could be programmed by the player-analyst. For example, on one assignment they plugged in the subscriber list for "Soldier of Fortune Magazine" along with fifteen other parameters, two of which were recent purchasers of any amount of nitrate fertilizer or kerosene. The slot machine punched out nineteen names, one of which, was Jerald G. Farmer who was a childhood buddy of Timothy McVeigh. The significance of the connection was not recognized in time, of course, but you get the idea. The Slot Machine could access every source of electronic information in the nation that went out over an electronic circuit or the airwaves.

The document that Trask had been sent up by the NSA/FBI coordinating committee included a few of the interesting hits by the HSDI analysts. The one which stuck out was the accidental declassification of a geological exploration satellite package and the leasing of the package to a chain of dummy companies. The AeroNutronics GeoExplorer was a state of the art system designed solely for oil exploration. It had flown once already and was rumored to have found many vast new fields. It had even confirmed the Saudi sized fields in the Mekong Delta of Vietnam, one of the never made public reasons we fought the Vietnam War. The ANGX-5 reconnaisance package could be launched with a variety of boosters or the space shuttle. After it went "on lease" its chain of custody with the actual hardware was long gone from the refrigerated clean rooms of AeroNutronics. The paperwork was perfect, the first big lease payment appeared in the corporate account of AeroNutronics, but nobody could find out who authorized the transaction. It was the biggest fuck up anybody could remember in the community. It happened fast and now the ANGX-5 could be anywhere.

The NSA sicked the Slot Machine on the problem. They plugged in dozens of parameters including high net worth companies that could benefit by using it, leases on clean facilities, large purchases of imaging analysis equipment, and the bingo item, names of experts that the perps might hire who could interpret the data.

The name of one of the foremost interpreters of intelligence and satellite imagery popped up on a Slot Machine run who had just been issued a 10-99 from his employer. The guy was on a consulting contract with an oil company called TriAmCo Energy. The guy was recently retired and had a resume in intelligence like Von Braun did in rocket ships. The imagery analyst's name was Lawrence Feldman.

Trask's encyclopedic memory instantly recalled TriAmCo as being one of the only solid investors they could locate in the Russian shuttle restaurant deal. In a way he was relieved. The idea that the Colombian cartels were getting their hands on a space bomber began to dim as a workable possibility. But now, one mystery only yielded ground to yet another. The game is afoot, he thought.

Trask immediately called Benchly on the secure cell line. "Carleton, bring it on back to the barn we got some mighty interesting news."

"Well, I got some plum interesting news for you too sheriff, but you aren't going to like it."

"Well, come on home, hoss, and we'll drank some red whisky and talk about the meanin' o' life."

Chapter 42

John Good had once again been summoned to McCall's office for some inconsequential bullshit. There was no more time to be wasting with McCall. The mission was getting to the critical stage and his expertise was needed to keep the entire affair from unraveling around their ears. McCall had no idea of the repercussions if the mission was discovered and leaked to the government, which most certainly had been deeply penetrated by many facilitators who had not proved immune to conversion like Feldman.

Looking across the desk at J.B. McCall, Good saw a deeply religious and patriotic man who loved his country but had not a scintilla of understanding how the system actually worked. He looked at McCall and saw a man with the illusion that there were inalienable rights granted by the creator that all men were created equal. He saw a man who believed that the Bill of Rights actually existed and in some way would protect him from an over zealous government that could make him disappear without a trace or make him commit "suicide." Good sat with his arms folded, and waited impatiently to see what

the pathetic old man wanted. "What can I do for you?" he asked barely concealing his growing contempt.

"They have to be told as soon as they're finished at the Gagarin Center," McCall responded calmly.

"That's quite impossible," Good replied with a wave. "They'll have too much contact with too many people prior to departure. The opportunity for a leak is too great. No, we stick to the original schedule. And now I have work to do." Good pushed his chair back and started to get up.

"You're not going anywhere until I'm finished talking to you," McCall said; it was an order.

Good sat back down.

"We have to tell them because my son and Leanna Helms are having too much contact with the crew already and the cover story is already starting to crumble. Further delay will undermine our credibility with these men and will undermine their motivation for the job."

Good listened placidly, then began explaining as if to an idiot. "The Russians will follow orders, your son knows already, therefore Blalock is the only weak link, and as I have already indicated, I have that matter under control. We *will* have his cooperation."

McCall ignored Good's condescending tone. "John, I have not interfered in any way with your conduct of this mission until now. Not only will our men be told after the first phase of training, but there will be no more of that kind of talk." McCall painted on a big smile. "And I would remind you that this is Texas, and boot hill is full of men who have made less innocuous comments."

Good remembered something about a big dragoon revolver he kept in his desk. And there was that article in the Fort Worth Star-Telegraph where some New York tourist got shot for flipping off a good old boy in traffic. Texas had signs on the highway which read, Drive *friendly*. It would be easy enough to agree to whatever McCall was demanding, and he, Good, would just do later whatever had to be done…including what might have to be done with the elder McCall. In case of mission failure or discovery, the clean up to erase his involvement could get messy. "Very well," Good begrudgingly agreed, "we'll put the big briefing together when they finish phase one."

"Thank you," replied McCall, extending his huge hand. "I think you'll see that there's no downside to taking the high road with our boys and it'll pay handsome dividends in the end."

"Perhaps you're right," Good half smiled, his emotionless eyes glassed over like a dead mullet.

McCall took his arm and walked him down the hall. "I know you have work to do John and I'll let you get to it."

McCall peeled off to the elevator and punched in the day code to summon the car. Upon reaching the Taj McCall, he stopped at his secretary's desk. Anne Louise looked up and noted the serious expression. She stopped the word processor and waited. "Anne Louise, where'd I put my .454 revolver?"

"It's in your toy safe on the fourth floor."

"Fetch it for me in the next day or so and get me a big roll of duct tape. Don't tell anybody and don't let anybody see what you're doing."

Chapter 43

The days of Leanna's blitzkrieg work schedule that started at six AM and drove hard to nine PM were a thing of the past. Bobby Tranh walked in on her several times a week and caught her just sitting with her chin propped on her hand drumming a pencil with the other hand. She gazed out the window and was either watching the falcons or just staring into space. She had wanted to tell Matt the real mission a dozen times while he was in New York but she hadn't because it was so important to contain the information as long as possible. Mr. Good and Colonel Bremen had made a huge point on this matter and were extremely candid about the nefarious possibilities of a leaked operational plan. She now had Bobby and his family also exposed. Mr. Good was frighteningly graphic about how things could happen if the wrong people uncovered the mission. He disclosed the shocking truth about Clinton's White House attorney, Vince Foster to make his point. Leanna, not being one to shrink from the horrible, found her throat constricting and her gag reflex commencing as Good described what he knew. But what was agonizing Leanna at the moment, was her worry that Matt would feel betrayed when he found out the truth and that she had known all along and didn't tell him. It was a kind of lie by omission, she thought. The only man she had ever loved, besides her father, and she had lied to him on a matter of life and death. Uncle J.B. said they would be told as soon as they came home from Russia, but in the mean time, there were four more months to go at the Gagarin Center.

She picked up his latest letter and read it again. And for the seventh time she smiled when she got to the part about the practical jokes that he and Duane were playing on Colonel Yakov and Lieutenant Grosovitch. It seems that the latest one was especially bad. Grosovitch had put some of Matt's capsaicin cream into Duane's tube of Preparation H. Sitting all that time in a wheelchair, in spite of Duane's Schwarzenegger-like work out regimen, had caused him to have some big time hemorrhoids. Leanna skipped down to the third paragraph and reread it. "...the reaction was hysterical until I noticed the *I'm going to kill you* look in Duane's face...he was thinking that I did it. I barely got out of the building with my life and I had to shout my innocence down the hall; swearing on a real Bible that it wasn't me, before he'd let me back in the building. Would you believe that Yakov had one? We deduced by Holmesian logic that it had to be Grosovitch that did it because at the only time it could have happened, unknown to Grosovitch, Yakov was in Moscow, and I was suited up with Duane in the zero G training tank. Duane is plotting his revenge...keeps referring to Grosovitch that *whitey mother fucker*. Grosovitch, on the other hand seems to have taken a liking to Duane and showed up at lecture last week in a flowery island shirt unbuttoned down the front showing the T-shirt underneath looking amazingly similar to Duane's. Yakov chewed his ass and made him go change. Have also noticed that Duane seems to have started having occasional bouts of taking himself a little too seriously, he gets real quiet when I ask him anything about the mission."

Leanna smiled again, took a deep breath, and put the letter down on her desk. A cloud deck was moving in from the Atlantic, maybe some rain this afternoon. She could see thenorth tower from her office and its top two stories were already disappearing into the gray murk. New people working in the WTC always worried about some off course airliner crashing into the buildings. The falcons outside her window were hunkered down for a blow; the male had stopped hunting and was nestled up next to his mate with one wing across her back. The tip feathers of his wing fluttered as the blustery gusts began licking at the nest.

I wonder what Matt is doing now, Leanna thought.

Chapter 44

Some of the loudest most emotional meetings in the history of the joint chiefs were occurring far too frequently. The generals' aides in the outer office on one occasion sent a representative in and asked that they tone it down because it was upsetting the enlisted personnel who could hear the shouting. Just make up your minds what we are to do, and we'll do it, the major explained. The passivity of the executive branch in the face of mortal national peril was generating a supreme stress in the joint chiefs. The president's cabinet meetings were choked with fear and angst. Secretary of Defense McMillan observed during one meeting that this must have been the same thing that happened around the council fires of the American Indians when they agonized over what was to be done about the unstoppable onslaught of the whites. The latter day chiefs realized too late the blunder that they had made. Would they share the fate of the Indians? Was this the ultimate and final manifestation of what goes around comes around? Even with a full World War II type mobilization, the nation could not be ready.

The president then tasked the military with the impossible. The military was asked to do something with nothing. And while no one said the words, everyone was thinking the same thing. The cabinet had been compromised. This log jammed the decision tree from the beginning and it was Pearl Harbor all over again on a planetary scale. General Marshall was out taking his ride with orders not to be interrupted.

"Let it be said that this is the price we pay for electing a God damned draft dodger," was a final comment by Air Force Brig. General Thomas "Snake & Nape" Chestnut before he was escorted out of the room.

"We're having our faith tested," replied Marine Commandant Benjamin Atkins, "and if there is anyone here who doesn't believe in civilian control of the government, speak now because I'm going to punch your fucking lights out."

The chairman stood up and placed his arm on Atkins shoulder. "Ben, nobody is thinking about anything like that. Sit down, General, and let's see what we can do."

The stop gap plan concocted by the Joint Chiefs was called "Red Sea" and moved out on the highly limited places that action could be taken. Coordination with the Russians was good and while cooperation was also good, there was the feeling in intelligence that several Russians knew something that they were holding back. And the Russians had every reason to be holding back. They strongly suspected, as did members of the Group, that the highest levels of the American government had been compromised by facilitators. Disclosing to the joint chiefs might be a pipeline into the enemy camp and the mission of the Stork would be erased, along with the lives of the two hundred twenty-three insiders who planned and perpetrated the operation right under the noses of the political arm of the Russian Federation. Even at this late stage, as the truth of the extraterrestrial threat was being explained to world leaders, the mission of the Stork had to be cloaked under a veil of blood for anyone who leaked the secret. Two engineers at Tupelov and their families had already vanished when they became suspected as possible sources of leaks.

Red Sea foresaw only seven significant areas that had promise. First off, it provided funding and top priority to building as many X-35s as possible until the outbreak of hostilities. Second, The NORAD Bear Trap installation had to be completed to protect the central government when it relocated. Third, additional Bear Traps would be built around New York, Los Angeles, Los Alamos, and Seattle, parts permitting. Fourth, SDI would be completely abandoned and all personnel reassigned in construction of the X-35 ground and space systems. Fifth, the ICBM and bomber force would escalate as rapidly as possible its readiness until Defcon 4. The deadline for this was 1 February, prior to commencement of the Solar Max starting early in the year 2000. Sixth, stalling/deception tactics including a negotiated surrender, which could be dragged out providing more time to prepare. Inflatable dummy X-35s would be mass produced and stationed alongside the actual spacecraft. Seventh, preparation of the public by use of the media.

Crew selection was already underway for the X-35s and production of the space fighter was gradually ramping up at Lockheed-Martin and Boeing. Meetings were scheduled with key members of the Group's allied contacts to see what could be done about construction overseas. The Air Force, Navy, and Marines were combing the ranks of their pilots for the special skills it was believed would make the ideal space fighter pilot. They were told nothing about the assignment except that it was of utmost national urgency. The screening process used a series of off the shelf video games and holographic arcade-like simulators, which had been tweaked for higher fidelity.

They initially dubbed the X-35 the Australus because most of its flight testing was done at the new Area 51 in the Australian outback. The original Groom Lake test base had gone main street America under the prying eyes and ears of Art Bell and the saucer nut culture. The Australus was the aircraft they were actually working on when the X-33 was cancelled which was nothing more than a test platform for the more advanced X-35. The Australus looks a little like an old Chance Vought Cutlass, but more triangular and fatter. The wings are about twice as long but are thicker and with less sweepback, only twenty-three degrees. And while capable of reaching and sustaining an orbit out to five hundred miles, the Australus operates in near Earth space without the use of orbital mechanics. It can be launched vertically by tilting it back at a seventy-five degree angle on its wing tip launch pads raised into position by the retractable telescoping monopod in its belly. It can also take off and land like an ordinary jet fighter using a conventional looking landing gear. The Australus is not encumbered by heat absorbing tiles like a shuttle because it reenters the atmosphere at a low speed until the wings begin to fly. A normal recovery is about twelve hundred knots until down to around thirty-five thousand feet when it continues to slow to airliner speeds of around six hundred knots. The Australus is a Remotely Piloted Vehicle and while it can be flown from its own cockpit, in actual combat, it would be remotely piloted using a human pilot, inside a ground based cockpit simulator. The cockpit in the aircraft has a backward leaning seat similar to an F-16 and a rigid neck and helmet brace for high G maneuvering. Once reaching Interface Altitude (IA), however, the cockpit seat fully reclines and the pilot's sensor helmet slides aft into a receptacle which holds the head rigid. The pilot's body slides aft also like he is going into a magnetic resonance medical machine. The cockpit is then filled with a blue looking stuff called fiber-gel that has the consistency of jello. After the cockpit fills with the fiber gel, a microwave signal is energized which stiffens the gel encasing the pilot in a solid mass preventing movement in the extreme Gs expected in space combat. The system was abandoned when it was quickly realized that the primary control mode, that is remote piloting, was far more effective. The extreme G loads experienced in the manned mode of flight was lethal to human pilots.

The location of the duplicator/simulator Command Control Facility (CCF) would be the closest secret ever maintained by the American military. The location was a former nuclear safe bunker built by Fortune 500 companies during the Cold War. It was two miles deep in solid granite and basaltic rock and was the deepest manned base ever constructed. Multiple direct hits by H-bombs would not penetrate the facility. The X-35 crews, and other personnel were blindfolded while being transported to and from by helicopters, then vehicle caravan. All our eggs would be in one basket, but at ten thousand feet deep, we felt that the basket was safe. Nothing we knew about the EBEs suggested they had anything that could get to our pilots this deep in solid rock. The code name for the base was "Cactus" and it was located deep in the Adirondacks of northern New York near the small town of Iron Mountain. A committee of leading intellectuals were sequestered there in 1963 and told to write a report on the possibility and desirability of peace. The committee consisted of the Who's Who of nineteen sixties science, business, and the humanities. Rumored among the members were Victor Maslow, Maynard Keynes, and Conrad Loring.

The flight simulator visual system for the Australus consists of wrap around graphical displays incorporating internal and ground radar feeds, live video from onboard cameras, as well as a laser stabilized optical tracker for up close maneuvering. The spacecraft has an advanced automatic collision avoidance system (AACAS) which would prevent it from hitting another X-35 in the violent swirling dog fighting that was envisioned in near earth orbit. Combat closing speeds of over fifteen thousand knots were expected. No human pilot could withstand the G forces that would be experienced if it were flown like a conventional aircraft with an onboard pilot. The tactical systems are controlled by the AAAI, the first quantum computer adapted for military use. (Advanced Adaptive Artificial Intelligence) The X-35 propulsion system uses the Pratt & Whitney G-1A-15 Magnetodrive once it reaches Interface Altitude (IA) of 400,000 feet. The G-1 engine taps the unlimited supply of magnetic flux energy of the earth's magnetic field and can vector the repulsive flow in any direction. A vast oversimplification of how it works would be to imagine what happens when two like poles of a magnet are placed together. The repulsive force, known as the Biefield-Brown effect, is what the G-1 channels and magnifies. When operating in the Southern Hemisphere, it reverses engine polarity and captures the opposite repulsion effect. If a dogfight had to cross the equator, the X-35 is vulnerable for a few seconds until the engine switched polarity. The G-1 engine is ninety-five percent ceramic and its only moving parts are the triple redundant centrifugal flow liquid nitrogen pumps for the engine cooling system.

The heart of the engine is the Trans Gravitic Converter (TGC) which simultaneously converts magnetic lines of force into energy and vectors the thrust to produce the high acceleration and turning capability. The TGC does this by generating huge amounts of electrical power as the space fighter crosses the electromagnetic field lines of the earth. The mechanism is similar to the way a generator makes electricity by spinning a permanent magnet within a field created by an electromagnet. The field energy can only be trapped when the X-35 is travelling at an angle to the lines of force. This is why the Australus is always launched from the ground on easterly or westerly headings. Long spidery sensor/collectors of superconductor magnesium diboride in the wings channel the Earth's field energy into the powerful ceramic core of the G-1. The G-1 sits right on top of the TGC that amplifies and creates thrust by repulsion. One byproduct of TGC operation is tremendous heat, which is handled by a liquid nitrogen radiator, not unlike the one in your car, except the cooling lines honeycomb the interior of the engine allowing direct heat transfer to the cooling agent. The engine coolant then circulates through the two weapons amplifiers if the weapons are in use. If the weapons are not firing, the coolant just continues in a bypass circuit within the engine. The second byproduct of the G-1's operation is the creation of excess electrical energy to the tune of about ten thousand megajoules. The excess energy is stored in three sandwich layers of skin over the entire aircraft.

The substances which make up the three layers are classified Top Secret Level 20 only two below the maximum security classification of Double Gamma. The outer layer of skin, which you would see from the ground, is an extremely pure, extremely thin layer of silver only microns thick. The intense electrical charge continues to build in the airframe until it reaches a preset point at which it trickle discharges harmlessly into space. This excess energy is stored in the skin of the aircraft and acts like an electrical capacitor, which powers the Raytheon-Tessla dual RT5 Argon laser and particle beams. The weapons fire alternately, nanoseconds apart, through a spherical nose turret, and were found to be highly effective against captured ETE materials in ground testing at Wright Patt.

It was not known how the weapons would perform when those targets are under power and intelligent control. The nose turret is perfectly spherical and is locked into position mechanically until the weapons system is energized. At that point the turret floats on frictionless maglev bearings and rotates like greased lightning. One test, conducted in Australia, had four super sonic drones fly past an X-35 in a powered drop test. The X-35 used the first operational quantum computer and the engineers programmed it with the sum of human knowledge on military tactics, history, and game theory including professional sports. The advanced attack computer was set on full automatic. The test was not only for the weapons, but they wanted to see how "aggressive" the artificial intelligence would be. Theoretically, the AAI would search its vast memory and apply the tactics it thought would work under the conditions…then adapt as necessary to defeat the threat. Nobody really knew what it was going to do.

Test day arrived and they dropped an X-35 unpowered like a glider from a B-52 at 35,000 feet, then flew four drones by it for target practice. The X-35 engaged the four drones when they were ninety degrees abeam. One ducked under, one pulled straight up and the other two broke right and left respectively with the Australus going right through the middle of the formation. Even though the closing speeds were under 6000 knots, the RT5s disintegrated the four drones in less than a second; all four literally burned in half detonating their fuel tanks in a blinding explosion. The engineers' mouths dropped open as they watched through their binoculars when the X-35 executed a totally unexpected maneuver. After totally destroying the drone aircraft, the Australus was not satisfied. It rolled inverted and executed a split S dive and went after the pieces of the four targets as they fell through the sky. The RT5s continued firing until they vaporized every piece of the four targets down to the size of a softball. It was an awesome display, even for the engineers who designed the system.

From the ground to interface altitude, the X-35 is powered by two Russian, Proton P14 liquid fuel rocket engines. When the Russians decided they couldn't master solid fuel, they built the most reliable liquid fuel engines ever built. The P14s use liquid oxygen as the oxidizer and almost anything else for fuel. They can use kerosene, JP4, JP5, Jet A, B (commercial airline fuel) and even auto gas in an emergency. All that is necessary to use an alternative fuel is to switch six selector valves on each fuel control with a three cm socket wrench. This enables the X-35s to be launched from almost anywhere you could get a truck of LOX. The system was Russian, simple and reliable. The engines fire simultaneously for a vertical launch from it's monopod launch gear, or one at a time if you launched like an airplane off a runway using its retractable landing gear. Even if one of the two engines failed on takeoff, the remaining engine using a longitudinal accelerometer which sensed the reduction in thrust, increased power to 150% on the remaining engine. This would get you to Interface Altitude where the G-1 Magneto-Drive takes over at fuel exhaustion. The G-1 would operate at lower altitudes, but they found that man made sources of electromagnetic energy, power lines, radar, etc. distorted the shape of the Earth's magnetic lines of flux energy. When the engine tried to convert the distorted field waves, it tore itself loose from its mounts. The Autoland Auto recovery system allows the space fighter to glide in for a landing at any airport with a 5000 foot runway and an operating ILS that is within range of a TACAN station. The short landing capability is achieved by the deployment of a drag chute on main gear touchdown and firing a retrobrake when the nose gear touched down The retrobrake is a forward firing solid fuel rocket booster from the Navy's ASROC system. Ground commands from human pilots flying the duplicator/simulator would normally direct it to its operational base. But in case communications were lost, the X-35 would select from an onboard database of suitable alternate airports, fly there and land automatically. It would start with bases that could support X-35 tactical operations and work backwards to civilian airports in descending order of preference based on proximity to X-35 support IE availability of LOX, and so on. The idea was to save the aircraft in the unlikely event of a power outage or major communication failure from the Central Command Facility.

In addition to the beam weapons, the space fighter has a very nasty system, called with some understatement, the Proximity Device (PD). The PD is an EM pulse enhanced five megaton nuclear warhead programmed to detonate anytime the X-35 gets within two thousand meters of anybody not in the satellite orbits database or not squawking the correct IFF setting which presumably would be an enemy spacecraft. Outside two thousand meters the RT5s engaged the target until it is either destroyed or gets out of range. Inside, 2000 meters, kaboom! No ETE ship. And since the X-35s are unmanned and built with a design philosophy that emphasizes sheer weight of numbers and cost effectiveness, it was thought that this would be an acceptable tradeoff. Before his suicide, General Hammond theorized that we could build and replace X-35s a lot faster than the EBEs could replace their manned ships and get them here from wherever the hell they came from, likely many light years away.

The X-35 is, of course, flown from the ground. But once airborne, up to a hundred aircraft can be flown in a single formation. A fly by would be such a tight formation it would look like they were all attached together. This system requires the use of special atomic clocks on the aircraft and in ground equipment co-located with the data uplink transmitters from the human piloted flight duplicator/simulators. This system is the Advanced Automatic Collision Avoidance System or AACAS. This is also the one which keeps our spacecraft from running into friendly satellites or each other in dogfights. One tactic that can be disclosed is called "The Rabbit Drive." When NORAD identifies

Bill Broocke

a Fast Walker, an intruding enemy space craft emitting a strong EM signature, several widely dispersed, line abreast formations of X-33s would converge to either force the enemy spacecraft down into the SDI envelope to be picked off by a kill vehicle, or lower to be vaporized by a Bear Trap battery. If they stayed high and fought it out, all the better. Another gaggle of X-35s would be vectored in for a turkey shoot. If the enemy ship wouldn't stand and fight, or be herded down into the teeth of our defenses, and just zoomed vertically out of reach, he would escape. But doing that, he would also be denied access to near Earth space for whatever nefarious purpose he had in mind. The X-35s never required refueling or rearming once in space. As the ships came off the production line, it was anticipated they could stay on patrol in space for months. Eventually, near Earth space would be saturated with thousands of X-35s crisscrossing every corner of the planet in hunter killer formations.

The strategy was to deny an adversary access to near Earth space by swarming him with a lethal welcoming committee of expendable weapons. If he escaped intercept by X-35s he would be vaporized over our cities by mass concentrated fire of plutonium powered beam weapons.

One of the interesting features of the duplicator/simulators is that the control stick was put back. The pilot flies barehanded with his right hand with his bare left hand on a throttle. The throttle never moves and the stick only becomes moveable on the glide back to Earth after the mission when the aerodynamic flight controls become active, similar to the space shuttle. This was done to keep the pilots happy. However, once past IA on the climb out, the

Flight Guidance System switches to the intercept mode. In this mode, brain impulses detected by the pilot's special helmet and "confirmed" by motor reaction stimuli picked up by the sensors on the control stick made the aircraft react accordingly. The X-35 flies by thought waves, but the control stick sensor validates the thought wave as a flight control command. The pilot flies the X-35 until he gets a target lock at which time he can fight mano a mano Mustang vs. Messerschmidt style or use Auto Engagement. The AE mode of the attack computer can attack as a single ship or coordinate the attack with other X-35s computing optimal use of aircraft in the three dimensional trigonometry and speeds in space combat. Simulations at Wright Patt suggested that an ETE ship encountering three X-35s hunting in the coordinated attack mode, had an eighty-two percent chance of getting his ass blown clean off.

The visual system in the simulator is spectacular and uses enhanced holographic projection with real time visual feed from cameras on the aircraft. The computers combine all this imagery and paint it distortion free and with absolute clarity on the inside of the simulator's canopy/screen. If a squadron was deployed at Lambert Field in St. Louis, for example, a pilot flying the mission from the classified duplicator/simulator location, could look over his shoulder and see the Arch as he sat there waiting for the launch order. On the initial tests, the pilots ate this system up. The simulated takeoff was quite real. The simulator thundered and shook as the mighty Proton boosters ignited. The G forces were simulated by tilting the duplicator to the vertical position and slightly deflating the seat and back cushions on takeoff. The test pilots had one big complaint. When the simulated attack blasted an alien ship out of the sky, there was no audible explosion. The fact that this was exactly what would happen is space didn't carry any water with these guys and they kept bitching. The programmers finally put one in with a highly satisfying visual and audible explosion, which buffeted the duplicator. It even had a debris field complete with alien bodies blazing by the cockpit. The test team really liked the modification. Their spokesman, a blood and guts Air Force Wart Hog driver from the Gulf War, summed up their opinion of the modified visual effects. He said that *it was only fitting since they weren't able to get up there and kick the shit of them in person.*

Most of the ICBMs in the ground silos had been spun up and were having their targeting and guidance systems updated to be able to accept new targets on a moment's notice. We now had two thirds fewer missiles that we did ten years ago, with the Russians in the same boat. The subtle alien plan to disarm us had worked, and no one had any faith that ours, or the Russian Rocket Forces, had any deterrent effect whatever. And the bombers would most likely be slow moving sitting ducks if they attempted to go anywhere to confront alien activity. The sense of anger and despair in the halls of the Pentagon was soul shattering and as the months wore on, you couldn't find a single smile in a hundred miles of corridor. "Snake & Nape" Chestnut finally flamed out completely. Building security found him sitting at his desk, staring straight ahead, unable to speak…the office hazy with stale cigar smoke. At first they thought it was a stroke, but then realized he was mentally and emotionally erased. They couldn't even treat the poor bastard because they were afraid he might disclose something outside the tightly cleared people who were working on the problem. Chestnut spent three years in the Hanoi Hilton and was nearly beaten to death with bamboo clubs on numerous occasions. He had hundreds of cigarette burns on his back where the North Vietnamese guards had tortured him. He took all they had, and now, with his nation and likely the world facing an imminent disaster, he realized that there was nothing he could do.

They found him sitting, staring straight ahead, the cigar in his right hand burned down below his charred fingers. He just sat there, the purple ribbon of the Medal of Honor around his neck with both hands tightly clutching the armrests of his chair. In his left hand he held a gold chain with a locket on the end which contained a picture of his wife Linda, who had been killed by a drunk driver while he was a prisoner of war. He had never remarried. By any definition, Tom Chestnut was a great American patriot. But, none of this mattered now. He was already someplace else. All he had to give was gone.

A week later, a Navy Commander disappeared and was never heard from again. He hadn't had access to any of the sensitive materials, but it was the first time it had happened without anybody finding a body. It looked the like the guy just went over the hill. And church attendance went way up. Wives and families of the Pentagon personnel were surprised when the fathers of the service families suggested that they start going every Sunday. The service chaplains were even being asked to hold prayer breakfasts in the Pentagon officers mess.

Red Sea plunged ahead despite the desperateness of the hour.

Air Force Systems Command began installing the Bear Trap around Cheyenne Mountain with the components it had on hand. By a special deal from the US, the strike at the Korean plant had lifted and the critical tactical displays began to show up. The estimates on national coverage began to increase as more parts were located and a few more cities could be protected. The SDI was formally cancelled, plagued by technical problems, suspected sabotage, and friction by congress and the cabinet. The latter, having two members who were especially vociferous about what a waste of taxpayer dollars it was. The limited Bear Trap and X-35 Australus construction were coming out of the black budget, however, and the two certain opponents in the cabinet had not yet found out.

Maj. Gen. Troy Hamilton, Commander, Space Command, U. S. Air Force, had been the MacArthur of the High Frontier. His visionary scheme of the triple layered planetary defense, using swarms of deadly space interceptors, SDI and the Bear Trap, had died with him, in a quiet little roadside park near Arlington.

Our plans were in ruins.

The aliens were right on schedule.

The mighty caldrons of the sun were beginning to boil their storms of shit and the enemy was coming on chariots of death. We were not ready.

Chapter 45

The initial fun and games of flight training with a bunch of pilots was gone. Duane was more serious than ever. Blalock took Yakov aside one day for a heart to heart discussion about the mission. "Dimitri, so what do you think?"

"About what?"

"The mission."

"You mean the real mission, or the bullshit mission they told you in America?"

"The real mission."

"Well, Matt, I told you about the two schools I had to attend before they sent me here to train with you and Duane. Does that sound like we're going to get rich finding vast oceans of oil?"

Blalock looked at his friend. "Nope. Looks like we've been lied to. But let me tell you Dimitri, the guy behind this is a great man who fought in the, uh, Great Patriotic War…and I just can't bring myself to believe that he lied to us without a good fucking reason."

"My people have placed this mission on a priority equal to anything in our history Matt."

"So you think that the Stork will be carrying some kind of weapon?"

"Yes."

Blalock scratched his head. "The Russians and a handful of Americans team up with an old orbiter that's been under a tarp for ten years and are going to do something with a nuke? Goddamit, it makes no sense. What the fuck are we going to do?" Blalock took off his ball cap, pushed his hair back and stared off through the giant windows of the Gagarin Center's reception building.

Yakov placed his hand on Blalock's shoulder. "We will do what we have always done, my friend. We will do our duty."

Mercifully, the schedule had been changed around and the crew would be going back to Texas for the mission briefing before going to orbiter systems school at the Tupelov factory. This relieved the angst that was building up in the four pilots and gave Duane something to say. It will all be explained when we get home, he kept saying. No, I don't know any of the specific details, he said, which he didn't. He knew the overall plan, but the intelligence was just starting to come in from Lawrence Feldman's sources on the intent and plans of the EBEs.

Feldman had assured Good, Bremen, and J.B. McCall that his sources, mostly from people referred by the Group, were unimpeachable. As the ETE plan began to take shape, painstakingly pieced together from people with fragmentary knowledge, and the Group's fifty-year database, Feldman and his team were filled with a dread they had never experienced. The amoral intentions of this alien race defied human cognition and paled into nothingness any science fiction plot ever written. The monsters of the id, that felled overnight the mighty Krell, from their "towering pentacle of greatness," was a Mother Goose story compared to what the EBEs had up their ass.

Blalock, Duane, Yakov and Grosovitch sat together in business class on the Delta flight from Moscow to Atlanta. The flights were full to DFW and so they had to split up and travel in pairs. Grosovich wanted to go with Duane so Yakov flew with Blalock. Going through the metal detectors, Yakov was blown away by the courtesy of the airport security and secondly the WH Smith Newsstand that had hundreds of different magazines and newspapers. In the atrium of the Atlanta Hartsfield Airport the piano player was banging away on the baby grand. "My God, do all American airports have these luxuries?"

"Oh yes," Blalock assured him, "Even the small ones, like Atlanta."

The four pilots rendezvoused at the DFW executive terminal where the sleek, shining G-4 was waiting. The flight to Plainview was a blur to the four since they were lagged out from the long overseas hop. Tex Lambert was waiting with the Lincoln as the G-4 glided to a halt in front of the TraAmCo hangar complex. Tex gave Matt and Duane a big bear hug, followed by the more customary effusive Texan hand shaking. Tex then eyed warily the two Ruskies with just a nod.

"So, how long's it been since you boys had a good burger?"

"Right on Tex," Duane answered. "Too damn long," Matt agreed.

"We've never had one," Yakov said.

They pulled into the Burger King and gorged themselves for the next hour.

TriAmCo was a changed place. Wackenhut guards were everywhere. Most of the company administrative employees had been moved to another part of the fifty-acre complex. There were tweedy jacketed professor types wandering the halls and Russians in their seedy looking civilian clothes that were completely out of place. Making the Russians look even more ridiculous were their new cowboy boots, presumably to fit in.

The entire GHQ building had been taken over by what appeared to be about three hundred people that Duane had never seen before. There was zero levity and even Ann Louise, who was still there on the top floor with his Dad, was seemingly a little depressed. She had a hug for Duane and Matt and even the Russians, and the usual big bowl of fresh baked chocolate chip cookies and an iced cooler of cold milk. She never forgot anything.

Anne Louise ushered the four immediately into J.B. McCall's office where J.B. was waiting with more bear hugs and hand shaking. "You boys are the first friendly faces I've seen around here in months. Lotta shit going down."

The Russians' heads were on a swivel like they were at the Christmas show in the Hayden Planetarium. The opulence of the office rivaled the palaces of the Czars. "Sit down everyone," J.B. gestured, "make yourself comfortable. Look," J.B. started, "I guess by now you've figured out that the oil mission was a cover story. I'm so sorry I had to do that, but after the big briefing, I think you'll understand why we did it."

Matt noticed the look on Yakov's face as they glanced at each other. That must be the Russian version of *oh shit were fucked,* he thought.

"OK, that's the bad news," J.B. continued, "Here's the good news." Three of the guys we're flying in for the mission briefing can't be here until next Wednesday. This means you guys can take a five day vacation. Colonel Yakov, you and Mr. Grosovitch can go anywhere you want in the G-4 on TriAmCo. Here's a credit card that will get you anything you want. Have a ball. I'd suggest San Francisco. It all goes on my tab."

J.B. handed the platinum Visa card to Yakov. "I'm going to send Tex with you to do the driving."

Yakov shot another look at Matt.

"Dimitri, this is a good deal, we'll talk after the meeting." Yakov seemed visibly relieved not ever owning a credit card or having the slightest idea what a tab was.

Then J.B. looked over at Duane. "Duane, son, I'm sorry to say that you'll have duties here at HQ. Commander Blalock, I believe there is a certain spell binding beauty in New York who is breathlessly waiting for you to call."

Anne Louise came in about then with tea for the two surprised Russians, coffee black with one package of the blue stuff for Matt, and a diet coke on the rocks for Duane. On the silver serving tray was a small linen envelope with a royal blue colored wax seal with Matt's name written in flowing script. Matt grabbed the envelope, tore it open and read Leanna's note. Smiling, he leaned back in his chair, and handed the note to Yakov, who read it, whistled once then passed it to Duane. Duane's only comment was, "Holy Shit man!" Grosovitch snatched the note out of his hand. Eyes glued to the page as he finished the message, Grosovitch slowly handed the letter back to Blalock. "How many women such as this live in your country?" Grosovitch asked incredulously.

"Near as I can tell," Blalock answered, "Leanna is the only one."

"And it is a good thing," Yakov interrupted, "or all of you would have been killed in bed long ago." The five men laughed.

Leanna was sending a Falcon the following morning. The message, in a far less graphic description, said that they would be spending the weekend in her apartment. They would not be going out and that he should *prepare* himself. The p.s. was interesting. Leanna had inquired, teasingly, that since she had not been with a man since meeting Matt, that would he please be sure his will was up to date?

When the meeting was over, on the way out the door, Duane turned to Matt with a forced serious look on his face. "You know, pal, she might not be kidding about that will."

Chapter 46

Trask and Benchly sat next to each other at the conference table at the weekly department meeting. The heads of all the departments were there and the task, as always, was to decide what to send to the President for his weekly long range intelligence briefing. There was the usual information about suspected locations of Osama Bin Laden, threat analyses for the various embassies, what the drug lords were up to down south, and the Russian, Chinese, Indian and Pakistani military activity for the week, such that it was. Trask was paying about half attention to what was being said and he was letting Benchly chair the meeting. In his red diagonal folder that he'd brought to the meeting he had some photos from the HIROTT (High Resolution Orbital Tracking Telescope). He had the only copies, but when there was a pause in the tempo of the meeting, he distributed a copy to each of the department heads. The room fell silent for several minutes.

The silence was broken by Steve Wallins. "What the hell is that thing doing up there? It shouldn't have got above fifty miles!"

Trask looked down the long mahogany table and steepled his hands in front of his face. "My sentiments exactly," he said. "Would anyone care to advance a theory?"

"Is it emitting?" somebody asked.

"No way. We have nothing on this," replied Gerald Billings, whose department monitored emissions from known eight thousand orbiting objects in conjunction with NASA.

"It's not emitting radio waves, but it is emitting something else," Trask continued.

"Every time it passes within a hundred miles of one of our RAD-5s we get a radiation reading that goes off scale."

The eight men were staring holes in the photographs.

The object in the photos was Cosmos 874, an NPO Energia RD-170, the largest liquid fueled booster in the world. It was just up there, going round and round being real quiet.

"The French?" somebody queried.

"No, Kourou is closed for operations until all the new construction is finished," somebody answered.

Carson Benchly shifted his weight in his chair and cleared his throat. "Leonard, among other applications, the RD-170 is the booster the Russians were planning to use to launch their space shuttles."

Trask didn't raise an eyebrow, but looked down the table making contact with each man. "Gentlemen, the operative word in Carson's astute observation is *launch*. What we need to find out, is what the devil a complete booster is doing out there all by its lonesome."

Chapter 47

Matt rode in the front seat with Preston as they motored into Manhattan from New Jersey in the big Rolls. The falcon crew that picked him up this time weren't quite as talkative as the last two guys but it didn't matter, Matt was still jet lagged from the day before and he'd slept the whole way. He learned that Preston was a former Royal Marine who had fought in the Falklands and had been the guy who sunk an Argentine landing craft in Port Stanley harbor with a Carl Gustav 84 millimeter anti-tank missile. You learn a lot about people riding in the front seat.

The black limo made landfall on the Manhattan side of the GW Bridge and you could see the yellow crud from a million exhausts floating in the concrete canyons. Blalock and Preston were instantly enveloped in the queer synergy of bedlam and the slow choking rivers of steel and rubber.

They pulled up in front of the Trump Tower and Preston popped around to the boot and got out Matt's green, banged up B4 bag. "Daresay they aven't seen the likes o' that kit coming through the front door o' this place eh, Capn' Blalock?"

"If the stiffs who live here knew half the places that bag has been, both of us would get the heave-ho."

Preston nodded with a short laugh. He had an instant mind picture that would have fit almost any pilot in any air force in the world. They shook hands and Preston motored silently off. That was the last verbal conversation that took place for the next two hours.

Bill Broocke

Matt punched the bell on Leanna's penthouse. The first thing he was going to find out was exactly everything she knew about the mission. Leanna answered the door barefooted wearing a short, tiny translucent purple silk nighty, loosely tied at the waist. The perfect nakedness and the poetic architecture of her body caused Blalock to swallow hard. She stepped into his body digging her nails lightly into the back of his arms, arching her back slightly so that her pubis pressed softly but firmly against Matt's. He grabbed her around her tiny waist roughly pulling her to him. Leanna softly melted into him, gently transferring her weight to her arms now around his neck, bringing her left leg up and behind Matt's right thigh, digging her heel into the small of his knee. Matt tried to speak, but Leanna crossed his lips with her right forefinger and then kissed him. Her lips were warm and wet and tasted faintly of strawberries. Her mouth opened fully as Matt responded to her. She then cupped her left hand softly behind his head digging her nails lightly into the base of his skull. Leanna could feel Matt's pulse through her fingers and she waited as they powerfully tasted one another. When his heart began to race, Leanna knifed her long velvety tongue deeply into his mouth, almost into his throat. She snaked her tongue slowly, with intense precision around his entire mouth. She could feel her own heart rate beginning to climb. She then released the nail pressure slightly on Matt's neck so that his heart rate would stabilize. Her heart beat continued to increase until their two hearts were pounding together like synchronized engines. Leanna's tongue was alive, like a hot sweet worm, filling his mouth and slowly screwing itself into the reptilian pleasure center of his brain.

Matt got light headed as his blood rushed into his loins and began experiencing a painful building pressure. His testicles felt like they had swimmer's cramps as a stinging sensation commenced at the base of his glans. Leanna unzipped his pants and dropped slowly to her knees taking him into her mouth in one fluid movement. She sucked strongly, messaging the bottom of his erect penis with powerful strokes of her tongue. The release was immediate. Leanna swallowed again and again and as the ejaculate surged into her mouth. Matt climaxed with such intensity he saw flashes of light even though his eyes were closed. Gasping for air, he sunk backwards slightly against the front door of the apartment. Leanna rose to her feet and they kissed again. There was just a trace of stickiness to her tongue. She had swallowed every drop.

Abruptly she released her embrace and clasped her hands in his and led him backwards into the room. She guided him into her bedroom and untied the thin silken sash of her garment and let it slip silently to the floor. She slid up on her bed and lay back against the big pillows with one leg slightly arched. She reached down between her legs with her left hand and her middle finger disappeared inside her. She began arching her back with each thrust and Blalock stood there dumbfounded, getting out of his clothes clumsily. He went to the end of the bed and climbed up on it walking toward her on his knees. Leanna stopped masturbating, opened her legs and reached out. He mounted her in a second. She threw the pillows away, which were under her head and arched her back again to show him the angle at which she wished to be penetrated. Leanna held him strongly with her heels and calves locked behind his legs. She moved her hips left and right as

Matt squeezed into her. She relaxed her PC muscle until he had fully inserted himself. Matt gave her long slow strokes as she got comfortable with her grip on him. She then slowly locked her heels into the small of his knees, and after several more strokes; she made eye contact with him and squeezed hard with her PC muscle as he withdrew. The grimace of pleasure on his face was acute and once satisfied she was squeezing properly, she guided them both into a pulsing rhythm that would gradually build to a crescendo. After twenty minutes she could feel Matt getting close. She allowed her own animal drives to gradually release until she was completely free and becoming a wild animal. She put her mouth close to his ear, and cried out each time he stabbed her. They raced for the moment of release and she allowed her instincts to arc weld into his until she knew they had perfect synchronicity. At that point, she contracted her PC muscle like a satin vice, and clawed her nails into his back. Their simultaneous orgasms were like overdosing on endorphin by syringe, and being hit by lightning at the same time. Blalock uttered a guttural moan as he convulsed into the insatiable Leanna.

Matt awakened at four am with Leanna in his arms. They were sleeping cheek to cheek and he tasted something salty on her face. It was dried tears. He pulled her closer to him and she opened her legs slightly, running her soft right foot down the back of his left thigh. He kept the pressure on her back with his hand and she moved into him more tightly. In a moment, she pulled him slowly on top of her and it began again.

When the sun finally peeked over the steel and glass Sierras of Manhattan, a morning breeze was furling and unfurling the lace curtains by the sliding glass doors that opened to the spacious patio deck of the penthouse. Leanna sat in bed her back to Matt and he brushed her long dark hair, which was well below the shoulders. Her hair was silken and thick and accepted the turtle shell brush without protest. He kissed her lightly on the nape of her neck and along her shoulders. Her skin was flawless, the color of buttermilk and touching her was like touching a velvet doll. That was the point he decided not to ask her about the project. The spell of the moment would have been shattered and the little joy he had experienced since losing Diane would be evaporated. They had hardly spoken since he arrived. "Leanna, I love you," he whispered in her ear.

"And I love you too, my darling," she turned, putting her arms around his neck.

And so that was how Matt and Leanna finally got it together. Anne Louise Parker's devious plan had worked like a champ. The rest of the four-day leave was like a Movie-Tone newsreel in the forties.

Flicker flickety flash! See billionaire heiress Leanna Helms with mystery man dining at Daniel.

Flicker flickety flash! See Matt and Leanna sailing New York harbor in the company's eighty-five foot ketch.

Flickety flash! See Matt and Leanna enjoying Mozart's opera, Cosi Fan Tutte at the Lincoln Center. See Matt lean over asking, "Would somebody please tell me what the hell is going on?"

Flickety flash! See Matt and Leanna dancing cheek to cheek at the Rainbow Room.

Flickety flash! See Preston pulling up in the Rolls to take Matt to the airport on the last day. See Leanna crying as she sends her man off to war.

Blalock exhaled deeply as they pulled away from the curb in front of Trump Tower. Leanna's response to him leaving confirmed that Mr. McCall had something truly important for him to do, something truly shitty, something desperate. But he had a good crew, Dimitri and Duane and a good back up with Alexi. Whatever it was, he thought, what the hell, it's happening on my watch.

He rode in the back of the limo this time and Preston knew something was awry. He'd seen the look before, hunkered down on Sapper Hill overlooking Stanley harbor at dawn on April 2, 1982. Preston and his mates were dug in, scared shitless, wondering what the hell they were going to do. An overwhelming Argentine armada was heading straight for them.

Chapter 48

Cosmos 874 was in a low, shaky orbit. After a few more passes the HIROTT got several more and higher resolution photos of the Russian satellite. It was not the complete Energia booster but only the last three stages. Instead of a traditional orbit package, it had just put itself into orbit with three remaining stages, presumably fully fueled.

"How long can it stay up there like that," Trask wanted to know.

"Leonard, there are only two factors that have a bearing on that question. One, the fuel and oxidizer. The Russians use Syntin for fuel, which is nothing more than a really good brand of kerosene. The oxidizer is liquid oxygen and it likes being in space just fine. The other limiting factor is that low orbit they're in. NASA says that they can't maintain that for much more than six months before the orbit decays and she comes home. And with the solar max beginning to peak, it could come down even sooner by being literally knocked down into the atmosphere The impact force from the mass coronal ejections from the sun will be hitting us seven times per day when the max is at its worst. That's why we had to send a space shuttle mission out there to shove the international space station a little higher."

Trask twiddled his thumbs as he looked directly at Benchly. "What's going on with the alleged Bogota restaurant?"

"The shuttle is being readied at Tupelov to be flown to the long runway at Kourou and then overland to Bogota where the site preparation is almost complete."

Trask was slowly shaking his head. "Lookee here, hoss, we have a spacecraft that theoretically can be refueled in orbit and now we what is essentially a huge fuel tank in orbit waiting for something to happen."

"Well, I'd say you're on to something there, boss, except for one thing."

"That being what?"

"That being that we know for a fact that Tupelov has ripped the guts out of it even to removing structural parts. The two factory guys we have on the ground say that it would be a deathtrap to fly without the stuff they've pulled out."

"What about the ejection seats? Do they still work?"

Benchly crinkled his brow. "Will have to get back to you on that one, sheriff."

"When the seats are pulled out and I'm having rack of lamb at the grand opening, I'll have this burr out from under my blanket."

"Next item," Trask leaned back in his chair and stretched. "So what's all this happy horse shit on crop circles?"

Chapter 50

Benchly had been talking for about twenty minutes on the subject of the crop circles, giving his boss the history and showing slides in the darkened office. The beautiful and ornate patterns were truly interesting, Trask was thinking. Must have taken hundreds of college students with real teamwork to pull these things off in the middle of the night. Yes, there was no underestimating the abilities of dedicated hoaxers, especially the Brits who made it a national pastime.

The slides were flashing by and Trask was getting flicker vertigo as Carson Benchly droned on. But then Trask bolted upright in his chair.

"This is the one that got everybody's attention over at CIA," Carson said. It was one of the simple circles with the north-south bisector line running through the middle.

"The bisecting line is oriented exactly true north within hundredths of a degree and oddly, birds will not fly over the darned things. The complicated circles," Benchly switched back to a previous ornate design, "the birds fly right over, no problemo." Benchly continued explaining that they were located in areas of zero radar surveillance, and that they were in proximity to certain non-coastal metropolitan centers except for the two near the NORAD command base and Russian NORAD near Kuransk. "And here's the zinger," Benchly continued, "we found one up here in northern New York State near the town of Hudson." Benchly clicked the next slide with a map of the world showing all the bisector circles, then he clicked a slide of the continental US and the lone simple circle sitting way up there in New York.

"Leonard, this is the one that nobody gets. The guys over at the company say that if we can figure out what this one is doing up here, it would probably unlock the puzzle of the bisector circles."

Trask took a slow deep breath. One of the advantages of being the Director of the National Security Agency was that you knew everything, even the stuff above Double Gamma, the ultra secret about the extraterrestrials.

Benchly noticed a definite alarming change coming over his boss. "Leonard, what in God's name is wrong?"

"I know what your bisector circles are, Carleton."

"What? Tell me."

"They're bullseyes…target coordinates."

"Incredible! How do you know? Bullseyes for whom?"

"Get the Secretary of Defense on the scrambler."

Benchly was getting concerned. "Leonard, who's going to be shooting at us?"

"For got sakes man, stop babbling and do what I'm asking!"

Benchly grabbed the green phone on Trask's desk. "Get me the Secretary of Defense. This is urgent." Benchly put the phone back on its cradle. "Leonard, how could they be targets? They're all out in the farmlands. Wouldn't target coordinates be right on top of our cities and defense bases?"

Trask came back from the screen where he was examining the bisector circle near Hudson, New York, right next to Iron Mountain. Somebody had learned the location of "Cactus" the Central Control Facility for the

X-33s newly designated the SF-35A...where all the hardware and all the pilots were buried two miles deep in solid granite.

Chapter 49

Blalock, Yakov, and Grosovitch all arrived back in Plainview on the afternoon before the day of the big briefing. It seems that Yakov and his adjutant had run into a Russian language instructor from San Diego State and three of her students at Perry's down on Union Street. The instructor and Yakov hit it off like Forrest and Jenny. She was actually a Ukrainian who had been in the country for only two years and obviously had heard of Yakov. The three young women with her practically fainted when their teacher explained that Yakov was the sole survivor of the brave helicopter pilots that capped the reactor at Chernobyl and had been awarded the Order of Lenin, the old Soviet Union's equivalent of the Medal of Honor. Before the night was over, Yakov and the woman were holding hands under the table and the three coeds were fighting fiercely for the affections of Alexi Grosovitch. All in all it had been a very successful mission, Yakov had reported with one eyebrow lifted for emphasis. Matt said that he had not broached the subject of the Stork and its real purpose with Leanna because everything was going so well, he didn't want to break the charm. Besides, he trusted J.B. McCall. J.B would not ask them to do anything that didn't need doing. So everybody was still in the dark on the morning of the big briefing.

They entered the big conference room and found that the places had been set for them but no names for the twenty plus guests that sat at the front table of the room. The guests were at a long table along the front with a lectern, and the four pilots sat at a smaller table for four facing the long table. A set of briefing books were stacked in front of each chair with a yellow legal pads and pencils.

At 0800 sharp, J.B. McCall came in leading the twenty plus other people. Matt leaned over to Duane on his left. "The second guy there, is that who I think it is?"

Duane nodded.

"He was on Apollo 13 right?"

"Yep," Duane agreed.

The twenty-five guests all took their chairs and got comfortable, although there was a great deal of stress apparent in their faces, except for the astronaut, who seemed relaxed. There was more than the normal clearing of throats and sipping of water as J.B. McCall stepped to the lectern.

Chapter 51

J.B. McCall stood ramrod straight at the lectern, took a sip of water and looked at the four pilots sitting in front of him. "I guess by now, you've figured out that we aren't going oil hunting." Duane glanced down momentarily at the blank legal pad in front of him, then to his right at the three faces of his friends who had turned toward him.

"I'm sorry that Duane or I could not tell you the actual mission earlier on, but as we begin this briefing, I believe you'll understand the reasons that we could not do so. We are about to embark upon a mission of such import that the fate of the entire population of our planet hangs in the balance. We have assembled here the best minds available to brief you on the target, the enemy, and what we know about his intentions. I have liquidated almost fifty percent of my net worth to finance this project along with another investor whom you have already met. What you are about to hear will sound fantastic at times, and utter lunacy at others. I can assure you, however, that everything you are about to hear is factual and has been verified and cross confirmed from many different sources. If at any time in the briefing you have a question, just speak up. The entire mission briefing will take all of today and tomorrow. Day three will consist of meetings with teams of experts in various disciplines to round out the overall effort of the first two days. Are there any questions so far?"

There were no questions.

"Good, I'll yield the floor to Colonel Lowell Bremen. Colonel Bremen is the former Deputy Director of Army Intelligence and retired just before joining us here at TriAmCo. Colonel Bremen...."

Bremen got up from the long table without notes and walked around to the lectern where he punched the screen button. A large white screen unreeled slowly from the tubular canister attached to the back wall. The lights dimmed and an old black and white combat film flickered onto the screen of the USS Yorktown with a deck load of B-25s with their engines running. The deck was pitching with salt spray blowing over the bow and onto the lead plane commanded by Colonel James Doolittle, the famous air racing pilot and aeronautical pioneer of the 1930s.

"They caught us by the short ones at Pearl Harbor," Bremen began. "Most of the Pacific fleet was burning on the bottom of the bay. We knew they were coming and we did nothing. Roosevelt, needed a way he could galvanize public opinion into war against the Axis. Little did he realize that this would be the result." The screen faded into combat footage of Pearl Harbor and battleship row, with massive explosions blasting ship after ship, which rolled hull up taking their crews to their deaths. Japanese planes flew low, strafing the docks cutting sailors in half in clouds of blood as they ran for cover. "We knew they were coming and we did nothing." Bremen paused and let the four men absorb the horror of the footage, which had been classified for sixty years as too grotesque to release to the media. Scenes of dead and dying soldiers and sailors in camera vitae continued for another five minutes...hundreds with heads and limbs blown off, laying a huge pools of their own blood where they had bled out before they could be helped. The movie then faded out from the carnage of Pearl Harbor and faded back in to the deck of the Yorktown with the B-25s with their engines running. "Gentlemen, another Pearl Harbor is coming, but this time it won't be a remote naval base in the Pacific, it's going to be the entire planet."

Yakov muttered something emphatic in Russian and Grosovitch repeated it.

Blalock leaned to his right and put his hand up to his mouth, "Dimitri, was that *oh shit* in Russian?"

"Not exactly," Yakov replied softly, "It was w*e're fucked.*"

"Teach me how to say that later, OK?"

"I would be glad to."

Bremen, who was fluent in Russian and two other languages, stopped momentarily and made eye contact with Yakov. "Colonel Yakov, I couldn't have phrased it better myself. But, we have a surprise for our visitors. Our sources tell us that they are highly intrigued by our unique belligerence as a civilization, and that we have surprised them again and again with our unpredictable aggressiveness. All we need, gentlemen, is one more surprise." Bremen paused as the film clip continued. The B-25s released their brakes and roared down the carrier deck into the morning mist…and into history.

"Gentlemen, you are going to be our thirty seconds over Tokyo…pull this off, and you buy us the time we need to mobilize the world and mount a credible defense."

The four new saviors of the world sat in stunned silence. Bremen switched off the projector. "Gentlemen, I would now like to introduce Dr. Landrom Steele."

Steele was a slightly built man who walked with the grace of a dancer. His sunken cheeks and toned frame indicated a man who took good care of himself. He came to the lectern from the end of the table and shook hands briefly with Bremen who returned to his seat. "Gentlemen, if what you have heard so far has blown your mind, you ain't heard nothing yet." Steele paused for a molecule of mirth to rise from the four astronauts. Grosovitch half smiled, but that was it. Steele cleared his throat and launched into his presentation. "I m a member of a top secret twelve-person committee known as the Group. Membership in the Group has changed over the years. But, the knowledge of the Group's existence has been known to less than one hundred members of the Federal Government. The Group's responsibility for over five decades has been to monitor, assess and collect information about extra-terrestrial activity and to divine their intentions, and capabilities. We were formed in 1947 and our first chairman was Admiral Roscoe Hillenkoetter, the first director of the CIA. Other distinguished members included Dr. Vannevevar Bush, who worked in the Manhattan Project; James Forrestal, our nation's first Secretary of Defense; astronomer and cryptoanalyst Dr. Donald Menzel, and eight other distinguished scientists and military officers including General Nathan Twining. For the next three days we are going to brief you on fifty-three years of cumulative research by this committee and provide an update of the enemy's latest plans and dispositions by Mr. Lawrence Feldman recently retired from the Jet Propulsion Laboratory. The flying saucer culture correctly identified the existence of the Group several years ago, but through the extensive disinformation program that was in place, we were a hundred steps ahead of them and able to easily confuse their research with bogus documents referring to ourselves as the *Majestic 12*. I give you this brief history of the Group so that you will have complete confidence in our information, which has been collected, and verified with the most absolute scientific accuracy at our disposal. Are there any questions at this point?"

Blalock held his finger up.

"Commander Blalock, go ahead with your question."

"We've been in here for almost two hours now, and I think we need a break."

Yakov leaned to his left and whispered in Blalock's ear, "Thank you, commander, the mark of true leadership, Lenin would have given you the Order of the Tomb Urinater."

"Don't get me started Dimitri, I told you at the Center that we were only *even*."

Yakov put his arm around Blalock's shoulders and laughed. The four filed out of the room without waiting for permission.

"Well, er, I suggest we take a fifteen minute recess," Dr. Steele said to the empty table in front of the lectern. Steele turned to the now standing remainder of the speakers who were stretching and drinking water, a few filing out of the room themselves. He made eye contact with Dr. Aaron Sullivan, the consulting psychiatrist for the mission, and walked over. "A little on the rude side, wouldn't you say?"

"I'd say we have four guys with the cajones to maybe pull this thing off," Dr. Sullivan responded, smiling.

Seemingly startled, Steele replied, "Oh yes, yes, I see what you mean."

When the briefing resumed, Steele finished his presentation, which was the history of extra-terrestrial contact. The majority of the time was used to cover the spacecraft that crashed near Corona, New Mexico. The four pilots learned that the rumors that had circulated for years were true. An extraterrestrial scout ship while performing a reconnaissance mission over our only air base with atomic bombers near Roswell, New Mexico had crashed. Alien bodies were in fact obtained and the wreckage collected and sent to Wright Patterson Air Force Base where the Air Materials Command began an exhaustive investigation of its properties. Over a period of forty years, analysis of the extra-terrestrial technology led to the development of high tenacity materials such as Kevlar and the microcircuit. Silicon wafers with microscopic lines of finely etched silver were sent to Bell Labs which when combined with the recently invented transistor solved the heat and size constraints of conventional circuits. The micro revolution began which resulted in the fantastic leaps of computer technology of the sixties and seventies. Hand instruments harvested from the ship were found to be able to cut through solid objects with a beam of light and led to the discovery of the laser. The engineers could find no wiring anywhere in the ship. Instead, they found fine hair-like bundles threaded throughout the guts of the spacecraft and when light was passed over the broken ends, light came streaming out the other end of the fibers in a rainbow of colors. Fiber optics were a direct result of this discovery. The investigators could not find an engine or any kind of control mechanism such has a control stick or rudder pedals. It was later discovered that the engine was in the skin of the ship and used the magnetic field of the planet for propulsion.

Pratt & Whitney eventually unraveled the secrets of the gravity engine and developed the G-1A-15 Magnetodrive used in the SF-35A. Development of the G-1 engine was a heroic effort by the P & W engineers, in which nine men gave their lives attempting to disassemble the propulsion system of the alien ship. Twenty-three other engineers later died from a previously unknown type of thyroid cancer.

"For the next fifty years, the EBEs conducted a thorough military reconnaisance of the American and Soviet weapons capabilities. The two powers, while in a genuine global competition, became alarmed over ETE intentions and secretly agreed to build two massive arsenals of death. If the EBEs attacked and were able to neutralize one of the arsenals, the remaining arsenal would fire everything it had. We did not know their actual intentions during the Cold War, and so the responsible actions were taken by both super powers and that was to assume the worst case…that the EBEs were hostile."

The four pilots, whose attention was frozen solid by the revelations, didn't ask for a break for the next three hours as Dr. Steele rattled off the stunning truths of the greatest conspiracy in recorded history. "As of the present time, we have recovered nine ETE ships in various conditions. One lost a torpedo duel near St Augustine with one of our attack submarines. Another ship was shot down near Frankfort with a Nike Zeus, and the Navy bagged one in 1963 when an alien ship went into a hover at ten thousand feet right over the top of a missile cruiser. The most striking recovery, however, occurred in 1954. A completely intact saucer configuration ship was left sitting on the ground at an abandoned air base in Utah. We transported it to the Groom Lake facility and left it on the ramp for nine months until it stopped humming. This was by far the greatest find of all since all its systems were operational."

"Why did they leave us one of their ships, for God's sake?" Steele looked over at Duane.

"We don't know for sure, but we think it might have had something to do with the hot pursuit policy the Air Force had instigated with the Air Defense Command. Every time an ETE ship appeared, we launched everything we had in an attempt to force or shoot it down... we wanted that technology. We think they decided to give us one to so we'd stop pursuing-- which we did, by the way. Several members of the Group also expressed the opinion that the EBEs were supremely confident of their technology superiority and probably thought we'd never figure any of it out. This, of course was not the case. Other members of the Group wondered why only the west was harvesting crashed alien spaceships, and if their technology was so superior, why did they keep crashing?"

Yakov spoke up. "Is it possible that the UFO cosmonauts only wanted the Americans to have their technology so that we could be defeated?"

Steele nodded. "Not only possible, Colonel Yakov, but probable. Mr. Feldman has done extensive research into this question and will be briefing you in this matter tomorrow morning."

"Incredible!" Yakov exhaled in Russian.

"Even people from outer space hate us," Grosovitch answered in English.

Duane leaned forward and caught Alexi's attention. "Maybe your boy Lenin fucked with Darth Vader's Preparation H."

Blalock doubled over. A flurry of Russian ensued between Grosovitch and Yakov.

"Colonel Yakov, who is this Darth person Duane is babbling about?"

"I have no idea, but you had better curb your practical jokes. I am beginning to suspect that the African-American is similar to the African elephant…both have a long memory."

Dr. Steele could not hear the entirety of the conversation at the crew table, but looking at his watch, he noted it was six thirty.

"Gentlemen, this seems like a good point to break for the day. Your briefing books have a significant amount of information that will fill in the gaps of what was presented today."

The crew of the Stork gathered their notebooks as Dr. Steele walked over to their table. He shook hands with each man.

"Thank you for what you are about to do for all of us," he said.

And he meant it.

Day two of the big briefing kicked off at eight AM with two people missing from the speakers' table. Dr. Steele introduced Larry Feldman with a brief bio on a few of his stellar accomplishments. Steele told how Feldman had uncovered the alien plan and brought it to McCall, who had contacted Good who orchestrated the massive clandestine buildup. How the Group had embraced the Feldman plan in the face of paralysis of the central government, due to the fifth column effect of numerous and high placed traitors promised to be among the survivors and who had been converted by the facilitation process. It was a convoluted and tortuously complex story. Steele went on to explain how they had tested Feldman's skin for ultraviolet sensitivity and through tests proved that Feldman's skin showed no adverse reaction to continuous 1000 millirem UV bombardment for over twelve hours. This dosage would have fried normal human skin in minutes. In addition, they made him breathe an atomized mixture of $HNO2$ (nitrous acid) and nitric acid at concentrations which would normally eat a hole in a thin piece of steel sheeting. Feldman stayed on the special respirator for 36 hours, only breaking for meals, with no degradation of his lungs' alveoli and able in some unknown way to extract the oxygen from the lethal substances he was inhaling. Steele continued and said that Feldman has discovered that a few facilitators remained loyal even after the mind alterations were completed, and by debriefing this handful of people was able to collectively determine the complete alien plan for Earth and its people. The Group made significant contributions with its vast repository of data on extra-terrestrial activity collected for fifty years, especially transcripts of actual telepathic conversations with selected individuals in the intelligence community. The alien plan was incredibly subtle at first, and in a way humane and symbolic of the great race that they once were. "But all have sinned and fallen short, this fact eluded even them, and they went their evil way for they knew not what they did."

Dr. Steele completed his long monolog then turned to the seated people behind him. "Let me now introduce Mr. Lawrence Feldman."

Feldman had a manila folder crammed with notes as he walked up to the lectern, pushing his glasses back, which had slipped down his nose. The four pilots were all thinking the same thing. Those had to be the thickest glasses they had ever seen on a person. "Good morning gentlemen. After the brief synopsis by Dr. Steele, I'm glad to see that no one is weeping in the aisle."

Blalock and the two Russians looked at each other and then at Duane. Duane spoke up. "Mr. Feldman, my fellow crew members don't know about Demming."

"Perhaps you should explain, and I believe that several of our guests were not present when it happened either," Feldman answered, looking back at the table and getting a couple of nods.

Duane started. "Matt, as you know, we interviewed several other candidates for mission commander before you, one of which was a hot shot shuttle astronaut named Duke Demming. When we first started the recruiting process Mr. Feldman came in and gave an abbreviated version of what he's going to take all day doing with us. When we got the part about the evil plans of the enemy, Duke had some kind of seizure and started crying...got down on his knees and started talking in tongues...completely snapped his radish. We checked his folder later, and sure enough, he was in one of those holy roller denominations...we completely missed it."

Matt looked over at Yakov who was sitting with his arms folded and Grosovitch then back at Feldman. "Well, I just checked my crew, and nobody's crying yet...of course we haven't heard the whole story...we reserve the right to do all our crying later." Yakov laughed under his breath. Grosovitch just stared. Feldman reshuffled his papers and adjusted his glasses again, coughed once into his hand then took a sip of water.

"It sounds as if you are going to be able to handle the information satisfactorily."

Yakov passed a note to Blalock. "First you give Stingers to the Mujadeem, now this. You Americans aren't going to be happy until you finally kill me."

Blalock deadpanned and wrote underneath, "Think of the glory comrade, you'll be in the history books."

Yakov wrote right next to Matt's scrawl, "I'm *already* in the history books." And indeed he was. Yakov tore the page off the legal pad, wadded it up and tossed it dead center into a waste basket by the door about thirty feet away.

Feldman was ready to get started at last.

"We think there is a high probability that EBEs from various star systems have been visiting Earth for some time. The records are all holographic, of course, and are subject to widespread subjective analysis. The evidence from the last fifty years, however, is substantial, and we know a great deal about the EBEs from not only collected data but from the EBEs themselves, who until 1963 were periodically communicating directly with us. Firstly, we know that there are two basic groups of extraterrestrials who are interested in us. They appear separately and together and while their agendas do not coincide in many areas, one group will not interfere with the activities of the other. The group with whom we are concerned on this mission have been labeled by the flying saucer lunatic extreme as the Nordics. This is due to their very humanoid appearance. The second race, who are aiding the Nordics, we refer to as the Greys, so named because of the grayish cast of their skin. We refer to the aliens as ETBEs because we do not recognize them as human. ETBE stands for extraterrestrial biological entity. We will shorten this to EBEs for purposes of this briefing."

Yakov interrupted, "Mr. Feldman, I am puzzled as to why it is so important to dehumanize these people with your abbreviations…would not a highly advanced race also contain and likely practice advanced concepts of humanity?"

"Not necessarily," Feldman countered. "Consider results when the technologically advanced European race encountered the Aztecs. But there is a far more practical reason to deny their humanity, Colonel Yakov. And that reason is that we are going to kill them.

If we define them as human, we technically could be committing murder." Feldman shuffled through his notes and produced a 1963 legal opinion from Assistant Attorney General Norbert A. Schlei. "A copy of this document is in your package, but let me quote, '*Since criminal laws are construed strictly, it is doubtful that laws against homicide would apply to the killing of intelligent, man-like creatures alien to this planet.*'

We are looking at every detail of this operation to prevent possible repercussions upon your return."

"You mean we could be tried for murder?" Yakov asked incredulously.

"Extremely unlikely, Colonel Yakov, since the alleged crime would be taking place outside of any jurisdiction…but we felt obliged to at least look into this aspect. I believe when you hear the balance of the briefing, you will realize that this is a mission of self-defense, pure and simple."

"Continue your statement."

Feldman pushed his glasses off his nose and back onto his face.

"As I said, the last fifty years have been the most fruitful due mainly to our improved technology, and it was in this time frame that the EBEs decided to inform us of their intentions toward us that have been in progress for over a hundred years. In 1923, the EBEs placed a surveillance ship in orbit around Jupiter. When it detected the EM pulse from our first atomic test in 1945, it communicated with their central authority that is located in a planetary system of the star Tau Ceti forty light years away. The atomic test demonstrated we had reached a predetermined point in their process of qualification in their search of the galaxy for suitable places to perpetuate their species. Their home planetary system was gradually being absorbed by a small black hole, which they had captured and had been used to power their civilization for thousands of years. It had become uncontrollable and was warping the fabric of time and space making a mass evacuation of their society necessary. The problem was that while they could take a great many on their huge ships, the vast majority of their dense population would be left behind. Time was running out, but after hundreds of years of looking, they found a planet with a suitable species for the plan to prevent their extinction."

"If they were going to take our planet, what did they need us for?" Grosovitch asked.

"Their original plan was a humane and noble strategy that would result in the deaths of most of the alien population and no deaths of anyone on planet Jebus, their term for Earth. Their plan was to land as many colonists as possible on Mars, which they called the planet Malek. Mars was similar to their home world and then they would introduce their unique DNA slowly over many years into the population of homosapiens. This would allow perpetuation of their species by interbreeding, but at the sacrifice of five hundred billion sentient EBEs. Their high code of ethics and religion would not allow them to displace or take lives of other intelligent life. This was their great dilemma…to perpetuate their species without taking the lives of another race."

"This is the goddamdest story I have ever heard Mr. Feldman."

Feldman looked up from his notes at Blalock, "Perhaps you won't judge Mr. Demming so harshly now."

Feldman looked back at his notes and plunged on. "Then the unexpected happened. In the process of melting the remainder of the Martian ice cap as they terraformed, as it were, to get Mars to the climate of the home world, they made an alarming discovery about Earth. It seems that a cometary impact on Saturn had created subtle changes in Saturn's orbit which affected Earth's climate and caused the ice age. We have verified this with the work of our own scientists, by the way."

"So why would they care about an ice age on Earth if they're changing Mars into their home world? I'm totally lost in all this." Blalock asked.

"That wasn't the problem, Commander Blalock. The problem they discovered was that the worlds' nuclear arsenal, if detonated in a major war, could have the same effect, slightly scaled down, as a comet hitting Saturn. The subtle shift of Earth's orbit would cause Mars to have an ice age, reversing their entire plan and causing complete extinction of their race. This is when desperation began to set in and personal contact with their representatives was suddenly stopped. A consensus began to build toward a new plan, a more invasive plan that would include interbreeding and hybridization but also wholesale elimination of the Jebusites and annexing the planet for their own purposes. Desperation, self - preservation, the gradual erosion of their acute reasoning powers by exposure to the propulsion systems of their spacecraft, and other factors made them turn to their deity for divine intervention to solve their problem. Their deity responded and told them that Jebus and Malek would be their home and to take the two planets and annihilate the current occupants."

"Mars had occupants?" Grosovich asked.

"Yes, we were told that Mars had sea mammals and some were saved and genetically reproduced in Earth's oceans."

There was some stirring at the table with the pilots when Matt had a question.

"Where the fuck do these assholes get off thinking they can come in here and just take our planet?"

Feldman began to feel a little queasy, but took another sip of water before he answered. "Unfortunately, uhhh…there is precedent here on our own planet…the westward expansion of colonial America annexing Mexican and native territories…er…uhh and of course Israel." Feldman collected himself and continued, again pushing his heavy lenses back onto the bridge of his nose. "The alien plan was further complicated by a decision that they made in the late fifties. Concerned that we might accidentally engage in a global nuclear war they decided that in order to defuse the problem, one side had to achieve some kind of victory without using the arsenals. The EBEs allowed us to obtain their technology, at first by crashing their ships right next to our top laboratories and later handing one over intact at a closed air base in Utah. The great technology breakthroughs of the alien technology culminated in the design of the B-2 bomber, which broke the back of the Soviet Homeland Defense Radar Net."

"That is correct," Yakov spoke up.

"When the B-2's existence was disclosed, we knew it was over…we had no rubles left to completely replace our defense radars."

"And then the law of unintended consequences struck," Feldman continued.

"We were able to capitalize upon their technology so effectively that we began to realize that we could mount a potential defense against the EBEs using their own technology against them. The EBEs monitoring our technology racing forward by leaps and bounds realized that the gradual plan of DNA introduction had to be scrapped. If they stuck to the original timetable of hundreds of years, we would have been able to fight them before it was completed. Their final plan is what we're facing within the next six months using the solar max to cloak their movements.

"Their plan is twofold. One, they intend to create massive electrical discharges in the atmosphere similar to lightning which will burn the nitrogen in the air creating NO_2 and N_2O_4, which when combined with water vapor create highly acidic nitrogen oxides. This creates a lethal atmosphere killing all surface air breathing creatures and prevents photosynthesis in plant life. In a matter of hours, all air breathing animals on the Earth's surface would be killed and the plant food chain disabled. The level of nitrogen oxides created would wipe out the complete ozone layer in a matter of minutes. This would allow an unshielded bombardment of ultraviolet radiation that would cook to death anyone emerging from an underground bunker during daylight hours."

"Jesus Christ," Blalock exclaimed. There was some general discussion at the pilots' table after Feldman's last statement. Yakov and Grosovich were shaking their heads in disbelief. Blalock seemed to take a consensus about something.

"Mr. Feldman, how much time do we have?"

Feldman turned to the panel behind him.

One of the seated members spoke out. "The threat window will open in six months."

"What about your leadership, what is being done to prepare the people," Yakov wanted to know.

Another voice came from the seated men, "The decision was made years ago that the people could never be prepared for the knowledge of the existence of the EBEs. With hostilities imminent, the decision has just been made by the President on advice from the cabinet, that telling people now would create rioting in the streets which would disrupt the contingency plans to meet the threat."

"Many of us wanted to get this information to the people years ago," Feldman added, "But we were blocked at every juncture. Now, when the cooperation of the people might save lives, they're way behind. The government now has their asses in a crack, because they not only would have to tell the people that the UFOs are real, and admit they had been lying for fifty years, but that they are also hostile. I think you can see the hole they've dug for themselves. It would be a big pill to swallow."

"If everybody is going to be killed in hours, how will they keep their DNA going?" asked Grosovitch.

"Seven percent of the population are immune to the new lethal atmospheric conditions... people like me...they call us facilitators...they're going to use us for breeding stock."

Feldman took his glasses off and rubbed his eyes with his right hand. Then in a complete departure from the cool professional intelligence officer persona added a footnote.

"When they come for me, there will be fucking alien bodies piled high in my front yard because I'm going to kill as many of these cocksuckers as I can...before they..." Feldman caught himself and paused. He then felt around the top of the lectern for his glasses then put them back on.

"Excuse me for that slight digression, gentlemen, besides, I think this mission has a high probability of success and well....let me continue."

Feldman told of what they knew of the alien physiology, that there were internal organs, but nothing that seemed similar to that found in man, and there were fewer of them. There was no stomach and no excretory system and nothing that resembled food was found on their ship. Some of the Army pathologists who had examined the bodies advanced the theory that perhaps these were only some kind of android created for exploration and space flight and that we had not yet met their masters.

Feldman continued until one PM when they broke for lunch. The final hour was a withering barrage of contact reports from hundreds of pilots, including former President Jimmy Carter and aviation pioneer William Lear. Feldman folded his manila folder and readjusted his glasses for the last time. "Gentlemen, we are faced with the most dangerous enemy conceivable...vastly superior in technology, virtually beyond our understanding, relentless in purpose, driven by the instincts of self preservation like cornered animals, and imbued with a Jihad fanaticism that they are doing the will of Allah. They think our planet is a gift from God...their promised land, and they intend to take it."

The afternoon session of day two was a briefing by the Apollo 13 astronaut. He was considerably more relaxed than the previous speakers. Balding and hitting his late sixties he was trim and in good shape, he came to the lectern with a quiet dignity and confidence that immediately got the four rookies attention. He dimmed the lights and started the slide projector from the controls on the lectern and once again the big screen unreeled from the wall.

"Well, I trust everyone had a nice lunch contemplating our invincible foes from outer space who want to waste us." The four chuckled and the tension was broken for a few more minutes. "I'm here to brief you on the flight plan of the mission, the details for which are in the large blue notebook. As you can see it is extensive...that's the bad news. Here's the good. Ninety-five percent of this mission will automated and run by the onboard computers...so there is nothing to worry about, worry about, worry about." He was citing the punch line of an old airline joke. Blalock and Duane laughed; the Russians didn't get it. "What you are going to do is a plan devised but not used by NASA on the Apollo program. Not because it wouldn't work, but because as it turned out it wasn't necessary. You're going to do what is called the EOR profile which stands for Earth Orbit Rendezvous. You will launch in a modified and stripped-down Russian shuttle from Kourou here in French Guyana. The slide projector popped in a slide of the sprawling European Spaceport ideally situated almost exactly on the Equator. This allowed launches to take advantage of the Earth's greater rotational speed and put significantly larger payloads into orbit with less fuel.

"There are no European launches scheduled for the next four months due to a massive construction program they kicked off last year. A handful of our people are there now and Tupelov will send another one hundred twenty technicians when the Stork is flown in on its carrier aircraft. There are only twelve people in the French Arian organization who know that there will be a launch of the Stork and only two of these guys know where it's actually going and why. Everybody else thinks it's going to be sent to Bogota and put on static display and converted to a restaurant similar to what they did with Buran, the first Russian shuttle, now set up in Gorky Park.

"After the launch, you will make four Earth orbits and rendezvous with the Energia RD-170. Mr. McCall will go EVA after the automatic docking maneuver and assure a positive lock is made between the two vehicles."

"That's what we were practicing in the zero gravity simulator at the Gagarin Center, " Duane observed.

"Correct," the space veteran continued. "After docking with the booster, you will do a systems check on your navigation and propulsion systems prior to the LIB or Lunar Insertion Burn. The shuttle does not carry enough fuel by itself to escape from the Earth's gravity well, but the big Energia has plenty of power to get you there no sweat. Enroute trip time is approximately five days. Upon arrival at the moon, you will do a LOB or Lunar Orbit Burn from the remaining fuel in the Energia which will put you into a transpolar Lunar orbit at seventy miles with a perigee of thirty five miles. You will make three orbits. The first orbit will be a reconnaisance to locate and identify the Shard and the Tower which protrude from the Aries Basin. The astronaut hit the slide advance button and another photograph popped into view. It was an oblique photo of the moon's South pole showing the distinct unnatural extrusions of the two alien bases with several cigar shaped ships docked nose in to one of the structures. The astronaut turned to address Feldman who was looking up at the photo from almost beneath it.

"Mr. Feldman, I believe this is the one you were looking for?"

"Son of a bitch!" said Feldman. "They tried to renumber the photo sequence, but I caught them red handed."

"Thank God that you did," the astronaut responded.

"These pyramidal structures extend five thousand feet above the surface, are highly reflective and perfectly black almost as if they have an obsidian surface. The next slide clicked in which was a close up of the two structures. "As you can see, magnification doesn't help much, but radar sounding by Clementine before she went off the air gave us this." The next slide showed a radar sounding graph of the Lunar surface directly over the alien artifacts.

"Holy shit, they're huge!"

"You got that right. These scale lines down the side of the image here represent one hundred meters each. The Shard and the Tower come together one thousand meters below the surface with the remaining sides of both structures extending beyond the radar sounding depth of forty-three kilometers. That's twenty-three miles down for those of you who haven't switched to the metric system yet. The alien base may fill up half the inside of the moon for all we know…this is only as far as we can see."

"How the hell are we going to knock out something that big?" Blalock asked.

"We're not sure that we can, all we want to do is ring their chimes and delay their operation."

Click flash, the next slide popped in.

"After positively identifying the targets you will update the guidance system on your weapons for the remainder of the orbit. During orbit number two you will deploy the LMX to the surface with Mr. McCall who will set up the ground based laser illuminator."

Click flash. "After deploying the Lunar Rover, you will be seeding your weapons which will trail out behind you in deteriorating orbits slowly descending into the target. Orbit three you will retrieve the surface team and undock from the Energia for firing the last stage of the booster. The Energia third stage contains a one hundred megaton thermonuclear warhead with a subsurface bunker penetrating casing. It has a sensor fuse that will not detonate the device until another nuclear explosion is sensed. The forth and final orbit will commence the EIB or Earth Insertion Burn by the internal engines on the Stork. Upon establishment of an Earth insertion trajectory, you will arm and fire the weapons you have previously seeded into orbit. They will home on the laser illuminator pods seeded in the weapons package backed up by the ground illuminator. Once the weapons have glimpsed the illuminated targets, the rest is going to be like the Persian Gulf. When the first twenty megaton warhead detonates the one hundred megaton device will also go off."

"That's going to get their attention," Blalock commented.

"Either that or just really piss them off." Matt nodded at Duane in agreement.

"Gentlemen, there is more." The four stopped talking among themselves and looked back at the lectern.

"After the combined one hundred twenty megaton explosion occurs, for the next hour every six minutes the target will be hit with another twenty megaton ground penetrating warhead. At the completion of the nuclear attack there will be another interval of two and a half hours to allow the target to cool down to approximately twenty degrees Celsius. At the end of that interval, we believe that it is highly likely that at least part of the target will be opened up. At that point a simultaneous chemical attack will commence using fifteen enhanced capacity BLU-80 Bigeye chemical weapons containing GB5, the latest and most lethal of the nerve agents. The GB5 in just one of the warheads is enough to kill the entire population of California." The astronaut consulted his notes.

"Dr. Davadov, did I pronounce your name correctly?"

"Quite right." A stocky disheveled Ukrainian took some notes out of a well-worn leather case and rambled up to the lectern.

"Before I continue the flight plan briefing, Dr. Davadov will brief you on the third weapon system we will be using."

"Is pleasure to be part of important mission for life of world." Dr. Davadov was the only former Soviet scientist whose English was not flawless. "After chemical attack, remaining weapons in seeding orbit will fire rocket motors and strike target. As you know, Aitken Basin contains a great deal of water in the form of slushy permafrost. A great deal of surface water will be evaporated away by stream of nuclear explosions, but calculations show that a great deal will remain. The EBEs chose to build their base in the middle of massive permafrost of slushy water because we think they are using it for life support and possibly power."

"How would they get life support and power out of water?" Grosovitch asked.

"Water is one part hydrogen and two parts oxygen. Split them up and you have breathing air and hydrogen for fuel. Immediately after the chemical attack the remaining weapons will hit. These are biological warheads containing RTE, the most toxic substance ever created on Earth. It is a space survivable, genetically engineered combination of Rift Fever, Tularemia, and Ebola. These weapons will burst into the warm melted water surrounding the alien base. Tests on alien tissue samples showed that the RTE was extremely aggressive in attacking and destroying the cell membranes and infecting the host. You must assure that in the case of a hung weapon in the magazine, that it is not a RTE. You cannot return home with a RTE projectile on the Stork. A crash which released the RTE, theoretically could kill the population of the entire planet within a couple of weeks. And there is no antidote or vaccine. This toxin was developed specifically for this mission and as a result it is virtually unkillable in the sanguine conditions here on mother Earth."

Yakov was nodding his head. So, that's what that shit was for, he thought. If these gadgets work as advertised, we might just pull a rabbit out of the hat.

"God forbid, but what's going to happen to all this weapons material if the Stork does a Challenger," Blalock asked.

"Is good question," Dr. Davadov nodded and checked something in his notes. "The weapons bay magazine is a hardened self contained unit and will automatically be ejected from the Stork by rocket motor and lowered to Earth by parachute recovery. And even if this system fails, as long as the weapons have not been armed, they will not detonate, even with a massive malfunction of the RD-170."

"And after they're armed?" Duane continued.

"You will not arm the weapons delivery systems until the Earth insertion burn is

established on the way back, so should not be consideration."

"What happens if we get a hung bomb?"

The astronaut stood up and walked back to the lectern. "Gentlemen, we believe we have emergency procedures that will cover just about anything that will come up and we'll be covering this stuff in detail at Tupelov during systems ground school."

Duane leaned over to Matt and whispered in his ear as if he was continuing the astronauts comments…"so there's nothing to worry about, worry about…"

The briefing was extended for another three days as the four guys virtually interrogated the panel members who were not part of the original presentation. The Texas phase of the flight planning wound up on a

Friday, and Saturday morning they were on their way back to Russia on United out of San Francisco.

The school at the Tupelov plant was held in a small office with little more than the huge Shuttle flight manual and scores of slides of the various systems explained in broken English by one of the handful of designers that was still around who knew anything about the vehicle.

The Russian shuttle was much like the American spaceplane except that it had a sort of Russian loosey goosy design philosophy that was hard to grasp. Yakov explained that it was the same idea behind the AK47 versus the M16. The AK would keep firing after completely being submerged in mud whereas the M16 had to be continually cleaned and preened. "Whatever the malfunction, even if it's not in the book, there's always a way to fix it with a Russian design," he said over and over in school. Several of the interesting differences in the Russian ship included a "slot RAT," and photoelectric cells on the inside of the payload doors in case of a complete power cell failure. The slot RAT was a tiny slotted intake of the top of the fuselage that was manually opened with a screw cable device which took ram air during re-entry and powered a turbo-hydraulic pump to operate the flight controls in case the APU was inoperative. The two problem systems according to Yakov were that the thruster maneuvering jets had a separate fuel supply from the OME (orbital maneuvering engines). This meant you had to be cagey with fuel management on the thrusters so that you'd have enough to get the ship into the proper re-entry attitude of 22-30 degrees nose down when it was time to come home. The American shuttle used the same fuel supply for all orbit useable engines and did not have this problem. The other problem system was oxygen supply, although there was an onboard capability sufficient for the round trip to the moon, which used liquid oxygen augmented by a chemical oxygen generator and scrubber. Oxygen generating cartridges had to be changed every twelve hours and the scrubber unit had to be replaced every twenty-four hours. Unlike learning a new aircraft, shuttle systems problems were attacked by long complex checklists using decision tree designs. Unfortunately, it was all still printed in Russian and Blalock insisted that everyone painstakingly hand write the translations under the Russian text.

"I know what it says, why do I have to put this in English?" Grosovitch protested.

"Because we're going to be speaking English, Alexi...from here until we get home. I don't want to hear any more Russian out of you and Dimitri." The three noticed a definite change in the tone of Blalock's voice...still laid back and calm...but he was beginning to assert himself as the commander. Matt noted their expressions. Good, he thought. It's time we get serious with this dog and pony show we signed up for.

Systems school went by fast and was much like trying to take a drink of water out of a fire hydrant. Yakov knew the shuttle far better than the instructor did and time and again stopped the lesson to explain how some something really worked. Blalock's opinion of Yakov went higher every day. Yakov appreciated the easygoing nature of the Americans and their eagerness to learn without the gruff ego mania he had to endure with the Soviet cosmonauts and their lurking jealousy of him getting a plum assignment.

The crew was coming together at last. Duane commented on the last day of ground school, "What was that line out of "Independence Day?" He got blank looks from the other three. "You know, where Will Smith says *it's time to get up there and kick ET's ass?"*

"One last item, gentlemen," Matt announced on the last day of school, "and this is no reflection on Duane, we'll be taking Alexi on the mission to help out on the surface."

Duane nodded his head in agreement, he'd been thinking along the same lines. Yakov pounded Grosovitch on the shoulder, both men with shit eating grins on their faces.

"The chicks will not leave you alone when you come back the big hero," Yakov laughed.

"Yeah," Grosovitch smiled...the infinite possibilities unfolding before the fertile imagination of a single, twenty-five year old fighter pilot.

Chapter 52

Trask punched the intercom to Carson Benchly's office. "Carson, can you see me right now?"

Benchly knew that tone of voice, it was not a request or a suggestion and he put down what he was reading and headed over to the Director's office.

"Carson, the French are fueling one of their Energia RD-170s down at Kourou."

"That's odd," Benchly replied.

"Our information is that Kourou will be closed for launch operations for another ninety days when the construction is completed."

"You think that's odd, look at this."

Benchly looked at the satphoto images Trask pushed across the desk to him. Benchly put on his reading glasses. "Oh gosh, is that the Stork?"

"Yep, they flew it in three days ago and it disappeared into the hangar to the right of

the spacecraft. It was white when it went in."

Benchly swallowed hard as he scanned the photo. The Stork was hooked to a tug and was being towed toward the massive assembly/mating building at the French spaceport.

The Stork had been painted black.

"Still think that sumbitch is headed for the pages of Bon Appetite?"

Benchly felt a knot in his stomach.

"Carson, that crazy Texan is going to fly that sumbitch with our stolen recce package and the Frenchies are in cahoots with him."

"Clearly, this is a job for the State Department, boss."

"I've already sent them a message and I've notified the FBI that Mr. JB McCall needs to have another talking to."

Benchly handed the stack of photos back to Trask.

"Assuming you're right, Leonard, why did they paint the ship black?"

"Why indeed, and why do we have another RD-170 in a low equatorial orbit?

Carleton, old steed, I have all the questions. What I don't have are any answers."

The call from the FBI came later that day at the TriAmCo HQ. They would be coming out the following morning and would most appreciate Mr. McCall making himself available for an interview. In fact by the time the phone call came, Federal Agents already had the TriAmCo complex under clandestine observation. Bremen and Good were exchanging the binoculars looking at something out the window of the twenty-fourth story when McCall walked in on them.

"The FBI wants to come for a chat tomorrow morning, what do I tell em'?" John Good kept his back to McCall and left the room without speaking.

Bremen put the glasses down on his desk and walked over to McCall and shook hands. "J.B., the FBI has been here since this morning. The entire complex is under observation by long range sensors and a few lads in a Texas Highway Department van about three miles up the black top."

"This does not seem like a promising development," McCall exhaled.

"I hate being at odds with the good guys." Bremen was unconcerned. "J.B. we're about fourteen steps ahead of our friends out there. I wouldn't worry about a thing. Just have your meeting and deny everything. I'll take care of the rest."

The following morning, Special Agents Daryl Green and Michael Pomeroy were ushered into the Taj McCall. Neither man even flinched at the expansive grandeur. Green came out from Washington and Pomeroy was out of the Dallas field office.

"How about some coffee for you boys?" McCall asked cheerily.

Green began. "Mr. McCall, we didn't come out here to drink coffee. We have evidence that you have participated in the theft of top secret government property for conversion to your own uses. And we are specifically referring to the AeroNutronics Geoexplorer. If it was up to me I would have hauled your ass out of here last night for interrogation in Dallas. Pomeroy here seems to think that you deserve some special treatment based on your government service. I however…"

Pomeroy cut him off at this point. "Agent Green, may I have a word before we continue Mr. McCall's interview?"

"Feel free to use the conference room gents." McCall stood up and ushered the two federal officers to the oaken door, behind which was the conference room. The two agents disappeared into the room and closed the door. McCall went back to his desk and called Bremen. "Lowell, they're here and I think they're fixin' to really get in my shit."

"They'll be getting the call any minute, relax," Bremen answered with serene self confidence.

Chapter 53

Trask had called a special meeting of all department heads and the representatives from the joint task force from CIA. The FBI had not been invited. "We are here to evaluate some rather disparate intelligence we have collected and try to figure out just what the hell is going on and what we should brief the president about it. You all have had twenty-four hours to review the packages which we provided. Carlton you're up."

"Okay, here goes." Carleton walked to the front of the room, pulled his laser pointer out of his pocket and the lights dimmed. The projector then displayed the first image. "Six months ago an elaborate ruse was started in Bogota, Colombia to create the idea that a private group was going to erect a Russian space shuttle and use it as a restaurant." The projector clicked.

"As you can see they went to some rather elaborate extremes to pull this off. A month after construction began, the GeoExplorer MK5 satellite disappeared from AeroNutronics Ford under complex circumstances. The loss of this technology represents a major blow to our intelligence capabilities and compromises extremely sensitive data on the whereabouts of petroleum and other resources. The package was stolen by this man."

The next slide showed J.B. McCall walking out the front gate of the Botanical Gardens in Cayenne, the capitol of French Guyana, two years prior while he was there negotiating drilling leases.

"By an incredibly complex network of dummy corporations and most likely cooperation of insiders, the GeoExplorer was declassified on paper only and then leased to a series of dummy companies. We believe the satellite will be taken into orbit by a Russian space shuttle similar to this one."

The next slide showed the Buran touching down on its maiden and only space flight near Baikonar. "The next issue, which complicates the matter, is this." The next slide was a recent photo from the NIROP showing the RD-170 in the low equatorial orbit. "We still have no idea what this is all about. And here is the piece de resistance on the Russian shuttle."

Benchly punched in the latest slide they had from a Keyhole 10 of the French launch complex. Murmurs went up around the room. "What you see is correct gentlemen. The Russian shuttle has not only been painted a deep space black color, but as you can see in this image, the technicians have completely removed the landing gear."

"Are they going to leave the GeoExplorer in orbit?" somebody asked.

"It would make sense...no evidence that they stole it in the first place," another voice answered.

The room was chattering. "How are the cosmonauts going to get home with no landing gear?"

Benchly kept going. "Now, the crop circles. Careful analysis of their locations reveals a disturbing trend of that suggests that they may be target markers of some kind. The one up here in Hudson New York was the key. The only strategic target in this vicinity is the CCF for the SF-35s."

The guy from CIA raised his pen, "But the circles are not directly on top or even close to the alleged targets they are supposedly marking, and there are no circles anywhere near the coastal cities."

The theories were flying thick and heavy when Trask's secure cell phone chirped once. "Un-fucking-believable," Trask muttered into the handset. "You have positive confirmation? By a Aeronutronic's employee? Unprecedented!" Trask folded up his cell phone and rapped the side of his water glass with his pen. The intense discussion quieted down.

"There's been a further complication…the GeoExplorer has been found."

The room, at that point went dead silent for about thirty seconds, then erupted in something akin to, but not exactly what you'd call chaos. These men were seasoned veterans of everything that could go wrong in the world.

Yep, they found the GeoExplorer safe and sound. It was still wrapped up in its fancy Mylar protective cocoon in a rented, air-conditioned storage building only five miles from the AeroNutronics plant. It had been there all along.

*   **

Special agents Green and Pomeroy emerged from TriAmCo's big conference room and seated themselves again in front of McCall's carrier-sized desk. This time Pomeroy spoke first. "Mr. McCall we admit to the possibility that you were given some bad advice concerning your involvement with these people who have stolen the GeoExplorer. If you'll just give us an explanation to the best of your knowledge, given your esteemed record of citizenship and service to our nation, we are prepared to make a recommendation to the Attorney General not to…."

Right then Special Agent Green's cell phone went off.

"What? They found it? Ahhhhhh shit! Uhhh, thank you….understood."

Green punched Pomeroy on the arm.

"We have no further business here."

"What's the big news boys?" McCall queried.

Green, in a completely subdued, tone says, "Mr. McCall, we're sorry to have bothered you…uhh, well, come on Pomeroy, lets go."

Everybody shook hands and that was the end of the FBI until two months later.

Colonel Lowell Bremen, Deputy Director of Army Intelligence, (Ret.) had outfoxed the KGB for over thirty years. Spoofing the feds was like taking Cub Scouts on a snipe hunt, but Bremen's greatest challenge was still ahead.

Chapter 54

On July 25, 2000, the Stork's crew arrived in French Guiana and checked into the Mercure Ariatel near the airport. The same day, the NSA issued its first Emergency War Warning in its history, when collective sensor intelligence from dozens of sources noted a massive concentration of vehicular activity in Lunar space. Seven coronal mass ejections per day like photon tsunamis were washing through our surveillance satellites and one after another was being literally fried to an electronic death by the worst solar outbursts in recorded history. Every day, every hour, little by little, we were going blind. Leonard Trask along with key members of the NSA and CIA had evacuated to the huge underground FEMA base near Altavista, Virginia. Carlton Benchly stayed behind. There was no pass for his wife to go with him to the bunker and he told his boss that he would not leave her.

Trask, a widower, shook hands with his second in command at the Land Office the day of departure then went to a closet and pulled out a rifle case and handed it to Benchly. "Carleton, I hope to God you won't need this, but it might come down to it."

"Thanks Leonard, I hope you're wrong." Benchly and Trask shook hands once more and that was the end of it. The press was told that a Camp David retreat was gearing up when in reality president and his cabinet were packing up for evacuation to the most secure place in the nation, the NORAD air defense base buried deep in Rockies. A skeleton staff was left in the White House who had no idea what was happening except there certainly were a lot of people leaving town all of a sudden.

Also on July 25th, the CCF went active, two miles deep beneath Iron Mountain, New York. The fifty-fourth SF-35 had just finished post - production testing and was leaving the Lockheed Marietta plant by C-5 for Cape Canaveral where half the fighter wings would be based. The other half would be at Vandenberg, the availability of liquid oxygen being the limiting factor in the early deployment phase. The crews were already settled in and the simulator/duplicators were coming on line as soon as each SF-35 finished its pre-launch checks and established data/control link with the CCF. The lengthy preflight testing was seriously shortened due to the onset of the crisis and also due to the fact that the SF-35 did not require an onboard pilot. One of the first things the crews did was change the name of the fighter. "Australus" was a little too wimpy and the SF–35 was re-dubbed the Lightning 2, in honor of its distinguished WW-II namesake built by the same company. The Lightning crews in their ready rooms were on chalkboards and computers literally twenty-four hours a day working on tactics to use against the EBEs. Airbus and British Aerospace were almost completed tooling up for SF-35 production and Marchetti in Italy, and Mitsubishi in Japan had the plans to the space fighter and were proceeding as quickly as they could, but were far behind the Americans and the French/British effort.

July was the so-called dry season in French Guiana. Even so, it was hurricane season and a minor depression was ginning up twenty five hundred miles west of San Juan. And while the mornings are usually clear this time of year, the counter clockwise flow off of the low pushed up against Guiana's Atlantic coast. It then drifted across the Maronhi River, lifted up over the Tumac-Humac Mountains then released its moisture in wavy curtains of rain that drenched the countryside for hours on end. When the mornings were clear, early risers tasting the sweet damp morning air witnessed magnificent sunrises over the Atlantic framed in golden edged towering clouds. And on the Earth, fuchsia blooming Bougainvillea, covered trellises, fences and rusting iron gates of the old French colony. Bordered to the north by the ocean, the west by Surinam, and Brazil to the east, the tiny nation is ninety percent rainforest and mangrove swamps. The rainwater cascades through the streets of Cayenne down the worn wagon ruts in the narrow brick roads of the old city and into the gutters where it is efficiently drained away by the sewer system installed by Napoleon's engineers over a hundred years before. Until the French built the European Spaceport at Kourou, a hundred kilometers west of Cayenne, French Guiana's main claim to fame was being the location of Devils Island and its famous prisoners Henri, 'Papillion,' Charriere, and the French Army officer Alfred Dreyfus.

Of course, all this was about to change. Within a single decade, Kourou, its great patriotic Governor Stephen Phinera, and the part the two played in the historic mission of the Stork would be common knowledge among the school children of an entire world. It was July 25, 2000 and the huge leather-backed turtles were laying their eggs in the humid nights on the beaches of Mana, the coastal town near St. Laurent Du Maroni. The crew of the Stork had no idea of course, but it was quite possible that if the plans of the EBEs succeeded, the great sea turtles of Mana would never make their trek to the warm wet sands of Guiana again.

Blalock and his crew called a couple of taxis and had themselves delivered to the visitors center just outside the front gate of the sprawling EuroSpace launch complex.

Blalock looked at his watch, he was on time, where was the contact? The crew was browsing, looking at the displays, when a tall, tanned, lean looking guy, wearing Arian blue technicians' coveralls, came through the front door, looked around the room and made a bee line for Blalock.

"Commander Blalock, welcome to Kourou. My name is Mike Mancusso."

Chapter 55

The president and his cabinet sat in the viewing area behind the rows of consoles that were a hundred feet set back from the huge multi situation display. From this position, deep inside Cheyenne Mountain, the duty commander, Marine General David Chetwood would be able to command and direct America's entire nuclear and conventional defense had the president not been present. For forty years, men had sat at Chetwood's position prepared to take the nation through a nuclear holocaust. Men who were selected for this assignment were the smartest and the steadiest combat officers in the entire military.

Chetwood had served in Vietnam, Somalia, the Persian Gulf, and Kosovo. He was a mustang who started off as a rifleman humping the paddies of III Corps, and made it to two stars picking up a Ph.D. in history from Harvard, along the way. Chetwood's expertise was war fighting. The buzz on the guy around the Pentagon was that after Commandant of the Marine Corps, he'd be the next Chairman of the Joint Chiefs.

Chetwood was noticing something unusual about the ETE formations as they joined up their ships in Lunar space. Of course, there was no way of knowing what they would do when they arrived in Earth space, but he was hoping against hope that what he saw developing was a trend.

Consulting with the other branch chiefs on the secure line to their underground base outside Washington, the War Staff at NORAD felt that the attack would come in two or three phases. The EBEs would probably conduct one last reconnaissance, then an attack in mein or attack in sections using whatever weapons they had, cutting up the targeted surface of the planet a piece at a time. Upon leaving Lunar space, the EBEs were coming in five large formations of just over a hundred ships each. Each formation looked like the letter "Y" and the five formations flew in trail in the direction of the single vertical stroke of the letter. It looked like five capital letter Ys stacked on top of one another, travelling toward the bottom of the page. For some reason, they did not seem to be in much of a hurry, and the ETA of the lead formation was about seventy-two hours.

The USA, Russia, France, China, and the UK were on Defcon 2 for the second time in history. One entire console, the width of the massive room, directly in front of General Chetwood's position was dedicated to communications with the allies. The Chinese confirmed our estimates of numbers, type of formation, and ETA, and this caused something of a stir, since we had not been aware that they had advanced to this level of sophistication. Everyone's missiles were spun up, every available bomber in the air or on runway alert. Each awaiting targeting coordinates in the event of an actual landing of forces, though not one planner thought this would happen until the inhabitants of the planet had been neutralized. Fighter Command was conducting continuous patrols over major cities and defense installations and the US Navy and Russian Navy had attack submarines guarding the approaches to each nation's major coastal cities. One Russian Kurst class boat, that could not get home in time after the Defcon 2 went into effect had been attached to the US Navy and was patrolling the east coast off New York, down to just north of Norfolk. We did the same thing with one of our fast attack boats which was off Murmansk when the shit hit the fan. It was strange, Russian boats protecting our cities and American submarines protecting the approaches to a Russian city and all the nations of the Earth unified for the first time to meet a common threat. Even Nigeria, the most intractable, most corrupt government on the planet sent a secret message to the president. They were switching a significant portion of their refineries over to the production of Syntin, the preferred fuel for the SF-35s.

The last thing the EBEs wanted was a massive nuclear exchange. And while the threat of this had deterred them for forty years, we had now disarmed from Cold War levels and stupidly, kept the population ignorant of the existence of extra-terrestrials because we thought they *"couldn't handle it."* Now, it was too late to evacuate the cities or build enough shelters. A massive nuclear exchange with an unaware and unprotected population would merely do the alien's work for them.

Chetwood was the first to figure out why the aliens were taking their time. It became evident when NASA sent over the sunspot warning. Record sized storms were raging on the surface of the sun and were expected to create coronal mass ejections totaling close to a trillion tons of solar material. We could expect arrival of the associated CME in seventy- four hours. It would likely blind the remaining satellites and drown radio and telephone communications for at least twenty-eight hours. That, combined with the trajectory of the enemy formations, gave Chetwood the first glimpse into their intentions. They would hit North America first during daylight hours when coincidentally Earth was between the Moon and the Sun. They would then engage their weapons, peeling us like an apple as the Earth turned on its axis, attacking behind a blinding curtain of lethal rain from our home star. The sunrise after their arrival would be the last for each continent and its people. It was brilliant and worthy of a truly advanced intelligence, to combine the limitless power of the sun with their own advanced means and technology. We would be gone before the whimper left our lips.

We had such great promise as a species, Dave Chetwood mused to himself. We had many falls as we stumbled up from the primordial ooze, but we got up each time and kept going. We climbed out of the Rift Valley and made our way into Europe and Asia. We killed and maimed but we also built the pyramids and listened on one knee to the new messages of hope and love from Jesus, Buddha, and Krishna. We came into the age of reason and used our technology to conquer the sky then reach for stars. Unless we got a big break, Chetwood summarized; the great promise of the human race would not be kept.

There was something gnawing in the back of Chetwood's mind and once it surfaced into cognition, he called a meeting.

There were four general grade officers present at the meeting besides Chetwood. He flashed a slide on the screen of the lead formation on its arcing approach to an up sun vector, the heading upon which it would slide into Earth space. "Does anybody remember MacArthur's analysis of the classic blunder of the Japanese commanders in the Pacific?"

There were several heads nodding yes. But Air Force Brig. General Brad Simms shook his head no.

"Dave, I guess I'm the dumb one in here, better tell me."

"Brad," Chetwood began, "This is the longest shot I've ever called, but here's what I think these fuck heads might just do....and if they do, we've got a shot."

Chapter 56

All hell broke loose on the EuroSpace Complex when they rolled the mated, Stork-Energia RD-170 vehicle from the main assembly building. The two hundred some odd technicians of French Aerospace and the guys from Tupelov were steeped in the currency of secret operations and were no strangers to classified military missions being launched out of Kourou. But, the rest of the base personnel had never seen a space shuttle mated to one of their big boosters, and painted black, the Stork had an apocalyptic look to it that scared the hell out of everybody. The first buzz that swept the base was that the Americans were involved. Then people noticed the small red star on the left wing of the iron black ship, and the word began spreading and no amount of spin control could contain it. Several European reconnaisance satellites in the work-up bays awaiting launch were detecting high levels of plutonium in the vicinity and the significant background signature of nuclear weapons. Pre-launch testing was giving the technicians alarming off scale readings. You didn't have to be a Hercule Poirot to figure out that all this had something to do with the Stork.

The French birds had been sleeping peacefully in heir nests until the Russian shuttle showed up, then they went crackers. Louis Bleriot, the Base Manager and descendant of the aviation pioneer was one of the two Frenchmen that knew what was going on, where it was going, and why. Bleriot, a fencing master in the art of political dueling where the contestants had dirigible sized egos and 180 IQs deftly parried the increasingly

Bill Broocke

worried inquiries until the call came from ITN. They wanted him to confirm information they had about a Russian space shuttle being launched at Kourou. He stalled them by saying there was a classified military operation but that he was authorized to give them an exclusive on the story if they would withhold broadcast until after the launch, which was imminent. Unfortunately, the story had leaked farther than ITN. Two members of the Prime Minister Chirac's cabinet had been leaked the story by an ITN correspondent. None of the three would pass the ultraviolet skin test. One of the cabinet members made an overseas call to Guiana's governor Stephen Phrinery for confirmation. Phrinery gave his absolute assurance that the Russian shuttle story was a huge hoax that originated over the Internet which even had fake telephoto images of a black space shuttle mated to a big booster. That he, himself, had gone out to the launch complex to check out the rumor, and that all was in tranquility except for the construction crews finishing the big expansion project. Governor Phrinery was the other Frenchman who knew the inside story.

Despite denials, an encrypted e-mail originated from the one French cabinet member and successfully arrived at the e-mail address of a cabinet member for the American President. "Possible interfering military operation commencing in Kourou," it read. Secretary Hayes-Udall deleted the message and headed over to Harrison-DuPont's NORAD VIP quarters to discuss what should be done.

"Brad," Chetwood continued, "The Japanese commanders in the Pacific, even when enjoying a numerical superiority, time after time committed their forces piecemeal. We chopped them up like mincemeat.

Instead of one massive coup de mein on Guadalcanal, they made dozens of individual Banzai charges right into the teeth of our machine guns."

"Why the hell did they do that?

"Brad, they did it because they did not understand the concept of force economy. They thought that by holding back they could defeat us and not expose larger numbers of their forces. Instead, all they did was march straight into a Marine hamburger machine. They did this time and again in an effort to hold down casualties…instead it guaranteed maximum losses."

Chetwood turned to the conference room's tactical repeater display and pulled out his telescoping metal pointer. "As you can see, the EBEs are forming up in trail and coming down the attack axis single file, one after another. If they only employ part of their force and we give them a bloody nose…well, it's a long shot. But remember what we know about them. They say they have never fought a war and they found our peculiar warlike nature surprising and extremely rare in their travels. They told us how precious life was to them and what a benign race they were. So, unless they were bull shitting us from the git go, they are departing from the natural benign predisposition of their race into an area where we might have an edge. We've spent our entire recorded history perfecting our ability to kill each other in exponentially more efficient ways. My general recommendations are as follows, the details you will provide for the final draft of the battle plan.

"One, Get every flyable SF-35 up ASAP. Brad, have them cover as much as the CONUS as possible, you tell me the best way to do this.

Two, get all our fighters up and keep them there. Ground all civilian aircraft. Any target not squawking the correct IFF code will be considered hostile and attacked immediately. The orders will be to attack ETE ships at any cost including using nuclear missiles over the cities. If we can't hit their spacecraft with missiles, we have to ram them."

Air Force General Brad Simms looked up from his note pad. "My boys will know what to do," he said.

"We'll have to coordinate this with our allies, Chetwood continued, "we can't tell them what to do, but tell em' this is what we are going to do. I think they'll follow.

Same deal with the submarines and surface forces. They have to aggressively attack any ETE ship they encounter submerged or over the sea. Fire everything they've got including tactical nukes near the cities. There can be no holy ground. Even if we don't catch the son of a bitch until he's inside the Golden Gate, hit him with anything and everything that we've got. I don't care if half of San Francisco disappears in a fireball, if we get the bastard it will be worth it. Success of this plan is based on aggressiveness. We must aggressively attack and continue to attack the enemy with everything we've got. If there is only one pilot in one F-15 left in the air, I want that man to fire all his missiles or ram the enemy to score a hit."

Chetwood made eye contact with Sims. "Brad, once the battle is joined, I expect all pilots to fight until out of fuel. We will be relentless in this attack until either they or we are vanquished." Chetwood nodded to his aide who walked around the conference table and distributed a fifty page double spaced outline.

"This is a work in progress, gentlemen, I need your best thoughts and your best people working on he final version."

The CCF, deep inside Iron Mountain, was a hive of activity as SF-35 crews climbed into their duplicators and uplinked to their specific aircraft on both coasts. Forty-nine SF-35s were mission ready when the launch orders came. Cape based crews, even though they were safely under two miles of solid granite, could see from their cockpits crystal clear views of the launch site. They could see the ice on the LOX hoses being retracted by the NASA fuelers. The could see a line of majestic, shattered opal clouds out over the Gulf Stream, and seagulls wheeling and soaring down the wave torn beach. The patrol plan was devised by Maj. Bert Stahl, who would command the east coast group. He called it "Von Schliefen's yo-yo." Nobody knew if it would work since nobody had ever fought in near earth space with a space fighter that could do 12,000 knots and make ninety-degree turns that pulled twenty "Gs." But the idea was to create two patrol lines. One line would be anchored at the Cape. The other patrol line would be anchored at Vandenberg.

The two lines of twenty odd Lightnings would sweep back and forth across North America like two giant opposing windshield wipers. When an enemy ship was encountered, all nearby SF-35s would go to pack attack mode. Reinforcements would roll up the patrol line toward the fight like a yo-yo catching the intruder in a massive crossfire of energy weapons or taking him out with a contact kill with the Proximity Device. Assuming the alien ship didn't go vertical, the computer study of Stahl's strategy showed that there was a forty-nine percent chance of a beam weapon kill and a seventy-four percent chance with a proximity engagement. There were five hundred bandits sliding in on the up sun line, and there were forty-nine interceptors standing between them and the annihilation of the planet. Somewhere in the guts of even the most gung-ho SF-35 driver, was a fleeting notion of thankfulness that they were two miles under solid granite. Hand flying one of these machines "out there," would be suicide.

There is no such thing as absolute safety in war, and in the end, two miles of solid granite might as well have been the skin on a bowl of pudding. Of the original one hundred fifty-two pilots who flew the early A models of the SF-35, only fifty-four survived the Tau Ceti War.

Chapter 57

It Was T minus six hours at launch complex six at Kourou. It was a gray gusty morning. The wind was buffeting the big green leaves of the sea grape trees outside the trailer that had been set up for the Stork's crew to suit up. There was a twelve hundred foot ragged cloud deck and had this been NASA, the launch would have been scrubbed long before now. The depression twenty-four hundred miles east of San Juan, was picking up steam, but fortunately not moving toward the coast. Lines of low cumulostratus floated in from the ocean at T minus four hours as Blalock and his crew were strapping into their seats. Off to the east the first rumble of thunder was heard. The cockpit was cold from the external air conditioning ducts that had been stuck through the entry hatch. Blalock in the Commander's seat looked over to his right at Yakov who met his eyes. Both men knew what lightning could do to a giant rocket full of liquid oxygen and fuel, not to mention the electronics. Yakov and Blalock were all business and Dimitri continued reading the challenge and response checklist.

"External/internal power selector?"- Pilot
"Internal power selected." - Commander
"Aero surface check?" - Pilot
"Auto check complete, green light." - Commander
"Orbiter main engine gimbal selector?" - Pilot
"Armed and launch position." – Commander

The Tupelov engineers had reduced the Stork's non-fueled empty weight by an incredible forty-eight percent. They ripped out the chemical toilet, the galley, the rest facilities, and even sections of load bearing structure had been vacuum drilled with millions of small holes to reduce weight. Since the crew was going get home with a nylon letdown by ejecting at low altitude, the landing gear was removed. This alone saved over eight thousand pounds. The Stork would be launched with its main engines on standby. With its light weapons payload, the Energia RD-170 could easily get it to orbit for rendezvous with the second Energia which would be used for the Lunar Insertion Burn. Russian shuttles carried three times the internal fuel of their American counterparts and the Stork's onboard engines would be used for establishing its orbit around the moon, the Lunar Orbit Insertion (LOI), and for the return home, the Trans Earth Injection (TEI). Designed for thirty flights, the structural integrity of the Stork had been sacrificed to the point that two flights was all the engineering life left in the ship.

Matt and Dimitri continued the long pre-launch checklist for the next hour.

"External tank oxygen vents?" - Pilot

"Vent valves closed, pressure building." - Commander

"Main propulsion helium pressure?"

" MPS Helium isolation A, B, six switches open."

"Abort check?"

"Not applicable, abort to orbit only."

It was decided that given the deadly cargo, that an abort to orbit was the only option for a launch problem. Unless there was a malfunction below fifteen miles, the Stork could fire its main on board engines and achieve a low orbit. There, it would eject the weapons into a high permanent orbit with the rocket booster on the magazine. Since the RD-170 had never had a launch malfunction, and the weapons casings were designed to survive a crash, this was considered an acceptable risk.

The checklist continued for another two hours…

"Alternating Current sensor to Monitor." Blalock cycled the switches.

"AC Bus sensor switches, all three, off for one second then monitor."

"APU Prestart?"

"APU started, pressure normal."

"Launch computer?"

"Code Tango launch program loaded & running."

"Prelaunch checklist complete," Yakov finally announced.

"Thank you sir," Matt nodded, keying his mike.

"Kourou, pre-launch check completed, we're ready to go."

"Stork, this is Kourou, we have green panel and you are go for launch. T minus two minutes and counting."

"Roger, Kourou we are go for launch," Blalock responded.

The flight director was standing at his console observing up and down the small number of controllers and the three silent American security officers who had arrived with the Russians from Tupelov. A green light was illuminated on a short stansion over each controller's position. In case of a problem, the controller would give a verbal warning and hit either the hold switch, which turned the light to yellow, or the red switch illuminating a corresponding red light, which called for a launch abort. The flight director had all green except for a flashing yellow on his phone. It was an inbound emergency call on the secure comm line.

"What the hell," he yanked the phone up. "Yes? What? Immediately." Stunned by the call from the Prime Minister himself, the flight director opened the clear guarded cover to the abort switch and moved his hand to actuate the switch. Suddenly he felt the cold barrel of a pistol in his neck.

"Don't move." somebody said behind him. The director made a lunge for the abort switch. Mancusso buried his commando knife into the back of the director's hand and four inches into the laminated desktop. The director's muffled scream was silenced by the roar of the mighty Energia as its main engines ignited.

"We're going to light this candle, asshole," Mancusso calmly whispered in his ear.

The other controllers tried to monitor their instruments and look back at the flight director at the same time to see what the hell was going on. The building rumbled on its foundations as the massive RD-170s cleared the launch tower in a storm of fire and smoke.

The Stork was away.

The G loads steadily climbed as the ship accelerated. Vibrations shuddered through the fuselage of the shuttle creating strange harmonic noises in the cockpit, which made the instruments hard to read. "They took out so much structure, it's not as stiff as it should be," Yakov shouted into his helmet mike. The massive engines literally burned a hole in the clouds as it climbed. Out of fifteen thousand feet, the cockpit suddenly lit up like a flash cube had burst outside each windshield. Simultaneously a muffled explosion bolted the crew sideways against their shoulder harnesses and the cockpit went dark. Three red warning lights lit up on the electrical control panel and a flashing master warning in front of each pilot.

"Oh shit," somebody said.

***

The first time anybody sees an SF-35 launch, they're usually speechless for at least a minute. The Russian P-14 engines have a roar to them that would put goose bumps on a corpse. The first SF-35 launch took place at sundown on July 30, 2000 at Cape Canaveral, only seconds later the second group launched out of Vandenberg. Twenty-four Lightnings blasted into the gathering night at two-second intervals heading out over the Atlantic. The SF-35 doesn't lift off slowly, like a typical liquid fueled spacecraft. The Lightning comes off the ground like it was fired from a gun, its twin Proton engines shrieking like banshees.

Climbing out of 150,000 feet, the lead Lightning was flown by Maj. Bert Stahl. Von Shliefen's yo-yo was his baby, so he got to honcho the first patrol. He looked back over his left shoulder and could see the rest of the group climbing into the night on the tips of flaming arrows of white fire. He started a shallow turn to the north and checking the TSD (Tactical Situation Display) he could see the group instantly turning to match his. Punching up through the terminator, the boundary of the sun and the shadow caused by the earth, he was in the light of the setting sun. The reflection of the sun off the mirror-silvered skin of his wings was quite distracting, he'd have to mention this to the visual programmers. Passing 350,000 feet, the roar of the P-14s started dying away as their fuel exhausted. Stahl's fighter coasted easily above Interface Altitude at 400,000. "With silent mind I've trod, the high, untrespassed sanctity of space," he thought. The stars were positively vibrant even with residual beams of magenta from what was left of the day, angling in a tangent from the western horizon. But the stars to Bert Stahl, and to every SF-35 pilot would never be the same. Ex Astras Peligras was emblazoned on their new squadron patch. "From the stars, danger." Stahl imagined he felt a prickly, static induced wave of gooseflesh, as the Pratt & Whitney G-1 engine came to life. With no moving parts except the turbocooler, flying right next to an SF-35 would be a lonely experience. It was as silent as death, Stahl thought, exactly what I have in mind for these little green cocksuckers. The group of twenty-four SF-35s took their interval and began forming the patrol line as Stahl headed due west to set up the southern edge of the coverage area. The glow of New Orleans was already coming up over the nose and you could follow the lights of shipping traffic up the Big Muddy. Down and to the left, the Gulf of Mexico was alive with thousands of tiny brilliant pinpricks, flaming gas fires blowing off from oil platforms.

Stahl's Lightning levelled at the patrol altitude of 300 miles on a heading of two eight zero degrees. The five flight leaders had checked in and all aircraft were station keeping normally. Stahl keyed his mike. "Cactus, Cactus, Ripper Five on station."

"Ripper 5, Lightning control, we've got you."

The sun was up again and Stahl could see the Baja Peninsula and the Pacific coast gliding silently toward him. Momentarily, the twenty-four SF-35s would make a right turn into a line abreast formation to begin the first northern sweep of the big wiper blade. Stahl glanced down at his ground speed indicator. It was steady on 5500 knots.

Stahl closed his eyes. Oh God, he prayed, please help us to stop them.

***

"We've had a triple AC power cell failure," Blalock called out as he punched out the master warning. All five CRTs had white "Xs" across the screen and had gone dark. Red warning flags had popped into view on the standby panel, which had conventional round gauges in case you lost your visual displays. The cockpit had gotten dark with only the emergency lights for illumination. An instant later the cockpit lit up again as the Stork climbed above the weather into the clear. As near as they could tell, only good thing they had going for them was the emergency DC computer bus was still powered. The flight plan for the whole mission was in the computers. Jesus, Blalock thought for a nanosecond, this is like the simulator check from hell. Out of instinct from his airline days, Blalock called for the Loss of total AC checklist. Yakov sat there, just thinking. He did not pull out the triple AC power cell failure checklist. This was because there wasn't one. There was no written procedure for this emergency. The designers, in their wisdom, with geometric logic had calculated that such a remote event was impossible. The entire ship could be powered from one power cell through ingenious automatic and manual transfer buses and the slot rat generator when in the atmosphere. In fairness to the designers, it should be noted that they

401

never imagined a launch through the middle of a thunderstorm and being hit by lightning.

Yakov finally spoke up. "Matt, there's always a way with Russian technology, I can fix it."

"Do it, man and quickly."

Booster separation was occurring about then and had they experienced a separation malfunction, their first clue would have been the Stork veering wildly off course and disintegrating. The master fault annunciator, where most of the warning lights were located, needed at least one power cell powering one AC bus to be working. Yakov was shouting a series of instructions in Russian to Grosovitch who was riding in the lower deck with Duane. Grosovitch struggled out of his seat under the three G, load and pulled himself to the companionway.

"Do you see them yet?" Yakov shouted.

"Yes, behind the mounting braces for the galley, right?"

"Right, that's them."

Duane passed Grosovitch a fire axe, who grabbed it by the business end to use the insulated handle to push with.

"Are the relays open? Can you see a yellow ring around the big black buttons?" Grosovitch keyed his interphone,

"Yes, I can see the yellow rings!"

"Thank God," Yakov exhaled.

"Push them in Alexi, any order!"

The Stork had long since completed the roll program and was now at orbital speed and altitude. Systems were coming back as Grosovitch pushed the surge relay control breakers back in one at a time. Red flags were clicking out of sight in their round dials and the CRTs came back to life with a lot of snow at first, but then cleared up. Normally, the access to these relays was a ground maintenance function, but removal of the galley made them accessible in flight. Yakov had correctly guessed that the power cells were still on line and only these ground fault relays had popped from the lightning strike.

Now the hard part, they needed multiple orbits to catch up with and dock with the Energia booster they would need for the trip to the moon. The booster wouldn't even be on the Stork's tracking radar for another four hours. Despite the rocky launch, the Stork was directly behind the booster on orbit. It was a matter of slow overtake, mate up, then a six minute burn on the big Energia for the seventy-five hour trip.

Everything was getting back to normal until Duane made a discovery. In the severe buffeting on the launch, the storage locker door for the oxygen generation canisters had sprung open. Canisters were floating out and Duane was catching them and putting them back. The Stork's internal liquid oxygen system was only good for six days. A chemical oxygen generator like the one used on the Mir was added as a backup to increase the endurance on the life support system.

"Matt, aren't we supposed to have twenty of these oxygen canisters for the chemical generator?"

Blalock perked up.

"That's affirmative. Jesus Duane, how many do we have?"

"I can only find six, either they didn't put enough in here or the rest of them are floating around the cabin here someplace."

"That's just fucking great," Matt muttered. Yakov was busy calibrating the tracking radar with terrain features. Blalock nudged Yakov in the shoulder.

"Hey, Dimitri, you getting any of this?" Yakov finally finished and was satisfied with the radar and looked up smiling.

"So, they didn't load enough canisters?"

"Looks that way, any ideas?"

Yakov reached down into his nylon flight bag netted to the right of his seat and pulled out a bundle tossing it end over end through the weightless environment to Blalock.

"What the hell," Blalock caught it with one hand. It was a package of ten canisters.

"I tell you with Russian technology there's always a way." Blalock sailed them down the passageway to Alexi who handed them off to Duane. Blalock was not amused.

"But we're four short."

"We can do it with sixteen," Yakov responded evenly, "as long as we don't have too many long-winded speeches by the mission commander." The tension in the cockpit noticeably eased.

"I'll be a paragon of brevity," Blalock promised.

"Dimitri, your Russian technology is killing me, man, I hope you got a hat full of rabbits, because we've already used two of them."

"Murphy was a Russian," Duane chimed in over interphone.

Yakov reached over and chucked Blalock on the back, "Hey Tovarish, now you know what I felt like in Afghanistan when your American technology blew my bloody tail rotor off...what we need is some vodka." Yakov had an infectious, bear-like laugh. Blalock pretended to be looking for something on the overhead panel.

"Say, where's the flight attendant call button on this crate, we need Muffy up here with a bucket of long necks."

The Stork plummeted on, gradually overtaking its ride to the moon, from dark to day, the view from orbit was all the four pilots had thought it would be. The big blue marble with spiraling weather patterns, brown trackless deserts with their vacuous swirling mists of timeless sand. The moon reflected like a bright silver dime on the blackened waters of the oceans like they were polished glass. It would have been even more beautiful if the cargo bay had contained almost anything else.

Dave Chetwood and the other four senior officers were literally holding their breath standing at their positions behind the long command console in the main situation room. The IMAX sized screen on the multi-situation display showed that the ETE force had detached four ships from the main body that were decreasing interval between them and sliding down the SEA-Axis. The main body now appeared to be holding position.

Admiral Turner was the first to speak, "Goddamit Dave, they're doing it."

Chetwood's deputy, seated to his right, had the Joint Chiefs on the secure line. The Chairman of the Joint Chiefs was listening in. They were looking at the same thing on their screens. "General Chetwood, do you people have a further assessment of this maneuver?"

"Yes sir, I think they're being cautious...They're going to test us."

"That's the consensus here as well."

"General, NORAD recommends going to Defcon 1."

"Defcon 1 is approved by JCS."

Chetwood turned to the president standing right behind him next to him.

Clinton nodded.

"General, the president has approved Defcon 1."

"Go to Defcon 1," Chetwood announced over the room PA

"How many 35s are up?" Chetwood's deputy hit the SF-35 status console. The big screen switched from the space mode to the planet mode and the current positions of the patrolling SF-35s were displayed as two perfectly straight lines of little yellow triangles, one hinged at the Cape, the other one at Vandenberg, sweeping slowly across southern Canada and the U.S. mainland. "Fifty-two SF-35s on station," Chetwood's deputy responded.

***

Leanna was doing everything she could to maintain an air of normalcy in her day to day routine. Helms Industries and its subsidiaries had over two hundred thousand employees who depended on her to keep all the big wheels turning in the infinite machinations within machinations. Her uncle was keeping her as informed as possible and she knew that the Stork had launched successfully. Information was now going to be sketchy since there was no elaborate mission control, and tracking stations all over the Earth, only an office at the Tupelov factory that was maintaining a listening watch on an unused military frequency. The Stork had no deep space communication capability. All it had was a dual UHF transceiver out of a Backfire bomber and a small directional dish. The radio was extremely powerful and used a suitcase-sized nuclear generator. It was designed to send back strike reports through heavy American jamming after an atomic attack. The last report said that the Stork was on orbit and overtaking the booster.

Leanna was filled with apprehension and realized that the next six days were going to be hell on Earth worrying about the only man she had ever loved. I need to get out of this office she finally determined and called Preston to bring around the Rolls.

"Trump Tower please, Preston, and wait while I change clothes. I want to just drive today."

In 1982, when Mathew Helms had hired thirty-seven year old ex-Royal Marine Sergeant Preston McKennon to drive his family, he had been impressed with the young man's bearing and quick wits. Mathew Helms thought that perhaps, someday, having such a man at the wheel with his wife and teenage daughter, might pay a handsome dividend. A father's love was about to reach out from the grave and across a sea of time. The dividend was due.

***

Yakov was running the final checklist on the Kurs automatic docking system with Blalock when the Energia booster finally came within view. The Kurs system had been used with success on the Mir station for years. But when the breakup came, the Ukrainians, who made the Kurs system would not supply anymore units to Russia until it paid its bills. The one on the

Stork and Energia was the last unit produced and, since it had been paid for in cash, the Ukrainians claimed it had been ground tested and would work as advertised. The system had been slightly modified to work with a Shuttle Energia system and the complete exercise had to be verified with a space walk. Four white flags would be in view on the attach brackets where the Stork would be mated to the booster.

Grosovitch had been in prep breathing 100% oxygen for last ten hours. Since the suits only provide 4.7 psi pressure and the Stork was at 14.7 psi, an astronaut going EVA had to decompress before going outside. If he didn't do the pre-breathing schedule, he'd get the bends like a deep sea diver. The Kurs system used the onboard radar of the Stork and a precision antennae and computer on the booster. The Kurs interfaces with the autoflight system and as long as all the components show green lights on the Kurs control panel, the docking is completely automatic and there is "nothing to worry about." Of course the MIR station had several close calls using the system, and of course these were the ones bought on credit. Grosovitch was suited up and standing by to go EVA in the airlock when the Stork kissed up against the long Energia booster. Grosovitch practiced with his MMU (Manned Maneuvering Unit) in the closed cargo compartment for about an hour until he felt comfortable to go outside. Duane opened one of the cargo bay doors and out he went, just like in the NASA films. Grosovitch went out of sight under the right wing of the stork in order to get a close look at the docking bracket.

"Commander Blalock, there is a problem." Blalock was just shaking his head.

"What's wrong Alexi?" Yakov interjected.

"I only see two of the four flags in view, other than that it looks like we are perfectly docked."

"Are you sure man? Do you have direct light on the windows…they're not fogged up or dirty?" Duane asked.

"Can you kick it with your foot?" Yakov wanted to know.

"I'm sorry Colonel Yakov, but I tried that, all it did was cause me to start turning summersaults."

Yakov caught Blalock's eye and exhaled disgustedly.

"I'm sure the locks are in…it's the flags that are sticking out of view."

"I've got to go out there," Yakov said.

"Dimitri, if we do another ten hours pre-EVA protocol, the flight plan is shot."

"Yeah, I know. I'm not going to pre-breath."

"What? You can't do that, you'll get bent sure as hell."

"I'm going to overpressure the suit."

"That's impossible, plus the suit will be so stiff you won't be able to do jack shit. What if you blow off a glove or a boot?"

"My friend, I don't like this either, but do you have a better idea? We can't go with only two locks engaged now can we?"

Blalock knew Yakov was right. Yakov was already working on the other Orlon B EVA suit.

"What are you doing?"

"Remember what I've always told you about Russian technology?"

"There's always a way," Blalock commented quietly.

Yakov took the back off the pressure regulator and adjusted it with a tiny Philips head screwdriver so it increased suit pressure to 12 psi. Yakov was suited up in twenty minutes, but Blalock insisted that his glove and boot attach points be wrapped with NASA tape.

"What the hell do you think you're going to do when you get out there?"

"I'm going to hand Alexi this." Yakov held up a small mallet out of the tool chest.

Forty-five minutes later Yakov handed Alexi the small mallet. Grosovitch administered several well-aimed bangs on the sticky flag windows and both of them immediately popped into view. Yakov, with Grosovitch following took a small detour on the way back to the airlock and flew their MMUs back to inspect the weapons magazine. There was an exclamatory flurry of Russian between Yakov and Grosovitch.

"I didn't like the sound of that," Duane said.

They were both back inside in another thirty minutes with no ill effects. After restowing the EVA suits, Grosovitch and Yakov floated to the upper deck. Duane was sitting in the pilot seat taking pictures out the window with his big Rolaflex when the two arrived.

It was T minus forty minutes for the Lunar Insertion Burn.

Yakov took a deep breath. He wasn't smiling. "Good we're all here, I have some more news. We have stowaways."

* * *

NORAD had been watching the Stork since lift off. Nobody was talking at Kourou except that base security had arrested three Americans who were being "very" uncooperative.

The intelligence on the Stork was sketchy, but the thing that really got the President's attention was the space bomber story that was attached to the Russian shuttle. Hayes-Udall seized the moment to voice her opinion.

"This is obvious. The Russians are in cahoots with the EBEs, we've got to take them out."

"It makes a hell of a lot of sense," Harrison-DuPont quickly agreed. "What other explanation could there be? We need to do it now, while we have time. We can ask questions later. Didn't the last report from the French say that they suspected that it was carrying nukes?"

The President turned to General Chetwood. "Dave, what do you think?"

"Mr. President, I think we ought to take a look for ourselves. "

"Do it."

Chetwood picked up the phone and punched up the CCF. "Cactus, this is Chetwood at Pine Tree..."

Bert Stahl's first twelve hour duty day was almost over when the CCF gave him a call. "Ripper One we got a special for you."

"Ripper One, roger, I'm ready to copy."

"Ripper One, proceed to the following coordinates and hold west on a heading of zero eight eight degrees five hundred mile legs at maximum speed, Angels one fifty. There's going to be a Russian spacecraft come by in about twenty minutes. We want you to look him over."

"Lightning control, Ripper One, we're on it." Stahl then copied the holding coordinates on his kneepad. They would be intercepting the bogey just above the equator.

"Ripper one flight join on me we're heading south. Ripper Five you have the group."

"Ripper five, roger. Hey Bert, we won't start the party without you."

"See that you don't, we'll be right back."

"Cactus Control, Ripper one, flight of five out of angels three zero zero (300 miles) for Angels one five zero."

"Ripper One lead, Cactus shows you out of angels three zero zero."

Stahl formed his flight into a diamond and all five SF-35s smoothly accelerated to 20,000 (knots) heading south.

***

Blalock was incredulous. "What do you mean, stowaways?"

"Matt there are four weapons back there in the magazine they didn't tell us about."

"You've got to be shitting me," Duane chimed in.

"I'm not shitting you, and I believe they have soft landing packages, like what we used on the early Lunapods."

"What the hell are they?"

"Matt, I have no idea, but check this my friends," Yakov looked from face to face, "the casings of the projectiles are covered with writing."

"You mean like, ET this you son of a bitch?"

"No, Duane, I did not recognize the language. Tell em' Alexi."

"I think a couple of the letters were Croatian, but I'm not sure. If it was Croatian it was very old Croatian," Grosovitch explained.

Blalock floated back over the commander's seat and strapped in, shaking his head in disbelief.

"We'll worry about this later. Duane, confirm cargo bay doors are closed and locked. Lets keep going on the pre LIB checklist."

They completed the checklist in ten minutes and had fifteen minutes to spare before auto-ignition. For the first time since lift off, things were finally settling down.

Ripper One had been holding in a left hand racetrack for about ten minutes when the TSD (Tactical Situation Display) picked up the Stork.

"Ripper flight, here he comes, guys. Everybody got em?"

"Ripper Two."

"Three."

"Four."

"Five."

Stahl tightened his left turn and joined up on the Storks left wing. "Cactus, we got the Russkie, but he's got one of our shuttles tied on the back of a big booster of some kind…and the shuttle is painted solid black!"

"Jesus H Christ……er, Ripper One I'm patching you though to General Chetwood at NORAD."

"Major Stahl this is Chetwood at Pinetree, how do you read?"

"Five square NORAD."

"Major Stahl, what do you see?"

"It appears that they have a space shuttle painted flat black riding piggyback on one of their huge boosters."

All four guys were strapped in on the upper deck of the Stork for the LIB with Duane behind Matt. At T minus ten Duane tapped Matt on his shoulder.

"Matt looks like we have company."

He then pointed off to his left. Blalock turned around. Yakov leaned forward loosening his shoulder harness so he could see.

"What next?" Blalock muttered.

And there they were, five of them, beautiful silver ships, sparkling in the sun, in a rock steady echelon formation fifty feet off the Stork's left wing.

"Is it them or us?" Grosovitch wanted to know.

"God they're beautiful," Matt said.

"If they're ours, I never knew we had anything like that."

McCall passed his Zeiss binoculars up to Matt.

"Take a look at the canopy and then right below the canopy." Blalock looked over at the lead SF-35's cockpit.

"Jesus, there's nobody in there."

"Look at what's below the canopy rail."

Blalock moved his field of vision downward, then smiled.

"Dimitri, take a look. They're ours."

"I do not recognize the cartoon character," Yakov responded indifferently.

It was sweet little ET with a big surprised look on his face with an SF-35 shooting a huge lightning bolt up his ass.

Yakov continued to study the lead aircraft. "You say they're friendly...do they know that *we're* friendly? Did anyone notice the turret looking feature on the nose? It's pointing at us."

Yakov handed the glasses back to Blalock.

"Probably some kind of visual system...my guess is that these things are remotely piloted."

"Mr. President, I urge you to take the Russians out now," Harrison-DuPont pleaded.

"Can anyone think of a downside to what the secretary is recommending?" the President queried."

The rest of the cabinet was silent.

"What do you think, General?"

Chetwood put his headset and boom mike on again. "Major Stahl, this is NORAD, you still there?"

"Affirmative, General, still here."

"We're trying to decide if this Russian ship is hostile to the United States, and we have unverified information that it might have nukes aboard."

Stahl wagged his wings at the Stork, the international interceptor signal for "you have been intercepted, follow me."

Matt noted the wings wagging on the nearest spacecraft. "Oh shit, he wants us to follow him down."

"Ain't likely," Duane cracked. "Shit, we couldn't if we wanted to."

Stahl selected "armed" pack attack and "Proximity disable" on the AAI and the other four SF-35s surrounded the Stork then locked their RT-5 projectors onto the target.

Yakov looked out his window and there was two other SF-35s on the right wing, but now the silver interceptors were starting to move out to five hundred eighty meters, the minimum range for a beam weapon engagement.

Blalock figured it out first. "Oh crap! Duane, strip off your flight suit and get your ass in my side window, these bastards think we're with the bad guys." Blalock tore out of the seat to make room. Duane was out of his flight suit in and instant and was doing exactly what the commander ordered.

Stahl moved up to ten feet wingtip clearance for one last look before moving out to attack range. "Son of a bitch," he whispered, as he disarmed the pack attack on the AAI. The other four 35s obediently followed lead and slid smoothly back to the left echelon. Stahl then went to max mag on the field intensifier for a close up of the Stork's cockpit. Stahl laughed out loud as he saw Duane pushing himself off back to his seat. Matt got up next to the window and did a tomahawk chop pointing out into space then pointing down toward the big Energia, then holding his hands apart showing something big. I got it Ivan, Stahl thought to himself.

"Pinetree, this is Ripper lead."

"Go ahead Major Stahl, this is Chetwood."

"Sir, I think it's a moon shot."

The Energia fired and the Stork began to leave Earth orbit. The SF-35s fell slowly behind and soon they were nothing more than glittering dots against the black velvet field of space.

Harrison-DuPont and Hayes-Udall were borderline hysterical. "You can't take the word of a fucking *pilot* for something this important," screamed Hayes-Udall.

"Send those goddamned jets after them, they can't be allowed to escape," shrieked Harrison-DuPont. The two women suddenly regained their composure and looked around the room. The room was completely quiet. Everyone was looking at them.

Harrison-DuPont, the quickest witted of the two, excused herself.

The vice president followed discretely out the door. DuPont paused at the ladies room door, then when she saw that no one was watching walked quickly to the first empty office she found. She picked up the phone and sat down. "Give me an outside line," she ordered angrily. Gore reached over her shoulder and took the phone firmly out of her hand and replaced it on the cradle. "There'll be no outside calls," he said calmly. He then turned and nodded his head. Two Air Force security police stepped forward and took the madam secretary into custody.

Chapter 58

The first four ETE ships arrived at an altitude of two thousand miles over North America at 1003 hours EST on 31 July 2000. Coronal Mass Ejections were wreaking havoc with our sensors although we never lost contact more than a few minutes at a time. The ships weren't as big as the ones in "Independence Day," but they were plenty fucking big, over a mile in diameter, perfectly circular and thinner than anything we had seen so far. The ships were only fifty meters thick but tapered sharply at the perimeter.

The first one to get here was heading for the big missile field east of Omaha. Lt. Commander Uriah "the Pariah" Levi was the group commander of twenty-seven SF-35s on a southern sweep from over the Canadian border, when the CCF transmitted the contact in range message. Commander Levi's call sign was the "Pariah" because just like his namesake Commodore Uriah Levi, of 1835, who tried to stop the practice of flogging in the US Navy, he was always in trouble.

The CMEs were raising hell with communications, but the flight leaders were able to piece the message together from Lightning Control.

"Here they come." The alien ship was hurtling toward the ground at over six thousand knots. By the time the group was able to get him on each of their TSDs his path was perpendicular to the surface and showed no intention of changing course or speed. The group accelerated to get between him and the missile fields. At six hundred miles, shit started happening. The curvy blue and yellow lines on the TSDs showed that the group would successfully intercept at angels two-ten. Levi sized up what he wanted to do in a nanosecond. He was going modify the yo-yo. The alien ship continued straight for the ground and showed that it was going to bisect the patrol line. Uri keyed his mike.

"Gunfighter 15, he's coming down right on top of you."

"Ah, roger that, we got him."

"Gunfighter fifteen and Gunfighter ten take your sections to pack attack now."

"Gunfighter 10."

"Gunfighter 15 roger."

"Gunfighter 5 and 25 lets go to angels 500."

Lt. Commander Levi knew that going vertical was the best escape maneuver the ETE ship could use and his plan was to modify the yo-yo with a mushroom cap to catch him if he tried to escape the fight by going straight up.

"Gunfighter lead, Gunfighter 15, I got a problem."

Gunfighter 15 had accelerated to 20,000 and the pack attack mode had not gone green on the beam guns.

"I'm pulling out in front of the flight and heading straight for the guy." The other ten SF-35s were also behaving strangely. They had slowed to 18,000 and were letting the single ship pull way ahead. The artificial intelligence used in the AAI was leading edge stuff and space fighting had never happened before.

"This is Gunfighter lead," Uri said, "don't touch nuthin'. Let the big dog eat. Let's see if this stuff works."

The ten SF-35s that were boring in for the attack had formed into a cone shaped formation with Gunfighter 15 on the pointy end and the other ten

Bill Broocke

forming a large circle ten miles in diameter trailing the leader by twenty-one miles.

"Damn, I'm inside gun range…Uri, the BWs are not firing…I think it wants to ram the son of a…."

The sky of near earth space at two hundred miles is a deep indigo, almost black. The curvature of the planet is an obvious feature, but in daylight, the view of the home world is a humbling sea of impressionistic pigment that could only be painted by a loving Creator. But all this scenery was suddenly obliterated into a field of snow white followed by a massive jolt in the cockpit of each 35 in the group. The visual system came back on and the rest of the Gunfighters witnessed a scene of savagery that no one would ever forget.

***

The TLI burn was completed and now the Stork was just coasting. Everything was back on line. Nobody had a clue what the stowaway weapons were about. Nothing on console twelve had anything to yield on the subject. The only thing to do was just deliver the package as planned and let the stowaways take care of themselves. If this had been a NASA mission, about now, the astronauts would be working their asses off with all sorts of bullshit. Blalock told everybody to take a nap, which they did. Grosovitch floated around for a while looking into lockers and reviewing the ground mission.

"I can't sleep," he said after a questioning look from Blalock.

"Good, you mind the store Alexi. I'm going to do a level one self-diagnostic. Wake me in three hours."

The mid-course correction burn went perfect. Yakov was punching away at his laptop checking fuel, oxygen consumption, then delivering a position and status report over the

canibalized UHF out of the Backfire.

"Tell them our ETA for earth return, Dimitri, and have them pass it to NORAD. We don't want any confusion on our heroic return after saving the universe."

"Yeah, that'd be a real bitch to get our asses blown cleeeeeean out of the sky by our own guys after we went through all this shit…whacking ET and his pals," Duane cracked.

"I heard that, home boy," Grosovitch blurted sincerely.

Duane eyed Grosovitch suspiciously.

The hours wore on. The Stork was functioning perfectly. They had the ship in a slow roll mode to keep from overheating the structure. The oxygen consumption curve was just below the line, figuring they were short four canisters. It'd be tight on the way home. They took more naps. They ate. Things quieted down. Matt took a moment for himself and took his water bottle out of his netted flight bag next to his seat. There was an envelope on top of his Tupelov manual that floated free. It was from Leanna. He tore open the envelope and the sweet scent of Obsession lightly permeated the cockpit. Grosovitch who was half asleep came wide awake. Yakov started grinning as he worked on the laptop without looking up.

"Matt, you gotta read this one out loud, OK?" Duane shoved him on the shoulder from behind. "Look, I promise I won't get a woody this time OK?"

Everybody busted out laughing. For the first time since he accepted the job of commanding the mission, he began to think they were going to pull it off.

***

Uri Levi pulled five SF-35s off each end of the patrol line and climbed the two flights to form the cap. They were passing Angels 305 when Lt. Paul Martinez flying Gunfighter 15, scored a proximity hit on the alien ship. Later analysis of the battle revealed that the AAI on Martinez aircraft rewrote its tactical program as the situation unfolded. As it closed with the target, and there was no evasive action, the AAI "decided" to collide with the enemy spacecraft before detonating.

The contact engagement blew a huge section out of the ETE ship that looked like a big shark bite on a surfboard. The alien craft slowed suddenly, stopped its descent, and started to accelerate vertically. The remaining SF-35s in the low group then did the absolutely unexpected. The ten interceptors enveloped the alien ship like electrons spinning the nucleus of an atom. The diameter of the circle was about fifty kilometers and the SF-35s were virtually invisible at the rotational speeds they were flying. The instant the last SF-35 was in orbit on the alien, they opened fire. The AAIs on each SF-35 were in complete synchronization. The beam weapons from all ten SF-35s fired without ceasing in blinding bursts of white energy. It was a savage, brutal assault more like piranhas ripping up a jungle animal. The attack first concentrated at the edge of the blast hole on the alien vessel. Twenty beam weapons fired continuously working on the wounded section, then worked their way across the middle of the alien ship, literally, cutting it in half. It was a violent gang rape of light sabers. Like a grasshopper torn apart by ants, the alien was cut to shreds by mandibles of pure photonic energy and hyper excited neutrons.

He never had a prayer.

The engagement lasted seven seconds.

Big pieces of the alien ship coasted vertically for another fifty-five miles from the sheer momentum of his last desperate act of salvation. The low group's AAIs activated the high group's systems, as the debris field blossomed. The final phase of the battle made the Great Marianas Turkey Shoot pale by comparison. The SF-35s mathematically swarmed the pieces of alien ship and continued firing on smaller and smaller pieces until there was virtually nothing left.

"This is Gunfighter lead, break it off, break it off," Uri's heart was pounding.

"Think we got em? (laughter)," somebody transmitted.

"(Laughter), got him and the dog he rode in on."

"Blew the hair off his nuts."

"Now, where's yo' daddy, asshole."

"Can the chatter Gunfighters, we got three more on the way, reform the patrol line."

The controllers at NORAD and Lightning Control were cheering and high fiving one another. Chetwood picked up the PA, "Gentlemen, this fight is just beginning, they have four hundred ninety-nine more where that one came from." This sobered everyone up pronto and the war room got back to business.

"What now?" the president asked.

"Here comes the next one," Chetwood said calmly.

Only minutes behind the first alien craft, number two had changed course and was descending out over the mouth of Hudson Bay, a long way from the nearest flight of SF-35s. In an instant he was too low for intercept by the Lightnings and moving too fast for air breathing jets to have a shot at him. He flashed by two flights of Canadian F-16s over Lake Winnipeg who got off a shower of missiles. The giant ETE ship effortlessly outran the missiles which arced impotently into the rolling sub arctic tundra and exploded. He then turned to the southwest and dropped below all radar coverage, what little was still working. Chetwood put his hand on his deputy's shoulder. "Paul, where's that heading taking him?"

"I'm working on the projection now, General."

The last known position and speed was plotted on the big screen showing North America. A dotted yellow line sprinted out across the map showing the ETE ship's projected course. The yellow line went directly over a small town deep in the Adirondacks of upper New York State. The joy and exuberance of only minutes before evaporated. Sphincters all over the room contracted and the cold unyielding veil of fear came out of the ether and grabbed everyone by the throat.

Chetwood folded his arms across his chest and pursed his lips as he turned to the president. "This is not good, not good," is all he could say.

"What is it that's not good, General?"

"Mr. President, he's headed for Iron Mountain, Lightning Control, and there's nothing we can do to stop him."

***

Ten hours before the Lunar Orbit Insertion Burn, Matt got everybody up for one last go around on the attack plan. They went through their notebooks a page at a time. This took two hours. Yakov preflighted the weapons. They then had a big meal and tried to take another nap. Matt and Yakov were was the only ones who could sleep. The adrenaline was pumping hard in Duane and Alexi. It was almost time for them to start prebreathing for their EVA which would start with the prelaunch checkout of the Harley-Davidson LEX. The one in the bay was a duplicate of the one they trained with in Arizona for two days.

"Not exactly your standard NASA paint job," Duane observed as he scanned the LEX with the cargo bay camera.

"I like it," Grosovitch answered, patting McCall lightly on the arm. "In case we run into some skanks we can pick them up."

Duane smiled then turned serious. "We run into any skank on this dog and pony show, I guarn-fucking-tee you they ain't going be so friendly."

Yakov leaned over to his left putting his hand up to his mouth so only Blalock could hear. "Sounds like Alexi's picking up American slang pretty good, don't you think?"

The proximity alert went off on the so-called UFO detector they put in.

"Shows dead ahead," Blalock commented. Yakov flicked the tracking radar from standby to active and after a couple up wavy sweeps, the scope settled down and a target was detected at max range. In four minutes it began to be visible and was moving into position directly ahead of them.

The alien ship about three hundred feet in diameter and looked like the ones in the grainy photographs that were saucer shaped with the conventional dome on top. A series of light flashes came from the dome, then paused. The series of flashes repeated.

"Duane is that Morse? Don't you navy pukes have to learn Morse?"

Duane floated up to the jumpseat between the commander's chair and the pilot and pulled out his pen. "Gimme something to write on?" Yakov handed him a small pad. The light flashes began again. Duane started writing. T-R-A-N-S L-U-N-A-R F-L-I-G-H-T

I-S   P-R-O-H-I-B......That's all Duane got. The Stork suddenly began shuddering. Loud powerful thuds jarred the cockpit, knocking stuff loose that had been secured by Velcro.

***

"Cactus control, this is Chetwood at NORAD, who am I talking to?"

"Go ahead General, this is Colonel Loyal Sung."

"Colonel Sung, the second bandit is heading your way, he got away from us. Should be there in about fifteen minutes."

"Thank you General Chetwood. I think we'll be OK, we're ten thousand feet down in solid rock."

The mystery of the crop circles was cleared up fifteen minutes later. The second alien ship dead centered the crop circle outside Hudson, New York and disappeared into the earth as easily as a CD dropped edgeways into a bathtub. The alien ship burrowed by some unknown mechanism through solid rock and basalt and upon reaching a depth of two miles began heading for the CCF, rolling along sideways like a quarter on a table top. F-15s arrived overhead and reported that the alien ship had gone into the Earth without exploding and disappeared in a giant crevasse like hole.

Seismic sensors at the CCF recorded off scale readings as the alien ship approached moving at over forty knots through solid rock.

"We think they're going to use these all over the world," Chetwood barked into the line to the CCF. "They're going to take out our cities from below.

None of the underground bases are safe including us, once they get through. I recommend immediate evacuation of the CCF."

"We won't be able to get everybody out in time," Sung replied.

"Save as many as you can, Sung…get the pilots out first…without them we're history."

The attack alarm went off throughout Cactus Control. "Abandon your duplicators and proceed to the elevators," Sung ordered over the public address. Forty-nine canopies flew up in the four duplicator bays and pilots with their computer crews scrambled out running for the elevators. When the pilots saw the enlisted troops staying behind, they balked at leaving without them and caused a major traffic jam. The two freight elevators were the fastest, but Sung ordered the gigantic blast doors to the service road to be opened for everyone who wanted to try getting out on foot. It was twenty-four miles uphill to the surface by road. The two vehicles that were already in the base were loaded like Tijuana transit buses, with guys hanging from the windows and sitting on the roof. The base was literally shaking itself apart as the alien ship got closer.

Rocks and electrical plumbing fell from the ceiling and the lighting system flickered on and off. Sung collected the backup tapes that contained the irreplaceable tactical data that was collected in the first engagement. Some of them had not completed

427

downloading. He waited. Lightning Control, invincible to attack from above, crumbled around his ears. The last tape finished downloading and he ran the box to his second in command, Major Paula Wills, who with two airmen was shredding documents in the command post.

"Get these to the surface, Paula, I'm going to set the charges."

"What about you?" she cried, above the thundering din of falling rock and impending cave in.

"I'll take the last elevator, you've got to save the tapes. Take your people and get the hell out of here."

Wills and the two airmen ran to the elevator and hit the # 1 button. When the doors closed, it was the last time anyone ever saw Colonel Loyal Sung. Every duplicator, computer and encryption system was equipped with phone book sized thermite charges that would incinerate everything to ash in a massive 35,000 degree solar furnace and would burn for days. Sung ignited the thermite then dived under the command console as the molten fireball enveloped the complete interior cavity of the base. He couldn't breathe and he felt himself being cooked alive as yellow combustion plasma swirled around him. The alien ship crashed through the wall of the five-story bunker in an earthquake avalanche of rock. Sung reached up to the desk over his head and grabbed the command destruct pad. When the alien ship was half way through, Sung yelled, "Banzai this you mother fucker," and hit the switch.

The five-kiloton destruct charge blew five minutes after Major Wills and her two airmen emerged from the freight elevator. It knocked everybody on the surface off their feet. Windows cracked in vehicles and the ground leaped. The sound of the blast was like distant thunder. A few seconds later, a gigantic cloud of gray dust bellowed out the mouth of the access tunnel like a Civil War cannon being fired. With the datalink broken, the SF-35s began to automatically recover to their launch bases. The AAIs obediently took the Gunfighters back to Vandenberg and the Rippers back to the Cape. They came gliding in one at a time on the shuttle runway at the Cape and the active ILS runway at Vandenberg. Crews were standing by with tugs, and as soon as one touched down and was towed off, the next SF-35 came swooping in for an automatic landing, popping its drag chute and firing the retro-brake.

They all came home but one.

Ripper 5 had a fried logic chip from the CMEs and instead of going home to Cape Canaveral, it decided to land at on runway 27R at Miami International. Approach control

had no idea who this guy was, but he setting up like he was going to try for runway two-seven right. They cleared everybody out of the way and in he came. Ripper 5 came out of high key at 20,000 feet abeam the end of the runway heading east toward Miami Beach and started its base turn over Little Havana gliding like a streamlined anvil. When the tower got their binoculars on the aircraft it blew their minds.

"Is it a UFO?" the local controller asked.

"We're going to find out pretty damned quick," one of the other guys responded.

"Let's see em explain THIS one," the supervisor said.

"Whoever you are, you're cleared to land on two seven right…welcome to Earth."

Ripper 5 flashed across LeJune road at its normal landing speed of 200 knots and cars swerved all over the highway from people astounded by the silvery futuristic aircraft.

Ripper 5 dropped its landing gear, plunked firmly down on the 1000 foot stripes in a small cloud of neoprene smoke. The drag chute rolled out behind and opened with a pop. The retro brake fired and the Lightning rolled quietly to a halt, right on the runway center line, smack dab in front of the American Airlines maintenance hangar.

Nothing happened for a while, until two American mechanics drove slowly out to investigate the big "UFO" just sitting there with voluminous clouds of liquid nitrogen hissing from the four turbocooler vents. The mechanics moved in cautiously for a better look.

"Hey Lenny, is greeting aliens from outer space in our contract? And what am I going to tell Linda if they send me home tonight as a vaporized lump of coal?"

"Use your usual excuse…blame it on management," Lenny answered.

"We'll be OK so long as there ain't no doves flyin' around."

When they saw it had Goodyear tires, they relaxed and called maintenance control to send out the biggest tarp they had. The fleet of fire trucks pulled up about then and firemen clambered up the side of the fuselage on ladders to rescue the crew. With all flights in the country grounded, stranded passengers in the terminal were glued to the floor to ceiling windows dumbstruck watching the scene unfold. Several were going around the beads saying Hail Mary's, two or three were openly weeping and hundreds were crouched behind anything they could find to avoid the certain explosion and flying glass. One guy was on the phone to channel four with a news tip. American covered the SF-35 with the huge tarp and towed it out of sight into the hangar.

The mechanics explained to an incredulous bunch of their pals in the break room, "We ain't shittin' you, the crash crews popped the canopy and there weren't nobody drivin' that sumbitch."

* * *

Yakov jumped in his scat. "Matt what the hell are you...?" The cockpit rocked with reverberations as Blalock held the trigger down on the sidestick controller. The faint smell of cordite permeated the cockpit as the 40 millimeter recoilless gun slammed fifteen armor piercing rounds into the alien ship at point blank range. Impact detonations showed at least five hits but nothing happened at first.

"Ohhhhh shit, now we've done it," Duane trailed off, making eye contact with Alexi to his right who had both his hands locked on the arm rests of his seat braced for impact, his eyes like a couple of banjos. The alien craft moved off to the right going into a slight right bank, like a child's gyroscope spinning down. Blue plasma flickered out of the impact holes and spread along the bottom surface of the saucer. The alien went into a steeper right turn, moved out further like it was drifting, then slowly passed out of sight behind the Stork. Nobody said anything for a couple of minutes, but everyone was looking at Blalock. "We shoulda' waited and copied the complete--" Duane began to say. Blalock cut him off in mid-sentence.

"Cut the crap Duane, we're here to nuke these bastards, you and Alexi start your EVA prebreathe and lets get on with it."

* * *

Two C-117s were on the way to Hudson, New York to pick up the SF-35 crews. Bert Stahl saw Paula Wills sitting on the ground with her box of tapes and walked over and kneeled on one knee next to her. Stahl ran his hand through his thinning hair and folded his arms across his chest. "Paula, my love, now it starts to get really interesting," he said.

Wills tightened the cloth dust cover she had on the box of tactical tapes and looked up. "What do you mean?" she asked.

"The Cactus is gone and we won't be able to replace the duplicators in time…we're going to have to man the 35s and fight the ETs up close and personal."

Wills started when she realized what this meant. The extreme turning performance of the fighter during space combat, could easily kill a human pilot with G forces alone, not to mention the proximity engagement in which the onboard pilot would be vaporized. Or just being close when another 35 scored one. The overdose of radiation would kill a human pilot within hours, probably be dead before the patrol was over. Stahl's baggy Nomex flight suit was covered with dust and perspiration stains. He slowly stood up, took a deep breath, wiped his forehead, and stared blankly straight ahead. Paula Wills looked up into his face. His mind was already up there, locked in swirling combat with beings who would annihilate us. She then reached over and took his hand in hers and firmly opened his clenched fist. She gently pulled his hand to her mouth and softly kissed his open palm.

* * *

The LOI had gone like clockwork and the Stork was in an apogee sixty perigee thirty-five mile polar orbit. Duane and Alexi were suited up and strapped in on the LEX as Yakov opened the payload doors. Flying upside down over the moon, McCall and Grosovitch looked up at the spectacular landscape that filled the sky as the payload doors opened like a curtain at science fiction opera. The gray lifeless planet drifted quickly by as they approached the launch point. Craters, craters everywhere, Matt thought as he compared the inertial generated position with what he could see on his Apollo charts. The Stork tracked like a dye and the lunar surface unrolled below them like a giant gray desk globe.

"Approaching launch point," Matt transmitted.

"Roger that, LEX is go for release," Duane replied.

"Five, four, three, two, one, release."

The LEX sprang off the payload bay dock with a burst of compressed air.

"Oyster, standby for deorbit ignition…confirm the parasol in deorbit mode."

"Roger that, Matt, Parasol is in the trailing position."

Matt watched the inertial timer start running down on the track display as they closed on the release point, "five, four, three, two, one, ignition."

"Whoa baby," Oyster laughed as the hypergolic engine ignited. The umbrella-shaped exhaust of the parasol engine lit up the backs of their EVA suits with an orange glow as they descended out of orbit on a long shallow arc to the landing site.

"How's it look, Duane?"

"Looks like it's working…"

Twenty minutes later the LEX was at 8,000 feet over the Aries Basin.

"Alexi, what's the parasol doing?" Duane asked over the suit comms.

"It's starting to move to the land position."

"Yeah, good, that's what the indicator says."

"Stork, we're throttling up for touchdown."

"Good luck Oyster, let us know when you're there."

The LEX came gliding in over a huge field of boulders. It was difficult to judge altitude and closure speed. There was nothing to compare the terrain with, since there weren't any known object sizes to judge by.

"Fuel remaining eighty-five seconds," Alexi called out watching the pressure gauge at his position. The LEX hit hard, bouncing back into the air and coming down on the right front tire. It rolled to the left in a careening series of bounces that finally dampened down and all four tires were on the ground.

"Is landing like aircraft carrier, eh bro?" Grosovitch stated more out of relief than a complaint.

"I've made worse." McCall keyed the mike. "Stork, we made it."

"Good work, we're almost out of range…set that sumbitch up and high tail it back we'll see you in a little while."

"Let's get the launch frame detached." Grosovitch obediently hopped out of his seat and got on each side and unscrewed the big wing nuts that held the LEX secure to the Parasol system.

Duane drove the LEX out like a boat being launched from a trailer. "OK my man, which way?" Duane asked.

"Straight ahead to that saddle then on to the right up that draw. I see our spot already." Grosovitch pointed, consulting his flip chart to be sure. The lithium ion battery showed full charge and the sure-footed LEX took out across the lunar surface like mountain goat. It made a rooster tail of dust as the four big tires dug into the gray powdery soil.

"Hey, Alexi, what's this fucking switch?"

"What fucking switch?"

"Right here." McCall pointed down to a small yellow guarded switch between the large handlebars with the word "Rumble" carefully stenciled above it in small white letters.

"It wasn't on the trainer," Grosovitch replied.

"Well, if we don't know what it's for we ain't going to mess with…."

In a flash, the impulsive Grosovitch reached over and hit the switch.

"Don't! Oh, shit!" Duane shouted over the suit comm, knocking his hand away. A second later the sweetest sound in the world came slowly up in the background of their helmet speakers. It was the melodious, throaty roar of a Harley Davidson motorcycle…and it was rigged to go with the throttle on the electric motor.

"Is hoping nobody can hear this but us," Grosovitch said.

The LEX rolled up and down in and around craters. Mountains twice the height of the Rockies loomed off to the left and the view was magnificent. "We'll have to come back again when can stay longer," Grosovitch observed. The LEX was as fast as the trainer and McCall let it out a little to estimate its capability in case they had to make a run for it later, but then throttled

435

back. It was a long way from home to have an accident on a Harley. Two white specks in the cosmic lunar wasteland, they pressed on in the twilight of the stars. It was another thirty miles to the set up position.

The parasol orbit chassis sat silently where they left it, like a boat trailer waiting for its weekend angler to come in off the bay. Sound does not transmit on the moon because there's no atmosphere to propagate the compression waves. But if there were, you would have heard the sound of drip………. drip……….drip. And you could have seen tiny puffs of fumes as the highly corrosive fuel reacted with the ancient clay of creation.

The parasol had a fuel leak.

It was the landing.

***

The number three and four alien ships came down as a pair. At an altitude of approximately one thousand miles they split. Three headed for the Eastern seaboard. The track projections left no doubt where number four was going. It was coming straight down on NORAD, the nerve center for the aerospace defense of the nation. Chetwood was leaning over the central console conferring with his battle staff when the president walked over from the viewing area. Chetwood stood erect and pulled his tunic down.

"What's the situation, Dave?"

"Mr. President, we need to get you and your cabinet to the topside bunker…we strongly believe that another one of their burrowing type space craft are coming for NORAD."

"What about Iron Mountain?"

"Mr. President, Lightning Control has been destroyed. All the SF-35s except one have recovered to the Cape and Vandenberg and the crews should be arriving by C-117 at any time now."

"Now what happens?"

"As soon as the crews get to their launch bases we operate the ships with onboard pilots."

"You mean we'll be having so-called dogfights in space with our boys after the EBEs?"

"Yes sir, but you must prepare yourself for casualties now. We expect heavy losses, at least at first, and of course, depending on whether or not the ETs finally figure out their blunder sending their forces in piecemeal like this. Frankly, the enemy commander has me completely baffled."

The president put his hand on Chetwood's shoulder, which seemed to surprise him

"Whatever happens, General, I can assure you it will not be the end of us. We have a heavily armed population thanks to the second amendment. Our forefathers were far more wise than any of us ever imagined."

"Mr. President we don't have much time. We need to get you to a safe location on the surface as soon as possible."

"And your people?"

"Mr. President, this is why you pay us the big bucks. We still have sixty F-15s overhead and we still have the missiles in case we need them...we'll have to stay and take our lumps...now, let's get you to out of here." Chetwood pointed the way as an Air Force Major with an armed squad of security police shepherded the presidential entourage toward the waiting vehicles to convoy everyone to the outside. The president shook hands with the five general officers and was gone.

Chetwood picked up his command phone and punched an extension. The response was almost instantaneous.

"Bear Trap Control, Colonel Echeverria speaking."

"Etchie, this is Dave, Como esta su frijoles caballo?" It was their standard joke since high school when they grew up across the street from each other in Tampa. Chetwood had gone the Air Force Academy, fighter pilot route. Colonel Alphonso "Etchie" Etcheverria wore glasses and was a computer geek. He got his Masters in information systems management from UCLA after getting commissioned out of an Army ROTC program at Tampa U.

"Mis frijoles son caliente as the fires of hell, mi general."

Chetwood half smiled. "Etchie, you got him on your TSD?"

"Affirmative."

"You got any ideas?"

"We're going to open fire at maximum range on auto engagement and keep firing until he comes through the ceiling ….and we've disabled the 10,000 cutoff…it's going to sound like a Cuban New Year's party up here."

"Etchie, if we come out of this, I want you to make me some of your famous black bean soup. OK?"

"Wilco on that NORAD, got to go, we have company."

"Good luck mi compadre," then Chetwood hung up.

Echeverria looked up and down his battery control team. Only one captain in the lot, and twenty-four first and second lieutenants in their twenties. Behind his back, his troops called him El Cid and they loved the guy. Somebody rented the movie one night during a lull in the intensive drills that were took place as soon as the Bear Trap went on line. There was this line at the end of the movie that they adopted as a sort of fight song. Everybody in his command called him Colonel Etchie, but only when nobody from the outside was around.

"SCAM status?" he queried.

"SCAM at 110% all control rods at five percent...she's running hot but in the green."

"RT status?"

"All batteries active and tracking."

"Attack computer?"

"Set on auto engage with 10,000 ft. safety on override."

"Six shooters?"

"Two turning per battery, pluto feed set on continuous."

As the alien ship continued downward toward Cheyenne Mountain the Tactical Situation Displays showed him approaching the 400,000 foot ring where the computer would start the attack sequence. Echeverria picked up the mike on his desk and selected PA.

"Listen up people. Monitor your systems and clear all malfunctions as soon as you can. I intend to keep firing as long as the system will operate. If we over temp the SCAM or exceed any system limitation, I want you to hack through all shut down faults and keep your battery in action. If we have a massive system failure, or we're knocked out by enemy action, and there is only one battery left, I want that team to keep firing its weapon on target until he comes through roof. They called us computer nerds in school…ladies and gentlemen it's time for the revenge of the nerds…let's kick some ass."

"For God, for Spain and Alphonso," the lieutenants cheered.

The alien ship crossed the yellow 400,000 foot marker ring on the TSD and the ground shook. The blue Colorado sky became alive with the white smoke of rocket trails as the big hypersonic Night Riders rode forth on towers of fire to meet the intruder. The battle for NORAD was on.

***

The combat information center was getting almost more information than they could process. Captain Nicholas Poboji ordered the Krasnodar to flank speed and reversed course to head north up the American east coast. The Krasnodar was a type 949A Antey class attack submarine NATO code Oscar II. The Krasnodar and its sister ship the Kursk, both longer than football fields, were designed to engage and destroy an American carrier task force. U.S. Navy communication traffic was fast and confusing as the messages were descrambled and sent up to the captain's monitor. A major naval engagement was in progress in the Atlantic off New York. An alien ship had landed in the sea and submerged two hundred twenty miles southeast of Sandy Hook and the Americans were in hot pursuit.

"Sir, the Americans are now transmitting in the clear."

"Put it on the overhead," Popoji ordered.

"Sir, they were having difficulty tracking the alien ship's position because it has accelerated to 180 knots submerged. That's four times faster than any torpedo they have." The last SOSUS station was two hundred miles away, and by the time the Americans had a position worked out and saturated the area with weapons, the alien was thirty miles somewhere else. The ETE ship was changing course randomly, but the Americans thought he was heading for the Veranzano Narrows Bridge and the entrance to New York Harbor. Pentagon analysts had postulated that to create the maximum damage, the burrowing ships would proceed to the city center then operate in an outward spiraling circle. Foundations of all structures would be destroyed and those above ground would crumble into rubble once the alien ship found the harmonic signature of the construction materials.

Popoji spoke good English and the growing desperation was evident in the American voices as the alien closed with the coast. Circling P-3s, dipping helicopters, and carrier based SA-3s swarmed the sky off the coast. Thousands of sonobuoys were being dropped. The Americans fired hundreds of their latest weapons at ghost targets. In the end they began firing in salvos at suspect targets hoping to get a lucky hit. Then the Americans began to run low on munitions just as another too late tactical plot came in from SOSUS. Krasnodar's intelligence team and sonar technicians listened in stunned amazement at the sound of distant underwater explosions. It was like a stream of staccato snaps from an infinitely long string of firecrackers. The Americans were relentless and the intelligence operators on Krasnodar had a windfall of data. They were receiving weapons signatures intelligence and guidance system data revealing technology that was unknown to them. There were large two explosions, then silence.

The Americans had used all their munitions.

"Let's fly the seagull," Popoji ordered.

The tubular antennae with the large teardrop shaped PF pod on top poked up through the whitecaps spilling off the other sensor antennae. The PF compartment opened and the kite unfolded its wings and soared into the Sunday afternoon like a Mylar pterodactyl. The long trailing wire spiraled into the sky and soon the Krasnodar had a five-thousand- foot UHF antennae.

Popoji picked up the mike. "Task force fifteen this is Krasnodar, do you read." There was a pregnant pause as the fleet communication officer finally figured out that he was talking to the Russian attack submarine assigned at the last minute to help patrol the US coast.

"Krasnodar, we're a little busy right now, what do you want comrade?"

Popoji, looked over at his executive officer who was just shaking his head. The Americans are so damned arrogant, they both were thinking. Popoji keyed the mike again. "Have you destroyed the target?"

"No Krasnodar, we can't lay a glove on him. He's too fast too track on SONAR and he's outrunning our weapons."

"Would you like us to engage the target?"

"Krasnodar, say your position?"

"Krasnodar is seventy-eight miles east northeast of Norfolk."

"Shit, you can't do no good from there, we can't hit him and we're right on top of him...Krasnodar you're wasting our..."

Popoji heard the rattle of a headset dropping on a desk and voices in the background.

"Give me the Russian," somebody said.

"Krasnodar, this is Admiral Phipps, can you attack from that range?"

"Yes, Admiral, I think we can help. The weapon, unfortunately, has a twenty-kiloton warhead. We will be striking perilously close to the city of New York."

There was a series of conversations in the background then Phipps came back on.

"Take him out if you can, Krasnodar, I take full responsibility, Admiral A.J. Phipps. Note the time, 1703 UTC. "

"Very well, Admiral, move your forces to the east, send us his last known position, and we will engage in seven minutes."

"Good shooting Krasnodar…and God bless you. Phipps out."

The Krasnodar, like most Russian warships, bristled with armament. It had 20 SS-N-19 "Shipwreck" surface to surface missiles and the type 65 and type 53 torpedoes. The Krasnodar also had four super Shkval Mark II long-range anti-submarine torpedoes.

The Shkval was fired like a short-range ballistic missile vertically out of the same tube that fired the SS-19s. When it entered the water in the target area it would do a three hundred sixty degree turn and pick the best target it could find. The faster the target, the more likely it would be selected. The Shkval had a submerged speed of 250 knots using a liquid fuel rocket engine and top secret, super-cavitating nose, which caused it to travel in a frictionless bubble of air. The West had nothing like it.

Task force 15 retired at high speed to the east and rigged for nuclear engagement. Steel gray prows crashed and plunged with white water as the fleet turned eastward and accelerated to maximum speed. Hatches were battened down, radiation filters and ventilators turned on and firefighting teams donned their anti-radiation suits. Phipps and his staff huddled around the CIC plotting table on his flagship. Nobody said a word and the tension was like a fencing foil folded in two. A young seaman with a headset manning the long- range radar looked up for a second and accidentally made eye contact with Phipps.

"I sure hope these Russkies can shoot, Admiral."

"They shot the shit out of the Nazis," Phipps responded evenly.

"Truth is stranger than fiction," Popoji said to his exec. "Who would have ever guessed that we would spend all those rubles building this ship to destroy the Americans, and now we are going to use it to save them."

"Maybe they will give us a ranch in Montana, like in the movie," the exec cracked.

Both men smiled.

It was an interesting thought.

"Take her to fifty meters and start the prelaunch check," Popoji ordered.

***

Colonel Etcheverria watched the target tracks on the TSD as the night riders green dotted lines headed to intercept the intruder's red solid line. Suddenly he got an idea. Instead of waiting for a contact detonation of the warheads then collecting up the misses to be reloaded after they parafoiled back to the launch point, he reached over to his panel and armed the command detonation switch. By firing all the weapons at once, the alien ship would have to fly through a twenty mile in diameter nuclear fireball. He could then use the Fletchettes and RTs to finish off anything that was left. The tracking lines came together. "I'm going to command detonate all the warheads simultaneously," he announced over his headset and boom microphone. He hit the switch.

They heard the explosions in Denver. It was like intense distant cracks of lightning. The downward component of the blast shuddered the Bear Trap command post one hundred feet below ground and some fine dust filtered down from the ceiling. The alien ship broke up. The multiple Night Rider bursts broke the ETE craft in two pieces. When the Raytheon-Tesslas opened up, everybody jumped clear out of their chairs. Nobody had ever heard live fire with the Bear Trap because we did not want to reveal our capability. The ten batteries with two weapons each fired with an explosive mind numbing shriek. It was deafening, even in the hardened underground bunker. The lasers fired a bright red pulsing beam while the particle beams were a brilliant, white plasma pipe of excited neutrons. The plutonium-tritium cartridges encased in high explosive, fed smoothly into the small cylinders of the one hundred foot diameter rotating drums of Reynolds 1209 stainless steel, like an atomic gattling gun. The criss crossing beams of energy first concentrated on the two halves cutting them into fourths and so on until the system autoselected random targeting and the individual batteries picked and chose their own targets.

Telepathic terror screamed from alien brains.

They had not known fear for ten thousand years.

Now they were being burned alive. The RTs fired and kept firing. The frightening rumble of beam weapon fire echoed from the distant mountains like an erupting volcano on a far way island.

It was violent, merciless and continuous.

It was machine war. It was the ultimate rape of the soul, unyielding, precise and performed with a supreme brutality unknown by man or alien.

It was death at the molecular level.

They planned to take our planet.

The plan wasn't going so hot.

Debris of the alien ship rained down for a solid hour on the Bear Trap site like cardboard aerial bomb casing that floats out of the sky after a fireworks show. Twenty- four computer geeks had their revenge.

There was loud cheering, high fives, and woof whistles that went on for five minutes.

Etcheverria pulled off his headset and tossed it on the commander's console, then leaned back in his chair and exhaled loudly.

**

Leanna was filled with angst and was on the cell phone hourly to Plainview to obtain word from the latest position report of the Stork. It was a beautiful Sunday afternoon in New York and she knew that if she didn't get out she would go mad. Preston was waiting at the curb in front of the Trump Tower and Leanna ran and jumped in the front seat with him while he was reading the Times. It startled the hell out of him.

"Come on, Preston, let's do the bridge loop, I need some fresh air."

"Which direction, Ms Helms?"

"Let's do the GW first then come home over the Narrows. I'll bet the ocean will be beautiful today."

Even with an off shore breeze, being Sunday, all the ordinary crud that messes up visibility in New York was absent. After a quick tour of scenic New Jersey, Preston and Leanna arrived at the approach to the Veranzanno Narrows Bridge and parked at the newly completed scenic overlook at the entrance to the bridge's on ramp. Leanna took out her binoculars. The rolling huge Atlantic swells had a peaceful feeling, Leanna thought. What was it that Freud said? We like the ocean because that is where we came from. Then she noticed something.

"Preston there's large fleet of ships way out there. I see geysers of water. Oh, I'll bet it is a training exercise."

"Better let me take a look, Mum." Leanna handed the binoculars to Preston. The horizon was dotted with scores gray warships. Two extremely large underwater explosions broke the surface with towering mushrooms of foam and fire, too far away to hear immediately.

"Ms. Leanna get in the car NOW!"

"What? I'm not ready to leave." Leanna was shocked by the tone of her chauffeur's voice, who the hell does he think...

Preston grabbed Leanna by the belt in the back of her slacks and rushed her into the back seat of the silver gray limo like a bouncer tossing a drunk.

"Get face down on the floor and stay there until I bloody well tell you to get up," he shouted. Preston dived into the driver's seat with Leanna on the back floor still protesting but now scared to death. The Rolls roared to life and Preston burned rubber peeling out of

447

the parking lot and onto the expressway. He floored the accelerator, heading for town, where there was plenty of concrete for cover. "This is a bloody long bridge," he muttered. Good Lord, give me just one more minute, he prayed.

Had they been watching, Preston and Leanna could easily have seen the jet black Super Shkval Mark II come down from the sky almost out of the vertical only five miles from the Veranzano Narrows Bridge. The thirty-three foot torpedo entered the water like a champion diver with hardly a splash, shedding the stabilizer chute as it disappeared into the wave tossed gray green sea. Bobbing back to its attack depth of ten meters, it began a slow left three hundred sixty-degree turn. Passing through a heading of 066 degrees, the unmistakable ultraviolet disturbance of a large displacement object was detected by the new guidance system. It was moving fast. The target was selected. The Shkval excreted a cloud of bubbles from its skin as the liquid fuel rocket engine ignited. The super-cavitating probe extended from the torpedo's nose and within forty-six seconds, the frictionless containment bubble formed as it accelerated to 250 knots, faster than the speed of sound underwater. The large object sensed something in its path and began a high-speed evasive turn. The Shkval turned to intercept.

It was too late.

***

The ETE base was visible as it rose from the lunar horizon forty miles away. The two massive pyramidal structures were squat and black but rose two miles above the surface. The plan called for flying directly over the structures to positively identify their positions and lock those coordinates into the guidance systems of the individual weapons. Once out of range, the weapons would be seeded into orbit in clusters to look like harmless scientific satellites. Duane and Alexi would rendezvous with the stork after positioning the back up laser target identifier on the next orbit. On the third and last orbit the Stork would jettison the Energia booster so that it would impact the alien base after the Stork had commenced its Earth Trajectory Insertion (ETI). After established on the road home and the ETI burn completed, the crew would activate the weapons systems which would rocket into the alien base according to schedule. The party would start with a one hundred twenty megaton combined explosion of the warhead in the nose of the Energia booster and the first twenty-megaton hit from orbiting ground penetrators. This would be the largest man made explosion ever conducted. After the twenty-four nuclear weapons had struck the base at ten minute intervals, ripping it open layer by layer, it would then be bathed in lethal nerve agent and the extremely aggressive RTE which would mix with whatever liquid water might be present. The RTE would infect and kill any living organism that survived the nerve agent and nuclear bombardment

Based on the best information available, assuming breach of the ETE structures, it was thought that the three weapons systems would have good results. There were far too many assumptions in the equation.

Still flying inverted; the Stork flew silently to almost directly overhead the massive black monoliths.

"These aliens are going to have to be pretty damned stupid to buy this bullshit, Dimitri. I never liked this part of the plan from the beginning…it's just asking for them to blow us a new asshole."

"I agree. Let us hope that we do not share the same fate as the Clementine. This would be an ideal time to engage the Ulithium P238 Space mod-u-la-tor," Yakov observed with mock sincerity. Blalock was not amused. Yakov updated the target position on console twelve and all systems showed a complete update.

"Where are all their ships, Matt?" Hundreds of ETE ships had been reported in the space around the moon.

"You got me by the balls." Then he whispered, "Uh oh."

A thin blue beam of light rose instantly out of the smaller of the two structures and hit the Stork without apparent effect. "Maybe some kind of sensor beam to detect our intentions," Yakov commented. Both men's guts were churning. The launcher magazine in the cargo bay contained the nastiest stuff ever concocted by the demented weaponeers of planet Earth. The Stork passed gently by the ETE base. There was no death ray or Romulan disrupter beams. No StarTrek phaser blasts from below or surface to air missiles. It was a tranquil passage and both men relaxed not believing their luck.

"Un-fucking believable," Matt said.

"Indeed," Yakov replied watching the base disappear to the rear from his side window.

"This just might work, my friend," Matt continued. Suddenly, a flurry of Russian profanity filled the cockpit. Blalock looked over to see what the hell was the problem. "What's wrong?"

"Matt, console twelve is dead!"

***

Major Bert Stahl led the third patrol with human piloted SF-35s. His body was encased in fibergel to absorb and better distribute the massive G loads of space combat. His seat was inclined similar to a beach chair, his helmet hard wired to his recently shaved head. The visual system was input directly to his brain by four surgically attached pickups into which the fiberoptic wiring was attached. It took some getting used to.

The unexplained lull in ETE activity had enabled the completion of six more Lightnings, but there was no time for training. Crews were prepped and launched as soon as the aircraft were available.

The EBEs then commenced a second wave of attacks. This time they sent four ships down to overpower the defense. Stahl as Ripper lead was just beginning his course reversal over Mammoth Lake, California when the contact message came from "Pine Tree" the new Lightning Control based inside Cheyenne Mountain.

At just outside one thousand miles, the four alien ships did a sort of upside down bomb burst maneuver and fanned out toward different targets scattered across the country. This time they were jinking all over the place. It was virtually impossible to tell what the ultimate target was going to be. Stahl ordered the group to slow to 250 kts effectively just maintaining position.

"Ripper group, this is lead, slow to two-five-zero knots, two-fifty…we aren't going for a head fake."

The TSDs showed the ETE ships changing speed and direction randomly as they hurtled down from space.

"Gunfighter lead, Ripper lead."

"Go ahead Ripper."

"We're slowing to station keeping speed until we figure out where they're going."

"Yeah we're doing the same thing. What about selecting pack attack and see what the AAI thinks?"

Damn good idea, Stahl thought selecting the multiple target engage preview function.

The AAI showed four geometrically dispersed flights of SF35s positioned directly under each inbound ETE ship moving along under it like a huge spider web basket ball net waiting for the shot to come through.

"Gunfighter lead, lets do it."

As overall tactical commander Stahl made the call.

"Attention all Gunfighters and Rippers, select pack attack now…and hold on."

The AAIs were in instant telemetric sync with one another and fifty-five SF35s accelerated to 20,000 knots and split up into four groups that covered thousands of square miles. Within minutes all fifty-five SF35s were in position under the falling enemy.

When the alien ships jinked, the flight of waiting Lightnings below him changed course to cut him off and just moved laterally underneath him as he came down from the ether. The AAI was fighting in a zone defense. The closer the alien ship got, the AAI tightened the interval between ships in each of the four welcoming committees. The pilots had been exposed so far to only six or seven Gs in relatively straight acceleration vectors and the AAI was making smooth shallow turns as it positioned everyone for battle. When the ETE ships got within sensor visual range the larger burrowing ships were being accompanied by one much smaller delta shaped craft in a tight formation. This was a new development and the tactical displays did not break out the two until they were within 800 miles where the resolution was good enough. At just inside 800 miles the purpose of the escorts became clear in a blinding fury of energy discharges which stabbed out of the blackness. Stahl's flight of eleven continued closing the target at maximum speed. There were two then three brilliant explosions a hundred miles away on either side of Stahl's Lightning as the alien weapon vaporized one ship after another setting off a secondary explosion when the proximity device detonated. The AAI's commanded a spiraling then counter spiraling corkscrew approach and the G loads came on like sledge hammer blows.

Two more discharges of the alien weapon, one miss, one hit. Almost within beam weapon range. The alien weapon began firing rapid fire with intense blue white bursts of light blazing down between the attacking Lightnings. Another hit! Who was it? Stahl was pulling ten G slams inside his cockpit as the AAI bored in for the kill analyzing the enemy tactics and adjusting. Down to seven out of eleven, Stahl thought, just trying to maintain consciousness as his aircraft violently changed direction and speed closing with the enemy. Then the Lightnings opened fire, but not at the larger ship. The night sky of space flickered like a disco strobe with nearly continuous laser and particle beam blasts. The alien delta ship was hit and tried to go vertical to escape annihilation. Three Lightnings surrounded him in tight orbits firing into the center as he desperately attempted to evade. The four ships climbed at high speed until the wounded enemy escaped into space above the five hundred mile ceiling of the SF35s. The remaining four fighters engaged the larger ship and within seconds, large dissected pieces were plummeting out of the sky after the beam weapons literally cut the alien ship into pieces. The battle lasted less than three minutes. The remaining three alien ships and their escorts experienced similar fates. The cost was heavy and out of fifty-five SF35s, twelve were lost to enemy action and seven more disengaged when their pilots' life signs showed dangerous trends. All seven pilots eventually died from internal bleeding or brain trauma from acceleration forces.

The ground crews could tell when a recovering SF35 was being hand flown or when the AAI was bringing it home. The AAI flight pattern was boxy and without improvisation and never made a victory roll on downwind. The square pattern flown by a Lightning coming home usually meant that when the crew chiefs evacuated the fibergel from the cockpit, their pilot was dead. War in space is no different than war anywhere. Good men die.

The arithmetic was simple. After two engagements, we had forty-three aircraft left out of fifty-five. The enemy still had four hundred ninety-two, plus an unknown number of escorts. The numbers were irrefutable. We were going to lose.

***

The Super Shkval impacted the submerged ET craft seven miles outside New York Harbor. The twenty-kiloton tactical weapon, the size of the Hiroshima bomb, evaporated the alien vessel and the resultant blast took out the main span of the Veranzano Narrows bridge leaving only a jungle of seared and smoking cables. The fuel tanks of cars caught on the bridge exploded as they fell into the ocean from the collapsing structure. The Lady in the Harbor was blown down and the shock wave rolled into town blowing out windows and starting fires almost to the middle of Harlem. Thousands of people on the Jersey Shore received flash burns and radiation poisoning. Thousands more were impaled by flying glass and other debris. By the Grace of God there was a northwest wind and the fallout cloud drifted out to sea. The final death toll would eventually climb to 20,298.

Leanna was face down on the back floor of the Rolls with Preston on top of her when the blast hit. The limo was stopped in a narrow alley between mountains of steel and concrete. The big sedan leaped as the concussion wave passed overhead like a mile high expanding half bubble. Glass from skyscrapers filled the day like glittering shards of lethal ice as big and small pieces pelted, penetrated and buried themselves in the roof and hood of the Rolls. After a long while Leanna stirred.

"Preston are you alright?"

Preston did not answer.

A three-foot section of aluminum tubing from a canvas awning frame, meant for Leanna, was buried in his back.

***

Yakov was unstrapped in a heartbeat and was heading down to the lower deck.

"Where are you going?"

"We've got to get power to the weapons...there's always a way with Russian technology," Yakov shouted, as he donned his wireless headset.

"Console twelve is dead, but the right hand essential computer bus is still powered...I think I can launch the weapons from down here. Unless the alien transmission wiped their memories, all the guidance systems have what they need."

"Do it, I'm showing eight minutes to release point."

"Three minutes to release point...how's it coming?"

"Almost got it." Yakov had a wire bundle pulled out from an access panel and was pulling it out to reach the right hand main AC distribution bus. If he had the right wires, he could energize the launch sequencer without going through console twelve which was shorted out.

"One minute to release point," Matt called.

Yakov touched the stripped wire to the copper bus bar in his gloved hand trying not to touch anything else that might make his body the circuit instead of the launch sequencer. The instant Yakov touched the two contacts together the four mystery weapons launched first, out of sequence with four loud thumps as the compressed nitrogen cylinders ejected the projectiles. Blalock was at the mission specialist station observing the cargo bay as Yakov held the wires together by hand.

"There went the four specials with the Croatian writing."

"Approaching release point....three, two, one, release."

The launch sequencer worked. The nukes came out first, then the chemical, then the deadly biological devices with RTE, genetically engineered to kill millions even in the vacuum of space. Matt wasn't counting they came out so quickly, bit it appeared that all the weapons deployed.

"Dammit, you did it, Dimitri...way to go man! Button up your shit down there and get up here quick we got to get ready to pick our moon rovers."

Duane and Alexi had the backup target illuminator set up almost immediately.

Lodged down behind a ragged crust of rock the illuminator just barely peaked over the top but had a clear shot at the top of the higher of the two enemy base structures. It would be vaporized in the first explosion, but it only had to work for the first orbital weapon. Alexi fired the pile rifle into the solid Bracia and secured the last stabilizing cable to it. Duane was revving up the LEX and the sweet Harley music filled both men's helmets. Alexi dropped the pile rifle and skip jumped toward the waiting rover.

"Now would be a good time for some payback for what you put in my Preparation H you Russky prick...let you hopscotch your cracker ass back to the Parasol."

Grosovitch climbed onto the back seat of the LEX. "How can make joke at time like this? Is going way too easy so far...am thinking comrade Murphy getting ready bust our balls!"

Duane floored the accelerator on the LEX, actually on the right handgrip, and a rooster tail of fine surface material flipped up behind the rover in a weird non-cloud of dust. They followed their tire tracks back to the Parasol and made the return trip in about half the time. Duane backed the LEX up onto the Parasol and Alexi leaped off and started reattaching the big wing nut locking fasteners on the Parasol's undercarriage. Duane booted up the Parasol's computer and tried to establish datalink contact with the Stork.

Duane heard a burst of Russian profanity, which he recognized as OH SHIT!

"Duane, we have a fuel leak!"

"How bad?"

"It's a slow drip!"

"Fuel pressure is normal, how much landing fuel did you say we had at touch down?"

"It was showing forty-five seconds on the landing timer when the engine shut down."

Duane climbed down off his seat and peered under the right front of the Parasol. A chemical reaction had burned a hole in the ground about a foot in diameter and six inches deep. "I figure forty-five seconds of fuel is three hundred pounds...fuel weight is about six pounds per gallon...that's about fifty gallons. Alexi, that don't look like a fifty gallon hole to me."

"Me neither."

"Strap on and let's ride the lightning...launch in seventeen minutes."

Returning to the Stork required launching at a one-time launch window then getting into a low elliptical eight by thirty-five mile orbit first and establishing contact with the docking computer on the Stork. The flight plan only allowed one attempt to leave the lunar surface and that is why the Parasol engine was selected because of its reliability. The Stork's docking system would then automatically fire the Parasol engine again and climb it on up to the Stork's orbiting altitude, slowing down and climbing into the docking rendezvous maneuver. Once the Parasol arrived at the Stork, no actual docking would take place. McCall and Grosovich would transfer over using their suit maneuvering units and enter through the main airlock. The Parasol and the LEX would just be left in lunar orbit. Once they got home, the Stork was going to be crashed after the crew safely ejected at low altitude, so there was no reason to take the rover with them.

"Oyster, this is Stork, how do you read?"

"I got you five square Matt. We're two minutes from lift off."

"The illuminator give you any problems?"

"Piece of cake. Alexi had the thing bolted into the rock in fifteen minutes."

"Shit hot...one minute to ignition on my mark...three, two, one, mark."

"Matt we confirm that. Docking link is established."

"We got the Bud on ice waiting for you."

"Sounds mighty good...twenty-eight seconds to ignition."

"Ten seconds."

"Four, three, two, one....."

"Oh, shit!"

"Duane, what's wrong?"

"Matt, we have no ignition, repeat no ignition."

"Use manual fire!"

"Tried that...it's no good."

"Is the Parasol tower locked in the takeoff position?"

"Affirmative."

The seconds ticked by. The Trans Earth Insertion Burn was the most critical maneuver on the mission and took everybody home. There was no second chance. Oxygen consumption was already below critical, thruster fuel, and the navigation computations to reach Earth were all based on this singular event in time and space and everybody knew it. Any delay would cause the Stork to either miss the Earth completely, or arrive with a suffocated crew with no thruster fuel to position the Stork into the correct reentry attitude. The wrong re-entry attitude would cause the orbiter to either skip out into space or dive too deeply into the atmosphere and burn up like a meteor.

The seconds turned into minutes…

Blalock and Yakov stared at each other.

"Dimitri, there's got to be a way," Matt said.

"If there is, I do not know it, my friend."

"Well, we're not leaving them."

"Matt, we have to. There is no other way. If we go around again, none of us will make it home, and there's no way of knowing if they will even have ignition on the second pass."

"Matt?"

"Go ahead Duane."

"I hope you're not thinking what I think you're thinking."

"What's that, Duane?"

"You're thinking you'll make one more orbit to see if we can get this piece of shit to fly."

"We're not leaving you, Duane."

"Oh shit. I knew you would do this. Look, you've got to. What does Dimitri say?"

"Dimitri isn't in command of this mission. Now listen up Duane. I want you and Grosovich to figure out why the Parasol didn't fire and fix it. We'll be back."

Yakov was shaking his head. "Matt, I feel the same way you do but the facts are…."

Blalock's nostrils flared and for the first time in his life he shouted in a cockpit. "Colonel Yakov, shut the fuck up and do what I tell you."

Yakov instinctively went silent…years in the Soviet military.

"Get on the Backfire and see if you can raise Tupelov. Have them contact NASA in Houston and see if they can recompute a new EIB."

"But what about thruster fuel and oxygen?"

"Never mind that now, we'll cross that bridge when we get there."

Yakov took a deep breath. Blalock had just signed everyone's death warrant. Yakov transmitted the problem in the blind over and over again describing their situation and when they would be line of sight again to get a transmission from NASA.

The crater-scarred lunar surface drifted by as the Stork passed the EIB point. They were now committed to another orbit and certain oblivion. Yakov was getting back in the game and was doing something with his laptop and the oxygen consumption program.

Neither man spoke for a long while until Yakov finished his calculations. His face was expressionless. "Matt...the oxygen...I think I found a way."

"I knew you would...you've been telling me that with Russian technology there's always a way...look, Dimitri, I don't expect you to understand this, but we Americans don't like to leave people behind." Yakov did not respond. His grim face spoke volumes but Matt did not read a word.

"Here's the problem, Duane. Damn!"

McCall looked where Grosovich was pointing inside the opened fuel control access panel on the Parasol. The parasol used a hypergolic fuel system which when the fuel and oxidizer mixed, it self ignited. This took a complicated fuel ignition system out off the long list things that could go wrong in space.

461

But the fuel-oxidizer mix valve was electrically operated and protected by a circuit breaker. The breaker had popped and the mix valve never opened.

"Can you reach that breaker from your seat Alexi?"

"Of course, why?"

"OK, lets strap in first before you reset the breaker…the son of a bitch might ignite when you push it in."

Grosovich and McCall were strapped in securely when Alexi reached down and reset the breaker.

Nothing happened.

"Well, now that that's settled, all we have to do is figure out when the Stork is going to…"

The Parasol engine fired at that instant.

White plasma blazed out of the nozzles and the Parasol-LEX rocketed into space. Boulders as big as a house turned into pebbles and two mile craters into BB gun pits on a window pane. The launch site disappeared below like they were shot out of a cannon. They say God looks out for children and fools and He certainly works in mysterious ways. But the Parasol's time of ignition for a second rendezvous attempt was within two seconds of what it should have been had the means to compute it been available.

"Stork, this is Oyster."

"Damn, Duane where are you?"

"Matt we just lifted off…we're approaching low orbit initial burn altitude now."

"Duane, the docking computer just went active…do you have a lock on?"

"Matt that's affirmative."

Forty-six minutes later, two filthy dirty, space-suited guys came through the inner airlock door and took off their helmets.

NASA mission control in Houston was all but abandoned as the battle raged in near Earth space over North America. The sea battle off New York plus three days and nights of attack, counter attack, and proximity devices going off lighting the night sky like super novas forced the government to admit the presence of not only extraterrestrials but hostile ones right out of Hollywood. The American people were at first outraged at the fifty year lie that had been perpetrated. The Trilaterals had a firm grip on the media, however, and an impassioned, patriotic, fight-them-on-the-beaches spin was blasted across the airwaves. It was the spin doctors' finest hour and the American people rallied.

The skeleton crew at mission control watched the geospace conflict over the big monitor screen that had tracked the Apollos and the American Space Shuttles. The electro magnetic pulses from the proximity engagements and the CMEs were wreaking havoc with the data link but they still could see the hopelessness of the situation. When the call came in from Tupelov, Scott Oldman, the duty controller first thought it was a joke. But the Russians were passionate as they described what was going on and what they needed. Yes, they had the old Apollo programs on file, somewhere. But no they wouldn't work unless NASA had piles of data about the Stork that could be plugged into the navigation models. There was no time and the task was too complex. Oldman told the Russians that there was no way they could conjure up the answers to their questions in time to do them any good. "We're sorry Tupelov, but I'm afraid we won't be able to help much. We'll take a stab at it, but you should prepare yourselves to lose your four Cosmonauts." Then Tupelov dropped the bomb.

"Houston, two of the Cosmonauts are Americans, Mathew Blalock is the commander and Duane McCall is one of the mission specialists." This information electrified the control room. NASA had always brought the astronauts home. This was the prime directive on all manned flights. People started making phone calls and standing at their desks punching stuff into computers simultaneously. Calls went out to two Apollo astronauts who were semi-retired in the Houston area and they were already enroute by car. The news that there were American astronauts in trouble spread like sheet lightning across a summer night. People were just showing up taking their old seats at consoles. Engineers were pouring over the meager stats that the Russians had provided on the ultra-modified Stork. In a matter of minutes the control room was humming with activity…American astronauts were in danger, they would be brought home. Nobody cared if it was a Russian shuttle or the Good Ship Lolly Pop.

One of the guys that just drifted in was a new engineer named Dick Sanders. He was a scrawny five feet zero red headed kid who looked about a decade younger than his twenty-five years and had just finished his doctoral in aerospace engineering. His two hobbies were space navigation and Apollo history. He sat quietly in one of the working groups blazing through data on his notebook computer as he listened to the discussions going on around him. After several minutes punching in numbers he hit the enter key and waited. The used Micron GoBook had only cost him three hundred bucks, a beggar's sum for the job it was about to do. The little GoBook did some thinking, then published its findings on five pages. Sanders looked the data over and did a ballpark reality check to see if it was rational. It looked close. There were only fifteen minutes left before it was needed and it appeared he was the closest to the solution. He turned the GoBook around so his group could see the screen.

"What do you guys think of this?" Everybody stopped talking.

"How'd you come up with that?" somebody said.

So he told them quickly going from page to page with his program showing where the parameters were changed and what he did. "This is from Apollo 14," he said finally.

"It's almost exactly what the Russians are doing, except of course, they are in a polar orbit, but I fixed that by doing this. Sanders clicked the screen to a page of equations. The engineers hummed, looked at the young engineer, then looked back at the screen.

"Let's go for it," one of the sitting guys announced.

"Yep"

"I agree."

"This will give them a shot."

They went around the table until there was consensus. Sanders picked up the notebook and took it over to Oldman's console followed by the rest of the ad hoc committee.

"Mr. Oldman, we think this will work."

The transmission from NASA's directional deep space net was crystal clear and a vast improvement over the unreadable frying static from Tupelov. Two minutes from Trans Earth Insertion all the data had been entered into the Stork's computer.

"Five second to TEI," Yakov counted down.

"Three-two-one, ignition!"

The Stork's engines ignited in an ecstatic plume of blazing combustion and the four Cosmonauts were hugged back into their seats. The thundering Russian engines pounded

like a million beating hearts. Matt saw Leanna's face, then an image of massed marching bagpipers at Edinburgh playing "Amazing Grace". It's funny what the mind does, he thought to himself, staring straight ahead at the big blue marble of home. Maybe he would have Leanna in his arms again after all. The TEI lasted for seven minutes then silence.

"It's time to finish the job," Matt announced.

"Matt, I have the access panels off and I've got all the wires rerouted from console twelve to the weapons launcher." Yakov was on the lower deck with more bundles pulled out.

"Any time, Dimitri."

Yakov shoved the rewired plug into the receptacle on the right hand computer bus.

Since there were no lights on the dead launch console, they had no idea if the weapons they had seeded into orbit went active or not. All they knew for sure was the launch transmitter that would signal them was getting power.

"Dimitri, any reason why we can't just leave the transmitter plugged in?"

"The comm dish will be pointed aft so we won't be able to communicate with NASA, but other than that, none that I can think of."

"We can turn it around when we're closer to home…meantime let's keep giving our packages the go signal…is everyone in agreement on that?"

"Makes sense to me," Duane responded. Grosovitch also nodded.

Yakov sailed back from the lower deck and strapped into his seat. "I've been thinking about the thruster fuel problem," he said. "It will take some timing but it can be done. Someone has to go out and manually position the ship using his suit maneuvering unit."

"You mean just push the nose into the right attitude?"

"That is correct, Matt. The trick will be to do it not too soon or the attitude will drift out of parameters...and don't wait too late or the man outside will be torn away and incinerated by air friction."

"I'll do it," Duane said.

"Bullshot, I should do it," argued Grosovitch.

"This job is gonna take timing and a sort of natural rhythm that, well, you whiteys just don't have." Alexi started to complain again, but McCall just grabbed him in a headlock and knuckled his hair. "My Pappy is paying for this little vacation and so I'm pulling strings, and besides, the word is bull-shit." Duane laughed.

"Both of you are going," Matt interjected. "The Stork has too much mass for just one suit. Duane you take the spare suit. Alexi, what do you have left on yours?"

"It has about forty-five minutes of oxygen and half a tank of suit fuel."

"OK, you stay out there until both of you get us in position then Alexi, I want you to high tail it back to the airlock when you get down to ten minutes of air...you got it...? ten minutes!"

"Yes, Commander, I will do as you say."

Yakov looked up from his oxygen calculations and slightly nodded his head. Assurances of cooperation from Grosovich in situations such as these were not altogether reliable. Yakov remembered when he had first met the young MiG-25 pilot who would not let him go to Moscow to face the KGB alone despite direct orders to stay behind.

"Dimitri, what else?" Matt queried.

"Since the correct reentry attitude is minus six to minus thirty-three degrees nose down, I suggest you shove her right into the middle at minus twenty degrees nose down....you'll have to be talking them through this by reading the attitude off your ADI. And remember, they'll need some lead time to get the nose stopped after they get it moving."

"Do the suits have enough maneuvering fuel?"

"Since we barely have enough thruster fuel to pitch over to tail first for the reentry burn, it doesn't matter. Either the suit trick works or it won't," Yakov stated matter of factly.

"OK," Matt said, "let's all try to get some sleep and conserve oxygen...Dimitri, what's your plan on that?"

"I need to go down to the lower deck first, I'll explain when I get back."

"Roger that," Matt responded.

**

The mood was grim at the sprawling TriAmCo HQ in Plainview, Texas. The Stork was overdue and space flight is a slave to the tyranny of numbers. All the numbers were irrefutably stating that the Stork was lost. Even if it was on the way home, there was no thruster fuel to position the ship properly for reentry and the one and only transmission they had received was extremely bad news. They were taking another orbit in an attempt to pick up the two guys down on the surface and all consumables were critically low for a successful return.

NASA had transmitted data for a new EIB, but no response had been received. Tupelov had calculated that even if another orbit and amended EIB data were used, the crew would die of oxygen starvation eighteen hours before their ETA. Leanna ordered Sky Guard to maintain a continuous watch on the moon until the Stork returned. The Stork was now long overdue and no explosions had been seen on the lunar surface. The numbers were irrefutable. The Stork was lost and the mission had failed.

John Good and his staff had shredded all the classified documents by the time the final word came from Tupelov that there was no way the Stork would be returning. J.B. McCall sat at his huge mahogany desk in the Taj McCall staring at the photo of his boy full and strong climbing up the side of an F-4 on some carrier deck. Ann Louise had wanted to stay, but he had sent her home to be with her family. The SF-35s were being gradually overwhelmed by the sheer numbers of the enemy. The casualty rate was brutal and dozens of pilots were killed on every patrol by organ failure and stroke from the intensive stress of space combat. But the phones rang off the hooks at Canaveral and Vandenberg from men who wanted to get into the fight. And they came. Some flew themselves cross country and just showed up. Several actually went AWOL from their line squadrons to get into an SF-35 unit.

They were killed by the score.

They still came.

McCall swiveled his big chair and gazed out the picture windows at the north Texas plains. It was early evening. There was a low deck of clouds and light rain falling. And the wind blew. A small dust storm was kicking up and the lights in Plainview had not come on.

Everyone had gone somewhere. There were no headlights on the distant highway. People were holed up like animals, waiting to die. There was nowhere for McCall to go. No family, son killed in space, his house just a big, empty building without Jessie.

He thought of the afternoon in Tuskeegee when he was about to blow his stack at the bus driver putting the German POWs on ahead of him, when Jessie reached over and held his hand. She was by God the best thing that ever happened to him for forty years. McCall thought about luck, and the day that second lieutenant Matt Blalock III had boomed the TriAmCo building busting his fish tank…the sharks…then later when Matt had come for the big briefing and didn't know that McCall knew all along who had buzzed Plainview that day in 1969. It had been fun watching the reaction on Blalock's face when Ann Louise, by pre-arrangement, had come in and made her little announcement about the boy in his little white jet. Then McCall's eyes fell again to the photo of Duane on his desk. If I was a crying man, he thought, I guess this would be an acceptable time. McCall caught some movement out of the corner of his eye and looked to his left.

John Good came in with a leather folder in his hand and walked over to directly in front of McCalls desk. "I'm afraid, Mr. McCall, that this is not a day for good news."

"I surmised as much by the reports," McCall answered leaning back in his chair.

"Unfortunately, for you, Mr. McCall, the news is going to get worse."

Good unzipped the leather folder and produced a silenced, nine millimeter Walther PPK, and pointed the pistol directly at McCall's head.

"What the hell do you think you're doing?" McCall blurted.

"Mr. McCall, it is now necessary to eliminate all connections with me and my future whereabouts. The fight must continue and it will be necessary to sever our relationship in a permanent manner."

"Dammit man, I gave my only son to this enterprise and half my fortune, and you question my loyalty?"

"Mr. McCall I have always been amused by your colorful back-on-the-plantation aphorisms, but even for a megalomaniac like you, don't you think it's a big jump from jungle bunny to Jehovah?"

McCall eyed his great grandfather's big dragoon pistol in its walnut display case on the side of his desk.

"Just keep your hands in your lap, Mr. McCall and don't be reaching for anything on your desk…this has to be done. Where I am going you cannot follow…"

McCall laughed, taking Good completely off guard.

"And who the shit do you think you are, you twisted skunk? Rick Blaine? Are you now going to demand that I turn over the letters of transit?"

Good's pistol arm was shaking with anger. "I think we've had enough conversation." Good squeezed the trigger.

A mighty blast blew out the front of McCalls desk as he fired the .454 revolver he had duct taped to the side drawer inside the bottom of his desk. The bullet missed Good and went through the gnarled oak wall paneling. It continued through the stainless steel elevator doors and exploded into the back wall of the elevator car blowing out a chunk of the concrete block elevator shaft. Good dodged to his left throwing his left arm up over his eyes but then caught himself and steadied his aim once again.

Then the pistol shot. J.B. convulsed as the bullet struck.

The shot came from McCall's left and the ear numbing report from the Colt .45 military was followed by the clang of a brass shell casing hitting the wood floor.

Good's head exploded like a ripe red watermelon, his brains splattering against the wall in a shower of gray and bloody goo. Colonel Lowell Bremen lowered his aim. There was no point in checking for a pulse. Bremen turned his gaze to McCall.

"J.B. are you OK?"

"Yeah, yeah, I think so…" McCall said, shaking like he had the DTs.

"J.B. I'm sorry. I didn't figure out what he was up to until it was damned near too late."

McCall trembled as he walked slowly, almost stumbling around his desk and stood next to Bremen over Good's body.

"Why? Just tell me why?" McCall pleaded.

The two men stood next to one another and stared at the prostrate man in a widening pool of blood soaking into the hand made Khurman rug.

"You wouldn't understand… we needed men like Good once. In his own way, when it really mattered, he was a great patriot. You know he lost a son too? Not too many people know that…shot down over northern Russia in an RB-47. Wife left him years ago…he couldn't tell her what he was doing…hell, his name wasn't even John Good."

"But why did he want to kill me?"

"I don't know JB. I think somewhere along the line he just got lost…lost in a wilderness of mirrors."

***

"Dimitri, what's keeping you down there?" Blalock called over the wireless intercom. No answer. "Alexi, he's got his headset off, go see what's keeping Yakov, we need to implement this oxygen conservation plan he's cooked up."

Grosovitch pulled himself down to the lower deck. "Alexi what's happening?" Now Alexi wasn't answering.

"Duane, take a look down there and see what's going on."

Duane started to head down the passageway when he met Grosovich coming the other way, tears smearing all over his face.

"Christ man, what's wrong?"

"It's Colonel Yakov," he choked.

"What about him?" Duane demanded.

"He's dead."

Grosovitch bawled like a little kid and held up a small, red, empty pill box.

Blalock unstrapped and darted down the passage to the lower deck.

Yakov had strapped his body out of the way, next to the storage lockers, taken the capsule, then died quietly and alone. There was a note stuck under the band of his wristwatch.

I estimate that this will give you another twenty hours of oxygen. As I have told you many times, with Russian technology there is always a way.

Sometimes it is a hard way.

Take care and safe journey my friends, Dimitri.
Blalock wiped his eyes.

"Godammit Dimitri, you didn't tell me you were going to do it this way."

Matt wiped his eyes with his sleeve and after several minutes got his composure back. When he got back to his seat, Duane had his arm around Grosovich who was beyond grief. Duane looked up hoping for a miracle. Blalock shook his head.

The Stork plunged on for its rendezvous with history. The infinite void of space enveloped the microscopic traveler who dared to trespass on its soulless frontier.

A frontier that did not know courage, or the greater love that a man has when he lays down his life for his friends. In the cosmological scheme of things, across a billion trillion light years in the vast distances that reach beyond the farthest galaxies, nothing that happened here mattered a wit. Suns were born in the dust, stars collided, and the overlapping continuums of the universe blended magnificently into one another in a mind blinding collage of time and gravity.

But Somebody had been watching and a decision was made...or maybe it was a freak burst of cosmic radiation, but thousands of burned-through microcircuits in the orbiting arsenal of death around the moon became suddenly realigned. Circuits closed, electrons flowed, solid-state laser gyros glowed to life, orbiting target illuminators suddenly sprayed downward onto the alien base. The backup illuminator placed by Duane and Alexi on the crater rim came to life spitting its tiny pencil beam of infra red light across the canyon rims and onto the top section of the tallest EBE structure. The first nuclear device then fired its engine and rocketed its ground penetrating warhead deep into the lunar crust between the two black pyramids.

***

"Holy shit! Look at this." The two grad students on watch at the Sky Guard base on Mount Cerro Puntas, Puerto Rico jumped out of their chairs and about gave themselves a concussion against the too-low ceiling in the old WWII radar emplacement. A brilliant white flare had occurred at the lunar south pole. About the time the flare had died down another smaller flare burst into view. This continued for hours as the continuous stream of nuclear bombardment laid waste to the EB lunar structure turning it to a pool of molten silica. Psychics around the world later reported the telepathic death screams of thousands.

The enemy space fleet disappeared.

Lightning patrols started coming home with victory rolls on the downwind and showboating approaches that meant the crews were alive. The crew chiefs cheered each time they spotted their bird in the pattern doing some kind of airborne hijinks. One of the Marine pilots did an unauthorized engagement of the G-1 engine on short final and pulled straight up into a seven G vertical climb accelerating to 10,000 knots going completely out of sight. The TGC made some kind of distortion in the atmosphere that created a thick bellowing trail of radiant sparkles like Tinker Bell. It was spectacular. The Pratt & Whitney tech reps were not amused when a grinning Marine captain popped his canopy after being towed in from the runway. The tech reps pulled the access panels and the G-1's guts might as well have been oatmeal they were so torn up. The

TGC was totally wrecked. "That's the Marines for you," one of them said.

***

Duane and Alexi slowly positioned the nose of the Stork into a minus twenty degrees nose down attitude. But getting the nose completely stopped was proving to be nearly impossible. There was too much mass and not enough thrust from the suit units. No matter what they did it would start drifting ever so slightly and it would soon be out of proper reentry attitude.

"Matt?"

"Yeah Duane."

"I'm going to have to stay out here to the last minute or she'll drift out of parameters."

Matt wanted to order him inside immediately, but he knew Duane was right.

"OK, Duane, but when I give you the word, you haul ass back in here, you got it?"

"Don't worry, I'll need no motivation on that one."

"OK, Alexi, no need for you to stay out there, come on back and let's get ready for the approach."

"Yes, Commander, I'm on my way."

Blalock pulled out the reentry checklist and began setting up the ship for the final leg.

"Commander?"

"Go, Alexi."

"I'm here in the payload bay...I think we have another problem."

"Why am I not surprised? What's the problem Alexi?"

"It appears that we have a hung bomb in the magazine...it's one of the RTEs." Blalock checked his altitude, still plenty to jettison the weapon into space, but it was getting tight. This is the only one they could not go home with. Detonation of an RTE warhead over land would kill every human within five thousand miles and maybe beyond since there was no antidote for the genetically engineered bio-agent.

"I suggest we fire the entire magazine into space using the separation charge," Grosovich suggested.

"Sounds good to me, let me know when you're clear."

Grosovich maneuvered himself out of the payload bay and around the other side of the ship. "I'm well clear."

"Duane, are you clear?"

"Yep."

Blalock lifted the red painted panel cover in the floor just below his seat, pulled the safety clip and flipped the magazine jettison switch. The Stork vibrated for an instant with a small thump as the tiny separation charge detonated which would shove the payload gently out of the cargo compartment.

"There she blows," Matt commented.

Grosovitch flew his suit unit back around the Stork and up over the lip of the open payload bay doors. Another flurry of Russian profanity.

So far nothing good had ever followed one of these outbursts, Matt thought.

"What's wrong Alexi?"

"The magazine...it didn't separate."

Blalock checked the altitude, five minutes from interface with the atmosphere.

"Duane, I'm showing five minutes from interface, leave the nose where ever it is right now, it will have to do, get back to the payload bay and pull that RTE out and get it clear of the ship…it'll burn up when we interface."

"I'm halfway there now." Duane was shooting from the chin of the Stork's nose up and around and into the payload bay. Alexi was standing off to one side looking for something in a side panel. "Commander, doesn't the magazine have a manual locking system that can be accessed from back here? It appears the separation charge fired, I see scorch marks at the base plate of the magazine, but it looks like the locks did not automatically disengage."

"I think I see it. Yep, it's an RTE and it's stuck." Duane was directly over the top of the magazine looking down into its innards with his flashlight. "I'm going to pull it out by hand." He reached in and grabbed one of the retracted steering nozzles on the strap on guidance package. He then noticed a brown fluid leaking from a seam in the warhead canister. The droplets adhered to his arm and drifted up and expanded across his visor partially obscuring his view. The jolt from the separation charge must have damaged the warhead. McCall had enough toxin on his EVA suit to kill the combined populations of Los Angeles, Tokyo, and Buenos Aires. *Oh fuck*, he thought to himself.

"Uh Matt, I've got the problem solved…I can manually pull the projectile out and shove it into space…uh, no problemo."

"Goddam, about time for some good news. Alexi, get your ass into the airlock, we're coming up on interface, this is going to be damned close."

"Is prefer to wait for Duane. I have eight minutes of air," Alexi argued.

McCall gave the RTE a mighty heave and it came sliding out of its tube and then on away from the ship slowly drifting away. "There, that did it, Alexi get into the airlock, I'm right behind you," Duane shouted over the suit comm.

Grosovich waited until he saw McCall physically heading in his direction before going into the airlock. Once inside, Grosovich moved to the far side to make room for Duane. McCall sailed up to the airlock but instead of going inside, he closed the airlock door suddenly, jamming his flashlight into the outer actuating handle to keep the door from being opened from the inside.

"Duane, what the hell are you doing?" Blalock said sternly, watching the proceedings on the payload monitor. Grosovich bolted to the airlock door and attempted to open it from the inside. The flashlight held.

"Matt, I can't come with you. I got the RTE all over me...the warhead casing was cracked by the separation charge."

"Duane, are you sure it's not just fuel from the guidance motors...maybe it's just a fuel leak...this thing's been leaking like a sieve the whole mission."

"No, I'm not sure...but I can't take the chance."

"Look, you let me make that decision; I'm the commander of this mission. Pull that fucking flashlight out of the door and get your ass in here."

"Yes, get your ass in here," Grosovich echoed. "You know you must always obey commander of mission. Is basic rule we learned even in Russian Air Force," Alexi's voice was pleading and angry.

"Alexi, my friend, you are so full of shit...I know you too well." Duane said softly.

The Stork hit interface altitude at 400,000 feet.

"Matt?"

"Duane, go ahead."

"Tell my Dad that I…"

There was a sharp screech of static as Duane's suit comm microphone vaporized from air molecules incinerating it by atmospheric friction.

Chapter 59

The Stork buffeted badly on the re-entry. Matt had both hands on the stick as he flew the Stork manually with no simulator practice and nothing to describe the maneuver but the flight manual. The windshield glowed a rosy red and pieces of ablative material tore loose from the nose and flitted by the cockpit like orange meteors. "Hang on Alexi, I don't have much practice at this," he shouted over the suit comm.

"Is having NO practice," Grosovich corrected.

Out of 300,000 feet the Stork stopped shaking and started flying. Once below Mach 1.0 the Stork smoothed out and handled beautifully. "Where are we Alexi?" Matt kept his eyes glued to the flight instruments.

"Coasting in over North America…southern Canada maybe."

"Thank God," Matt muttered, "we're over land." Matt banked the ship to the right and stole a glimpse out the right window. It was Puget Sound. Blalock rolled left and there was Vancouver Island. Matt then rolled the Stork into a sixty degree bank to the right and took up a one-twenty heading. They were now descending out of 125,000 feet.

"Where are we going?" said Grosovich.

"Montana, I hope…get ready, we're going to punch at 10,000."

Grosovich locked his shoulder harness and lowered his helmet visor that automatically energized the bailout support system.

"You're going first, Alexi." Grosovich nodded.

Passing 15,000, Matt reached halfway across the center pedestal with his right hand. Grosovich grasped it and they shook hands. The Black Stork flew as advertised, like a streamlined safe from a ten story window. Out of 12,000 Matt keyed his interphone. "Eject, eject, eject." The third eject command was unnecessary. There was a hole in the roof with a hurricane blowing through it where Grosovich was seated a second before. *Good boy*, Alexi, Matt thought, smiling. *Let the record reflect that in the end, you finally followed orders.*

Matt took one last look around the cockpit, lowered his visor and raised the seat handles. Out of 9,000 he squeezed the grips.

The Black Stork crashed in a large pasture five miles west of Whitefish, Montana. It pancaked in, skidding about five hundred yards, then when one wingtip dug in, flipped over tearing off both wings and the vertical stab. The rest of the fuselage wreckage went another half mile with big pieces flinging off at an angle. A few busted up sections of the fuselage finally came to rest against a stand of amber Tamaracks. The reentry and crash was visible for a hundred miles in every direction.

Alexi came down in a clearing, but he could see Matt's red parachute going down in the tall trees several miles away. Grosovich unsnapped his harness and set off for the commander in a dogtrot. An hour later, he heard someone blowing a whistle. Grosovich bounded through the underbrush like a hurdler and changed course slightly each time he heard another whistle blast. The whistle blasts were closer, but shorter and growing weaker. "I am coming, homeboy," he shouted.

Alexi was breathing hard as he burst through the last barrier of brush to Matt's position. It was not good. Matt was beaten to hell coming through all the branches with blood all over his face. One leg was broken, bent at an impossible angle. His right thigh

was speared by a three inch branch which was still sticking in the wound with a small trickle of blood dripping off the end of it.

"You look like shitsky," Alexi tried to appear unconcerned.

"I feel like I look," Matt groaned summoning a forced smile from somewhere.

Alexi began unsnapping him out of his gear and then cut a six feet section of riser from his chute. He applied the tourniquet above the puncture and twisted it until the blood stopped dripping off the branch. Grosovich picked Matt up easily and hoisted him into the fireman's carry. Matt cried out in pain as Grosovich headed back the direction from which he came. "Is good news," he said to the unconscious Blalock, "Is road where I came down."

483

The two park police were still watching the couple sitting in the rain by the Vietnam Memorial. "Can't believe they're still out there," one quipped. The monument technicians gathered up their etching tools and had left after Duane McCall's name had been added to the wall of heroes. The Lincoln Memorial was ablaze with lights and darkness enveloped the Mall. The compassionate Lincoln gazed down from his gigantic chair, as if he knew the incredible events that happened to his union that he died to preserve.

Leanna folded up the letter she was reading before the rain completely obliterated the writing. Matt had his arm around her from his wheelchair. Leanna dabbed her eyes a few more times and walked over to the black marble wall and touched the new name that had been added. A tingling sensation filled her hand yet she could not pull it away. Her body shuddered. An image appeared as if projected from the inside of the wall.

It was Duane, walking toward her on two strong legs in his navy flight gear.

His hand reached out from behind the Wall and touched hers as a reflection in a mirror.

"Matt, look!" Leanna gasped, covering her mouth with her fist.

"Take care of Matt, Leanna, he really loves you," Duane said with that irrepressible smile on his face. Blalock looked up.

"Matt, it's Duane!" Leanna cried. Leanna looked back at the Wall, but Duane was gone.

"What's wrong baby?" Blalock rolled himself from the side of the park bench over to the base of The Wall where Leanna was trembling.

"I saw something," she said. Leanna wiped the tears from her eyes with her shirt sleeve then leaned over and kissed Matt on the forehead. Matt placed the long package gently at the base of The Wall beneath Duanes's name. Leanna grabbed the handles of Matt's wheelchair and rolled him with her strong body over to where the Rolls was parked. Still wearing a soft body cast for his multiple broken ribs, Preston was moving in slow motion as he carefully got out to open the door for Matt and Leanna. "Stay put, Preston," Leanna ordered.

"Thank you Ms. Leanna." Preston slowly hiked his leg back into the driver's seat.

Leanna stowed the wheel chair in the boot and climbed in next to Matt.

"Where to, Mum?"

"The Mayflower Hotel, Preston."

The big Rolls murmured out into the demented river of steel that used to be called light traffic and was now the Washington rush hour.

"What's going to happen at the Mayflower?" Matt asked innocently, turning to face her, smiling with Bambi like naivete.

Leanna's eyes narrowed as she looked at him directly, her piercing blue eyes locking into his like missile radar. She put both arms around Matt's neck, lightly applying pressure with her nails. She then rolled her body slightly to the right bringing her knee slowly up between his legs bringing a firm pressure. She kissed him on the cheek, then touched her lips to his ear, "You know, sometimes you talk too much," she whispered.

***

The female park ranger picked up the elongated object and removed it from the olive drab canvas bag the couple had just laid below the new name on The Wall. "It's just a bunch of beer cans taped together." Her partner, smiling, gently took it out of her hands, looking it up and down as if examining some ancient artifact.

"I haven't seen one of these since Cam Ranh Bay," he said. He placed the tube on his shoulder like a bazooka and aimed it into the rainy night. He remembered being young...the faces of his buddies in faded jungle fatigues...young faces shouting and singing...a tinny distant strain of music..."We got to get out of this place...if it's the last thing we evvvver do"....he smelled the musky perfume of bar girls..."We gotta' get out of this place...to build a better life for me and you..."

The ranger tenderly slid the long metal tube back into its case and turned to his clueless partner.

"Just a bunch of beer cans my ass! This, my good woman, is an *elephant* gun!"